Land of Broken Promises –
By: Margaret Penfold
ISBN: 978-1-927220-90-0

All rights reserved
Copyright © Dec. 2014, Margaret Penfold
Cover Art Copyright © Dec. 2014, Brightling Spur

Bluewood Publishing Ltd
Christchurch, 8441, New Zealand
www.bluewoodpublishing.com

Names, characters and incidents depicted in this book are products of the author's imagination or are used fictitiously. Any resemblance to actual events, locales, organizations, or persons, living or dead, is entirely coincidental, and beyond the intent of the author or the publisher.

No part of this book may be reproduced or shared by any electronic or mechanical means, including but not limited to printing, file sharing, and email, without prior written permission from Bluewood Publishing Ltd.

Other titles by Margaret Penfold:

Land of Broken Promises series:
Patsy

Coming Soon:

Land of Broken Promises series:
Dalia

For news of, or to purchase this or other books, please visit:

www.bluewoodpublishing.com

Land Of Broken Promises: Maftur

by

Margaret Penfold

To Ray and Sean, Thank you for all your help this year, With love, From, Margaret

Dedication

To all the marvellous writers at Leicester Writers Club and particularly Jean Chapman and David Martin who have given me so much help. To the brave hearted men on PPOCA forum who have answered innumerable questions about their experiences in Palestine – To Evelyn Hall who helped a sloppy writer with her copy editing. To my offspring who have given me so much moral support.

Chapter 1

Maftur was twelve when she met the boy she wanted to marry. That day, back in 1933, a khamseen—the hot wind that could drive even the most sane to commit grievous bodily harm—was blowing over Haifa. She was sitting on the flat roof of the substantial al-Zeid family apartment block built into the Carmel mountainside. A clay oven, only used at Ramadan, Eids and large family occasions, protected her from both flaming sun and searing wind. A faint whiff of pine and thyme wafted across the roof from the undeveloped upper slopes of the mountain.

She'd been worrying about betrothal ever since she had stopped being a child and had become a woman. Since that horrible day, she'd had to wear either a hijab or a school hat at all times, even indoors (except during PE lessons, of course), and Granny had gone on and on to her mother about sending her photos to the marriage arranger.

It wasn't that she was against getting married, but she had other things to do first. Most of all she wanted to become a secretary, wear beautiful clothes all day and be the envy of other women who had to stay at home and look after children.

This afternoon she was trying to escape uncomfortable thoughts, and at the same time obey her father's order to study English for at least two hours a day during the summer holidays. She was reading 'Swallows and Amazons', borrowed from the school library. No one in that book had to worry about getting married.

Nothing could come between her and the story, until something hit the oven and fell to the floor with a rustling sound. She raised her eyes from her book to find a green kite at her feet.

Her gaze followed its string rising and falling across the roof and parapet. The string continued in a wavering arc over the recently-tarmacked road before stretching up to the second floor of a house further up the mountain.

A boy she had never seen before stood on a balcony holding the end of the string. She wondered if he could be the son of the president of the local chapter of the Arab Women's Association. Mrs. Shawwa was always boasting about her boy away at school in England. She picked up the kite, crossed the roof and held it over the parapet so he could reel it in.

The two younger of her three brothers, Dodi and Dindan, came running over from the far end of the roof, where they were rebuilding a car engine in the shade of rainwater tanks.

Fifteen year old Dodi snatched the kite from her and demanded, "What do you think you're doing, Maffy? Have you forgotten you're a woman now?"

She fingered the ends of her hijab. How could she ever forget?

Dodi let go of the kite. It plunged earthward but the stranger reeled it in before it touched the ground and held it in both hands, examining it for damage.

Dindan, only a year older than herself, shouted up to the boy, "You'd do better flying your kite from our roof."

The boy placed open hands against his ears, cupping them to indicate he couldn't hear.

Dindan raced down the fire escape that led to a backyard level, with doors on the second storey of their building, and ran up steps cut into a steep bank to the road above.

Dodi went back to work on the car engine but Maftur continued to watch Dindan as he stood in front of the boy's house shouting up to the balcony.

The strange boy shouted something back and, a few seconds later, emerged from his front door, carrying the kite.

The two crossed the road, ran down the steps and climbed up the fire escape. Maftur could see the stranger wore grey flannels, and one of the new-fashioned polo shirts worn without a tie. He looked too old to be playing kites—more Dodi's age, perhaps even older, a young man not a boy. She could understand why his mother talked about him so much. He was very good-looking, although his hair was Brylcreemed flat, English style.

"Dodi, this is Ismail," Dindan shouted. "He's home for the holidays. He says we can help him fly his kite."

Ismail looked at Dodi. "To be honest, I'm more interested in your car engine than the kite. I've been watching you carry parts home on your handcart all week. I was only flying the kite to check it still worked. I haven't seen it for three years."

He took a packet of 5-flavour Lifesavers from his pocket and offered one to each of her brothers. Then, to Maftur's amazement, he held the packet out to her and ripped the paper at the side. "You can choose whichever flavour you like," he said with a captivating smile that extended to his kind-looking eyes. He split the side of the packet with his fingernail.

Maftur was conscious of a strange feeling at the pit of her stomach as she smiled back and chose a tangerine sweet. Then she saw Dodi's glare and remembered to lower her gaze, as became a woman no longer a child. She felt her cheeks burn.

Dodi ushered the other two boys back to undisputed masculine territory, leaving Maftur standing alone. It was horrible having to change the way she behaved just because she'd become a woman. Three weeks ago, Dodi wouldn't have told her off for picking up a kite and sending it back to a boy. Of course, they had never particularly liked their little sister meeting their friends but she hadn't minded, because she didn't particularly like those friends. This Ismail was different though. What other boy would not only have offered a girl one of his sweets but even allowed her to choose the flavour?

All she wanted to do for the rest of the afternoon was lean against the cold clay oven, and dream about Ismail and wish he were one of her Beirut cousins. If he had been she would be allowed to ask her parents to include the Shawwas in the list of potential in-laws when they sent her photo to a marriage arranger. She then dreamed about her father turning all modern and letting her help choose her own husband from the families of his friends as well as his relatives. Well, no one could spy on her dreams.

She couldn't stay out here forever, however. She had to help her mother put the final touches to a special meal welcoming home an uncle, aunt and her two closest cousins, who counted as her sisters because they all shared the same four grandparents.

She glanced at the watch her parents had given her on

her first day at Haifa High School. She was already late!

Racing down from the roof to her parents' apartment on the second floor, she discovered her mother had set out only enough cushions round the low olivewood table in the dining room for the women, from which she deduced that the men would be eating separately in the liwan. The liwan was a room that traditionally opened directly onto a balcony but, three years before, while the family apartment block had been in the process of being built, her mother and Aunt Bahia had both insisted on separating their liwans from the balconies with sliding glass doors. Maftur was puzzled by that night's arrangement. It was unusual, nowadays, for men and women to eat separately at family-only meals.

She checked the liwan to make sure everything was in order, with enough cushions set round the table, and brass bowls filled with water in front of each cushion. There didn't seem much left for her to do. She hoped her mother wouldn't be angry that she hadn't come down earlier.

She went back into the women's quarters, into the almost unbearably hot kitchen, unsure of her reception. To her relief, her mother greeted her with a smile.

"There you are, Maffy. We're not having the little ones tonight. Zubaida is looking after them, but Granny is feeling well enough to join us, so you can set up a high seat and trolley table for her in the dining room. Place it so she doesn't feel cut off from the rest of us, and make the trolley look as pretty as you can."

So Granny was coming and that was why men and women were eating separately. Maftur doubted if Granny had ever eaten a meal in the same room as a man in all her life.

When she was very little she had lived with all her Haifa relatives in the big house down town that was now only used as offices and warehouse for the family business. There had been just one large kitchen in that house with Granny in charge of everything. In those days, Granny wouldn't let women and children have their meal until the men had finished eating. Maftur remembered her mother and Aunt Bahia constantly going on about having apartments of their own so they could live in the 20th century and run their own households.

With Ismail still at the back of her mind, she wondered

how his family ate. Would they behave more like her parents or her grandparents? She knew from her mother that they had only one kitchen, but that could be because they had no close relatives in Haifa.

Maftur forced her attention back to the matter in hand. She enjoyed making Granny's trolley pretty, especially as it gave her an excuse to use the new electric iron on a small hand-embroidered tablecloth.

She was arranging jasmine in a silver vase when her cousins and their parents, her father's brother and her mother's sister arrived, together with her eldest brother, her sister-in-law and her grandparents.

She had been looking forward to her cousin-sister's return. The first fortnight of the school holidays, while Sabeen was being paraded in Beirut before an array of potential mothers-in-law, had been lonely. She was glad men and women would be eating separately tonight. Her mother and Aunt Bahia would be able to talk freely about the visit to the marriage maker, and she and her cousins would be allowed to join in the conversation, provided they did so politely.

The men, including her two younger brothers who still lived at home, stayed talking in the lobby, but the women came straight into the living room. While her mother helped Granny, who suffered from arthritis, to the high armchair her father had bought especially for his mother's visits, Maftur admired the new clothes her aunt and cousins had bought in Beirut. Aunt Bahia wore a hat similar to one that had appeared in her mother's March edition of Paris Vogue. "There's nothing like it in the Haifa milliners yet," her mother had said when she had shown her the picture. Sabeen looked very demure and grown-up in a gorgeous silk crepe hijab patterned with climbing flowers in shades of orange on a pale blue background. Sister-in-law, Janan, had also dressed up in her best thob for the occasion. Beside the others, Yalda, head still uncovered, looked very much a child although she was only a year younger than herself.

"The little ones are worn out, so I'm really grateful to you for lending us Zubaida to look after them," Aunt Bahia said, as they all settled in the family living room.

"She enjoys playing the part of nursemaid again every so

often," her mother replied. "How was your journey?"

"Still a nightmare on that mountainous stretch between the border posts. The rest is a lot better than it used to be, though, so I shouldn't grumble."

Too busy helping her mother brings in trays of coffee and iced lime, Maftur didn't get a chance to chat to Sabeen and Yalda who sat in polite silence, hands on their laps.

The men entered the room. When she had served them tea, she helped her mother in the liwan, setting out, with a precision her mother couldn't expect from any servants except Zubaida who was otherwise occupied, dishes of lamb stew, saffron rice, liver and aubergine, stuffed peppers and marrows and piles of warm pitta bread. Her mother checked that the men could comfortably reach each dish with their fingers. When all was set, she signalled her father to lead in the male contingent, and left him to play host, with two male servants standing against the wall.

"We'll give the men an hour before we eat," her mother decreed.

With the door into the liwan firmly closed, the grown women, who had all been educated in Beirut, settled down to gossip in French. Maftur understood French well enough to follow the conversation, although she and her mother usually spoke Arabic at home. Her mother said it was more patriotic.

Aunt Bahia sounded excited as she told them, "The Old Man himself came down from Damascus and spoke to our Sabeen, asking her lots of questions. He gave her these photos with his blessing."

She displayed three photos of eligible male cousins. None appealed to Maftur. All looked serious, full-faced and too virtuous for words. They reminded her of her pompous eldest brother, Kamal.

"What an honour, the Old Man taking such an interest in a great-granddaughter," Granny said. "That's never happened before."

"That's what I thought at first," Aunt Bahia replied, "but it turns out the Old Man visited one of our Jaffa cousins in May, and before that a cousin from Damascus."

Maftur's mother shrugged her shoulders. "The Old Man has too little to do now he doesn't go into work every day.

Anyway, which photo did Sabeen choose?"

Aunt Bahia held up one.

"What's so special about him?" Maftur whispered to Sabeen.

"I had to pick someone," Sabeen whispered back. "That one has a kind face and your sister says he's always laughing."

As far as Maftur could see, the chosen face showed not a hint of laughter nor could she detect any extra kindness in the smug features. She hoped, when it came to her turn, one photo would stand out from the others.

The older women began reminiscing about the family of Sabeen's new fiancé. Eventually, when that topic petered out, Maftur's mother asked, "And how was my Parveen?"

"Healthy, happy and looking forward to seeing you in a fortnight's time," Aunt Bahia replied. She picked up her capacious bag and took out a bulging envelope. "She sent photos of your grandchildren."

Her mother's face lit up. She oohed and aahed as she pored over every baby and toddler picture, and then passed them over to Granny who looked at them judiciously and found for each a striking likeness to one or other of Maftur's many aunts, uncles and cousins.

When the photographs reached her, she made a show of interest. She knew she ought to love all her nephews and nieces, but babies looked so alike. She glanced up and saw Aunt Bahia give her mother a sideways look.

"Parveen says, will you be seeing the marriage arranger when you go up at the end of the month?"

Her mother frowned. "She knows full well what her father and I have decided."

Maftur watched Granny stare at her mother suspiciously. "And just what have you two decided?"

Her mother stared back defiantly. "We're keeping Maftur at school for the next four years. We're having no more dealings with marriage arrangers until Dodi has taken his examinations and settled into work."

Granny pressed her lips together and glared.

Her mother lowered her eyes. "It's no good looking at me like that, Belle-mère. It was your son's decision."

"Hmm," Granny said, "and just who batted her eyes to

persuade him into that decision?"

Maftur kept her face expressionless and her eyes firmly on her lap, but inside she was elated to discover that her mother really was sticking to a promise made a year ago, after she had read an article in the women's page of al-Karmel advocating equal education for girls and boys. Her mother must have spent much of the intervening time persuading her father it was his idea.

Now she wouldn't have to leave Haifa and her friends before taking the examinations that would turn her into a qualified typist. More than anything else in the world she wanted to become a secretary, work in an office and have all her friends envying her clothes and freedom.

* * * *

Three weeks later, in the nursery of a large house in Beirut, Maftur was on her knees building a castle out of wooden bricks with her nephews, nieces and second cousins. Her big sister, Parveen, lived here, part of a large family ruled over by Father's eldest brother, Uncle Harun.

She was surprised how much Parveen's children had grown in a single year. Although still uncomfortable when expected to croon over the latest baby, she enjoyed playing with the toddlers now they could talk.

Her mother came to the door. "Maftur, your father wants to see you in the liwan."

She felt a surge of panic. A formal interview in Uncle Harun's liwan? This was worse than receiving a summons to the Headmistress's office. She rose to her feet, her chest heavy, unable to think of anything she had done while in Beirut that could have brought dishonour to the family. All her time had been spent either in the women's quarters, here, or out with her sister and mother visiting relatives.

She stared at her mother, hoping for a hint, but she just turned and picked up one of the children's hairbrushes. Her mouth filled with saliva as her mother attempted to smooth her hair with the too-soft baby brush, saying, "I wish you had time to change." Then, when she replaced the brush, "But you will have to do as you are. Hurry along now."

The children cried as she left the room, not wanting her to leave. She turned to make sure they were calm, before trotting down the marble stairs.

When she opened the liwan door she saw her father was not alone. A very old man—so thin he was almost a skeleton—sat ramrod straight on the room's single armchair, his wrinkled neck as vertical as his backbone. The only people she had seen looking so old were beggars, but this was no beggar. His face was clean-shaven. His top quality fez pointed directly to the ceiling. His immaculate brown checked suit fitted perfectly, despite his lack of flesh. His liver-spotted hands, with rings on every finger, clasped the top of a carved ebony cane. She knew, without her father having to tell her, that this was the legendary 'Old Man', her great-grandfather, head of the silk manufacture and export business that employed most of her male relatives. No one knew his exact age but Granny had reckoned he must be over one hundred.

"Stand there, child," he ordered as she gave a little curtsy after closing the door. She stood still, while he looked her up and down. She hung her head in embarrassment.

"Now, turn round slowly."

She obeyed, conscious of her father sitting on a stool beside her great-grandfather, willing her to look her best. She wished she had been forewarned, so she could have dressed for the occasion.

"Your father tells me you are staying on at school until you are sixteen."

She remembered Sabeen saying this great-grandfather of theirs had questioned her and several other cousins after the marriage arrangers had started working on their behalf, but she wasn't seeing a marriage arranger, so why did he want to talk to her? Was he angry with her father for allowing her to stay on at school? She didn't know what to say for the best. She gave a slight nod, hoping she wasn't getting her father into trouble.

"How do you feel about that?"

Still looking down, she forced out the words. "I am happy to obey my father, sir."

"Lift up your head and look at me when you speak to me, child. Tell me, do you enjoy studying, or are you staying at school just to please your father?"

9

"I like school, sir."

"What are your favourite lessons?"

She knew she ought to say cookery and household management but hated lying. Giving her father an apologetic look, she answered, "English literature and history, sir." She glanced at her father again, dreading his anger. To her surprise, he smiled, almost as if she had given an answer he wanted to hear.

Her great-grandfather leaned forward. "What about French?"

"I like reading French stories, sir, but I don't like our French teacher."

"German?"

"I am sorry, sir, but I have never learnt German." She slipped her father an apologetic smile.

"Can you read Arabic?"

"Yes, sir, but I am only allowed to read Arabic books at home. We are forbidden to speak Arabic at school."

The old man nodded and leaned back. "That will be all, child. You may leave, but do not forget to keep working hard at school and go on reading Arabic, especially poetry, in your spare time. If you get a chance to learn German at that school of yours, take it."

She gave another little curtsey and made herself walk sedately out of the room. Once she had closed the door she ran back to the nursery, hoping her mother wasn't still there. She didn't want to confess that she had just ruined her marriage prospects, but her mother *was* there and looked at her expectantly.

"What did your great grandfather want?"

"He asked about my favourite lessons."

"Anything else?"

"He said I should read Arabic poetry."

"Was that all?"

"I think so."

"He didn't give you any photographs?"

Maftur felt her cheeks flame in shame. "No."

Her mother, however, looked relieved. "You've done the best you could, habipti. Now just forget about it."

Chapter 2

Three days after they returned from Beirut, her mother hosted a meeting of their neighbourhood chapter of the Haifa branch of the Arabic Women's Association (AWA).

Maftur helped set out the living room, placing a table in the centre, surrounded by cushions. The servants set glasses out in the kitchen ready to fill them with mint tea. It would be Maftur's task, as daughter of the house, to serve her mother's guests when they arrived. Aunt Bahia, sister-in-law Janan, the chapter's secretary and even Granny came to help, although Granny's contribution was to sit in her high chair and deliver instructions.

Everything was in order long before the meeting was due to start. While the four older women chatted, Maftur settled with her embroidery on a cushion near the door where she could see their faces and hear the conversation.

Granny had another dig at her mother about not waiting too long to seek out a marriage broker.

"Let me remind you, Belle-mère," her mother retorted in exasperation, "that the Damascus branch of the family values education."

Granny widened her eyes. "So you are casting your net in Damascus now, are you? Won't Maftur be lonely up there?"

Maftur put down her embroidery, shocked by the idea of having to live in Damascus, a place she had never once visited, a city even further from Haifa than Jerusalem—and Jerusalem was almost twice as far from Haifa as Beirut.

She saw Janan look at her mother. "I thought Abu Mussa's grandsons were all married."

"So they are," Aunt Bahia, replied. "Noor, you're not letting Maftur be a second wife, are you?"

Her mother faced Aunt Bahia. "Second wife, Bahia! I should think not! The Old Man's youngest son, Ahmed, is the one my husband has set his sights on, and I happen to know that the Old Man is sympathetic to the idea."

Maftur started working out relationships. This Ahmed

must be Grandpa's brother as well as her great-uncle. Surely they weren't going to make her marry an old man! One thing—as they weren't calling him Abu he didn't already have children. She willed her mother to look her way, but her mother was listening to her grandmother.

"Little Ahmed spent a year with me after his mother died. She was only eighteen, bless her, when the flu killed her. My father-in-law, who must have been over eighty by then, was heartbroken. That was two wives he'd lost since the war had started. The remaining wives also had the flu, so they sent the child to me—a lovely little boy. I was sorry when his father sent him to school in Beirut but at least I still see him once a year."

Now Maftur knew which Ahmed they were talking about. He wasn't even as old as her eldest brother. He had come to Haifa when her great-grandfather's oldest son, Abu Mussa, had collected rents from property his father had owned on Mount Carmel. She had assumed this Ahmed was Abu Mussa's son. She had never talked to him but, while she and her mother had sat in the sewing room, she had heard him, often enough, ordering her two younger brothers about in the living room. Although Kamal dubbed him 'that arrogant young pup', Dodi and Dindan had trailed after him every time he visited. The way he treated them, she couldn't think why they admired him so much. Even though he wasn't so very old, she didn't want to marry someone so full of himself.

She could keep quiet no longer. "Are you saying, Umm, that you and Baba have already chosen my husband without first giving me three photos to choose from?"

Her mother had the grace to look shamefaced, although Granny glared at the insolence of a young girl interrupting a conversation between married women.

"Of course not, habipti," her mother answered after a pause. "There's no firm arrangement in place. We're not even going to talk of marriage for you until you've finished school."

"It will be too late by then, Noor," her grandmother snapped. "Don't forget Ahmed was born in nineteen-fourteen. By the time Maftur leaves school, he will be married already, so Maftur would have to be his second wife."

"I will never let my daughter be a second wife."

Well, that was something at least.

Aunt Bahia added, "Your husband makes things very difficult for you, sister dear. When Maftur leaves school, all the other men of the right age for her will already be married."

Her mother looked defiant. "The Old Man says Ahmed wants to finish university and travel round Europe before he marries. Anyway, it won't be the end of the world if the match falls through. There will always be an honoured place in my household for my Maftur."

Her mother's attitude to her marriage would have been very different, Maftur reflected, if her eldest brother and sister hadn't already provided her with five grandchildren. She didn't like the idea of being a maiden aunt. Every family she knew possessed at least one, but no one gave them the respect accorded to married women. Perhaps, she reflected, it would be different if the maiden aunt went out to work as a secretary.

Other women of the section began to drift in. All, Muslim and Christian alike, wore Parisian-style dresses and couture straw hats finished with lacy veiling as modelled by Lilian Bond, although no hats were quite as up to date as the one Aunt Bahia had bought in Beirut.

While Maftur took round mint tea and honey cakes, their president, or Mrs. Shawwa as her Anglophile husband preferred her to be called, officially opened the meeting. Maftur hoped Mrs. Shawwa would talk about her son. Before she had met Ismail she had found Mrs. Shawwa's bragging about the prizes her Ismail had won for his schoolwork or the runs he had made at cricket tedious, but now she wanted to find out as much about him as possible. She had caught glimpses of Ismail during the past two days when he'd helped her brothers reconstruct the car engine. He'd even smiled at her once, but she hadn't dared smile back while Dodi kept such a strict eye on her. She was sure if her eldest brother, Kamal, had still been living in their apartment, he wouldn't have been as strict as Dodi.

Mrs. Shawwa asked Janan to make a rota for delivering food parcels to the families of men imprisoned in Acre, after the British had arrested them at an anti-Zionist demonstration that had got out of hand. Maftur hoped her mother would take her when it was her turn.

By the time Maftur refilled glasses, Mrs. Shawwa had moved on to the second item on the agenda—deciding who would write letters of protest to the District Commissioner, the High Commissioner, the English Prime Minister, and anyone else AWA central committee had decided had influence. Subject matter included the prolonged detention of Arab demonstrators, the failure of the British to include Palestinians in the top echelons of government, and the government's slow progress in building village schools.

When discussion came to a temporary halt while Janan, the section secretary, recorded the name of each volunteer against a letter's recipient, Maftur seized the opportunity to ask Mrs. Shawwa if she wanted her cup refilled. That lady looked at her as if seeing her for the first time.

"Your mother tells me you have attended demonstrations ever since the Arab Women's Association opened the Haifa branch."

Maftur recalled the earliest demonstration. Mothers had taken their children, even the smallest babies. When the chairman had read out the AWA proclamation starting, "We, the Arab wives and mothers of Haifa," many women had lifted their babies above their heads, and her mother had laid her arms across the shoulders of both herself and Dindan. She had felt almost as important as Dodi and Kamal, who stood behind them ready to protect their mother if the police used batons on protesters.

"And you now attend Haifa English High School?" Mrs. Shawwa continued.

Somewhat puzzled by the lady's interest, she confirmed the statement.

Mrs. Shawwa smiled. "Then I have a task for you, and if you complete it satisfactorily, we will enrol you as a full member of AWA."

Maftur clenched her fists and tried not to show her excitement. Sabeen was a whole year older but had never been offered an opportunity like this.

"What do I have to do?"

"Deliver a speech in English at our next demonstration, calling on the government to build more village schools for girls. Do you think you can do this?"

Maftur was sure she was capable of writing a speech, but delivering it in front of hundreds of people was another matter. She looked around. Her mother gave her a smile, her face glowing with pride. She had obviously heard what Mrs. Shawwa had said. She could let down neither mother nor country. She nodded, temporarily unable to speak, and scuttled off to the kitchen to ask Zubaida to make more mint tea, and set about calming herself. She must act like a proper grown-up from now on, if Mrs. Shawwa really meant it when she said she could be a full member of AWA.

By the time she returned to the living room, everyone was discussing the next demonstration. Janan argued that, with so many people coming to Haifa for the harbour opening, they should hold up an embroidered banner demanding Palestinian Independence.

Mrs. Shawwa banged her gavel loudly to end the discussion. "The opening ceremony celebrates the achievements of all the people of Haifa," she stated. "A day to put aside National politics and honour our city. We will make a banner for the harbour opening, but it will be a banner of celebration, not protest. The day before the opening is a day for protest. For that demonstration, we will meet outside the district house to demand that the government build more schools for girls. Maftur Shawwa will deliver a speech on behalf of our chapter."

Maftur remembered the last time they had protested outside the district commissioner's house. One of the AWA central committee had tried to kick in the front door when no one had answered her knock. The same lady had hit a policeman when he had tried to stop her kicking the door. That incident had shocked her mother.

"Don't you ever do anything like that, Maftur," she had warned. "The only reason that woman was not arrested is because she has an influential husband."

Maftur hoped no one would start kicking doors down while she made her speech.

Aunt Bahia frowned. "Surely Maftur is too young to take on that responsibility? Someone a year or so older would be more suitable."

Mrs. Shawwa shook her head at Aunt Bahia. "Are you

forgetting, Mrs. al-Zeid, that the Central chapter chose a nine year old to deliver their speech last year? Now, is there any other business?"

Her mother looked around the room. "Does anyone know if the garden party in aid of the blind is open to anyone who can afford a ticket, or is just for the British?"

"Anyone," Mrs. Shawwa told her. "The charity's chairman told my husband he hoped all Haifa's citizens, regardless of community, would support the cause."

Janan laughed. "He's holding it on a Saturday, and he wants Jews to attend?"

"I don't know that he's got it altogether wrong," Aunt Bahia said. "You've only to look at our neighbours. They're Jewish, but they go swimming on Saturdays."

"Could we go to the garden party as a group?" her mother asked.

The president nodded her agreement. "It's certainly a worthy cause."

"Do you want me to organise a charabanc?" Janan asked.

Mrs. Shawwa pursed her lips. "With only twelve of us, we wouldn't fill one, but it's an event to which we can take our children, and have our husbands accompany us."

There was general murmur of approval, and everyone promised to let Janan know the numbers by the end of the week.

After the visitors had left, Maftur was about to race up to the roof to tell her cousins about the speech she was going to make, but her mother kept her back.

"You'll be coming to the garden party with me and your father," she said. "I want you to see the house the Quigleys live in. It belongs to the Old Man. It may well become your home when you marry. I wish I could think of a way to let you see inside."

"Will Aunt Bahia and Uncle Abu Rakim be taking Sabeen and Yalda?"

"I am sure they will, but don't say anything to your cousins about the Old Man owning the house."

For the next few days, she and Sabeen hoped that, now they were women, they could wear either a glamorous hijab or a real Parisian hat to the garden party but, to their disappointment, both her mother and Aunt Bahia insisted school straw hats were appropriate on this very British occasion. However, she and Sabeen united in refusing to wear hats with elastic that came under their chins. In the end, they compromised on plain-coloured cotton hijabs.

There were eight from their family going to the garden party—her parents, Sabeen and Yalda, Aunt Bahia, Uncle Abu Rakim, and Janan. The little ones were to stay behind with their respective nursemaids, and all three of her brothers said they wanted nothing to do with the British, despite both her father and Uncle Abu Rakim pointing out attendance could be good for business.

The day of the garden party arrived.

Most members of their AWA section were already on the charabanc when their family boarded it outside the al-Zeid building.

The charabanc turned the corner and stopped again in front of the Shawwa's house. Maftur was delighted to see Ismail accompanying his parents and married sister from Nablus. He looked very grown-up in black trousers with a sharp crease, a blue, broad-striped blazer and a striped blue tie, the whole outfit being topped by a straw boating hat. She was even more pleased when his parents chose the seat in front of the one where she, Sabeen and Yalda sat. Her nose was only a few inches from the back of Ismail's neck. He smelt better than her brothers, a personal odour, nothing to do with his brand of soap. So busy breathing in the smell, she didn't hear a thing her cousins said while the charabanc skirted a wadi on a road no more than a dirt track. They turned onto another dirt track crossing a small rocky plateau to a mountain spur that offered a magnificent vista of the Mediterranean to the south of Haifa.

They drew up in front of gates opening onto a long drive, lined with tall flame-shaped cypresses. Once the passengers had disembarked, the driver moved the charabanc to the end of the road and parked beyond double gates leading into the agricultural area of the estate. While waiting for the grown-ups to get moving, Maftur and her cousins tapped their feet to the rhythm of band music floating in the air from beyond the drive.

Mr. Shawwa went over to Maftur's father, taking Ismail with him. She heard her father introduce Uncle Abu Rakim. The three men, deep in conversation, started up the drive, with Ismail tagging behind. Mrs. Shawwa, her mother and Aunt Bahia followed Ismail.

While she and her cousins brought up the rear, Maftur watched out for the house that might one day be hers, but all she could see at first were purple bougainvillea and part of a window with a black iron shutter.

The music grew louder and more of the house came into view. It was two storeys high, stone built, and roofed with red tiles like the houses in the Greek Colony, except that a watch tower, topped by a crenulated parapet, rose at the far end.

At ground level a flight of four broad stone steps with carved stone balustrades on each side led to a pair of elaborately carved wooden doors. The bougainvillea, that covered most of the wall and gave the house a friendly look, had been cut back round the black iron shutters that flanked the windows.

A gravel path, lined with red geraniums and plants with purple velvet leaves, circled the house. A placard with the words 'THIS WAY' pointed to the right. Two British women sat at a table next to the path, selling tickets. The men paid and they all went round the side of the house to a large lawn dotted with tables under striped umbrellas. Many were already occupied with people sipping lemonade through ice. Seated on a semi-circle of seats in front of a cactus hedge, a band in Police uniform played marching tunes.

A tall, middle aged British man in a cream linen suit and straw hat swooped down on Mr. Shawwa, confirming his wife's often repeated assertion that her husband was on close terms with the British. Maftur listened to Mr. Shawwa introducing her father and her uncle as volunteers, willing to help the British administration organise the October opening of the new harbour. Eyes cast demurely down while listening, she learnt the British man was a Mr. Quigley who lived in this house that might be hers when she married.

"And will you join our committee, too?" Mr. Quigley asked Ismail. "We need to involve our younger citizens."

She marvelled at the confident way Ismail replied to this

important British government official.

"I would very much like to have been involved, sir, but unfortunately I have to return to England before the harbour is opened."

"And what about your good ladies?" Mr. Quigley asked Ismail's father.

Mr. Shawwa introduced his wife as the president of the local Woman's Movement.

Mr. Quigley called out to a slim woman in an out of date hat who was chatting in a nearby group, "Ann, my dear, can you join us for a moment?"

The lady, presumably Mrs. Quigley, came over, bringing with her a girl of Maftur's age but taller, wearing a straw school hat kept on with elastic under her chin. It looked like a Haifa High summer uniform hat but had a dark green silk band with an embroidered shield. Perhaps her mother had been right and she should have worn her school hat.

"Mrs. Shawwa," Mrs. Quigley said, "this is my wife, Ann. Ann my dear, Mrs. Shawwa is president of one of the chapters of the Women's Movement that you wanted to know about, and these other ladies all belong to the same chapter."

Mrs. Shawwa introduced all the ladies of their AWA section to Mrs. Quigley and then, much to Maftur's surprise, introduced her. "This is Maftur al-Zeid, who is studying at Haifa High School. She will be relaying our thoughts on village education to the District Commissioner in October."

Mrs. Quigley smiled at her. "How very brave of you, Maftur." She turned to introduce the girl beside her. "This is my daughter, Patsy. She attended Haifa High until a year ago. Now she goes to boarding school in England and is home for the summer only. I don't know how I would have managed without her today."

"Your daughter goes to school in England?" Mrs. Shawwa exclaimed. "So does my son. He has been at Harrow for four years."

Mrs. Quigley acknowledged Ismail with a brief smile before saying, "Have you ladies time to take a cup of tea with me? I do so want to hear about your movement. Men in this country engage enthusiastically in the political side of things, but you practical women are the ones who keep things running smoothly."

Mrs. Shawwa beamed. "But, of course, we would be delighted."

This promised to be one boring afternoon. Sabeen's and Yalda displayed faces as expressionless as she hoped her own was, but the British girl was not so careful.

"Do you need me any longer, Umm Pat?"

"I'm sure you don't want to be stuck here with grown-ups all afternoon, Patsy," Mrs. Quigley said. "Why don't you take these young people and show them around? Find yourselves some lemonade. Tell the ladies in charge I'll pay, and ask Cook for a box of her special biscuits."

Maftur had difficulty keeping her face straight when her mother said, "Mrs. Quigley, my daughter was saying as we came up the drive, what a wonderful view there must be from the top of the tower. Could your daughter take them up there?"

Trust her mother to seize the opportunity to get her inside the house.

"An excellent idea," Mrs. Quigley said, and turned to her husband. "Now, Sean, I imagine you men want some time on your own. I'll tell people you're in the rose garden if anyone needs you. We women will be at the big table furthest from the band."

Mrs. Quigley and the AWA members marched off in one direction, and the men in the other. To Maftur's surprise, Ismail remained behind.

Sabeen gave her a nudge and whispered, "Our parents must know a boy's with us, so I suppose it has to be all right."

"Ismail," Patsy said, "how are you getting on in Haifa? Did you find all your stuff intact?" Then she swivelled round, her face reddening. "I'm so sorry. I didn't mean to be rude, turning my back on you like that. I haven't seen Ismail since coming home. We got to know each other, talking on the journey between Lydda and Haifa, after the rest of my group had changed trains. Would you mind hanging on here while I ask Cook to set us up with lemonade and biscuits?"

Maftur watched the British girl race—as if still a child—to a tent where servants were coming in and out with trays of glasses, cups and pots of tea. She was out again in a flash and beckoning them to follow as she ran towards the house.

Maftur felt a pang of jealousy when Ismail set off at a run, but then he turned his head, "Come on!" he called. "What are you lot dawdling for?"

"It's okay," she whispered to Sabeen. "Our parents can't see us."

So they all ran, as if at school games. Yalda succumbed to a fit of giggles at the older girls behaving in such an unseemly fashion. They caught up with Patsy outside a narrow door fitted with patterned glass panels and flanked by a pair of mud scrapers decorated with dogs' heads.

"At the top of the tower," Patsy told them, "we can see as far as Chateau Pelerin."

She opened the door and they followed her into a lobby full of old coats, wellingtons and garden tools. An open baize-covered door at the far end of the lobby revealed a comfortable-looking room with carpet, armchairs and a writing desk. Maftur marvelled that one day all this might be hers.

Patsy started up carpeted stone stairs. Maftur followed, not wanting Sabeen or Yalda to notice her taking an undue interest in the Quigleys' private quarters. Patsy paused on a landing and then continued up a narrower uncarpeted spiral staircase.

Maftur paused to peer out of a slit in the walls just wide enough to take a rifle barrel, and Ismail bumped into her from the rear. He hastily apologized and she felt embarrassed, but not all her discomfort arose from Sabena's disapproving gaze or Yalda's unsuppressed giggles. She didn't want Ismail to think her clumsy. At the top of the steps, from a landing surrounding the stair well, a ladder reached up to a trap door. Patsy was already climbing the ladder and pushing it open.

Sabeen whispered, "If you insist on climbing up, let Ismail go first so he can't see up your skirts."

Maftur turned red. She hadn't thought of that. By then, Patsy had hauled herself onto the roof and was pulling at the ladder to extend it. Ismail started up. Maftur followed, glad that Patsy had extended the ladder so she could step gracefully onto the roof. Yalda was just behind.

Sabeen came up as well. "You two need someone to keep an eye on you."

Looking over the parapet, Maftur saw her father and at least a dozen other men sitting at a table in the shade of a rambler-covered gazebo, surrounded by geometrically laid-out rose beds. All had paper and ink wells. Presumably, they were the harbour committee Mr. Shawwa had mentioned.

She moved to the other side of the tower. Her mother and the other women of their AWA Section sat in deckchairs on the lawn. It didn't matter if they could see her. They wouldn't know she had had to climb a ladder to get to the roof.

She looked over to vineyards and apricot trees beyond the cactus hedge and hoped her great-grandfather was not going to sell the rest of the estate.

Patsy came and stood beside her. "People in Ottoman times needed this tower to watch out for bandits. They must have been very brave to build a house here in the wilderness."

The way Patsy talked made Ottoman times seem like history. Maftur wanted to tell her that it was her great-grandfather who had built the house, and he was still alive. Instead she said, "I envy you spending your childhood here."

Patsy looked sad. "You only appreciate something when you no longer have it."

"It's the same with me," Ismail said, and came to lean on the parapet next to Patsy. Maftur felt another twinge of jealousy, although she wouldn't have known what to do if Ismail had stood next to her. Sabeen would probably have had a heart attack.

"I still miss Nablus. Now I feel hemmed in by buildings."

Maftur wondered why both Patsy and Ismail were sent to England when there were perfectly good schools in Palestine.

"But Mount Carmel's a wonderful place for exploring," Patsy said.

Yalda pointed to some ruins far to the south. "Is that Chateau Peveril?"

Sabeen glared at her, presumably for making herself conspicuous.

"Yes," Patsy replied. "There's a big archaeological dig going on there this year. I wanted to help but it's all closed down for the summer."

"What made you want to help?" Ismail asked.

"I'm going to be an archaeologist when I grow up."

Maftur was so interested in that statement, she spoke up without thinking. "I didn't know women could be archaeologists."

"Of course they can. All the staff excavating with Miss Garrod are women."

"Not just the staff, but the labourers too. It's an all-female dig," Ismail added.

Patsy raised her eyebrows. "How do you know that?"

"Because both my mother and sister are in the Women's Movement. My sister was very excited about it the year before I went to England, and wanted to join in, but my mother didn't approve."

Maftur wished she could speak to Ismail directly like Patsy, but with Sabeen and Yalda watching it wasn't possible. She wanted to be part of this conversation, however, so addressed Patsy. "Do your parents know you want to be an archaeologist?"

Even that question gained her a sharp dig in the ribs from Sabeen.

"Of course. My father would love me to be an archaeologist. He says I'll have to work hard at school, though, to pass all the right exams."

Maftur wanted to ask what exams you had to sit to be an archaeologist, but knew, if she provoked Sabeen any more, she might report her to their mother.

There was a short silence then Ismail asked, "What else were you going to show us?"

"Lemonade and biscuits," Patsy said, "and cook has promised us ice cream, as well. So let's get going."

Sabeen was the first to reach the top of the ladder, determined to clamber down without anyone looking up her skirt.

Chapter 3

Maftur was sure her brothers were up to something. They had stacked orange boxes to screen off their end of the roof.

Whatever it was had nothing to do with the car engine. The boys had finished assembling it before Ismail Shawwa had sailed back to boarding school. The engine now stood abandoned next to the clothes-line, much to the annoyance of the women who demanded its removal, but it was too heavy for anyone to lift, and the boys refused to dismantle it.

They were pursuing their mysterious new hobby, with the assistance of various fellow members of the Arab Youth League. Their most frequent visitor was the brother of Maftur's best friend at school, Ai'isha. Maftur's brothers and Ai'isha called him Fizzy, but Maftur didn't think that was his real name.

While the boys were busy at their end of the roof, Maftur, Yalda and Sabeen spent most of their after-school time that second half of October behind the Greek oven, making a banner to mark the opening of Haifa Harbour to supplement the one the ladies of the AWA's local section were creating. The ladies probably wouldn't have thought of it if their president, Mrs. Shawwa and her husband hadn't been invited, along with important guests from all over the Middle East, to sit on a platform with the High Commissioner.

While Maftur cut material into shapes and sewed them onto an old bed sheet, she heard frequent sniggers and the occasional loud guffaw from behind the orange boxes. Most of the boys' conversation, however, was carried on in whispers, too quiet to be intelligible.

Maftur worked with even more diligence than Sabeen and Yalda, despite the fact that she hated sewing. They would be holding up this banner not only in honour of their city but also of Ismail's parents. While sewing, she mentally rehearsed her speech for the demonstration.

They finished their banner at last.

While the others took it indoors, Maftur went over to the

parapet to gaze down the mountain slope at the 400 acres recently reclaimed from the sea, where builders were now erecting dazzling white stores and hotels. She couldn't remember a time when Haifa hadn't been one large construction site.

She missed the giant crane that for three years had lifted enormous rocks into the sea to form a breakwater, but the harbour engineers had moved on to the other end of town to work on a refinery and quays for oil tankers.

Out in the bay a liner sailed purposefully towards the harbour where cargo ships were already anchored, awaiting their turn to be loaded with boxes of the earliest citrus fruits. The official harbour opening, she reflected, was merely a ceremony. The new harbour was already in full use.

Dodi emerged from behind the orange boxes and stood beside her, carrying a pair of binoculars which he focused on the liner.

"Look at that!"

To her astonishment, he actually handed her his binoculars.

"Look carefully. That ship's flying the new German flag, but it's full of immigrating Jews. That's what you are celebrating with your silly banner."

Maftur focused and made out a red flag with a central white circle. Inside the circle was a cross with all four arms bent at right angles.

"How do you know it's full of Jews?" she challenged. "It's most likely bringing people back to the German Colonies who've been visiting relatives."

"It was in the Youth League's newsletter, donkey girl. Germany is emptying all its Jews into Palestine as fast as they can get them out. Because of this new harbour you're so proud of, Jews are now coming directly to Haifa from Bremerhaven. They are even advertising kosher food on that ship."

He took back his binoculars but Maftur continued watching the liner. Her cousins, Sabeen and Yalda, joined her as it reached the harbour.

"I wish those buildings didn't hide the new square," Sabeen complained. "I want to see how much they've done."

"The platform's going to be huge," Yalda said. "A girl in

my class says the Endor Cinema is lending the government six hundred velvet seats to go on it."

The thought of standing in front of 600 important people while supporting a banner gave Maftur a sudden attack of nerves. "All those people staring at us!"

Visualizing the scene, she realised why her small role at the harbour ceremony made her so much more nervous than giving a speech at the demonstration. People on that platform would be looking down at her. When she made her speech, people would be looking up.

A voice said, "They won't get the chance to stare. We won't be there."

She swivelled round and saw Aunt Bahia standing behind them, arms folded, lips compressed.

Maftur's thoughts immediately turned to her ailing grandmother. *Has she been struck dead suddenly like Ai'isha's grandfather last term?* The thought turned her too numb to ask, so it was Sabeen who put the question. "Why not?"

"The Nablus branch of AWA has asked us to boycott the Harbour celebrations. The Jaffa branch has already agreed to do so."

Relieved that her grandmother wasn't the cause of Aunt Bahia's concern, Maftur was less irritated than she might have been when triumphant laughter rang out from behind the orange boxes at the other end of the roof.

"Sabeen, I'm off to a full AWA meeting at HQ," Aunt Bahia continued. "I want you supervising down in the kitchen. Yalda, you stay up here and keep an eye on the little ones. Maftur, your mother wants you to help Zubaida." She turned and left.

Sabeen shrugged as if she didn't care, but there were tears in her eyes as she said, "Well, that's that, then."

"I don't think we need give up on the celebrations just yet," Maftur said. "I can't see people with invitations surrendering their places on the VIP platform that easily."

The longer her mother was out at the emergency meeting, however, the less certain Maftur became that the women of Haifa would ignore the boycott call.

When her mother finally returned, looking tired and not too happy, Maftur feared the worst. She gave a quick check round the kitchen to make sure everything was as it should be, before asking, "Are we supporting the boycott?"

By that time, her mother had removed her hat and handed it to a servant to take upstairs. She paused to tie on her kitchen scarf before answering. "Mrs. Shawwa asked us what it would look like if she boycotted a festival her husband had helped organise. Members who had been invited to sit on the platform, or with husbands on the committee, agreed with her."

"What about everyone else?"

"Several ladies who'd been upset when their husbands hadn't received an invitation were loud in support of the boycott, but in the end we voted against it by a narrow margin."

Maftur's spirits lightened but she was surprised to see her mother still looking worried.

"Aren't you pleased, Umm?"

"We're being hypocritical. If the harbour had been built in Jaffa, the Haifa branch would have supported a boycott unanimously."

Knowing she would be able to hold up the banner after all, however, Maftur wasn't too worried about the morality of the issue. She ran back to the roof. It was deserted. No sound came from behind the orange boxes. On impulse, she slipped behind the barrier, terrified in case anyone came up and caught her in male territory. She saw a furled banner, similar in size to the one she and her cousins had laboured over, propped against a water tank next to several cans of paint. She opened the banner out slowly to stop it rustling. The boys had divided it horizontally into three stripes, black, white and green. The central white stripe bore the slogan –

KEEP PALESTINE ARABIC

As she unfurled the banner further she saw, painted across the stripes at one end, a red triangle, in the middle of which was a stylized image of a black hand.

She put her hand to her mouth as she realised the enormity of what her brothers were doing, but at the same time she felt a thrill of excitement.

The 'Black Hand' was the symbol of an outlawed organization fighting for Palestinian independence, led by a really handsome Syrian, Sheikh Izz ad-Din al-Qassam.

Dodi and Dindan had once boasted that they would run away from home and join al-Qassam when they were old enough. She had wished then that she were a boy, so she too could fight for her country, but she had grown up since and was more sensible. She knew holding up that banner in full view of all the police guarding the platform would be even more dangerous than joining the gang. Her brothers would be arrested. Then what would her parents feel? Her father would be furious, if only because it would be bad for the family business. Her mother would be devastated. Although she supported action against uncontrolled Jewish immigration, her children were more important to her than politics.

For her family's sake, she must stop her brothers hoisting that flag. But how? Snitching wasn't an option unless she wanted her brothers to make the rest of her life a misery. If she hid the banner, the boys would still have time to make another, and they would guess who had taken it.

The best plan, she decided, was to get up earlier than anyone else on the day of the harbour opening, and spill pots of paint over it, doing her best to make it look like an accident. She re-furled the banner and propped it up carefully before returning downstairs.

Supper that night was not a happy affair. Dodi and Dindan glared at their mother as she reported the outcome of the women's group meeting to her husband.

When Dodi declared that she and the rest of the Haifa women had let down the whole Arab cause, their father yelled. "Da'oud. How dare you address your mother like that? Leave the room and wait for me in the Liwan. I expect to find you concentrating on your homework when I come in."

Dodi slunk away, his face sullen. Dindan followed. Her father did not call either of them back, just glowered.

"You would think that by their age they would realise a new harbour is good for business," he grumbled. "Mind you, I'm surprised Mr. Shawwa took the stand he did against the boycott. The rowdies in Nablus are liable to attack his estate when they find out."

"I am not so sure they would," her mother replied. "Mrs. Shawwa says they are grateful to her husband for not selling his land to Jews like several other Saudi landowners."

"He can't rely on that gratitude much longer. There's big trouble brewing, habipti, and I'm worried about our business. The Arab Executive has called on us to strike, but my father has ordered us to keep the warehouse open, so this morning the Muslim Christian Association sent hooligans from the Arab Youth League to threaten to set our buildings on fire unless we close. When I see Da'oud and Adad after the news, I'm ordering them to leave that League."

"But you ordered them to join only a few months ago," her mother protested. "You told them it was an excellent way to make useful business connections."

"It seemed so at the time, but not now the Muslim Christian Association is using it."

Whatever her father said, Maftur knew the boys would only pretend to obey. They had too many friends in the League to leave.

Her father tuned in their wireless to listen to announcements on the Empire Broadcasting Station. He was proud of that wireless. He had been one of the first to buy one after the BBC had advertised the new service. Her mother had suggested right from the beginning that she should listen to the announcements every night with them, before getting on with her homework.

Tonight they heard that the High Commissioner had decreed a curfew in Haifa, Jerusalem, Jaffa and Nablus for four nights. She had to stay in every evening, anyway, so it wouldn't affect her, so long as they lifted curfew in time for the fireworks on Tuesday. Her brothers would be upset, though, as they usually went out to see friends after they had finished their homework.

"I suppose the curfew's a result of the strike," her mother commented.

"Not just the strike," her father replied. "Didn't you hear the second announcement? The High Commissioner has banned a procession in Jaffa from marching round the whole town. Why the people there want a procession, I can't think. It's bound to cause trouble."

"If we sit back and do nothing, soon there will be as many Jews as us in the country," her mother said. "How else can we make our feelings known, except by processions and demonstrations?"

Maftur liked the way her mother argued politics with her father when there were no visitors around, although she knew it shocked Granny.

Her father pushed his glasses straight as if that made it easier for him to pontificate. "These demonstrations have nothing to do with getting rid of Jews. Jaffa's boatmen and the citrus growers are behind it. Once all the large cargo and passenger ships dock in Haifa, Jaffa boatmen will lose custom and citrus growers will have to pay extra to send oranges further up the coast."

"All very well," her mother argued back, "but they can't expect the government to pull our harbour down, now it's up, so why carry on with the protests?"

"They can try to force the government to rebuild Jaffa harbour. It wouldn't surprise me to learn that even Jewish citrus growers aren't secretly supporting these strikes. Most people down south are citrus growers first, and Arabs and Jews second."

Her mother waved her arms in dismissal. "All those narrow streets in Jaffa between the main road and the port! They'd have to pull down half the city to make it work."

"Whatever the cause, habipti, there's trouble brewing and I don't want my sons involved."

Chapter 4

The morning after the Haifa Women's Association had voted to support the harbour opening, Fizzy called for Maftur's brothers before school. Dodi and Dindan rushed off to get their satchels.

"Come back and wait for your sister and cousins," her mother ordered as they made their way towards the front door.

They stopped reluctantly.

"Get a move on, Maffy," Dodi growled. "You're such a slowcoach. Dindan, go over the corridor and buck up our cousins."

Maftur couldn't see why her brothers had to accompany her to school. It wasn't fair. Boys could go off by themselves where and when they liked, but girls could go nowhere without a male escort. She took her time collecting her coat and school hat.

Out on the street, the boys raced down the hill. Maftur, Sabeen and Yalda followed more slowly.

As they walked past their neighbours' house, Miriam Khan, who also went to Haifa High, came out and joined them as usual. Miriam was in Maftur's class, and counted as a friend, although not her best friend. That was Ai'isha.

Miriam's family were Jews. She was one of only two Jewish girls in the senior section of Haifa High. The other was an English Jew who had entered the High School section by way of the British Preparatory classes, but Miriam was an Arab-speaking Jew. Her family had lived in Palestine longer than Maftur's.

Far in front, the boys stopped at the junction of their road and the one leading to Haifa High.

"You'll be all right by yourselves the rest of the way," Dodi shouted. "Plenty of other boys are taking sisters to school. They'll look out for you. We have to meet a friend, and, Sabeen, if you tell your mother we didn't go with you all the way, I'll tell your father you asked me to let Fizzy take you to school without the rest of us."

Sabeen was too embarrassed to reply.

"You dirty-minded donkey," Maftur shouted at him. "Your lies will catch you out one day."

But the boys weren't listening. They had already run off in the opposite direction.

"Don't take any notice of him, he's just a bit of camel turd," Maftur comforted her cousin but Sabeen, Yalda and Miriam looked so horrified at her obscene language, she felt she had only made matters worse. They walked on in silence.

In the schoolyard, Maftur and Miriam separated from Sabeen and Yalda to join their own class already in line on the netball court. Ai'isha Tata beckoned her to the place she had saved, and whispered, in some excitement, that Fizzy was skipping school that morning to attend a special meeting of the Arab Youth League. He'd made her promise not to tell her parents.

Maftur deduced that was why her brothers hadn't seen her and her cousins all the way to school. They were attending the meeting too, despite everything her father had said the previous evening. She wondered what was so urgent that a League meeting had to be called during school time. It would have to finish in time for Friday prayers. Her brothers might get away with skipping school but her father would know if they weren't at the mosque.

At supper that evening, Dodi and Dindan were quieter than usual but kept grinning to each other as if relishing a particularly juicy secret.

Her parents talked about the harbour opening ceremony. The emir of Transjordan would be there and a whole trainful of important people from Egypt, Syria, Lebanon, Turkey and Cyprus.

"We must find somewhere that allows a good view of the platform," her mother said. "I want to see the clothes the women will be wearing, especially those from Egypt and Lebanon. I don't think anyone's coming from France, more's the pity. Where will you be standing, Abu Kamal?"

"With the rest of the committee that weren't honoured with invitations," her father replied, "checking that nothing goes wrong."

Maftur wondered if her mother realised how crowded the

square would be. They would need to leave in the middle of the night to bag a good place, but how could they if there was a curfew?

After the meal, her father tuned in the wireless again.

"A banned procession in Jaffa has gone ahead in defiance of government orders."

Both Dodi and Dindan waved their arms in delighted excitement until their father's grim stare subdued them.

"Fighting broke out between the police and a huge crowd of demonstrators. Shots were fired, people killed."

Her mother gave a gasp. "You must go to the warehouse at once, Abu Kamal, and telephone Uncle Mussa to see if everyone in Jaffa's all right."

Her father jumped up, put on his jacket and fez. "Boys, come with me."

Maftur and her mother turned their attention back to the wireless, eager for more details. The presenter read a message from the High Commissioner. He had ordered a curfew in all cities, from midnight until seven in the morning. However, to Maftur's relief, the great man declared he would not allow any disturbances to interfere with the harbour celebrations.

Father and her brothers returned only a few minutes later. "We heard gunfire," he explained. "A neighbour told us there's a mob rampaging downtown, so we came home, but there's no need to worry, Umm Kamal. None of our family's so stupid as to be out on the streets during riots, not after what happened in Jerusalem."

Maftur shuddered as she recalled the riots in Jerusalem only three weeks earlier. If the police hadn't driven the mob into the old city and locked the city gates, the papers said the rioters would have looted modern Jerusalem and burnt it to the ground.

The suqs in Jaffa and Haifa didn't have fortified walls with gates. What would happen if the mob came surging up their street?

A knock sounded on the front door. Mahmoud, the houseman, brought her father a message.

After skimming through it, he told them, "An order from The Muslim Christian league to strike tomorrow or face the consequences. I am going to collect my brother and Kamal. We must try and make Father see sense."

Maftur's school wasn't open on Saturdays so the strike wouldn't affect her, but as soon as their father had left the apartment, Dodi and Dindan waved their arms in delight.

"You needn't start rejoicing yet," her mother told them. "Your school hasn't sent letters home. So it will be lessons for both of you tomorrow unless we hear otherwise."

Her father returned a good hour later, to report her grandfather had at last agreed to close the warehouse.

Next morning Maftur watched her brothers set off for school with a meekness that surprised her until she reflected that they were probably about to attend a meeting of the Arab Youth League instead. Her father remained in the dining room reading both newspapers—the daily Filastin which he usually took to work with him and the weekly al-Karmil which he read at home before passing it on to her mother. Her mother liked it because its women's page reported on female issues not only locally, but also regionally, and internationally. When she had finished with it, her mother passed it on to her.

Her father read aloud a report in the al-Filastin, claiming thirty people had been killed in the Jaffa riots. Maftur had often wondered what was in the al-Filastin. Hesitantly she asked, "Baba, do you think I could read your paper when you have finished with it?"

He looked up in surprise, but seemed to give the question serious consideration. Eventually he replied, "No. It is too fiery for you, ya Maftur. I will order the Palestine Post. It will help with your English as well. Your brothers, too, could benefit from reading a moderate paper."

So the Filastin was too fiery for her to read? Maftur determined to sneak a look at it when she got the chance. Meanwhile, at least she had won the right to read a daily paper.

"Well done, Maftur," her mother said when her father retired to the men's quarters. "I've been asking him to order the Palestine Post all year. If he thinks your brothers will read it, though, he's very much mistaken. They won't look at a Jewish-owned paper."

Alone with her mother, Maftur felt free to ask, "Umm, how can we be sure to bag the best place to hold our banners if the curfew goes on until seven am?"

Her mother gave a complacent smile. "You thought I

hadn't done anything about that? Four of us are sending our housemen down to the square before midnight. The police say they can sleep there during curfew, provided they take a tent."

The apartment door opened and Sabeen walked in, dressed in going-out clothes. "Aunty Noor, since there's no trouble in town this morning, our mother says Yalda and I can go with our houseman to pick the most suitable place for our banner. May Maftur come with us?"

Maftur looked at her mother, willing her to agree.

Her mother smiled. "I can manage here by myself this morning. I would have sent our Mahmoud with you as well, but he's out buying vegetables. The square is close to the police station, though, so you should be safe enough. Don't go any further than the square, and return immediately if there's any hint of trouble. Sabeen, I know you're too sensible to let the others wander off. Maftur, don't forget I want to hear you practice reading your piece about village schools this afternoon. You still need to throw your voice more if you want people to hear you."

On their way down to the square Sabeen nudged Maftur and pointed across the road. "What are your brothers doing out of school so early?"

Maftur followed her gaze and saw Dodi, Dindan and two other boys dart into a greengrocer's shop still open despite the strike. She was terrified Sabeen would report back to Aunt Bahia.

"Please don't tell your mother you saw them. They'll blame me for sneaking on them."

Sabeen frowned. "But why are they skipping lessons?"

"I haven't the faintest idea," Maftur lied, but added more truthfully, "My brothers don't tell me anything."

A little later, she and her cousins were standing on the square which only three years earlier had been a small harbour called the Kaisersee.

"Look, there's a bandstand," Yalda shouted.

"That's for the police band," Maftur told her. "It's famous all over Palestine. The father of a girl in my class is in it."

Workmen, all Jewish judging by their clothes, were attaching gaily coloured bunting to tall poles and erecting an enormous wooden platform.

Maftur ran to a spot close to the front. "Our AWA section should stand here."

The others agreed. While Sabeen talked to Jibril, her houseman, making sure he could find the spot again, Maftur stared round at huge hoardings advertising the academy award winning film 'Cavalcade' being shown at the Endor cinema as part of the celebrations.

"We must make sure our parents take us to that."

"And the fireworks," Yalda said. "I'm so excited I just can't wait."

Sabeen suggested it was time to return home. On the way back they passed a new hotel. Looking up at its curving stone balconies, Maftur saw a sad-looking girl of her own age staring down, and gave a friendly smile and a wave. The girl waved back, returning the smile. Maftur hoped she had made someone a little happier as she hastened to catch up with the others.

Back home her mother greeted her with the words, "I'm so glad you're back. Mahmoud is still out. He's never taken this long shopping before. I was afraid there was trouble again."

"We didn't see any trouble," Maftur said.

It was another hour, however, before Mahmoud burst into the kitchen, perspiring heavily. He set down an empty basket.

"Umm Kamal, all the shops in town were shut because of the strike and there was a huge crowd milling around the suq. I went to the expensive greengrocers I had seen open on my way down, but by the time I arrived it too was shut and there were young boys throwing stones at cars, with no one stopping them. I met a man I knew. He told me a crowd from the suq had just run into the square and were tearing down the platform."

Her mother threw up her hands, saying, "Thank goodness the girls were back before trouble started," and sat down to draw up an alternative menu.

Maftur ran up to the roof where Sabeen and Yalda were teaching younger girls a new version of hopscotch, and told them what Mahmoud had reported. They moved over to the wall overlooking downtown Haifa and the sea, leaving the little ones to play on their own, and saw the roofs farther down the hill crowded with people. A thin plume of dark grey smoke, the only visual clue that anything was wrong, rose from behind the buildings hiding the new square.

"Look at that," Maftur shouted. "That's where we were only two hours ago."

Now they were listening for it, they could hear shouts and yells rising from down town Haifa. A few minutes later, they heard sharp reports.

Maftur gripped the edge of the parapet. "Are those gun shots?"

A swarm of tiny figures raced up King George Street.

The smaller children stopped playing and joined the older girls at the parapet, the littlest demanding to be picked up. The crowd drew closer. Amongst them, they could see Dodi and Dindan. Instead of entering their apartment block by the front door, the boys limped past the building and rounded the bend.

Everyone rushed to the other side of the roof and saw the boys walk slowly down the steps to the backyard and then climb the fire escape. As her brothers clambered onto the roof, Maftur saw they both had torn shirts, and there was a large bruise on Dodi's arm.

"Take the little ones downstairs," she ordered Yalda, "and don't say anything to the grown-ups."

Dindan reached the roof and sank down, blood trickling from a cut on his forehead.

"You needn't stand there staring!" Dodi snapped. "Dindan and I slipped over the edge of a wadi after school, trying to get a bird's nest. Luckily, an olive tree growing on a ledge broke our fall, otherwise you'd be attending our funeral. Maftur, get a bowl of water, some iodine and other stuff from the medicine cabinet."

"You can forget the bird's nest story," Maftur retorted. "We saw you running up from town. We'll only keep quiet if you tell us what you were really doing."

Dodi shrugged. "Very well, if it will stop you snitching, I'll tell you when you've brought the water."

Maftur knew Dodi would mentally rehearse his story to make it as impressive as possible and looked forward to hearing the result.

While she and Sabeen bathed Dindan's wounds, Dodi started. "We took a banner we had made for the harbour opening down to the suq to join the rest of our League. There were thousands of men there already. Because our banner was the best, one of the leaders let us go to the front when we marched to the police station. A whole lot of British police wearing tin helmets rushed at us with their batons. That's where Dindan got hurt. Many men turned off down a side street but Dindan and I found some bricks. We threw them at the police. The police tried to hit us but we ran faster."

When they returned downstairs their mother accepted the boys' bird's nest story without question. Their father appeared more sceptical when their mother relayed it, but he was more concerned with the aftermath of the riot. "They'll have to cancel the celebrations after today's events."

Maftur felt a sense of outrage. "The High Commissioner promised he wouldn't let riots stop the celebrations."

"He'll just have to break his promise," Dodi sneered. "There's no way he's going to get that stand rebuilt in time."

Maftur could almost smell the satisfaction oozing from every pore in his body.

Dindan joined in to support his brother, "Even if they did, we'd only…"

Beneath the table, Maftur felt Dodi's leg skim past hers to deliver a sharp kick to Dindan's shin. Her younger brother froze mid-sentence.

There was a knock on the front door. Mahmoud brought in a letter and gave it to her mother. "Abu Ismail's houseman brought it for Umm Kamal."

Her mother tore the envelope open and skimmed through the message. "Oh, Maftur, I am so sorry. After all your hard work on the speech, Mrs. Shawwa says in view of the recent riots AWA are cancelling tomorrow's demonstration."

Maftur was stunned. She had so looked forward to showing how capable she was.

There will be other times, dear…"

But not in front of the district commissioner, with the newspapers sending reporters.

Her mother looked at her father. "Baba, you're on the

committee. What will they do about the stand, with all those important visitors coming?"

Baba shrugged. "Its destruction is not yet official." He rose to tune in the wireless. The High Commissioner himself spoke.

Maftur listened intently. To her dismay, he announced that in view of the twenty-one tragic deaths over the past few days, festivities would be inappropriate, so harbour celebrations would be severely curtailed. He had cancelled the luncheon for important foreign visitors. Instead of a grand public opening, he would read his speech to a small group of government officials. The curfew would continue so there would be no firework display.

Maftur sulked but Dodi and Dindan grinned widely.

"He can't guarantee the safety of the VIPs he's invited," Dodi said. "So he's going to look very silly."

Her mother gave Maftur a sympathetic glance. "Never mind, dear, we can all still go to see Cavalcade on Wednesday afternoon, unless—" She looked at her sons "—your principles won't let you attend that part of the celebrations."

Her father glared at the boys. Under his stare, the boys faltered.

"Of course we want to go," Dodi said.

* * * *

The harbour opening was the most miserable day Maftur had ever spent. The headmistress had cancelled the promised holiday, but it was obvious neither pupils nor teachers wanted to be at school. In the evening, instead of fireworks there was a dreary radio-telephonic speech by the British Secretary of state in London, restating British policy on their government of Palestine as mandated by the League of Nations.

"Just think," her father said in an awed whisper, "that message is coming by telephone and radio, yet all of us can hear it at almost the same time that man is speaking."

It didn't make it any more interesting. The Secretary of State sounded too pompous to be real.

"There is, under the Mandate, an obligation to facilitate the establishment of a National Home for the Jewish people in Palestine, but

at the same time there is an equally definite obligation to safeguard the rights of all the inhabitants of Palestine. The Mandate carries with it a clear duty to Arabs and to Jews. That duty will be discharged fully and fairly without fear or favour."

"Does he have to use such difficult words?" her mother complained. "I don't know what he's talking about."

"Neither does he," Dodi muttered.

Chapter 5

Ramadan started in the third week of December that year. Maftur really enjoyed the meals after sunset had ended the daytime fasts. Although they never ate luxury food during Ramadan, her family's cooking skills made simple communal meals delicious.

While Granny intermittently stirred the harees (best described as a sort of mutton porridge) in the great clay oven on the roof for five hours, the other women created side dishes in their private kitchens. Aunt Bahia made Shourabat Adas (lentil soup), Janan put herself in charge of the tabbouleh and other salads, while Mother and Zubaida between them concentrated on the small meat pastries served as starters.

By the second week of January, the weather had turned bitter. Granny, however, while grumbling about the cold despite the extra clothes she had piled on, continued to use the outdoor oven.

Maftur hoped the weather would turn milder before Ramadan ended. Their family had invited at least one hundred people to what they expected to be the last meal of the month, so they would have to eat it in the open.

Grandpa came up while Maftur and her family were finishing their pre-dawn meal, and told them Granny had complained of stabbing pains in her side and chest during the night. Now she was talking wildly and seemed to be seeing things that weren't there. What should he do?

"I'll come straight away," her mother replied, pushing her plate away. "Dalia, get the thermometer and bring it downstairs."

However, when her mother tried inserting the thermometer in Granny's mouth, her grandmother mistook her for a demon forcing her to break her fast. When she eventually succeeded in taking Granny's temperature, she ordered Grandpa to go out and call a doctor at once.

As Granny wheezed painfully on the bed, with sweat pouring down her face, Maftur, her mouth dry with fear, gazed down at her and whispered, "Is Granny going to die?"

"Not if I can help it!" her mother replied. "But all is the will of Allah. You run up and tell your Aunt Bahia she is now in charge of the oven, and ask your father to come down before he goes to work."

"Isn't there anything you want me to do?"

Her mother kissed her hair. "You can stay home from school and help prepare for Eid. I wish we could cancel tonight's meal, but we've invited too many. Oh, and while I think about it, Abu Mussa is due in Haifa the day after tomorrow. He's supposed to be staying with Granny and Grandpa, so we'll have to put him up. Luckily, Uncle Ahmed is not with him this time. Tell the housemaids to air the guest room and put in clean bedding, while you help Cook and Zubaida in the kitchen. Can you remember all that?"

She repeated the instructions and her mother smiled. "One thing, although I'm leaving you in charge, always accept advice from Zubaida and Mahmoud. They know what they're doing. Now go upstairs and don't come down again unless I send for you. You'll have quite enough to do."

Maftur was determined to get everything right. She gave her mother's messages to Aunt Bahia and her father, before going to the kitchen where Zubaida was up to her wrists in flour.

Zubaida took her hands out of the mixing bowl and washed them under the tap as Maftur passed on her mother's orders.

"You'll have to deal with the meat pies and the tahini sauce, Maftur, while I supervise the housework. The rest is all in hand for today and for Eid too if, Allah willing, the moon shines tonight. You must find out from your father whether the men will eat in the family dining room or in the Liwan when Abu Mussa comes."

Later, while Zubaida fried pine nuts and the scullery maid peeled and chopped onions, Maftur rolled out the dough to make pastry squares. Outside the kitchen window, it had started to snow. She stopped work and pressed her face to the glass. The pines on the top of the mountain were turning white but the snow wasn't settling on the bushes in the yard.

A shivering Mahmoud came through the back door and

put down the baskets of shopping. "The baker will deliver the hot bread after the first evening prayers."

He stood by the paraffin heater to warm his hands. "I've never known such a cold Ramadan. People in the suq were saying that Jerusalem has had snow."

"That should put a damper on tomorrow's demonstrations," Maftur commented.

Zubaida, who was checking Mohammad's accounts, sighed in exasperation. "Why anyone should want to mix Eid with politics, I'll never know."

Aunt Bahia entered the kitchen carrying a bucket of soaked lentils, a sheep shoulder bone, a bowl of clarified butter and a string of onions. "Zubaida, I'll have to leave you to cook the lentil soup. Sabeen and I will be up on the roof concentrating on the harees."

"Is the snow settling there?"

"Not by the oven. I've told Fibril to sweep the parapets and the men's end of the roof."

Maftur spent the next half hour picking through lentils before passing them through a sieve.

The scullery maid chopped yet more onions.

A beam of sunlight lit up the kitchen. The snow had stopped. The sky showed blue.

Maftur set about mixing sweet dough, creating a variety of extravagant fig, date, nut, almond, pistachio and walnut biscuits and dessert bases that wouldn't be eaten until Eid. It was hard being surrounded by these things after nearly a month's abstinence from sweet stuff but it was even worse later when, after a whole day without food or water, she had to suffer the exquisite torture of a kitchen filled with the aroma of cooking pastries.

Zubaida and Mohammad went upstairs to organise the setting up of tables.

Her father arrived home shortly before sunset as everyone was busy ferrying meat pies, lentil soup and salads upstairs. "The doctor says your grandmother has pneumonia and pleurisy."

She looked at him, aghast. People died from pneumonia.

"The turning point should come tonight. Your grandfather and I wanted to stay but your mother says we won't be any use in a sick room. She'll send word if your grandmother takes a turn for the worse. Meanwhile, you are not to go down with food before sunset, or it may upset Granny, if she's conscious enough to notice."

Maftur joined the rest of the family on the roof. Clouds had returned and hid the setting sun. Warmly-wrapped visitors came up, using the stairs or the fire escape, and waited for the muezzins to call out adhans.

Once prayers had been said, the feast started. Maftur and Sabeen took small bites from their meat pastries to acknowledge the breaking of the fast, before taking loaded trays down to Granny's apartment.

Sabeen returned to help her mother after she had kissed Granny's hand, but Maftur lingered on. "Please let me stay here to look after Granny while you go upstairs, Umm."

"That's sweet of you, dear, but I haven't taught you yet what to do in a medical emergency. Your Aunt Bahia is coming to keep watch later, and we will take turns sleeping. You go on up now. If the moon shines tonight I don't want to see you again until you're in your new Eid finery."

Maftur hesitated. "You'll tell me if anything bad happens during the night."

"I will. Even if you are asleep I will wake you up but, imshallah, all will be well. Now go, so I can eat that fine meal you brought."

Maftur went up to join the others, feeling that if anyone could get Granny through this illness it would be her mother.

On the roof, everyone was talking, eating and laughing despite the cold, the older women keeping warm as they gathered in front of the oven, the elderly men sitting at the other end, well wrapped up in blankets. She wondered how they could all be happy while Granny was so desperately ill.

It was still cloudy. Everyone was sure they would have to wait another day before they could celebrate Eid. Then Mahmoud, who had been told to listen to the wireless in the dining room, rushed through the doorway to announce the new moon had been seen in Jerusalem. Eid would begin in the morning. Everyone cheered.

* * * *

After a restless start to the night, expecting a message to arrive any time, Maftur woke early. If it hadn't been for her concern over Granny, she would have been excited. This was the first year she had been old enough to join in the Eid prayers, the only public prayers the women in her family ever attended. For the first time she felt really and truly grown-up.

Zubaida came in carrying a bowl of soft, moist dates and a gold carrier bag that held her new Eid clothes.

"Eid Mubarak," they cried in unison.

"Is everything all right with Granny?" Maftur asked.

"Your grandmother is still very ill, but your mother sent a message to say she has turned the corner and you are not to worry."

For the time being she had to accept that. She pulled out the contents of the bag. Court shoes in patent leather with pretty curved heels, and sturdier shoes for rougher conditions, a well-cut woollen coat in navy, far more elegant than her school gabardine.

She was slightly disappointed to find, instead of the two-piece woollen costume with the bias cut skirt she had longed for, a tartan dress similar to the one she had received the previous year, but at least the skirt was longer. Last of all, there was a warm cashmere hijab, soft white with a shadowy beige cedar of Lebanon motif. Maftur had really wanted a hat but realised it would not have been appropriate for Eid. Even Janan wore a hijab to Eid prayers.

As soon as she had washed and said her prayers, she munched at the dates, the first sweet thing she had tasted since the start of Ramadan. As with last year, she found they had far more flavour after the long abstinence.

As Maftur viewed herself in the mirror, Sabeen came in, also in her new finery and with her hands already hennaed. Maftur wanted to rush downstairs to see Granny straight away, but Zubaida insisted on drawing henna designs on her hands before letting her go.

"Janan and I will be in the foyer waiting for you both."

"Eid Mubarak! My, you look so beautiful," Aunt Bahia called out, as she and Sabeen ran into Granny's entrance hall.

"Eid Mubarak," Maftur automatically replied, although her mind wasn't on the greeting. "How's Granny?"

'Still sleeping but, praise be to Allah, the crisis has passed."

"Where's Aunt Noor?" Sabeen asked.

"In bed. She's been up nearly all night, but I'll wake her so we can take the children to watch the procession. Now, Sabeen and Maftur, it's time you set off for prayers."

"Is there nothing I can do to help here?" Maftur asked.

"No. Run along now."

Although her offer of help was sincere, Maftur was relieved she could attend her first Eid prayers.

Reciting 'Allahu Akbar' all the way, they took an icy goat path up to an undeveloped area of mountainside where most people they knew were congregating. Along with everyone else, they continued reciting until the formal prayers started.

With delicate new shoots of winter grass growing under her feet, and surrounded by hundreds of people all concentrating on praying, that morning Maftur felt Allah to be closer and more real than she had ever known.

After prayers, the men went off to join the marchers who were carrying the letter of protest to the mosque.

Maftur, along with Zubaida, Janan and Sabeen, went to meet her mother and the children, who all carried large bags of carefully wrapped parcels full of the sweetmeats prepared the previous day. Zubaida made her way back to the apartment block, but the rest of them walked down town to watch the marchers. Maftur hoped they would keep to the agreed route. It was deviating from the official route that had started the rioting in Jaffa the previous October.

Everyone in the crowd was waving and shouting Eid greetings. All the same, she wished the men had chosen a different day for their demonstration.

Before long the scouts and their musicians came marching past, carrying high the black, green, white and red flag of the Arab rebellion against the Turks. In the crowd, people waved miniature versions of the flag. Maftur watched her younger brothers, amidst a gaggle of schoolmates, presumably all from the Arab Youth League, march past, waving their flags more vigorously than anyone else.

Waving a huge red flag violently above their heads, a man dashed into the procession and took up position in the midst of the boys, causing a kerfuffle around him.

Maftur felt her stomach churn, certain this was the start of a riot. Her mother declared it was time to leave.

Maftur took one last backward look at the procession, relieved to see two policemen frogmarch the communist away, while the scouts marched on unperturbed. However, throughout the subsequent tour of relatives giving and receiving sweetmeats, Maftur worried about the safety of their menfolk.

She and her mother left the tour early. Her mother went back to Granny's flat and she helped Zubaida make ready cakes stuffed with raisins and dates. While, around her in the kitchen, the live-out servants discussed the likelihood of rioting starting after the Sheik had read the letter of protest in the mosque, she kept dashing to the Liwan to look down the street, relieved each time to hear and see nothing out of the ordinary. Eventually Dodi and Dindan returned in one piece surrounded by friends, and retired to the men's quarter.

When Dodi appeared in the kitchen to demand a tray of coffee, cakes and sweetmeats, Maftur seized the opportunity to ask what had happened down town.

"Nothing!" Dodi replied in a disgusted tone. "No one did anything. They just listened to the proclamation and walked away to visit relatives."

Chapter 6

Maftur skipped school again on the second day of Eid. Before helping out in the kitchen, she went to visit her grandmother who was out of danger but still very poorly.

"Don't be surprised if she doesn't recognize you," her mother warned. "She keeps thinking I'm her daughter."

Maftur raised her eyebrows.

"You never met her daughter, of course," her mother continued. "She died in the same flu epidemic as Ahmed's mother."

Maftur kissed her grandmother's hand and was glad her mother had issued the warning when her grandmother called her Parveen. Before she returned to work, her mother promised to let them know when Abu Mussa arrived.

She appeared while Maftur was filling dessert pastries with cream and nuts. "Abu Mussa says he wishes to eat with the whole family. You won't believe it but your Grandfather has consented to eat with us as well, so long as I don't tell Belle-mère."

Her mother then examined the four chickens Zubaida had rubbed with lemon juice. "There should be enough there for eighteen people. The little ones don't eat all that much. Did Mahmoud find decent eggplants?"

"The best in the suq."

To Maftur's delight her mother then said, "Your Aunt Bahia has kindly offered to sit with Granny, so I can eat with you. Remember to send her a beautiful tray."

"What should we prepare for your mother-in-law, Umm Kamal?" Zubaida asked.

"Bahia says not to bother. She'll make her beef broth and an egg custard, although I doubt if Belle Mere will eat much. Remember, Maftur, everything has to go well. Next to the Old Man, Abu Mussa is the most important person in the family."

Maftur knew she was being silly to feel overwhelmed by the responsibility, because Zubaida had everything under control but, all the same, she panicked she might let her family down.

Despite her fears, the meal went well, with the array of hors d'oevres looking even more appetizing than usual and the chickens cooked to perfection.

The men belched their satisfaction.

After desserts had been served and sampled, Janan squeezed her hand and whispered, "These pastries are well up to the standard everyone expects in my mother-in-law's household."

After the food had been cleared and coffee and nuts served, her father teased her mother. "Ya Umm Kamal, I see I can lend you out more often without suffering dire consequences, now Maftur can take charge of the household."

Abu Mussa responded, "Ya Abu Kamal. You are indeed a very fortunate man. Umm Kamal has trained your daughter well."

Maftur relaxed enough to follow the rest of the conversation intelligently. She discovered Abu Mussa had found a buyer for her great-grandfather's citrus groves at el Tireh, and would be going over the next day to clinch the deal. It saddened her to discover that her great-grandfather had decided to sell the groves.

She didn't often dwell on her matrimonial prospects since she had been granted the reprieve, but she had had occasional fantasies of inviting friends to picnic under leafy canopies, with the fragrant odour of orange blossom wafting over them, after she was married to Ahmed. There was something special about the bright green of citrus groves when the mountain range looming over them stood brown and grey in the heat of summer.

"Who's bought them?" Uncle Abu Rakim asked.

"A settler in the Hefer Valley."

Maftur watched Dodi narrow his eyes and lean forward, his top lip curling in contempt as he hissed, "You sold out to the Jews!"

Her mother's face went white. The other women and older children discovered a new-found interest in cracks in the ceiling plaster. Grandfather glared at her father. Abu Karim hung his head in shame. Even the small children stopped playing and looked on in awe, sensing something dramatic had happened. Only Dindan looked at Dodi in admiration.

"Da'oud," her father said very quietly, his fists clenched, "please leave the table and wait for me in my office."

Dodi stood up, straight-shouldered.

Abu Mussa held up his hand. "Please, that is not necessary, Abu Kamal. Let the lad stay. Admittedly, his manners need mending, but he has the good of Arabia at heart. Let him listen to my response."

Her father signalled Dodi to stand still.

"I am ashamed," her father told Abu Mussa. "Nothing I can do or say can eradicate the insult made to you in my house." He turned to Dodi. "Da'oud, remain by the door, apologise to your great-uncle. Then listen to what he has to say, with your eyes glued to the floor, and don't you dare say another word."

Dodi stood with downcast eyes as ordered after mumbling an apology, but his shoulders were still straight as Abu Mussa addressed him.

"Your great-grandfather, Da'oud, has turned down many would-be Jewish purchasers who would not accept his conditions. Mr. Leitner has agreed to leave the running of the orange grove to my father's very competent manager, until he chooses to retire. He is buying the orange grove as a gift for his daughter who is the same age as your sister. It will be her dowry. There is no dishonour in this sale."

Maftur wouldn't have minded betting that Dodi didn't agree with that last statement but was relieved to see him keeping his eyes down without answering back.

Abu Mussa's next words came as a surprise. "Ya Umm Kamal, I would be very happy if your daughter and her nurse would accompany me to El Tireh." She was indignant, though, at the term 'nurse'.

Nurse! Maftur thought. *Can't he see I'm too old to need a nurse?*

"That is very kind of you," her mother replied. "I am sure Maftur is greatly honoured."

Maftur would have felt more pleased by the unexpected outing if the grove was not about to be sold. She wished, too, that it had been summertime so they could have picnicked under the trees. On the other hand, if it had been summer she couldn't have worn her beautiful new cashmere hijab.

She sneaked a look at Sabeen's face and noted her compressed lips. It seemed hard that Abu Mussa had not invited her cousin. The day would have been more enjoyable if the two of them could have shared it. She hoped Sabeen was not angry with her.

After the meal, the grown men retired to the Liwan to smoke the narghili that Mohammad had set up. The boys went to their bedroom.

The women stayed on chatting but, after they too had left, Maftur's mother said, "Maftur, your great-uncle will be watching your behaviour closely tomorrow. Act modestly but, on the other hand, do not show yourself ill at ease or embarrassed. Keep your poise and dignity at all times and remember to keep smiling."

So this was another test, doubtless arranged by her great-grandfather!

"Umm," she started, "I don't feel too well. I—"

Her mother cut her short. "Then you had better get to bed right away. Tomorrow is too important not to have you feeling your best. You don't want to let down your father and me, do you?"

Put like that, there was not much she could do but go through the ordeal.

Next morning, dressed carefully in her new clothes and black patent leather shoes, she followed Zubaida into the back seat of the taxi. This was the first time she had travelled on the southern section of the coast road. On family visits to Jaffa they went by train.

Abu Mussa settled in the front passenger seat and they set off. Beyond the harbour, they rounded the half-moon-shaped headland, green with fresh winter grass, and reached the first citrus groves, at first a narrow belt of green, but widening as the rocky mountain range receded from the sea.

The sun was riding a clear sky. It was hot in the car. Maftur would never have believed it could have been so cold only three days before. Her cashmere scarf felt itchy.

A few minutes later, the taxi turned into a drive surrounded by citrus trees, and stopped in front of a small two-storeyed stone house with a tiled roof. A man wearing a well-worn brown suit and a red fez, nowhere near as smart as Abu Mussa's, waited on the veranda outside the front door next to a woman dressed in fellahin clothes.

"This, ya Maftur, is the manager, Abu Ibrahim," Abu Mussa said as the man came up to the taxi. "And this, ya Abu Ibrahim, is Abu Fuad's great-granddaughter."

Abu Mussa opened the back door of the taxi. Maftur jumped out, followed more slowly by Zubaida. Abu Mussa led them to the veranda and introduced them to Umm Ibrahim.

"You must have some of my lemonade and baklava. Come sit here at this table." Umm Ibrahim led them to a wooden table surrounded by half a dozen rush-seated chairs, before bustling back into the house.

Meanwhile, Abu Ibrahim had taken Abu Mussa to a table on the other side of the balcony. Umm Ibrahim brought out a tray containing glasses, cups of coffee, orange juice and two plates of pastries.

Another taxi came up the drive.

"This must be the buyer," Zubaida said.

Two men emerged from the taxi. The first wore the town clothes of a German Jew, homburg hat, black jacket and well-pressed grey trousers, but his face was deeply tanned as if he led an outdoor life. The second was Ismail's father, dressed British style, in a trilby and grey office suit. Behind the men, looking rather shy, came a girl her own age. She wore a plain blue dress not dissimilar in style to her own. Her well-polished lace-up shoes would have met with the approval of Haifa High's headmistress. Beneath her straw hat hung two auburn plaits.

Abu Mussa beckoned her over. She remembered her mother's instruction to be polite and poised, and walked over in as dignified and grown-up way as she could.

"Maftur, this is Dalia Leitner," Abu Mussa said. "Her father is buying the citrus grove as a dowry. Dalia Leitner, this is my great-niece, Maftur al-Zeid. She would like you to have lemonade with her and, afterwards, would like to walk with you round the grove."

Mr. Shawwa translated this into Hebrew.

Maftur realised she and this Dalia might have communication problems, but she smiled and beckoned towards the table where Zubaida was sitting.

She decided to try English. "I will be honoured if you would sit with me to partake of orange juice from your grove."

She hoped that was dignified enough to please Abu Mussa.

"Parlez-vous français?" Dalia replied.

Maftur was happy about that. Her French was as good if not better than her English and it was a more naturally dignified language.

"Mais oui," she switched over. "My mother and I speak French all the time. All the women in our family do."

"I do not speak French well but I speak it weller than I speak English," Dalia replied in broken French. "I am glad now that I worked hard at French to please a teacher I liked. Who is the lady doing the knitting?"

Maftur blushed. "Oh, forgive my manners. This is Zubaida." Under no circumstances was she going to admit that Zubaida had been her nurse. "She helps my mother run our household."

"Bonjour ma petite," Zubaida said.

"Bonjour, Madame."

Umm Ibrahim came over with another glass of orange juice. Maftur introduced her to Dalia and was pleased when Dalia came out with, "salaam wa aleikum," even if it was with an atrocious accent.

"The man in the grey suit is your arriere-grand-père?" Dalia asked Maftur back in French.

"No, he is my grand-oncle. My arriere-grand-père is very old. My grand-oncle conducts most of his business."

"Does your grand-oncle usually take you with him when he is conducting business?"

"No. I think he hoped I would keep you company. He told me your father was bringing you with him because this citrus grove is to be your dowry."

Dalia frowned.

"Dowry? No. I don't think so. The grove is so I can make my own living when I grow up if I cannot find work elsewhere. My parents will leave our farm to my brother."

Maftur did a quick calculation. If this girl were the same age as her, she would be grown-up before Abu Ibrahim was ready to retire.

"You will run the farm by yourself?" she asked, and was relieved when Dalia replied, "Only when the manager chooses to retire—that is part of the agreement."

Umm Ibrahim brought over two greaseproof paper bags and two small bottles of lemonade.

"For picnic."

After she had thanked the manager's wife, Maftur drained the last of the lemonade from her glass. "Are you ready to explore your new property?"

Zubaida put down her knitting, reached into her holdall and brought out a paper bag containing a pair of old school shoes. "Maftur, wait. The ground is muddy. You must wear these."

How dare Zubaida behave as if she was still her nanny? What would this Jewish girl think? Arguing, however, would be undignified, so she did as she was told while trying to glare at Zubaida without giving Dalia cause to think she was sulking.

As they set off Abu Mussa called after them in Arabic, "Be back at eleven-thirty, girls."

She glanced at her watch. "We have an hour."

"You're lucky to have a watch," Dalia commented, a note of envy in her voice.

That restored her pride.

They wandered through the orchard following the irrigation piping which, at this season of the year, wasn't currently in use. The weather today, in contrast to the previous week, was warm enough for the shade to feel quite pleasant, with lines of bright blue sky appearing between the rows of trees, while open blossom gave out glorious perfume.

They came across a group of Hourani workers, standing on ladders. They were picking oranges and placing them in a wicker basket balanced on the head of a woman who stood patiently, hands loosely clasped in front, head tilted slightly to the left to offset the basket's tilt to the right.

As she watched, one of the men climbed down the ladder, took the basket from the living statue's head, and replaced it with an empty one. Maftur found something disturbing about the woman's passivity, as if her spirit had left her body to allow its use by others.

If she married Ahmed, she would ask him to stop employing Hourani migrants on his other estates.

They wandered on until they came to a group of tall eucalyptus trees. A post stuck in the ground indicated a boundary. A thick branch lay on the ground. By mutual consent, they sat on it to eat the baklava in the greaseproof bags.

"What do you think of your grove?" she asked.

"It's beautiful, and much bigger than our little one at Bereisheet. It looks well cared for. I didn't like the way the Arab workers were using that woman though. I shall speak to Papa about it."

Maftur was pleased. Since she couldn't own the grove herself, she was glad it was going to Dalia. All the same, she needed to defend her countrymen.

"Those workers are not Palestinian Arabs. We don't treat women like farm animals. They're migrants from Syria who come every year for the harvest. The trouble is they are good workers. That is why my great-grandfather employs them." She looked around. "I've always wanted a picnic in an orange grove, and now I've had one, but a picnic in summer would have been even better."

"When I'm grown up, I'll invite you to a summer picnic," Dalia promised.

Chapter 7

The khamseen at the end of April 1935 was the worst Maftur could remember. Usually a khamseen lasted no more than seven days but this one went on and on.

The searing wind blew sand across the scarves that protected their faces as she and Yalda trudged home from school. The scarves looked silly below their school hats but since everyone was in the same state, it didn't really matter.

Maftur let out a sigh of relief when the janitor opened the entrance door to their apartments, and they could loosen their scarves. It was not much cooler on the stairs, but at least they were out of the wind.

She noticed the change of temperature as soon as she opened the lobby door.

Her mother was sitting on a chair beside an electric fan. She put down her embroidery and jumped up as Maftur entered. "Come straight to the sewing room when you've had a shower. I'll have a cold drink waiting for you there and two fans set up, one for you and one for me."

Maftur headed for the women's quarter. What a relief to remove her sweat-soaked school uniform and let the spray of cool water fall over her body.

Dressed in nothing but a thin cotton thob, she joined her mother in the sewing room where the two fans cooled the air, and a glass filled with ice and lime water stood on a small table.

Maftur sank onto cool ceramic tiles, and circled her hands round the cold glass. "We don't have to go to school tomorrow," she informed her mother. "The headmistress said the building's too hot. We've been given a load of extra homework instead." She lifted the glass and let the chilled liquid slide down her throat.

"It's the same at the boys' school," her mother told her while rethreading her needle. "Although I doubt they would have been let off if it wasn't Labour Day tomorrow. More people than ever are treating it as a holiday."

"Next year our school may take part in the procession."

"Apparently the Jewish schools are taking part this year. Since you are both off school perhaps you and Yalda would like to come with your Aunt Bahia and me when we take the little ones to watch. If the wind drops, that is."

In the living room next door, Maftur heard Dodi raise an indignant voice. "Fizzy, you're never joining in with the Jews?"

She only heard Fizzy's quieter reply because she was listening for it. It came dripping with the superiority of someone already earning his own living.

"I'm supporting my comrades in the rail union, that's all. Conditions of service are as important to us as to Jews."

"Detarame!" Dodi's response stopped short when a more mature voice cut in.

"Da'oud, your friend's right. The Jews are not our enemies. The only people holding us back are the French and British. We should co-operate with the Jews."

Dindan's surprised voice said, "But you support the Black Hand, ya Ahmed."

"Not in everything."

Maftur raised questioning eyes. "Is that Great-Uncle Ahmed in the living room with the boys?"

"Yes. He's in Haifa with Abu Mussa. Strictly speaking, he should not be here in our apartment. He came to lunch with your grandmother but, when our boys heard he was in the building, they rushed down and dragged him up. You know how they are about him. I decided it wouldn't matter so long as they kept to the living room and we stayed in the sewing room."

"Why's he here? It's not Rent Day!"

"No. That's something I want to talk about with you. Abu Mussa has come to Haifa especially to see your father."

Maftur digested this. "Abu Mussa wants to speak to father, not grandfather?"

Her mother nodded.

Maftur took her time working out the implications. "I'm to marry Great-Uncle Ahmed?"

"That's what your great-grandfather has decided, but only on certain conditions."

"But you said I could finish school!"

"And so you shall! That's one of the conditions."

"Why aren't you letting me choose from three photos?"

"Oh, that," her mother replied. "The marriage broker sent them."

She stood up, opened a wall cupboard, took out three photos and handed them over.

Maftur glanced through them and shot an angry glance as she held up two. "Sabeen rejected these two years ago."

"No, only one of them. The second is a younger cousin. I agree you would be a fool to choose either."

Maftur looked at the third picture. In contrast to the other two, Great-Uncle Ahmed shone out like a prince.

Her mother touched her arm. "The Old Man's third wife says Ahmed is becoming a lot less opinionated these days, and is turning into a very polite young man."

Maftur continued to stare at the photo. It was true. Great-Uncle Ahmed didn't look nearly as supercilious as the opinionated fourteen-year old she had met when little.

"Ahmed," her mother continued, "will start his studies at the American University of Beirut in October. You could end up marrying a very influential man. So, which photograph do you choose?"

* * * *

Maftur didn't see her father that night. He was still downstairs with Grandfather and Abu Mussa by the time she went to bed.

Next morning promised a day even hotter than the one before. She paid special attention to her morning prayers, trying to put herself in the right frame of mind to accept her father's decision, whatever it was. She entered the dining room, prepared to learn her fate, but her father and brothers had already left for the warehouse.

Impatient for news, she blurted out, "Umm? What did Baba decide?"

Her mother shrugged her shoulders. "An unofficial betrothal—no dowry to be paid for three years yet."

"So, I'm on sell-or-return terms."

"Not exactly."

Maftur detected a note of anger in her mother's voice.

"Ahmed has stipulated that if his father insists he go into politics, he wants a wife sufficiently educated to be an asset. You are to continue with your schoolwork and sit matriculation. If you do extra well you will have an increased dowry. If you fail the exam, the marriage is off." Her mother almost spat out that last sentence.

Maftur guessed her father leaving the house early indicated a strategic withdrawal on his part rather than devotion to duty.

"Incidentally," her mother continued, "your semi-betrothed has sent a pile of books as a semi-betrothal gift. He wishes you to read them all before the wedding."

Maftur stamped her foot. "I won't read a single one. I won't even look at them."

Her mother laughed. "If you don't look at them you won't know what not to read, will you? I went through them. You've already read three!"

* * * *

When Mrs. Norman read out the end-of-year exams results that June, Maftur was elated to find she had tied with Miriam for top place. Ai'isha was not far behind. They were all eligible to sit for matriculation the following year.

"However," Miss Norman told the class, "matriculation is merely a preliminary qualification for higher education. I would advise anyone not planning to go to university, teacher training college or nursing school, to sit City and Guilds instead of matriculation. Practical subjects like typing and needlework will be of far more use to those of you intending to leave school at sixteen."

Maftur realised then for the first time that the Matric syllabus did not cover secretarial subjects. She hoped her great-grandfather had used 'matriculation' as a portmanteau word for all examinations taken in the fifth form.

She watched her mother carefully as she opened the envelope containing details of subject options for both Matric and City and Guilds. Her mother took her time reading the lists.

"Which subjects do you want to take?" she asked at last.

"Typing, shorthand and accountancy," Maftur replied, hoping that would be the end of the matter.

Her mother raised her eyebrows. "But those are not matriculation subjects."

"They're as good as."

"They may be, but that doesn't alter the fact that they're not matriculation subjects."

"But, Umm, you know how much I want to be a secretary, and stay in the same class as Ai'isha. She has to take City and Guilds because she wants to start her own dress design business and—"

"It's no good, Maftur. Your great-grandfather has laid down his requirements."

"But, Umm, Baba said he was only letting me stay on at school so I could learn secretarial skills."

"That was before the Old Man said you had to take matriculation."

"Can't you ask Baba to persuade him to let me do City and Guilds?"

"No one can talk the Old Man out of anything once he's made up his mind."

"My teacher said we ought to take City and Guilds if we weren't going on to university."

"Your teacher hasn't betrothed you to your Great-Uncle Ahmed. Now that's the end of it."

At last the constraints of her betrothal, unofficial though it was, struck home in earnest. Maftur wanted to take herself off into a corner and cry her eyes out, but instead readied herself to argue with her father when he came home.

Her father, however, refused to get into an argument. "I am not going to be nagged about this from now until parents' evening. We'll settle the matter right now."

He sat her down to choose options from the matriculation list, and then wrote a letter to her teacher.

Maftur refrained from bursting into tears until she was in bed. Then she buried her head in her pillow and cried for her lost dreams, until her nose was sore and her head ached.

In the schoolyard next morning, she told Ai'isha that her father was forcing her to sit matric, but stayed silent about her unofficial betrothal. She didn't want to look silly if she failed the exams.

"That was unnecessarily speedy," Mrs. Norman commented when Maftur handed in her father's letter. "I think you should take it back to give your parents more time to reach their decision."

"No. My father's made up his mind."

The next day, a miserable Ai'isha told her, "I have to sit matric, too, all because of you, Maftur."

"What do you mean, because of me?"

"My father said if Mr. al-Zeid thinks the matriculation stream will ensure the best education for his daughter, I must take matric, too."

"I am so sorry." But secretly, she was pleased she and Ai'isha would still be in the same form.

Her friend shrugged. "I suppose I can take a proper dressmaking course when I leave school, if I don't get a marriage proposal first."

"You'll get a marriage proposal soon, you needn't worry."

"I don't think so. Our clan is short of eligible men and I have very pretty cousins. What about you? Will your parents stick to their promise to dismiss marriage proposals until you leave school?"

She resisted the temptation to tell Ai'isha about her unofficial betrothal, and changed the subject. "Are you doing anything special this holiday?"

"Just the usual fortnight's visit to Ramallah to visit my grandmother. We'll be going early because we have to be back in time for the Garden Party in Aid of the Blind. The railway workshop manager is hosting it this year. It may help Fizzy get promotion."

Chapter 8

By the spring of 1936, Maftur was too busy revising for end of term exams to be concerned with much else. She could hardly fail to notice, though, how arrogant Dodi had become since starting work.

That evening, as she struggled to make sense of the English 1832 Reform Act, Dodi returned home late in an even more belligerent mood than usual. He announced he wouldn't be going in to work the following day as he would be on strike.

Grandfather had insisted on keeping the warehouse open, strike or no strike. Maftur couldn't believe that Dodi had the nerve to rebel against Grandfather's orders.

"If you had one gram of patriotism," Dodi told his father that evening, "you'd urge Grandfather to close the warehouse. Uncle Assad has already closed the weaving factory and spinning mill."

Instead of shouting him down, her father tried reasoning. "Da'oud, shutting down businesses makes no sense. It won't persuade the British to refuse entry to Jewish refugees, and only plays into Jewish hands by making Arabs poorer."

Dodi continued arguing. Maftur wasn't sure whom she agreed with—Grandpa or her brothers—but knew that, if something weren't done, there would soon be more Jews than Arabs in Haifa. Only yesterday, when she had gone out with her mother to buy shoes, she had noticed most people in the new shopping centre were speaking either German or Hebrew. On the other hand, she couldn't help sympathizing with Jews who had lost their German citizenship and had nowhere else to go.

As Dindan looked up from his homework to support his brother, her father lost his temper and began shouting.

By mutual consent, she and her mother retreated to the sewing room, but she could still hear him shouting. Her mother picked up a French novel but sat rigid and tight-lipped in her sewing chair with the book upside down on her lap.

Maftur decided to escape to the roof, hoping she might

catch another glimpse of Ismail. She had seen him the day before, while she had been reading one of her English set books.

"I'm going to get some fresh air, Umm. Will you be all right by yourself?"

Her mother managed a smile and squeezed her hand. "Of course, habipti. I do wish, though, that the boys wouldn't set out to upset your father. When I was a girl, children always honoured their parents."

"They aren't deliberately making him angry, Umm. They just feel strongly that Palestine belongs to us and we should be governing it, not the British."

She didn't add that her brothers had become angrier with the British after they had shot down the charismatic leader of the Black Hand. She didn't think her mother was a great supporter of the Black Hand.

Her mother shook her head. "They should leave such things to their grandfather. He's head of the family."

It was useless trying to defend her brothers. Maftur kissed her mother's cheek and left.

It was a beautiful clear evening, the moon shining almost white above Mount Carmel, but the air still retained a hint of daytime warmth. She gazed over the road at Ismail's balcony. Even as she looked, however, a light came on behind the curtains. She waited, almost forgetting to breathe, as she willed Ismail to step out onto the balcony. The doors opened and there he was, silhouetted against the light. She wondered if the moonlight enabled him to see her.

He lifted his arm and waved. She gave a guilty wave back and then turned away, her heart thumping. Firefly memories flickered through mental darkness of half-forgotten days; Ismail in rambling clothes climbing the mountainside with her brothers; Ismail in business clothes walking with his father down the street; Ismail entering a cafe on Kingsway with an unknown friend. He had smiled at her on all those occasions.

She wanted more than a smile or wave. She wanted to feel his hand on her shoulder, perhaps even... Feeling even guiltier, she cut off that line of thought and walked to the other side of the roof. The new electric street lights revealed their night watchman, who should have been on the other side of town guarding the warehouse, panting and stumbling up the hill. He banged on the front door and yelled to be let in. Their doorman came out, arms akimbo, but the watchman pushed past him, shouting "Fire!"

Maftur scurried inside and looked down the stairwell. The night watchman was thumping on the door of her grandparents' apartment, still shouting, "Fire."

Her grandfather opened the door.

She raced down to her own apartment. As she entered the lobby, she heard the internal phone between her parents' apartment and her grandparents. She picked up the receiver "Maftur here."

Her grandfather's voice shouted over hers. "Fire at the warehouse! Maftur, tell your father, Abu Rakim, and Kamal. They must get over, at once. I'm leaving now. Tell your mother to sit with Granny."

Her mother was right behind her. "I'll tell your father. You go and get Abu Rakim and Kamal. I'll be with Granny if you need me."

Maftur rushed out of the apartment and ran across the corridor, throwing open Uncle Abu Rakim's front door. "Fire in the warehouse," she shouted.

Aunt Bahia came running. "Tell Uncle Abu Rakim," Maftur shouted. "Grandpa wants him at the warehouse."

In the nearest bedroom, one of the little ones started crying.

Maftur turned and raced off, bumping into Dodi as he bounded out of their apartment followed by Dindan. She fell. They rushed on without stopping. She picked herself up, ran up the next flight to Kamal's apartment, and shouted her message again.

As Kamal left, Janan bombarded her with questions.

Maftur held up her hands. "I don't know any more than you, except I saw the night watchman come in."

"Praise be to Allah, the night watchman's safe—but why didn't he put out the fire?"

Maftur left Kamal's apartment more slowly and went down to Granny's flat, to see how her mother was doing. She found her patting Granny's hand.

"We need sandbags," Granny was saying. "Tell the

servants to fill them."

"She thinks she's back in Damascus and the British are attacking," Umm explained.

"I'll make us some mint tea," Maftur replied.

A glass of mint tea! Always the answer to catastrophes in the al-Zeid households. She'd never made it before, but was determined to get it right for her mother and Granny.

She hurried into Granny's kitchen, now empty of servants who had their own rooms on the top storey, and picked a large bunch of mint leaves from the tub on the window sill. As she crushed them with a stone pestle, she thought about the home of her early childhood. Would it be burnt to the ground? Had her grandfather lost all his stock? Were their former neighbours' houses on fire too?

She ran to the family living room, looking for smoke but, on this level, the buildings across the road shut out any view of the other side of town.

She returned to the kitchen and placed the crushed mint into a saucepan with sugar, poured water on top, lit the stove and set the saucepan to boil.

She spooned some green tea into a jug and, as soon as the mint water began to bubble, poured it over the tea. She covered the jug and left the tea to stand, while she set three thick tea glasses onto a silver tray and placed a sprig of fresh mint at the bottom of each glass. She then strained the brewed tea into them.

Granny was asleep when she brought in the tea but her mother sipped it gratefully.

"You've made it so much better than cook. She leaves the mint boiling too long."

Maftur looked at Granny, still snoring and dribbling slightly. How different to the bustling efficient woman who had presided over the large household of her childhood. Would her mother be like this when she was old?

Eventually the men returned.

"Is the watchman all right?" her mother burst out.

Maftur realised she hadn't told her mother that it was the night watchman who had delivered the warning.

"Yes," her father replied. "There were seven in the gang so he didn't fight them. However, the young hooligans had some conscience, it seems. Before they set the door on fire, they gave the watchman a note for grandfather and told him to run for the firemen. The firemen put the fire out before it reached the stock but everything stinks of smoke. Praise Allah, the new stock hasn't yet arrived."

"What was in the note?" Maftur asked.

"If you do not close the warehouse, you will need more than a new door," he replied.

"Will you close the warehouse now, Beau-père?" There was a note of pleading in her voice.

Her grandfather slumped his shoulders. "We'll have to."

When Dodi and Dindan heard the warehouse was joining the strike they looked triumphant.

Her father turned on Dodi. "You're going to have to get a grip on reality, boy. Life is about hard work and perseverance, not striking. You needn't think I am going to let you wander around town getting into mischief. Next week you're on the train to Damascus. Your great-grandfather will find you a job there. As for you, Adad, if your school goes on strike I'll hire a tutor each day. As soon as your exams finish, you, too, will be on the train to Damascus."

* * * *

Maftur was surprised to find how much she missed Dodi. Her mother missed him even more, continually saying she hoped the strike would end so she could have her Dodi home. Meanwhile, Dindan withdrew into himself, probably, Maftur guessed, because he was dreading his own turn in exile.

"My father's calling a family conference," her father announced one evening. "With no let-up in the strike, we need to move operations out of Palestine."

The Al-Zeid men from both Jaffa and Galilee came for the business meeting, the women and children accompannying them to make it a social gathering as well.

Normally for a business meeting the men used Grandfather's Liwan for the conference. Granny organised the men's meal while Aunt Bahia, Janan and her mother entertained the women and children and provided them with a meal on the roof. This time, however, the men squashed themselves into her father's Liwan and Granny was out of commission. So it was decided that her mother should prepare the men's meal in her kitchen with a workforce composed of both her's and Granny's servants. Aunt Bahia would take the female visitors shopping in Kingsway's elegant new shops, while Janan and the nursemaids looked after the younger children on the roof, keeping them well away from Mahmoud, who would be turning a whole lamb on a spit in the clay oven. Maftur would have to skip school to supervise the women's meal in Aunt Bahia's kitchen, with Zubaida's backup and Aunt Bahia's and Janan's servants as her workforce. For someone who wasn't getting married until she was at least nearly seventeen, Maftur reckoned she was getting a good training in household management.

"Just stay calm and follow Zubaida's advice, and you'll do fine," her mother told her on the morning of the conference. "And if you can't feel calm, act it. Acting is the most useful talent any wife and mother can develop."

With her stomach churning all morning, Maftur followed her mother's advice and everything went off well.

The men had finished their meal and were back in conference by the time the women returned from town, ready for their own meal. Her mother came up to the roof and inspected the feast spread out under awnings, and complimented Maftur on getting everything just right. The women sat on cushions surrounded by their children. Talk at first was mainly about the shopping trip. The visitors agreed that Haifa, although as modern as Tel Aviv, was much friendlier.

"Jaffa and Tel Aviv are now two separate cities, one for Arabs and one for Jews," an elderly great-aunt said. "You are lucky in Haifa. You must keep it like it is—a city for everyone."

Later, conversation switched to family matters. The visitors were particularly interested in Dodi and Dindan. The way her mother talked them up, the Jaffa cousins must have had the impression both boys were models of rectitude and handsome masculinity.

She was back in the kitchen supervising the clearing up when Dindan arrived home from school later than usual. He took her aside and displayed a tattooed skeleton hand on the inside of his wrist. The skin around it burned an angry red.

"Bandage it for me, Maftur, and if Umm mentions it, remember I did it lighting a Bunsen burner at school."

"Why did you get that done? You know Umm is sure to see it once the bandage is off."

"Not if I put my watch over it."

"But why have it done in the first place?"

"That's my business. Just get on with covering it, and no iodine either, thank you."

After bandaging Dindan, she served him a large plate of lamb, rice, eggplant and tomatoes—not that he deserved it, but he was her brother after all.

"If anyone wants to know where I am, I'm revising in my room," he told her.

It was late at night before the relatives drove off and she could return to her own apartment. Dindan came out of his room. Zubaida brought in a fresh pot of coffee, and her father asked her to stay while he told them what the men had decided.

"As soon as we get permission from the Old Man, we're shifting everything except the silk mill out of Palestine for the duration. Uncle Mussa will open a new warehouse in Alexandria. We'll transfer the Haifa business to Lebanon. Abu Rakim and I will catch the bus to Beirut tomorrow to look for a warehouse space."

Her mother frowned as she handed round the coffee cups. "Your father's not going with you?"

"He's delegated everything to us."

"How long will you be away?"

"Until we've organised somewhere to live."

Her mother raised her eyebrows. "We're all moving out?"

"We'll be safer in Lebanon the way things are going."

"Where in Lebanon? Presumably not Beirut, or we'll be trespassing on Uncle Harun's territory."

"Remember the Old Man's house in the Damour Valley? My father's had his eye on it ever since mother started going downhill. They spent the first years of their married life there so he thinks she'll be happy there. He's in negotiation with the Old Man about buying a mulberry grove and spinning mill in the Valley. Many silk sheds in the Damour Valley went bankrupt recently so we could buy cheaply."

Dindan interrupted. "If the mills have already gone bankrupt, won't it be a risky investment?"

Their father beamed at him. "Well done, son. We'll make a business man of you yet. That was exactly the point I made to your grandfather, but he argues so many mills have gone now, the scales have fallen the other way. Chateau al-Zeid is only twenty-five kilometres or so from Beirut, habipti, so you'll see the grandchildren often."

Her mother evidently needed more encouragement than that. "If we go, will you change your mind about Dodi and Dindan having to work in Damascus?"

"So long as we come across a suitable silk mill. My father wants Uncle Assad to train them in silk production."

Her mother's eyes lit up. "In that case, I can't wait."

Dindan broke into the conversation again. "I don't want to go to Lebanon."

Her mother looked at him, eyes wide. "What?"

"I want to go to Damascus."

"Why?"

From the sharpness in Umm's voice, Maftur realised how deeply Dindan's statement had hurt her.

Dindan put on his most virtuous voice. "I will learn more about our business in Damascus." He stood up. "I must go to bed. I have my last exam in the morning."

Her father watched him leave with raised eyebrows, and then leaned forward. "There's another advantage to buying mulberry groves in Lebanon—I didn't want to speak about it in front of Dindan. When the trouble's died down here, the firm can make a fortune selling the Jezreel site to Jews."

Maftur kept her eyes cast down, so her father wouldn't realise her anger.

Chapter 9

Dindan was so eager to go to Damascus he caught the first train after his exams, despite their mother's protestations.

When Maftur told Ai'isha that Dindan had joined Dodi, her friend told her that Fizzy had left home too. There was pride in her voice, even awe as she said, "He's joined the rebels."

Maftur was astonished. "Fizzy—a rebel? Only last year, he was all for co-operating with Jews."

"That was when the Arab and Jewish rail unions still had a joint committee."

"Do your parents know what Fizzy's up to?"

"My mother doesn't like it much, as you can imagine. She worries the British will either shoot her little boy or put him in prison and hang him, but my father is proud of him. He says the time for making speeches is over."

Maftur was struck by how fathers could be so different. "My father thinks patriots are nothing but gangs of bandits out for loot."

Ai'isha nodded. "He's partly right. Fizzy grumbles that most gangs are only pretending to be patriots. The band Fizzy belongs to behaves like a real army unit." She added in an awed voice, "Their leader is an advisor to the Grand Mufti!"

"What's the leader called?"

"The Ghost of Sheik izz-ad-Din but Fizzy calls him Ghost for short."

"That's not his real name, surely?"

"No. Fizzy won't tell me the real one—says it's secret."

Maftur thought of the secret she had kept for Dindan. "Does your brother have a skeleton hand tattoo on his wrist?"

"How do you know? That's supposed to be secret, too. Fizzy hides it with his watch. He only showed it to me after I promised not to tell."

"Dodi and Dindan are in the same band as your brother."

"Not while your great-grandfather's supervising them, surely!"

Ai'isha was right. Her brothers were safe for the time being.

News from Lebanon was slow in coming, but at last her grandfather received a telegram.

"ALL PHONE BEIRUT WAREHOUSE TOMORROW"

He booked an international call from the phone line in their deserted warehouse.

Next morning, Maftur missed school yet again to join her family in a trek across town.

Grandfather took first turn on the phone. Father told him he'd rented a warehouse in Damour and was in negotiations for a mill with its own mulberry groves farther up the valley. He hadn't found accommodation. Unfortunately, Chateau al-Zeid was already rented out for the summer so they couldn't move into it until autumn, if they were still there then. It looked as if they would have to split up and stay with various Beirut relatives. Grandfather told him that in that case he and Granny would stay on in Haifa.

Her mother had the next turn. Her father agreed with her mother's suggestion that she and Maftur should stay in Haifa to support Grandfather with Granny.

"We'll still go up to Beirut for our usual fortnight though," her mother told her when she relinquished the phone.

Aunt Bahia took a long time when it came to her turn. After passing on the phone to Janan, she relayed her news. If the mill purchase went through, she, Abu Rakim and the children would camp out in the mulberry groves until Chateau al-Zeid became vacant.

* * * *

On the last day of term, one of the Christian girls in her form suggested they all meet up in the milk bar on Kingsway the following week.

Maftur wondered if her mother would allow her to go without a chaperone but, luckily, that week an article in al-Karmil had left her mother in rampant feminist mode.

"Of course you must go. Professional women have to

build up support groups, and it's never too early to start. Zubaida can walk down with you, but I'll ask her to leave you at the milk bar door. She can do some shopping for me from the suq and then wait outside until you are ready to come home. Don't leave her hanging about in the street too long, though."

Maftur felt very grown up as she and her friends huddled together round two tables pulled together, passing on gossip about their married friends. The Muslim girls giggled behind the scarves they constantly swept across their faces in sophisticated modesty while their eyes surreptitiously swept the room searching out good-looking young men.

When Fizzy entered the milk bar, scarves were drawn more tightly across faces and every girl at the table focused their gaze on him.

Looking fixedly at the ground, his cheeks burning, Fizzy made his way towards his sister. Ai'isha jumped up and drew him away. The other girls spent a busy five minutes ostentatiously not looking towards him, but their giggles became even more uncontrollable.

From the corner of her eye, Maftur watched Fizzy slink off and at the same time saw Zubaida outside the window in conversation with Ai'isha's chaperone. She sighed. Time to go home. She waited for Ai'isha to return, nudged her, and pointed to the window.

They prepared to leave, and everyone agreed they must meet up regularly throughout the vacation. As they walked towards the door, Ai'isha gave her a note.

Maftur read it, and stood still, staring at her friend in astonishment.

"Do you know what this says?"

"Fizzy just said it was from Dodi for you."

"But Dodi's in Damascus. Why send me a message through Fizzy?"

Ai'isha shrugged "Fizzy says the Ghost lives in Damascus. Perhaps he gave him a lift to meet up with Dodi."

Maftur read it. "Dear Sis, fetch the box that's under my bed and make sure you don't tell anyone. Get Ai'isha to give it to Fizzy before he returns to camp."

Ai'isha gave a gasp. "You have to go into the men's

quarter to get it?"

"Yes! When's Fizzy going back?"

"Tomorrow evening."

"So I have to get the box tonight and give it to you tomorrow. How will I get it to you?"

Ai'isha bit her lip. After a moment, she said, "I'll tell my mother you're lending me some of your books so we can discuss them. That way, she'll let me come over to your house without waiting to ask your mother."

Outside the coffee bar window, Zubaida was tapping her foot impatiently on the pavement and shooting malevolent glances through the glass.

"Right, but we must hurry home now. I'll see you tomorrow."

Maftur told her mother that Ai'isha was coming over so they could talk about books, and to her consternation her mother said, "I'll ask Umm Fikri to join me for a cup of tea at the same time."

Maftur felt puzzled for a moment until she realised Fikri was Fizzy's real name. She felt worried. With Umm Fikri present it would be even more difficult for Ai'isha to carry Dodi's box home undetected. She felt almost ill for the rest of the day at the prospect of the task ahead. What sort of trouble would she be in if her mother discovered her trespassing in the men's quarter?

That night, long after her mother had retired, Maftur picked up her emergency flashlight and, without turning it on, crept through the Liwan.

She opened the door leading into the men's quarter and closed it softly, then turned on her flashlight. The first door on the left opened into her father's study, but which door opened into her brothers' bedroom?

The nearest door on the right revealed a washroom. The next opened into a broom cupboard. The third, however, revealed a room containing two beds. She sidled in, conscious she was trespassing into the most forbidden territory of all.

She crouched down by the bed nearest the door, swept her flashlight under it but saw, right at the back, only a pair of old football boots and a bundle of magazines, covered in brown paper and tied neatly together with string. Curious, she prized away part of the brown paper and saw a women's uncovered head and a shoulder, bare apart from a bathing costume strap. She hastily tucked the parcel back. Beneath the other bed, she found a similar parcel and another pair of boots, but the bundle of magazines was nearer the front. She moved it aside and saw a rectangular metal box about a foot long pushed up against the wall.

Lying on her stomach, arm outstretched, she dragged the surprisingly heavy box towards her. She ran the flashlight over it and recognized Dodi's old bullet collection. Judging by the weight, he had added considerably to it since she had last seen it almost four years before. She carried it back to her room, wondering how Ai'isha would get it home. A paper carrier wouldn't be strong enough. Her mind buzzed, preventing sleep, as she wondered why Dodi needed his bullet collection so urgently. Was he intending to remain in Damascus when the strike ended?

In the morning, she placed the box in an empty shoe carton, stuffed another carton with loosely crumpled newspaper, tied the two together to match weight with bulk, and wrapped them in brown paper, hoping this parcel could pass for a stack of heavy books. She hid a few books from her bookcase under her own bed to leave appropriate gaps on the shelves.

Predictably, when Ai'isha arrived and picked up the parcel, she balked at the weight. "My mother will make me leave some books behind when she sees me struggling. What was in the box, anyway?"

"I didn't open it," Maftur replied truthfully.

She ran into the living room where her mother and Ai'isha's were discussing painful economies housewives had to make during a strike.

"The books Ai'isha needs to borrow are too heavy for her," Maftur said. "Can Mahmoud carry them in his shopping basket?"

"Of course," her mother said absent-mindedly, keen to resume her conversation.

As Ai'isha and her mother were leaving an hour later, Ai'isha asked her mother if Maftur could sleep over at their house when she returned from her annual fortnight in Beirut.

At least, Maftur thought, she had gained something as a result of doing what Dodi had asked.

Chapter 10

To Maftur's intense relief, her great-grandfather did not leave Damascus or ask to see her while they were in Beirut. She was disappointed, however, that there was no time in their packed schedule of family visits to visit the mulberry groves. She had fond memories of a visit to the ones at Jezreel when she was little, but her mother was already unhappy leaving Granny for so long so they didn't extend the holiday.

Back in Haifa, she and Ai'isha began their series of sleepovers. She spent most of the summer vacation helping Ai'isha design, cut out and sew fabulous summer dresses for themselves and their mothers.

Soon after they returned to school for the autumn term, the Arab Higher Executive called off the strike, while members of a British Royal Commission interviewed Arab and Jewish leaders as they investigated the future of Palestine. Shops and factories re-opened, patriotic guerrilla freedom fighters returned home.

Aunt Bahia and Uncle Abu Rakim remained in Lebanon, having moved into Chateau al-Zeid.

Maftur's father, Kamal and Janan returned to Haifa. Kamal and Janan moved into Uncle Abu Rakim and Aunt Bahia's larger apartment on the same floor as his parents. Kamal also took over Uncle Abu Rakim's former position as the warehouse's treasurer and chief clerk and, to her mother's delight, Great-Grandfather sent Dodi and Dindan back to Haifa to help get the warehouse back into shape.

The end of the strike wasn't such good news for everybody, however. Fizzy had lost his job at the railway when he had gone on strike and the only work he could find was casual labouring, but his father refused to let him stoop to that after all the money spent on his education.

One morning Ai'isha came to school looking happier than she had done for some time. "My brother's found a job, thanks to your Dodi."

Maftur raised her eyebrows in surprise. "How could our

Dodi help Fizzy find a job?"

"Dodi wrote to your great-grandfather. Fizzy's starting at the carpet factory in Damascus next week."

When her father discovered that Dodi had recommended Fizzy for a job in Damascus, he was furious with him. "How could you deceive Abu Fuad by recommending someone who's been a brigand for over a year?"

Dodi drew himself up indignantly. "I didn't deceive Great-Grandfather. I told him exactly what Fikri was doing during the strike. Fikri's not a brigand, he's a patriot."

"Abu Fuad must be going senile," her father muttered.

Recalling her own interview with her great-grandfather, Maftur couldn't imagine him turning senile but, on the other hand, she would never have believed that Granny, the stern matriarch of her childhood, could transform so suddenly into a confused old woman.

Soon after Fizzy moved to Damascus, her great-grandfather recalled Dodi and Dindan and sent another of his great-grandsons, Akred, to Haifa in exchange.

Akred, along with a new bride from Damascus—a third or fourth generation cousin, Tuqa—took over the apartment that had belonged to Kamal and Janan.

Maftur tried making friends with Tuqa but found they had so little in common that conversation was difficult. Instead of joining in coffee evenings with her new Haifa family, Tuqa seemed to live a vicarious life in Damascus, with one or another of her large family coming down by train every week to keep her company. The visitors made excuses to decline invitations to meals and never came to her mother's after supper coffee evenings. It didn't help that Akred didn't fit in at work. Her father and Kamal constantly railed against her great-grandfather for using Haifa as a dumping ground for unemployables.

If it hadn't been for Ai'isha, Maftur would have been very lonely that winter.

They resumed the sleepovers they had enjoyed during holidays and put them to good use, supporting each other with their course work, especially in maths. Maftur loved algebra, but found geometry bewildering. On the other hand, Ai'isha loved geometry, said it really helped when it came to designing dresses, but floundered with algebra. In return for help with algebra homework, Ai'isha showed Maftur how to use geometry to produce skirts cut on the bias, which were all the rage that year.

The comparative calm following the end of the strike was soon shattered throughout Palestine. Arab political parties, united during the strike, began feuding again. Men in Jerusalem and Jaffa, opposed to the Grand Mufti's party, received death threats, as did Arabs who worked in government institutions. In rural areas, although real patriots had stopped fighting, brigands passing themselves off as patriots held up taxis and buses demanding money to aid the fight for Arab freedom.

Haifa at first was safer than any other Palestinian city, thanks to the vigilance of an Egyptian-born CID chief. It wasn't long, however, before the town's reputation for comparative peace was shattered by a series of high-profile assassinations. All victims were influential Arab leaders who either opposed the political party led by the Grand Mufti or worked for the police. A relative of Ai'isha's father was one of those murdered.

"I never met the man so I can't say I'm too upset about him," Ai'isha confided in mid-morning break. "But the awful thing is my father is also in danger, so my mother wants to send me away. We've no relatives outside Palestine, so goodness knows where I'll end up. My mother hopes yours will have some ideas. She's visiting today."

That afternoon found her mother and Mahmoud outside the school gates as she and Ai'isha left the premises. Mahmoud carried a suitcase.

"Ai'isha," her mother said, "you're staying with us until matric is over. Then your mother will take you on holiday to Egypt."

Maftur felt guilty for being pleased that her friend was staying full-time. Revision went so much better when two of them worked together.

Ai'isha didn't stay long, however. Umm Fikri came over one evening. "My husband's out of danger, thanks to our Fizzy."

Her mother's eyebrows asked the question Maftur was having difficulty suppressing.

Umm Fikri gave a smug smile. "The Grand Mufti invited my son and several other young men to visit him in Damascus. My son told the Grand Mufti that his father only works for the British for patriotic reasons. When the mufti asked him to explain, he told him we need Palestinian Arabs in the public services to stop the Jews being in control when we become independent. The Grand Mufti agreed with him and promised to put my husband under his protection."

Maftur worried that Umm Fikri was exaggerating her son's influence with the Mufti.

Her father echoed her doubts when he came home. "I think, Maftur, that you had better not visit your friend's home until things settle down."

Her mother dismissed his fears. "Ya Abu Kamal, it's not Abu Fikri but your friend, Abu Ismail, you should be worrying about. I can't think how he is still alive, the way he speaks out publicly against the Mufti's party, and I don't know how Umm Ismail manages to carry on. I'd be a nervous wreck if I were her."

"I am sure the Mufti's party know that if they kill Abu Ismail, his heir will sell the Nablus estate to Jews out of spite," her father said.

Maftur resented the slur on Ismail. He would never sell land to the Jews. However, she had the sense not to spring to his defence. Trying to retain her sleepovers was more important. Unfortunately, her father remained adamant. So, what with Granny becoming more confused by the day and Tuqa remaining housebound and incommunicative, Maftur found her social life confined mainly to Janan who, after the birth of her first son, was now proud to be called Umm Sarim.

The political scene in Haifa took a turn for the worse in April when, after many failed attempts, assassins succeeded in killing Haifa's CID chief. A few days after the event that had shocked so many, Grandpa came storming upstairs while they were at breakfast. Without taking her father aside, as was his custom when discussing business, he burst out, "Some ruffian signing himself the Ghost of Sheik izz-ad-Din is demanding I pay a thousand piastres to support the Freedom Fighters, or else they'll burn down the warehouse."

Her father stood up, pushing aside his unfinished coffee.

"You'll have to phone the Old Man and tell him we're closing down and moving back to Lebanon until law and order is restored."

Grandpa quietened down. "Yes, that would be best. We can move your mother to Chateau al-Zeid."

Maftur's stomach churned. She pushed her plate away. If they fled to Lebanon now she would have wasted over eighteen months of swatting. She couldn't wait to get to school to tell Ai'isha about her father's threat.

Her friend sympathized. "Tell your parents you can stay with me until the exams are over."

She choked back a hysterical laugh. That was the last thing her father would allow.

After school both she and her mother waited impatiently for her father to return.

"Well," her mother demanded even before he had divested himself of his jacket, "have you decided when we're going?"

"We're staying put. I don't know what's got into the Old Man. He told my father to pay the Freedom Tax and he would reimburse us and says the Grand Mufti has promised Ahmed that no members of our clan will suffer if we attend to our business and refrain from interfering with politics."

Maftur wondered if the Grand Mufti knew of all the promises being made in his name.

"The Old Man should come to Haifa himself and see how things are here," her mother commented. "Then he wouldn't be so keen on us staying."

Maftur checked on the most important part of the conversation. "So I stay on at school until I finish matric?"

"Looks like it," her mother said. "Let's hope your great-grandfather knows more than we do."

Chapter 11

A few weeks before Maftur and Ai'isha sat their exams, Abu and Umm Fikri received an unexpected marriage proposal for Ai'isha on behalf of a younger son of an exceedingly rich Jaffa Uncle. The photograph of the proposed bridegroom so closely resembled Errol Flynn that Ai'isha had no hesitation in agreeing to a betrothal.

With considerable difficulty, Maftur kept them both focused on revision, even if geometry did revolve round creating a pattern for a Parisian-style wedding dress to fit the roll of expensive damask silk presented by the bridegroom.

As they pinned the finished pattern onto the luxurious material, Ai'isha promised she would create an equally fabulous wedding dress for Maftur when it came to her turn to marry.

Maftur knew she ought to feel grateful, but didn't want to think about her own marriage. She had still said nothing to Ai'isha about her conditional betrothal. The thought of it gave her so little pleasure that for a short time earlier in the year she had considered deliberately failing her exams. However, a combination of pride and the vision of becoming an old maid, never in charge of her own household, and with no children to look after her if she became as senile as Granny, put an end to that idea.

The exams came round at last. After each paper, Maftur could only remember questions she was sure she had answered incorrectly. Certain she had failed, she consoled herself that it would end her betrothal.

With so much depending on her exam results, normally Maftur would have been on tenterhooks all that summer of 1937. However, in early July, an event occurred of such horrendous proportions that it overshadowed everything else.

She had met up with her class-mates in the milk bar for a lunchtime leaving celebration—more a wake than a celebration, as this might be the last occasion when they would all meet together. For once her mother allowed her to go without a chaperone so long as she and Miriam went together.

Many would be marrying within the month, a few would go into nursing but most, depending on their exam results, would move on either to universities or teacher training colleges in Jerusalem, Beirut or Cairo.

It was an occasion for reminiscences. As they recalled the more hilarious incidents of their school years, their mood lightened. While their netball captain, Dewya, was in the middle of recalling a game where someone's knicker elastic had snapped just as she was aiming the ball at the net, the daughter of a particularly zealous member of the AWA committee arrived late, looking distraught.

"Sorry, everyone, but I had to stay and calm mother after the terrible news."

Everyone looked up, sympathetically worried. Miriam said, "What news?"

"An American paper has leaked the Royal Commission's report."

Maftur's stomach tightened. The Commission's findings couldn't be good if Catherine had made herself late to comfort her mother.

Most women however laughed aloud.

"Really, Catherine." Ai'isha waited for her giggles to die down before she continued. "I thought you were going to say someone in your family had been assassinated."

Catherine glared at her. "This is worse than any assassination."

"What was in the report?" Maftur asked.

"They're dividing Palestine into three and we Arabs will have the worst part."

Maftur pressed her fingertips to her cheeks. "That can't be true!"

"My mother says it is. The British are keeping some bits and giving all the fertile areas of Palestine to the Jews, even the citrus coast. The AWA committee's calling an emergency meeting."

"They can't steal our land from us just like that," Ai'isha said. "It has to be a hoax."

"Those Jews! We should have got rid of them years ago," Dewya spat.

Had Dewya forgotten Miriam was with them? Maftur

turned to look at her neighbour, but Miriam was already on her feet, walking towards the door.

"Miriam," she called out. "Please don't go. You know Dewya didn't mean you."

Miriam's best friend glared at the netball captain. She shouted, "I hope you're proud of yourself," and ran off to catch up with Miriam.

Maftur knew she ought to catch up with Miriam so they could return home together but thought Miriam's friend would resent her presence so stayed where she was.

There followed an uncomfortable silence.

"Which areas exactly go to the Jews?" someone asked eventually—more to break the silence, Maftur thought, than anything else.

"I can't remember exactly but I know they included the citrus coast, the Jezreel Valley, Galilee, Lake Hula, Tel Aviv and, I think, Haifa."

"Haifa! But they can't have that. We live here," Ai'isha protested.

"Who's having Jerusalem?" Dewya wanted to know.

"The British, along with Nazareth, Bethlehem and the Seven Sisters Road."

"The League of Nations won't allow it," Maftur protested. "It's against the Mandate."

"It's only rumour, anyway," the netball captain said. "For goodness' sake, let's talk about something else."

They all tried but the party spirit had evaporated. They split up to return home earlier than expected.

When Maftur arrived back at the apartment, her mother was in the sewing room, staring at the ceiling, her unopened embroidery bag on the floor.

She acknowledged Maftur's presence with a faint smile. "How did the get-together go?"

"All right." Maftur cut to the issue she was sure was upsetting her mother. "You've heard about the Commission's Report?"

"Your father told me at lunchtime. I can hardly take it in. Samaria, the only fertile area of Palestine left, except for a few patches down by the Jordan. The rest—just wilderness and desert."

"What will happen to people living in parts given to the Jews?"

"Your father says the British will force them to move out."

"They can't do that."

"Ask your father when he comes in. I don't want to talk about it anymore."

Her father came home earlier than usual after an evening in the coffee shop.

Maftur tackled him at once. "How did you get to hear the Commission's report before it was published?"

"Abu Ismail told me."

"So it's only rumour."

"Abu Ismail said the American paper that leaked the report was reliable. There's sure to be something on tonight's broadcast, so we won't have to wait long to find out."

That evening the High Commissioner made an announcement on the wireless. He confirmed the Royal Commission had recommended partition, and that the British Government had approved its findings. He urged all Palestinians to read the next day's papers.

Maftur's mother was in tears. "The British can't get away with this," she shouted as her father switched off the wireless.

"We'll not discuss it tonight," he stated. "We're all too emotional."

As Maftur stomped off to bed she thought of all those patriots who had resisted selling their lands, despite the high prices on offer. They were now going to lose them anyway.

A fresh thought burst into her mind. This partition wasn't just political—it would alter her life. No Carmel home for her now when she married Ahmed. She would live in Damascus where she knew no one, and what would happen to her parents? They weren't old enough to retire. How could the British do this?

Next morning she pored over the summary of the report in the Palestine Post along with accompanying maps. At least Haifa wasn't going to the Jews, but it wasn't going to the Arabs either. She couldn't eat her breakfast, she felt too sick.

A proposed compulsory transfer of peoples was in the plan, based on the swap of Greeks and Turks in 1923.

However, even the idiot commissioners admitted it would be currently impossible to fit 250,000 extra Arab fellaheen into the areas allotted to Arab Palestinians where only a few thousand Jews would be displaced. Fellaheen would be forced to emigrate.

The paper reported that the leader of the Royal Commission was going to explain that evening how the members had arrived at their unanimous decisions. Speaking from England, they would be rebroadcast in Palestine.

That afternoon on the hillside where Eid prayers took place, an emergency meeting of the full Haifa AWA was held. Maftur accompanied her mother, determined to play a big part in any action decided on. Even if their own section proved lukewarm, the main body of the Haifa Branch would demand action.

By the time the meeting ended, she had volunteered to do anything in her power to prevent the break-up of Palestine and found herself on the emergency action committee. Their leader was determined that Haifa should be the first AWA branch to present a protest to the High Commissioner.

Maftur's initial task was to collect signatures from all the residents in her street for their petition. Under pressure from the AWA committee, her mother reluctantly agreed to let her do it without a male escort, so long as it was only in their own street.

Because this was her first experience of collecting signatures, the committee asked an older woman, Leila Boutaji, to partner her. Maftur recognized Leila as having been head girl when she had first started at Haifa High School. She now worked as a shorthand secretary at police HQ at Khaiyet House.

As they set off, Maftur asked her how she felt about knocking on strangers' doors.

"My parents would be very angry if they knew I was doing it," Leila confessed.

"Why?"

"They'd consider it shameful and would also be afraid I'd lose my job."

"Would you lose your job?"

"I don't think so. However, it may affect my chances of

promotion."

"Promotion?" Maftur didn't know women could aim any higher than being a secretary.

"Yes, our office manager is leaving soon. I'm applying for her job."

This brought a whole new dimension to a secretarial career. Maftur determined to go on a secretarial course as soon as possible.

Standing in front of the first door and knocking was an unnerving experience, even though she knew the people who lived there. She watched with admiration as Leila confidently asked the manservant who opened the door if she could speak to the mistress.

When the woman came, Leila showed her the petition and asked her if she would endorse it, and also ask any other members of her family to sign.

The woman put her signature on the petition, but refused to take the paper inside.

"My husband would be very angry if he knew I'd signed," she whispered. "He says we must completely ignore the British after what they have done to us."

The reaction at the next house was very different. After the mistress had signed, she said, "Is it okay if I ask the servants to sign as well as the family?"

"Of course," Leila replied, "so long as they are all Palestinians."

They collected six signatures from that house and three from the next.

"Do you feel able to do the next house yourself?" Leila asked.

Maftur nodded, took the petition and steeled herself to knock. The mistress of that house was Armenian, who worked from home as a dressmaker. She rushed inside with the paper and came back with eight signatures.

Encouraged, Maftur knocked more confidently at the neighbouring house but the woman there refused point blank. "You ought to be ashamed of yourselves, you two, bringing dishonour on your families, tramping the streets on your own."

"Don't look so embarrassed," Leila said after the woman had slammed the door in their face. "You need a tough skin to be useful."

The next few visits were easy, and then they came to Miriam's house.

"I don't know whether we should knock here," Maftur said. "The family's Jewish."

"Arab Jews or Yekkes?"

"Arab."

"Go ahead and knock then."

It was the right decision. Miriam's mother signed the petition eagerly. "We've been neighbours with Arabs for hundreds of years. Who do the British think they are, trying to turn us into Europeans?"

They finished off the houses round the corner, including the Shawwas. Maftur could read the disapproval on Umm Ismail's face at what they were doing but knew she couldn't express it aloud while Abu Ismail was behind her, praising their courage for acting positively.

"Just my home to do now, thank goodness," Maftur said as they left the Shawwas' doorstep. "I don't think I've ever been so tired in all my life, but it was worth it. Can we have a short break before we return the petition?"

"I'd rather get off quickly," Leila replied. "I have to be at work extra early tomorrow to make up for time I've taken off today, but there's no need for you to go back to the centre. When we've collected your family's signatures, I'll drop off the petition on my way home."

"You're a real friend," Maftur said. "I feel so ashamed when I compare myself to you."

"No need to feel guilty. I was worn out the first time I collected signatures. It's the emotional stress. You'll get used to it, but don't fall asleep in front of the wireless this evening when the leader of the Royal Commission tries to excuse its stupid decision."

"I won't. I'll be too angry."

Chapter 12

Everyone in Palestine who understands English must be sitting in front of a wireless right now, Maftur thought as she listened to Lord Peel. He spoke English slowly enough for even her parents to follow his arguments, so they continued listening rather than waiting for the later Arabic translation.

"The Jews," Lord Peel began in that same plummy voice used by men heading the British government in Palestine, "had taken immense trouble to organise their case and had supplied skilled experts to answer questions from the commission. They had probed British shortcomings with refreshing tact and candour and had examined every article of the Mandate.

"The Arabs, on the other hand, at the outset had refused to provide witnesses. When they did eventually consent to speak, they had ignored the League of Nations' Mandate, insisting instead on the inherent right of the majority to manage their own affairs."

"That attitude of the Mufti's party is what ours has been complaining about," her father burst out. "The British are punishing the rest of us because of his obstinacy."

"The Mufti's a holy man," her mother reminded him, "so he has Allah on his side. It's his followers who let him down."

"Holy or not, I can't see our party supporting him. People will want proper action, not strikes that hurt us more than anyone else."

Maftur blocked out further conversation between her parents and concentrated on the voice from the wireless.

"As the inquiry went on," Lord Peel continued, "it became clear that, during the course of the mandate, the divergence between Arabs and Jews has widened. There is no allegiance to a common Palestine citizenship. People owe loyalty only to their own people and traditions.

"We found no other solution except to create two states—a Jewish state, free of all the limitations which the present mandate implies, and an Arab state where Palestinian Arabs, no longer denied representative institutions, lest they impinge on the obligations of the Jewish National Home, can be the masters in their own country."

How could this Lord Peel announce such devastating changes to their lives in this cold, detached voice? He used words and sentence construction her teachers had called old-fashioned. In emotional contrast to Lord Peel, she heard her mother's shrill voice.

"May Allah forgive him—we Arabs never will. It's not our beautiful fertile country he is returning, but deserts and wildernesses. Where shall we take our business?" she continued. "The firm has no need for us in either Beirut or Lebanon."

"It won't come to that," her father soothed. "It's only fellahin they'll transfer, not people from urban areas."

Maftur felt sure her father was being over-optimistic. She determined to go down to AWA HQ first thing next morning to help collate the petitions. She day-dreamed of the main committee asking her to join a delegation to Jerusalem.

Despite the many eager helpers at Haifa HQ, the Jerusalem Branch of the Arab Women's Association beat Haifa to staging the first official protest. Since press coverage for the Haifa presentation would now be minimal, the committee agreed to send just three committee members with their petition.

The disappointment didn't deter her. She flung herself into AWA activities, waving banners, writing letters of protest and speaking at protest meetings every day. She was forced to take a break from political activity though, for a series of weddings. Ai'isha's was the most important and, in the run up to it, she was allowed to visit her friend.

In some ways, she realised, Ai'isha's family were stricter on tradition than the al-Zeids. Umm Fikri always wore a hijab, for instance, and her grandmother was never seen in public without a full veil, but in other ways, the Tata's customs were more liberal.

The man Ai'isha was to marry had visited her even before the betrothal had become official. Ai'isha still didn't refer to him by name, however, just called him 'my fiancé'.

"My fiancé's not as good-looking as in his photo," she admitted one evening as they were putting the finishing touches to her Henna Day dress. "But I liked what I saw of him, which wasn't much, since I spoke to him from across the room, with both our mothers present, not exactly conducive to sparkling conversation. I dread to think what it would have been like if my fiancé's father's other two wives had come as well."

It then occurred to Maftur for the first time that when she married Great-Uncle Ahmed, her great-grandfather would become her father-in-law and, since he had more than one wife, she would have more than one mother-in-law to boss her about.

Thinking about marriage made her curious all over again as to what exactly happened on one's wedding night. One girl at school had said that your new husband made you take all your clothes off. Another girl had said that you didn't have to remove all your clothing but you had to do something so rude she couldn't bring herself to talk about it.

She'd tried asking her mother, but was told she would have to wait for an answer until the day before the wedding.

She built herself up to ask Ai'isha next time she saw her, if her mother had already told her, but felt awkward. It was easier to talk about it, somehow, when there were several girls together. So, instead she asked, "Will you live with all your in-laws after the wedding?"

"No. I thought I'd told you already, my future father-in-law's put my fiancé in charge of a new canning factory in the new Haifa Bay District. He's given us a modern bungalow there. I'll have my own kitchen and be in taxi distance of my mother and you."

Maftur felt pleasantly surprised. "I can visit you after you're married?"

"Until you marry yourself and go to Beirut, Damascus or Jaffa."

"I may not have to go that far. I may have a house on Mount Carmel."

"That would be wonderful. I'd miss you if you have to go farther." Ai'isha then reverted to her own wedding plans. "The Henna party's going to be old-fashioned. My mother's even borrowed the family money hat."

"Money hat?"

"Wait until you see it. It's centuries old."

"Will your husband come charging into the hall to carry you away?"

Ai'isha laughed. "No. It's only my mother who's getting carried away. My fiancé's side are all very modern. He'll be outside the mosque in Jaffa in a best Saville Row suit and newly blocked fez to meet me when I step off the coach, wearing that Parisian-style wedding dress we sweated over before the exams. We'll sign the wedding contract and listen to Mr. Shawwa's advice before going on to a western style banquet."

Maftur latched on to the mention of Shawwa. "Mr. Shawwa? The Abu Ismail who's our neighbour?"

"Yes, he's my father's lawyer and has agreed to be the officiant."

"Will he be going to the reception with his family?"

"Just his wife and one son, I believe."

So she would see Ismail on the charabanc taking them to Jaffa. She could hardly wait.

"The banquet is going to be out of this world," Ai'isha said, "which reminds me, whatever you do, don't forget your formal invitation. You'll need it. Security round my future father-in-law's house is worse than Acre Castle. It's been upped since the strike ended. The party my future father-in-law runs has split from the Grand Mufti's."

"The Shawwas have guards outside their house too," Maftur said. It worried her knowing Ismail might be in danger whenever he returned to Palestine. For some reason she couldn't fathom, thinking about Ismail gave her the courage to ask the big question. She lowered her voice. "Has your mother given you the wedding night talk yet?"

"No. She said it was too soon. She doesn't want me talking about it with my friends. She'll tell me after my Henna party."

Chapter 13

Abu and Umm Fikri had hired a hall not far from the suq for Ai'isha's Henna party.

Maftur finished the blue thob she would be wearing and laid it out on the bed, so her mother and Zubaida could admire the intricate embroidery on bodice and hem.

"We'll have to take a taxi," her mother said after she had seen it. "We don't want the old town's filthy roads ruining it."

Long before the taxi drew up in the narrow side street outside the hall, they heard traditional drum music. Inside, Ai'isha sat enthroned on a platform while her unmarried female relatives performed solo dances in her honour. Maftur could hardly control her giggles when she saw the money-hat made up with seven strings of tightly packed Ottoman Empire coins. Threaded jewels hung from the ear pieces. Poor Ai'isha sat bravely upright, her neck straining to support the monstrosity that quite spoiled the effect of her elegant thob.

For this first part of the Henna party, Maftur, her mother and other guests unrelated to the bride, were just spectators, while the bridesmaids, all female relations, presented the groom's gifts. Later, however, they joined the lines of women dancing dabkas and singing improvised songs, pausing momentarily to tuck into a magnificent display of sweet meats, while Umm Fikri and Ai'isha's aunts circled the hall offering sugared almonds to one and all. About ten o'clock in the evening Umm Fikri approached the throne and helped Ai'isha leave the platform. The dancing went on without a pause as Ai'isha left the room, and was still in full swing when the taxi that Maftur's mother had ordered to take them home at eleven pm, hooted outside.

Next morning, Maftur and her parents were outside Ai'isha's house by seven am. She and her mother mounted the waiting coach. Mrs. Shawwa, already seated in the second row from the back, had spread her coat and handbag on the seat to her left to save a place for her mother. Maftur took a seat in front. Other women followed and occupied nearby seats, careful to leave free those at the back of the coach. Eventually, a pale-faced, tearful Ai'isha, wearing her western-style damask silk wedding dress, and a delicate lace veil pulled back from her face, climbed unsteadily into the coach along with her bridesmaids. The women all clapped the bridal party as they made their way to the back. Once there, the bridesmaids set to, repairing Ai'isha's makeup. Umm Fikri, in a blue silk two-piece, counted the women. Satisfied all were present, she told the driver to call the men.

The men took over the front seats. Maftur caught a brief glimpse of Ismail as he stood aside to let his father precede him. He was more handsome than ever in a grey worsted suit and expensive fez. Her pulse raced long after they had passed Athlit.

Her mother and Mrs. Shawwa were deep in conversation, with her mother telling Mrs. Shawwa that she and her husband were looking for a bride for Da'oud.

Mrs. Shawwa reciprocated Umm's confidences by talking about Ismail. "He's gained his Juniors but there's no law faculty in that American University, so he's had to leave Beirut. Starting next term, he's taking classes at the Government Law School in Jerusalem. That lasts five years. A Jerusalem friend of my husband has taken him on as a clerk and will board him in his own house."

"Five years!" her mother exclaimed as the coach bounced over a still unfinished section of the coast road.

"Yes, but at the end of four years Ismail earns a Law Certificate. After five years, he obtains a Diploma qualifying him to practice as an attorney in Palestine. That diploma entitles him to join one of four legal inns in London, where he'll attend formal dinners for six months, and then he will be," she lowered her voice as reverently as if she were speaking of a minor prophet, "a barrister."

How strange Mrs. Shawwa is, Maftur thought as she listened. Most mothers, when talking of sons of Ismail's age, would concentrate on which branch of the family their son was going to marry into, but Mrs. Shawwa had said nothing about that.

"Will your son have to live in England forever?" her mother asked.

"No. He'll be back after a year or so to take over the day-to-day running of our law practice. My husband will then go into politics full-time."

During which part of this seven year program mapped out by his parents, Maftur wondered, would Ismail find time to marry, and who would he marry? Her mother had once mentioned that the Shawwas came from Saudi, so didn't have many relatives in Palestine, just a daughter in Nablus. Was Ismail already betrothed to a Saudi woman? Was some mother there suffering the same set of questions as her mother received about herself?

In Jaffa the coach stopped outside an imposing mosque. Abu Fikri, Abu Ismail, Ai'isha and her bridesmaids, all now heavily veiled, dismounted to the accompaniment of clapping and singing. As she sang, Maftur watched the bridesmaids pin citrus blossom to Ai'isha's veil and remove her shoes, before she and her father entered the mosque. The bridesmaids remained outside.

The coach started off again and wound through narrow streets until it reached the citrus groves on the outskirts of the city. It pulled up outside a pair of iron gates set in a tall stone wall. The driver hooted his horn. To Maftur's astonishment, the gates rolled open of their own accord.

The driver steered the coach into a huge pebbled courtyard, in the middle of which an ornate metal fountain spurted rainbows over golden carp, swimming languidly round a shallow pool. Surrounding the courtyard, uniformed men in navy slacks and shirts with white keffiyahs stood at attention, clutching menacing cudgels.

The courtyard fronted the most magnificent modern three-storey building Maftur had ever seen, more a palace than a house. A wide semi-circular staircase led to an enormous veranda, stretching the width of the second storey. A second fountain spouted high in the centre. Three fully-veiled women in black stood close to it.

Beside her, Umm shook her head in amazement. "I knew your friend Ai'isha was marrying into a rich family, but I never imagined anything like this."

"Saleem Effendi made his money from oranges," Mrs. Shawwa explained. "He owns all the citrus groves round here, and now he's expanding into juice canning."

After the men had left the coach, the women made their way across the courtyard and up the pink marble staircase towards the three women in black silk. The central one introduced herself and the other two as the wives of Saleem Effendi and welcomed their visitors.

A middle-aged woman, a housekeeper judging by her more rustic dress style, led them to the extreme left of the veranda, through french doors into a huge room panelled in glowing golden wood. Six outsize electric chandeliers hung from the high ceiling.

Close to the outside door, a female drummer beat out wedding music. Women were already dancing in front of a dais, on which stood an empty red velvet sofa. Amongst the women, Maftur could see a large number of bewildered Europeans being tutored in dance steps by Arabic guests. Small children played games of tag round European tables covered in damask, and laid out western style with knives, forks, spoons, side plates and glassware. At least one hundred dining chairs surrounded the tables. In front of each chair lay a souvenir menu decorated in silver.

The housekeeper led the Haifa contingent through the length of the room to a door at the end leading into an enormous room lined in polished grey marble. In the centre, another fountain played over a pool containing tiny goldfish. Hand washbasins surrounded the pool and beneath them, footbaths. Maids came to greet them, holding soap and towels. A row of cabinets containing western-style toilets lined the rear wall.

On emerging from a cabinet, Maftur approached the fountain where a maid washed her hands and feet and rubbed them with rose-scented ointment, before decorating her hands and feet in henna with a stylized citrus tree. Maftur felt as if she had entered a sultan's harem, but at least she didn't have to stay.

She and her mother re-entered the hall and joined the women already dancing and singing. Young women in white aprons over black dresses served mint tea and sugared almonds to anyone taking time out. Eventually the bride, bridegroom and bridesmaids arrived. The groom seated himself on the sofa while the bridesmaids escorted Ai'isha to the cloakrooms. The women sang songs in honour of the bridegroom—some obviously traditional to Ai'isha's clan. Eventually Ai'isha returned and sat next to her new husband while the bridesmaids danced in front of her, with everyone clapping to the music.

Waitresses filed back into the room, and stood behind the dining chairs holding up name tags. Two more waitresses brought a low table, placed it in front of the bride and bridegroom, and returned with a traditional dish of lamb and rice for the newly-married couple.

At a signal from one of Ai'isha's new mothers-in-law, the drummer laid down her sticks and everyone except the bride and groom found their chairs at the tables.

Maftur, whose rumbling stomach had received nothing that day except sugared almonds and a handful of dates eight hours earlier read the menu eagerly.

Grapefruit maraschino
Cold beef consommé
Grilled sardines
Lemon sorbet
Roasted quail in orange sauce
(Served with roast and mashed potato, spinach puree and carrots vichyssoise)
Tangerines in jelly
Petits fours
Coffee

The grapefruit arrived promptly. She was thankful her British education had included lessons in dining etiquette. Some older women were having difficulty with the western style cutlery. She wondered if the men had the same menu as the women, or would they be enjoying a traditional Arab feast like Ai'isha and her husband?

After coffee there was a general exit to the washrooms, while servants cleared tables and set chairs against the walls.

"Guess what?" Ai'isha called out excitedly, from where her bridesmaids were re-hennaing her hands and feet. "My father-in-law has given us a European honeymoon. We're taking the train to Port Said tomorrow to cruise to England. I'll see Big Ben, the Tower of London and Madame Tussauds. I'm so excited." She beckoned Maftur nearer and whispered in her ear. "My eldest Belle-mere is scandalized, so it's just as well we'll be going straight to our Haifa home when we return." She lowered her voice still further. "I owe everything to your father, Maftur. My husband insisted on marrying only an educated woman. If Abu Kamal hadn't made you take matric, I wouldn't have had to take it too."

"Educated wives are becoming fashionable," Maftur responded, privately wondering if it was merely a ploy on young men's parts to delay their marriages.

Back in the hall, dancing had recommenced and lasted until the bridesmaids carried off Ai'isha. The women then broke into chatting groups, while Saleem Effendi's middle wife, (Ai'isha's true mother-in-law) circulated, introducing members of the Haifa and Jaffa contingents to each other.

It was midnight before the Haifa men decided to leave. Effendi Saleem sent a carload of men, armed with knives and cudgels, to precede the coach.

If there was danger at any point, Maftur never knew it. She slept all the way.

Chapter 14

Soon after Ai'isha's wedding, Grandpa announced he and Granny were moving to Chateau al-Zeid. Maftur was with her parents at breakfast when they talked about it.

"Why now?" she asked.

Her mother sighed. "Half the time your grandmother thinks she is still in Chateau al-Zeid. They'll have Abu Rakim and Bahia's children around them, and enjoy frequent visits from their Beirut grandchildren and great-grandchildren, although what's wrong with the Haifa grandchildren and great-grandchildren, I don't know."

"Don't take it to heart, habipti," her father said. "The real reason he's leaving is that Palestine's become so dangerous."

Maftur wished her grandparents weren't leaving. The apartment building would no longer be a family home, but she realised her grandfather was right to be worried. Every day she read reports of highwaymen holding up cars, buses and lorries, and village bandits attacking Jewish settlements, or ambushing British police patrols. Added to the British threat to partition Palestine, any sensible person would move out given the chance.

"Moving their furniture will be a problem," her mother remarked.

Her father put down his coffee cup. "No, it won't. We'll do the same as when Abu and Umm Rakim moved. Send the stuff by boat to Beirut and then on by mule train."

Her mother shook her head. "You don't understand. We can't move your mother's furniture before she leaves the apartment—it will only confuse and upset her—but, on the other hand, her furniture has to be in place by the time she arrives at Chateau al-Zeid, if she's to settle quickly."

Her father folded his arms and sighed. "Why can't things ever be simple? I'll discuss it with my father and Kamal."

"And me," her mother said firmly.

"Yes, of course, habipti. We'll thrash it out at lunch-time."

"We'll need to phone your Uncle Harun while making our plans. Book a trunk call for one o'clock and I'll bring lunch down to the warehouse."

Maftur was out that day distributing leaflets for AWA.

"We sorted it in the end," her mother told her when she returned. "Here's the plan. After our usual fortnight in Beirut, you and I will stay with Bahia and Abu Rakim for at least a fortnight."

"I'll be in Lebanon when my matric results come out!" Maftur was surprised to realise the results still seemed important, despite everything.

"Akh Laa!" Her mother slapped her forehead. "How could I forget something like that?"

"It doesn't matter, Umm. I can wait to find out."

"It *does* matter. Your grandfather will just have to phone Beirut again. We'll keep to the same plan but move everything on three weeks—so, where was I?"

"You and I staying with Aunt Bahia."

"Yes. While we're on our way to Chateau al-Zeid, your grandfather will take your grandmother to Uncle Harun's. Kamal will pack her furniture and send it to Damour by boat. Your father will meet the boat and take the furniture by mule train to Chateau al-Zeid. Once the furniture's in place, Abu Rakim and Bahia will collect your grandparents from Beirut. We'll then stay on at Bahia's until we are satisfied your grandmother has settled in."

Her father agreed to the change of dates and added changes of his own. "I've been talking to my father. You and Maftur will stay on at Chateau al-Zeid until things settle in Palestine."

Maftur looked at him aghast. What about her work at AWA and her promised secretarial course? She turned to her mother for support.

"I'm not taking refuge in Chateau al-Zeid," her mother told her father next morning. "My place is with my husband."

"We'll talk about it once we're there," her father conceded.

Maftur realised that he had resigned himself to losing the battle. Later that day, she was glad they had postponed their visit to Beirut, when the AWA committee asked her to give a speech in English as the culmination to a massive protest march to the District Governor's HQ. Now was her chance to shine. She sat down each day to work at what might prove the most important speech of her life. She became so involved with it that the morning before the protest, her mother had to remind her to go in to school to collect her results.

She and a very nervous Miriam went together. The closer to school, the more important her results seemed. By the time they reached the yard she realised that the results were even more important to her future than her speech.

It seemed odd to be entering the building without Ai'isha, who was still on honeymoon. As she made her way to the reception area she found herself trembling, and had to use her hijab to wipe sweat from her eyes.

She took her envelope from the board with fingers twitching so much she had difficulty tearing it open. She unfolded the paper inside. She had passed with distinction. Her maths grade in particular was far higher than either she or her teachers had predicted. All her swatting had paid dividends.

In a dazed state she heard Miss Norman say, "Congratulations, Maftur, you've done us proud. With marks like that you will have no difficulty getting into university. I know you haven't applied, but it is not too late. Come in and see me next week after you've discussed things with your parents."

She refrained from saying she didn't want to go to university, and almost danced her way home, dreaming about starting a secretarial course, getting a job in the typing pool of a large firm, and eventually becoming a top-level secretary. The problem of her betrothal retreated to the back of her mind.

Her mother was ecstatic over her results and handed them to her father with pride. He sat on a cushion in the living room to peruse them, while her mother made him a glass of mint tea.

After congratulating her, he pounced on her maths marks. "I'll put you in charge of our accounts, Maffy. We need you at the warehouse. Akred is useless. Kamal still has to do the bulk of the paperwork himself, just when I need him pushing sales in Jerusalem and Safad. I'm sure your mother can spare you in the mornings."

She stared down at her father in dismay. He couldn't be doing this. It wasn't part of their bargain. Working in the family business would leave her even more restricted than at school. Anyway, she wanted to be a secretary not an accountant.

"You promised I could do a secretarial course," she shouted.

"No point now you're getting married," he said as he picked up his glass.

She wanted to yell, 'I don't want to get married' but, angry and shocked as she was, she knew such an admission would be too shameful. "I want to go out to work properly," she substituted.

"Don't be silly, dear," her mother broke in. "You can't work full time. You've your wedding to prepare for, and as for you, Abu Kamal, you have an urgent letter to write to your grandfather."

Maftur burst into tears, tore off to her bedroom, flung herself onto her bed and sobbed into her pillow.

Her mother came in a few minutes later and sat on the end of the bed.

Maftur lifted up her head and shouted, "You're nothing but a great hypocrite. You go on about women having the same education as men and yet you treat me like a baby factory."

Her mother looked at her for what seemed a long time before replying, "Maffy, your father and I gave you the same academic education as your brothers because men and women are equal, but being equal doesn't mean being the same. Allah gave women the privilege of bringing the next generation into the world, and the responsibility of rearing them in their most formative years. We must be grateful for that privilege. Allah gave men a different responsibility. They have to provide food and shelter for mothers and children. It is our duty to honour men for doing this, just as it is their duty to honour us for our role. Neither of us can fulfil our roles adequately if the other shirks their responsibilities."

It all seemed wrong to Maftur. She sat up to argue. "Umm, look at the widows who have to live on charity because all the men in their family are dead and they have no qualifications."

Her mother laughed. "I don't think you need worry about that. The men in our family make a habit of outliving the women."

"I'm not just talking about our family."

"Well, you should be. Family is more important than the individual for both men and women."

Maftur put her head back on the pillow. She was tired of arguing. She just wanted to sleep and forget everything.

Her mother kissed the back of her head. "Show us what you are made of at tomorrow's demonstration."

Next morning she rose determined not to let the events of the previous evening ruin her big day. Throughout the march, however, she found herself comparing what the British were doing to her country to her parents' partition of her life, leaving her with only areas of fulfilment essential for motherhood. By the time they reached their destination, the anger filling her mind fuelled the impassioned delivery of her speech. When she finished she had to wait for the cheers to die down before stepping back into the crowd.

After the committee had congratulated her, her father came up. "It seems your great-grandfather knew what he was doing, Maffy, when he chose you to be wife to his politician son."

* * * *

Great-Grandfather replied to her father's letter by return of post. At breakfast, in between spreading liban onto his pitta bread, her father read aloud the letter confirming Maftur's betrothal to Abu Fuad's youngest son, Ahmed Walud Khalid al-Zeid.

Her grandfather wrote:

Currently, however, Ahmed is engaged on an important political project, so is unable to name a wedding date. However, one of his stepmothers would be delighted to meet his fiancée during the family's next visit to Beirut.

The letter confirmed Maftur's impression that her fiancé was not exactly eager to relinquish his bachelor status. Why was it so much less shameful for men to resist marrying?

Her mother made no comment on the letter, except to speculate on which one of the Old Man's wives would make the journey from Damascus—unlikely to be the oldest who was well over 90. Even the youngest, Umm Ibrahim must be over sixty.

"How old would Umm Ahmed have been if she had lived?" Maftur asked.

Her mother screwed her forehead up as she calculated. "Almost forty. How time flies. Such a pretty little thing when she married—four years younger than you, Maftur. We weren't surprised when she didn't get pregnant for two years."

The prospect of the imminent interview with a future step-mother-in-law, combined with her parents' constantly-expressed doubts about the safety of their journey, prevented Maftur from looking forward to the holiday as much as usual.

The journey, at least, went off without incident, since a police armoured car escorted their bus all the way to the border.

In Beirut they stayed as usual in Uncle Harun's house with Parveen and her family, and began visiting various branches of her mother's family the day after they arrived. Maftur found herself cringing as relatives kept asking her mother what date she had chosen for her daughter's wedding. However, she had to admire the carefully studied nonchalance of the replies.

Despite the social embarrassment, Maftur couldn't help hoping Great-Grandfather would continue to prevaricate long enough for her to attend secretarial school, and get a proper job. She worried, though, that once one of her future stepmothers-in-law entered the scene, her mother would demand a firm date.

When they returned late one afternoon from yet another family visit, Parveen told them that Great-Grandfather's third wife, Umm Ibrahim, had arrived that morning, along with a personal maid and a man-servant.

An hour later, the dowager, Umm Harun, who nowadays never appeared in the public rooms of the women's quarter, summoned Maftur and her mother to her private sitting room.

Up until now, Maftur had never seen this great-aunt, although the servants lived in awe of her. Her legs felt stiff as she entered the room.

Umm Harun, whose wrinkled jowls hid her neck, lay propped up on cushions on a chaise longue almost too narrow to accommodate her extreme girth. Next to her, upright in a high-backed chair, sat a woman looking no more than fifty, wearing an expensive looking silk floral dress and a chic blue straw hat with net veiling. Umm Harun introduced her as Umm Ibrahim.

An ancient maid, presumably Umm Harun's personal servant, served mint tea and sweet pastries. Once the introductory niceties were over, Umm Ibrahim said, "I must congratulate you, Umm Kamal, on your daughter's exam results. She will make a good match for my son Ahmed."

So, Umm Ibrahim, Maftur thought, as she watched her mother dip her head to acknowledge the compliment, is staking her claim as my main mother-in-law.

It didn't take her mother long to steer the conversation to the subject of a wedding date.

"My Maftur is nearly seventeen already. People are asking why she is not already married. Do you know how long this important project will occupy Ahmed Walud Khalid?"

"Abu Fuad will determine that. He has brought Ahmed up to be the family's political representative, so Ahmed, you understand, needs a mature wife he can trust to keep state secrets. Before Ahmed and Maftur marry, Abu Fuad has requested that you have your daughter trained to a high standard in both typing and shorthand. This is essential if she is to be of real support to her husband."

Her mother compressed her lips, but Maftur liked the sound of the planned program. While her mother made a conventionally polite answer, she mentally rehearsed a response of her own. Taking advantage of a pause in the conversation between the women, she ventured to push her luck still further.

"Umm Ibrahim, may I have your permission to speak?"

Her future mother-in-law smiled benevolently. "Of course, chicklet. You must learn to speak up for yourself with other women. What is it you wish to say?"

"I am very happy to take a secretarial course, but if my work experience is confined to our family firm, I will not have a broad enough outlook to support my husband properly. When I have my secretarial qualifications, I would like to work first in the typing pool of the government Post Office in Haifa and then, when I have experience of British administration, I would like to work in the Secretariat in Jerusalem. This would be very useful to my husband."

She saw the horrified look in her mother's eyes, but Umm Ibrahim beamed at her.

"I can see why my husband picked you out for my son. You look ahead and plan. However, it would be wise to start your career in your father's firm. Ahmed has never worked in our business. He may be in danger of throwing himself into politics for its own sake instead of realising he is working on behalf of the family. If you have a good grasp of the family business you can help him stay focused. When you are eighteen you can spread your wings a little. Once you are qualified to work at the Secretariat in Jerusalem I will arrange for you to lodge with a respectable family until your marriage."

Chapter 15

The holiday in Beirut was over. Aunt Bahia and Uncle Abu Rakim made an impressive arrival in a chauffeur-driven Ford Tudor Standard, complete with two armed servants.

"We'll be a bit squashed," Aunt Bahia apologised, "because the Old Man insists we take guards wherever we go."

Maftur was curious. "If we can reach Chateau al-Zeid by car, why does the furniture have to come by mule train?"

"The roads aren't good enough for lorries," Uncle Abu Rakim replied. "Be prepared for a bumpy ride."

"Do we still have to make that long uphill walk at the end?" her mother asked.

"No. The Old Man had the path widened before renting out the house."

Maftur realised what Uncle Abu Rakim meant by a bumpy ride after they turned inland at Damour and took a rutted dirt road through mulberry trees, but the increasing beauty of the scenery made up for any physical discomfort. As the valley narrowed, she caught tantalising glimpses of cool green shade beneath trees overhanging a swiftly-running river at least six metres wide, even in the height of summer.

The jolting increased dramatically when the chauffer turned the car onto something little more than a goat track twisting up a rocky hillside. It terminated at a massive fortress-like structure high above the valley that had narrowed into a gorge. They drove through an arched gateway into a central courtyard surrounded by stone buildings.

"Every June, July and August the Old Man used to bring his whole household here, plus a small army of armed guards, and make his annual rounds ordering the best quality silk," Uncle Abu Rakim said. "Every time he married another wife, he added a new section. That's why it's so easy to accommodate my parents."

"What about water and electricity?" her mother asked.

"Heavy winter rains fill our huge cisterns with all the water we need, but we have no electricity."

Aunt Bahia sighed. "I do miss switching on lights."

For three days Maftur helped her mother and Aunt Bahia prepare Granny and Grandpa's rooms. Aunt Bahia had found out from Grandpa which apartment they had occupied when he and Granny were first married, and had done it up, converting one room into a modern kitchen with an American-style wood-fired cooking range, which also heated water and three radiators.

Maftur spent most of that week on a stepladder helping to fasten a lorry-load of rugs and carpets to bare stone walls. When her father arrived with the mule train, he sent her to search for the packing case labelled IMMEDIATE.

"I asked our father-in-law to label everything Belle-mère uses most often," her mother explained. "That way, even if we're still sorting furniture when she arrives, we can make her feel at home."

At the end of the week, her parents and Aunt Bahia went to Beirut to fetch Granny and Grandpa. To everyone's surprise, Granny settled down almost at once, and in fact, seemed less confused than she had been in Haifa. Occasionally she even called people by their own names.

Since Grandfather seemed happy to be left alone looking after Granny much of the time, Maftur and her mother found themselves with time to spare, while her father accompanied Abu Rakim to the spinning sheds, and Aunt Bahia educated her children. They spent mornings exploring the gorge, taking water colours and charcoal with them. They sketched romantic views of the river and tree-covered rocky cliffs, and spent two whole mornings painting a particularly beautiful crimson-leafed castor oil plant adorned with blood-red spires of blossom.

Despite the presence of armed protectors who accompanied them wherever they went, Maftur felt enclosed in a bubble of peace.

At the end of the week the bubble burst as she and her parents prepared to leave.

Aunt Bahia protested. "You've heard the news on the wireless. The situation in Palestine is awful. Please don't go back."

"We'll take our chances. Things have improved in Haifa since a new British officer's taken over and instigated 'stop and search' swoops," her father said.

"But the journey itself!"

"With luck the bus may have a police escort from the border."

Despite that rather less than reassuring conversation, they reached Haifa without incident.

* * * *

Back home, Zubaida handed Maftur a pile of postcards, all from Ai'isha. The earlier ones, postmarked Italy and Paris, had various views of the Coliseum, The Bridge of Sighs, the Eiffel Tower, the Seine, flower markets. The scribbled messages on the back were mostly about fabulous dresses and hats. The last card showed the Dorchester Hotel in London.

We're staying here for several weeks, thanks to my father-in-law. My husband gave me a Brownie camera for my birthday so I'll have oodles of photos to show you. I love it here but I'm a tiny bit homesick. Do write back with the latest gossip.

Maftur found it hard to reply. After all the exotic places Ai'isha had visited, her friend wouldn't be particularly interested in her stay in Beirut and the Damour Valley. She hadn't seen enough of their mutual friends to gather interesting gossip. All she could write about was her betrothal now that it was official, but even that was vague since she didn't have a wedding date.

The following week she started work. Her father had created an office for her in what had once been a servant's bedroom, and had had a nearby washroom and toilet renovated for her sole use. The office fittings included a primus and coffee percolator. A door at the back led to a balcony and fire escape, so she could enter and leave without going through the warehouse. Kamal had an office on the same floor, but the rest of the upstairs was used for storage.

She walked to work each morning with her father and Kamal, and walked back with them for lunch. Except in the busiest periods, she did not return to the warehouse in the afternoons. For her first two days Kamal worked with her, explaining the firm's accounting system. After that she was on her own, recording payments, sending out invoices, and costing orders, all carried out in best handwriting, sometimes in Arabic, sometimes in French, and occasionally in English. Sitting, working by herself all morning with no one to chat to was not the way she had envisaged office life.

Initially, she accepted the way the firm worked without criticism, but once she gained confidence she found the set-up old-fashioned. She itched to produce beautifully-typed correspondence, and promised herself that once she was a qualified typist she would press for changes, although she knew her father would tell her that the firm's organisation was not women's business. If, however, she could inveigle him into making that statement in front of her mother, especially on the day el-Karmil published their women's page, she would gain a powerful ally. Once her mother had an idea fixed in her head, she managed to wear down her father's opposition, grain by grain, until eventually he even forgot that the idea hadn't been his in the first place. A prime example of her mother's technique was the way she had transformed her father's attitude to private kitchens. He had moved from complete hostility to enthusiastic acceptance in the course of just three years. Unfortunately, she was unlikely to have three years to work on her own business ideas, unless Great-Uncle Ahmed was more capable of resisting family pressure than most men.

Although she was happy for Great-Uncle Ahmed to prevaricate about their marriage, she was greatly annoyed when her father employed the same tactics over her secretarial course. A fortnight before the secretarial school opened for the autumn term, she reminded him to book her into a typing course. He replied that since the situation in Haifa was currently so dangerous they would have to postpone it until things improved.

She was still sulking about her father's response when he came into her office the following morning.

"Two railway men have delivered a very large and very heavy package from Syria, labelled in French, 'For the sole use of Mlle Maftur Nour al-Zeid'. Do you know anything about it?"

She shook her head, mystified.

"You had better come downstairs while we open it."

As she followed him across the warehouse floor, she was

acutely aware of curious stares from the all-male workforce. She pulled her hijab tighter round her neck.

Once inside her father's large office that doubled as his hospitality centre, Acred meticulously untied the knots securing the parcel. She chafed with impatience while he carefully cut the thick brown wrapping paper so as to preserve it for re-use. At last he peeled back the inner paper to reveal a cardboard box with a picture of a typewriter, bearing the legend 'Made in Germany'. Attached to the box was a smaller package addressed to her father.

She felt a thrill of excitement, but came down to earth when she realised a German typewriter was likely to have a QWERTZ keyboard. If it came from Syria it might even have an AZERTY but it would be of no use to her for typing practice unless it had a QWERTY. She wanted to open the box immediately to find out, but had to wait while her father opened his package. It contained many typed sheets and a letter handwritten in Arabic. He read the letter aloud.

To my beloved grandson, Abu Kamal, from his grandfather, Abu Fuad, peace and blessings be upon you.

Please find enclosed the memoranda on the recent modernisation of our Damascus branch. I would be obliged if you would read it closely and as soon as possible change the Haifa procedures to fall in line with modifications in Damascus. We now type all letters, bills and receipts sent out in English, French and German and retain duplicate copies. Currently, the account ledgers remain handwritten in Arabic but we look to change this practice in the near future. Since the business in Haifa warrants only one secretary, I am sending only one typewriter. It has an English keyboard so the changeover to typing in Haifa will apply only to documents written in English.

In order to facilitate the changes, I have booked your daughter onto a beginner's typing course at the Premier Secretarial College on Kingsway, Haifa, every Tuesday afternoon for twelve weeks. Please find receipt enclosed. The teaching medium is English. Ensure that your daughter practices daily on the enclosed typewriter. Once she has gained a certificate of proficiency, she must use the typewriter in the office. It is possible that German may soon become our main commercial and political language so I have hired a German tutor for your daughter, a lady of good repute who will visit your apartment daily for one hour. Please make your daughter available for both this tuition and the typing course.

The typewriter and typing course, Maftur realised, were a direct result of her interview with Umm Ibrahim. She only hoped Umm Ibrahim had the influence to carry out her other promises. She wasn't quite so pleased about the daily German lessons. They would take up time she could use more profitably working for AWA.

The German tutor, an earnest-looking widow of about fifty dressed in a long black skirt and blouse, and with iron grey hair braided round her head, called at the apartment the next afternoon. Her mother arranged for her to visit every afternoon immediately after the lunch hour, except on the days Maftur attended her typing course, when she would attend the warehouse for an hour before lunch, freeing the rest of the afternoon to work for AWA.

Despite her initial reluctance, Maftur came to enjoy her German lessons. In conversation lessons Frau Hoffman would describe her childhood in Haifa's German Colony of the 1890s, speaking very slowly and clearly. "Such a quiet town Haifa was then, but we were very happy until the war came."

"That was a sad time for everyone," Maftur replied, thinking of her great-uncles who had been killed fighting against the British.

On the first afternoon of her typing course, Umm told both Zubaida and Mahmoud to escort her to the Premier Secretarial College. Zubaida watched her sign in at reception and reminded her that she and Mahmoud would be in the entrance hall to escort her home at the end of the session.

The classroom was full of young women, many younger than her. She was surprised to see so many Jews amongst them, not just Arab Jews but European ones.

Some women smiled at her in a friendly fashion. But she had no time to get to know anyone before the first lesson started. Learning to type was much harder than she had envisaged. She felt a real dunce as she sat at a hooded typewriter while the instructor named a key she had to find with a particular finger. Looking around, she realised the other women were struggling as well, and that made her feel better.

At the end of the session an Armenian woman, one of those who had smiled at her when she had come in, suggested she join others at Edmunds, a cafe on Kingsway, to recover from their ordeal.

She felt ashamed as she explained that Zubaida and Mahmoud would be waiting outside to take her home, but hoped to be allowed to join them the following week.

During the course of the week she kept reminding her mother how often she had emphasised that female networking was important. Her mother eventually conceded she could stay out an extra hour, as long, she said, as Maftur went straight to the cafe in the company of other women.

At the end of the following week's class she joined the others, Christian, Muslim, Jewish, and Armenian, in trooping across to Edmunds, a light and airy cafe built on the corner of Kingsway and a side street.

The women talked about jobs, clothes and, as they got to know each other better, even boyfriends and fiancés—in fact, anything and everything that interested them, except, by mutual although silent consent, politics and religion. Maftur approved of those exceptions. As far as she was concerned, religion was a private matter. She knew what she believed in, and didn't want to hear any views to the contrary. As for politics, she could talk her fill of that at home and AWA HQ. It was refreshing to spend an hour each week chatting on trivial feminine matters with contemporaries. She had missed Ai'isha during the past few weeks.

Ai'isha returned from honeymoon three weeks after the typing classes started. Maftur couldn't wait to visit her in her bungalow, four miles along the curving beach that joined Haifa to Acre, in a new mixed development of houses and factories.

Her mother booked her a return taxi fare, sending Zubaida with her.

Ai'isha was full of her visit to France and England and had brought back several albums of snaps. While a maid in a black dress with a white frilled apron wheeled in a trolley with a British teapot, china cups and saucers, wafer-thin cucumber sandwiches and an assortment of cream cakes artistically arranged on a three tier silver cake stand, she showed off her new camera.

Maftur admired the wafer-thin sandwiches the maid handed her on a china plate.

"We had sandwiches like this for afternoon tea at the

Dorchester." Ai'isha explained. "I asked the waiter how they were made. You have to cover cucumber slices in salt overnight, wash them and then soak them in lemon juice."

As they ate the sandwiches, Ai'isha displayed what seemed innumerable pictures of London, Buckingham Palace, the changing of the guard, Trafalgar Square with Lions, London Bridge, views from the top of the Monument, St Paul's Cathedral, Tower Bridge, both open and shut, and many other places with names Ai'isha couldn't remember. There were always at least two pictures for each location, one of Ai'isha looking gay and excited and wearing a different dress for every snap, the other of her husband, dignified in a suit and fez as if he were on the way to a business conference. Occasionally there was a third photo of both Ai'isha and her husband standing a few inches apart with their arms hanging by their sides.

"My husband asked strangers to take pictures of us," Ai'isha explained. "I don't know how he dared, but people always said yes."

Maftur put on an interested facade for as long as possible, and then looked around the room to make sure the servant had left.

"What was it like on the wedding night?"

Ai'isha turned a deep red. "It wasn't as horrible as I thought it would be after what my mother told me. In fact, once you get used to it, it's quite nice. I am sorry but I am not going to tell you about it. I might make it sound awful, when it isn't really. You'll have to wait until your mother tells you. Now I must show you the photos I took when we had a day outside London and went to Whipsnade Zoo."

After that first visit, Maftur shared a taxi with her mother and Umm Fikri to Ai'isha's home once a week, which considerably limited the time the two young women had for private conversation.

Although Ai'isha always seemed glad to see her, Maftur felt a gulf opening between them. Ai'isha was now enthusiastic about things Maftur found it hard to take an interest in, the new Miele vacuum cleaner, the Hotpoint cooking stove, marble tables and Persian rugs. She did, however, still listen to Maftur's accounts of her typing course and passed comments on politics, but not with the enthusiasm of their school days.

In November, when Ai'isha discovered she was pregnant, the gulf widened still further. Ai'isha focused solely on nursery furniture and baby clothes. She lost all interest in anything else, including happenings in Maftur's world.

Luckily, after-class meetings at Edmunds and working with AWA provided Maftur with stimulating conversation during the rest of the week.

Chapter 16

Afterwards Maftur always remembered 1938 as the year of the scarves. For her, the headgear problem started when the AWA executive in Jerusalem asked members, both Muslim and Christian, to show solidarity with their brothers fighting for independence by wearing only black cotton headscarves.

Maftur was quite happy to do so for a day or two, but hadn't anticipated a black scarf becoming her only head covering forever. Within a few days, however, any Arab woman, Christian or Muslim, appearing in public with anything else on her head other than a black scarf, was in danger of being stoned either as a prostitute, or an Anglophile.

She came to hate her black hijab but knew if she didn't wear it she risked not only her own safety, but that of her father and brother. Her dream of owning a Parisian hat receded into the realms of fantasy. Every now and then, however, she would open up her wardrobe and gaze longingly at her collection of beautiful silk hijabs patterned in her favourite colours to complement her dresses.

One evening in February while listening to the usual daily list of murders and robberies on the wireless, she was startled to hear a familiar name. Saleem Effendi from Jaffa, the announcer reported, had been shot dead while getting out of his car. His chauffeur was critically ill in hospital.

Maftur felt numb. The room changed dimension and colours dimmed. She stood up and rushed to the front door. She had to get to Ai'isha. Only the fact that the door was locked prevented her rushing downstairs and out into the street. As her mother led her back into the dining room, she realised that she would have had to return anyway to ask for taxi money.

"You won't do any good going to see Ai'isha at this time of night," her mother said. "And anyway, she's probably with her husband in Jaffa. I'll send Mahmoud round to Umm Fikri's house. If Ai'isha's home I'll go with you tomorrow. Your father will give you time off work. Go to bed now. Get a good night's sleep."

Maftur expected to lie awake all night, but must have dropped off into a nightmare where the Arabian flag of revolt flew over the blood-stained bodies of Ismail and his father.

She woke, the dream still vivid, her throat so constricted she could hardly voice her morning prayers. She had used all the water in the jug beside her bed to rinse her hands the previous evening. She went into the kitchen and found her mother already there.

"What are you doing up again?" her mother asked.

Maftur looked at the kitchen clock. The clock's hour hand was on eleven. She couldn't believe she had only been in bed two hours. She picked up a beaker and filled it with water, dropping it when a knock on the door startled her. The beaker smashed into pieces. Water spilt over the floor.

"Who's there?" her mother called.

The night watchman answered, "It's okay. Umm Fikri's houseman has brought a message."

Her mother let the watchman in and took the note.

"It's for you, Maftur."

Maftur's wet hands soaked the paper, stuck the edges together and smudged the ink. The paper tore as she prised the note open with trembling hands. Her blurred eyes had difficulty deciphering the words, but at last she made it out.

Maftur, you must have heard the news about my father-in-law. My husband's in Jaffa for the funeral. I'm at my mother's. Can you come round tomorrow, please?

She handed the note to her mother and began picking up pieces of broken beaker, as the watchman said, "Umm Fikri's houseman wants to know if he should wait for a reply."

As if wrapped in a transparent bubble, she watched her mother pick up a pencil from a pot on a shelf and take a sheet of paper from the pad she kept for grocery lists, and write on it. Her own hands still trembled as she mopped the floor.

Her mother handed the note to the night watchman, giving him a piastre for Umm Fikri's messenger, before saying, "Now, Maftur, get to bed and stay there. I'll finish the floor. If it's your father you are worrying about, you needn't. He has the sense to keep his political views to himself."

But it wasn't her father she was thinking of.

It was grey next morning, cold and drizzling. Even though they took a taxi, both Maftur's and her mother's coats were soaked as they walked the short distance from the taxi to the front door of Umm Fikri's house.

Maftur had scarcely entered the hall when Ai'isha flung herself on her, put her head on her shoulder and wailed, "I'm so frightened, Maftur. My husband's in Jaffa. The assassins will try to kill him too."

Umm Fikri spoke soothingly. "He'll be safe, love. The police will be there to protect everyone."

Ai'isha raised her head. "And where were the police when my father-in-law was assassinated? Tell me that. They knew he was in danger, making so much fuss opposing the Grand Mufti, but they did nothing."

Her mother opened her eyes wide. "You're not suggesting the Grand Mufti himself had anything to do with the murder? He can't help what his ignorant supporters do."

Umm Fikri put her hands to her mouth. "Of course she doesn't mean that," she said over her fingers. "Haj Amin is a good man. My son has met him and talked to him. He says he is very spiritual." She looked back to the kitchen to make sure the door was closed. "But you are right, it is a different matter with members of the party he leads." She turned on her daughter and hissed, "Ai'isha, you're only putting your own father as well as your husband in danger voicing these allegations. We must all learn to keep our mouths shut and our eyes averted."

Maftur recalled her dream in all its horror. If only Ismail's father would keep his opposition to the Grand Mufti's Palestinian Arab Party as secret from the general public as her father did.

She pulled herself together. This was no time to be dwelling on her own fears. She had to concentrate on Ai'isha. She didn't know how to help, though, and realised only Ai'isha knew what she wanted, and would probably only tell her when they were alone.

Umm Fikri led them into the living room, already set out with plates of honey cakes. A maid came in with Ceylon tea.

While the two mothers discussed what everyone could do to help Ai'isha, Maftur sat quietly trying to lend moral support purely through her presence. She watched Ai'isha's face to determine which suggestions her friend genuinely approved of, and concocted plans accordingly.

Ai'isha managed to get a word in. "Please may Maftur sleep over?"

Both mothers agreed before carrying on their conversation.

Ai'isha protested her mother's next suggestion that she stay in town until the baby was born. "I'd love to be with you, Umm, whenever my husband's away from home, but when he's back in Haifa Bay, I must be there for him." She looked pleadingly at Maftur and said, "If Maftur doesn't work in the afternoons, I would be glad of her company while my husband is at the factory."

Maftur nearly blurted out that she went to typing class and AWA in the afternoons, but she bit her tongue. Ai'isha had been her friend since their first year at Haifa High. Even if they had grown apart since leaving school, loyalty to her friend must supersede politics. She resigned herself to interminable conversations on baby clothes. "Of course, whenever you need me."

Maftur felt deeply frustrated that spring as she took a taxi to Haifa Bay every afternoon. She found it increasingly difficult to have a proper conversation with Ai'isha, who showed no interest in events outside the four walls of her bungalow unless she considered them a threat to her husband. On the frequent occasions the wireless reported violence in Haifa or Jaffa, she fell into such a panic that no one dared talk about current affairs in her presence.

In the real world patriotic Palestinians had forced rural police stations to close and passenger trains on branch lines to stop running. Whole swathes of Palestine were under the patriots' control, yet Maftur's own boring life revolved round typing invoices for silk rugs and sewing baby clothes. She bitterly regretted having no time to help the Arabic Women's Association.

The typewriter at work stared back at her accusingly. She could tell it didn't like being used by an unqualified typist. She had had to give up her typing course to be with Ai'isha.

One afternoon when Maftur arrived at the bungalow in

Haifa Bay, a fortnight before the baby was due, Umm Fikri met her at the door.

"Ai'isha started in labour soon after you left yesterday."

"Is she all right? Can I see her?"

"Yes, both Ai'isha and her son are fine. He weighed nearly four kilos."

But Maftur wasn't interested in the baby's weight. She was already dashing down the corridor to Ai'isha's room, excited that at last there was something tangible in this baby world to focus on.

She found her in bed, propped up on cushions, eating grapes.

"I am so glad everything went well. How are you feeling?"

Ai'isha gave a smug smile. "Fine. The midwife said I was built to have a large family. Do you want to see him?"

The baby lay asleep in the crib that Ai'isha had spent so much time choosing. Maftur felt a rush of tenderness as she stared down at the tiny human being. The baby stirred, gave a big yawn and opened his eyes.

Umm Fikri came into the room and stood by her. "Isn't he adorable?"

Maftur put her finger down and touched the baby's tiny but perfect hand. The baby clasped her finger. She felt a thrill of tenderness wash through her entire body.

"No," Ai'isha shouted. "You haven't washed your hands. You mustn't touch him."

Maftur jerked her finger away. The baby screamed and went on screaming.

She cringed back in guilt. Her hand felt huge and she could almost see the germs crawling all over it.

"Now look what you've done!" Tears of anger rolled down Ai'isha's cheeks. She struggled upright and lifted her legs to the floor. "My poor baby. He was so calm before you came."

"I'm sorry," Maftur said and rushed out of the room.

Umm Fikri ran after her. "Don't be upset," she said. "The baby will be all right. It's all so new to Ai'isha, that's all."

"Thank you, but I think I had better go home now. I'll come again tomorrow. Could you call a taxi, please?"

All the way home she reproached herself and, when she entered the apartment, flung herself at her mother.

"I'm just not ready for children of my own, Umm. I do hope Great-Uncle Ahmed continues to be too busy to marry."

Her mother stroked her hair. "Don't worry about it, pet. As soon as you have a baby of your own, everything will seem different. It's just you have no real experience of small children. You're fine with toddlers. They adore you."

Maftur, however, was sure her mother was wrong.

Chapter 17

For a while Maftur carried on visiting her friend daily, but it was becoming more and more of a chore.

Ai'isha had immersed herself in motherhood so completely that she regarded other people as only existing to admire her baby, preferably from a discreet distance. She employed a nursemaid to whom she could talk about him all day, and a good part of the night.

Before long Maftur felt she could curtail her afternoon visits to once a week without undue injury to her conscience. She went down to AWA HQ to resume work. Two of the more militant women cold-shouldered her because for so long she had put personal friendship before the cause. Her closer friends, however, considered loyalty to another woman more important than politics, so she was soon back to taking food parcels to the families of imprisoned patriots, and collecting signatures. These activities had to be put on hold again, however, when the family took their annual holiday to Beirut.

Her mother decided they must travel by boat since, by this time, no one in their right mind would risk taking to the roads in northern Palestine, even when escorted by an armed convoy. She managed to book a four-berth cabin for the women and a two-berth one for her father and Mahmoud on a luxury American cruiser, and the same accommodation on an Italian tourist boat travelling in the opposite direction a fortnight later.

A few hours before they were due to leave, Maftur's father told them he had some unexpected urgent business and had managed to obtain a last minute ticket on a flight from Haifa airport the following morning.

"Urgent business, I don't believe," her mother commented in an indulgent tone. "Your father has been longing to fly ever since Palestine Airways extended the route."

"Why couldn't we all go by plane?" Maftur asked. After all, she thought, my father isn't the only one who would enjoy the novelty of flying.

"Normally you have to book weeks ahead for a flight," her mother explained, "but your father managed to get a cancellation at short notice." She waved at their luggage packed with gifts for Lebanese relatives. "Besides, have you any idea how much all this would cost in excess luggage charges?"

They had so much luggage there was only room for Maftur and her mother in the taxi. Zubaida and Mahmoud had to set off early to walk down to the port. When Maftur and her mother arrived at the docks, Mahmoud had already picked two porters from the clamouring mob. He and one porter dealt with the luggage going into the hold. The other porter carried what they would need to the cabin. As their footsteps clacked along the metal gangway, Maftur couldn't think why, for a single night's journey, they needed two suitcases, a hatbox and an overnight bag.

The first thing her mother did, once they had found their cabin and paid the porter, was tug off her black scarf. "I won't need this again until we return, thank goodness." She opened the hatbox Zubaida had brought into the cabin and took out a hat and a pretty scarf.

To Maftur's delight her mother gave her the scarf. She tied it on and ran her fingers lovingly over the smooth silk.

As her mother pinned on her hat she said, "Zubaida, will you unpack and iron our evening dresses for dinner tonight?"

She gazed at her mother in surprise.

Her mother smiled. "Yes, Maftur, I have an evening dress for you. You can practice being a civilized young lady. Now stop sulking about the plane ride, and look upon this mini-cruise as part of the holiday."

Maftur wanted to wait and see what her evening dress looked like, but her mother was already outside the cabin, waiting.

They passed through a spacious lounge smelling of tobacco, where ladies with cigarette holders between their nail-varnished fingers sat on plump settees or upholstered chairs set round circular mahogany tables. Most were talking in loud Yankee accents, and exchanging photographs they had taken while touring Palestine.

A large stage dominated one end of the room. Her mother studied a notice on the wall.

"A Beethoven concert after dinner, tonight," she exclaimed. "How wonderful! What with all the curfews we've been having, I haven't been to a decent concert for ages."

They went out onto the almost deserted promenade deck, unable to hear each other because of the noise of the winding anchor chain and the ship's engines thrashing the water ready to leave. They watched tourists disembark from a newly-arrived Italian ship. Young men carrying clip-boards herded their charges into groups and escorted them to a desk where Palestine Police checked passports against their own lists, before allowing their owners out of the port area to waiting coaches.

Maftur noticed two young men surreptitiously join one of the groups and hand over their passports. The policeman scrutinized their passports for a long time and then called over a colleague who took the passports and led the men away. Everyone on the quayside stared. One of the men made a dash for the port entrance. The tourists huddled closer together, as several police converged on the fugitive and handcuffed him.

Out in the harbour a tug gave a mournful hoot.

Maftur put the incident out of her mind once they returned to the cabin. On her bunk Zubaida had laid out a gorgeous long-sleeved, high-necked blue crepe de chine evening dress embroidered with silver sprays of jasmine. A complementary blue silk hijab webbed with silver thread lay beside it.

"Do you like it?" her mother asked.

"It's beautiful," Maftur said.

"A present from your great-grandfather. Appeasing his guilty conscience, I presume. He's left money with Parveen so you can go shopping with her, and dress in a style suited to his future daughter-in-law."

Wearing her new dress and hijab, Maftur was sure everyone was staring at them when she accompanied her mother and Zubaida into a dining room lit by four chandeliers. Every table was covered in immaculate white damask and gleaming cutlery and glasses. Linen napkins folded into an elaborate boat shape decorated side plates. She worried that the other passengers might consider the three of them odd because they weren't showing bare arms, backs and cleavages like most other female passengers.

Zubaida whispered, "Stop staring around. There are enough young men gawping at you already without you going out of your way to encourage them."

Maftur let her mother choose for her and Zubaida from the elaborate menu. She ended up with a feast—vegetable soup, salmon fillet, beef steak and strawberry sorbet.

Afterwards the concert in the lounge made it a truly magical evening.

Next morning the ship dawdled along the coast to give passengers time to do justice to a huge breakfast.

Disembarking in Beirut they found their father at the harbour clutching their passport. It had only taken him forty-five minutes to fly from Haifa the previous day. Maftur wondered what would have happened if the plane had not taken off. It seemed silly that she and her mother didn't have a passport of their own.

"I'd have had to phone through to the British consul in Beirut," her father reassured her. "He would have seen to it that you were all right."

As they left the port, Maftur realised how drab Haifa had become over the past few months. The streets here were thronged with women wearing gay summer hats and floating gauzy dresses with hardly a black scarf in sight.

On the second day of her holiday, Maftur's big sister Parveen took her into the shopping centre to spend her great-grandfather's money. She had her hair cut and finger-waved. Afterwards they went to fashionable milliners and bought a wide-brimmed straw hat, its small crown wound with pale mauve ribbon, and decorated with artificial purple anemones.

Maftur felt like a million piastres when she visited Sabeen and her children. Yalda was there, too, with her new baby. Maftur was not in a baby frame of mind. She didn't ever want to see a baby again in all her life. What she really wanted was to talk to Sabeen and Yalda as she had before their marriages. However, she knew her duty and put on a doting face as the infants practiced winning smiles.

The fortnight passed all too quickly and before she knew it they were on the return ship. The Italian menu was very different from that offered on the American boat, but seemed less foreign. Once again she wore her beautiful evening dress and had to laugh at the expression on Baba's face when he saw her.

"I think, despite your long betrothal, it has hit me for the first time that my baby really has grown up."

Next morning Maftur and her mother reluctantly donned their black scarves before disembarking.

Very few genuine tourists left the ship at Haifa, the troubles deterring them. The passengers who accompanied them down the gangplanks were mostly European Jews hoping to stay in Palestine. These were rounded up into groups by Jewish guides, so Mahmoud managed to get their luggage towards the front of the queue leaving the docks. It was reassuring to have her father with them, passport in hand, as they approached the barriers, surrounded by armed police. The passport officials looked strange. They had abandoned their fezzes in favour of rural keffiyahs. The new costume didn't affect their efficiency, however. Her father was subjected to a barrage of questions before they were allowed beyond the barrier.

Out in the street the first thing they noticed was a cinema billboard onto which someone had pasted a large notice in Arabic. Maftur stared at it aghast.

In the name of Allah, the Beneficent, the Merciful! The Headquarters of the Arab revolution reminds all Arabs that the fez is not the true national headgear of Arabs. All Arabs must immediately remove their fezzes, the garb of the former oppressors, and wear the national keffiyah.

Her father and Mahmoud were already being besieged by hawkers all carrying bundles of white cotton keffiyahs and black iqals.

She looked up and down the street. There wasn't a fez in sight. Business men in smart suits now all had white keffiyahs waving round their shoulders.

"For goodness sake don't spend too long haggling. Just buy two," her mother ordered.

Despite her indignation, Maftur couldn't help laughing when they reached home, and the corner of her father's keffiyah kept dropping into his coffee. Her mother sent Mahmoud out to buy three better quality keffiyahs, and made her father put one of those on before allowing him out of the house.

After her German lesson the following afternoon, she and her mother made their way to AWA HQ. Leila greeted her enthusiastically.

The whole atmosphere had changed while she had been away. Everyone was confident of the Rebellion's success now the Black Hand was supporting the rebellion with proceeds from bank raids and bullion robberies.

"It's not the way I'd like us winning," Leila said, "but it's better than partition."

Chapter 18

They hadn't been home long before her father received a note from Ahmed saying he was unhappy about his future bride remaining in Palestine.

"Ahmed says," he told her mother, "that once the patriots have driven out the British, there will be civil war between the Arabs and Jews of Palestine. He wants me to send Maftur back to Lebanon until the troubles are over and advises me to send you as well. Ahmed is deeply into politics so is well-informed. I will take his advice."

Maftur had been looking forward to resuming her typing course in the autumn. She looked to her mother for rescue.

"My place is with you, Abu Kamal," her mother said. "Either you come with us or I stay here with you."

For once, though, her father remained firm against her mother's arguments. She realised, then, how much Ahmed's note had worried him.

Eventually her mother gave in. "Very well. I'll write to Bahia."

"Why Aunt Bahia?" Maftur asked. "If we have to leave, why can't we stay in Beirut?"

"We'll have our own apartment in Chateau al-Zeid," her mother said. "I thought you liked the Damour Valley."

"So I do—in summer. But I'll hate it in winter."

"The troubles may be over by then," her father said.

Soon after they took up residence in Chateau al-Zeid Maftur realised Ahmed was right to be worried about the situation in Palestine. Although Chateau Al-Zeid was not on a postal round, Uncle Abu Rakim brought the post home with him every evening from the silk mill, and that included the Palestinian newspapers that her father forwarded daily. The Palestine Post was full of massacres, bombings, kidnappings, assassinations and the destruction of hundreds of acres of Jewish crops and fruit trees. Everyone who could was escaping from Palestine.

Kamal sent Janan and the children to Beirut. Akred

moved back to Damascus. Her father and Kamal left the apartment block and took up residence in the warehouse, so they didn't have to walk to and from work. Mahmoud and his family moved into the warehouse too. The rest of the servants returned to their villages.

To Umm's intense delight, Dodi and Dindan came to Chateau Al-Zeid for a week at the end of September. They both looked extremely fit. Obviously their great-grandfather wasn't forcing them to spend all the daylight hours shut up in a warehouse.

Dodi was jubilant that, despite the brutal tactics of the British army, the patriots were achieving so much. "Do you know the British have brought in the RAF to bomb villages they suspect of harbouring activists and demolish the houses of anyone they think may have sheltered patriots, even if the unfortunate people were forced to hide bandits at gun point?"

"The Germans are supporting us," Dindan declared. "When we've liberated Palestine from the British they will help us get rid of the Jews. Then, Maftur, we will celebrate your marriage to Ahmed with the greatest feast the al-Zeid family has ever known."

"What has Palestine's freedom to do with Maftur's wedding?" their mother demanded.

"More than you would think!" Dindan replied.

Dodi glared at him before answering. "Nothing really, Umm. I guess Dindan is just getting carried away."

Maftur, however, was becoming more and curious about her younger brothers. With all their patriotic enthusiasm, she couldn't envisage them being mere onlookers in the struggle for independence, but they couldn't have done anything about it while working for her great-grandfather unless… She had always assumed that her great-grandfather was only interested in Syrian Independence, but a United Arabia would benefit the al-Zeid family business. If her great-grandfather was really aiming at a Pan-Arabic Union, then supporting the Palestinian Rebellion might be a step towards that objective. If so, what roles had he allocated to Ahmed and her brothers?

She recalled Dodi asking her to get him his bullet box two years before, and Ai'isha saying the Ghost was a Syrian. Surely the Ghost couldn't be her fiancé, playing the part with the blessing of her great-grandfather?

After a week her brothers packed to return to Damascus.

"Can't you stay longer than just a week?" her mother pleaded. "I am sure the Old Man will let you stay on."

"Sorry, Umm, we are really busy in Damascus," Dodi said.

Busy at what? Maftur asked herself. With Europe in a state of flux, the market for silk rugs wasn't exactly buoyant.

She read about a fresh surge of rebel activity inside Palestine. Patriots had gained control of the Old City. Independence didn't look too far off. She hated being in Lebanon while the Rebellion went on without her. If only she could have stayed in Haifa to work with AWA she could have played a heroic part in the Arab victory.

She pleaded with her mother to go home.

"Arabs being in control of the Old City doesn't mean it's safe in Palestine," her mother replied.

As it turned out the patriots' victory proved short-lived. The British responded to Arab successes by bringing in more troops and acting even more brutally. By the end of October, the British had regained control of the Old City and were bringing order back to rural areas. The battle for Independence was lost. Maftur felt guilty. If she had not abandoned AWA would the outcome have been different?

Then light shone through the gloom. Maftur couldn't believe it at first. The British had defeated the patriots, but all the same they announced they had given up the idea of partitioning Palestine. They released Arabs interned in military detainment centres and gave permission for top politicians exiled in the Seychelles to return to Palestine. The only reason for this change of heart must be that it was the will of Allah.

True patriots stopped fighting and came home. Only brigands and bandits continued to carry out ambushes and highway robberies under the guise of patriotism.

In December the rainy season started in the Damour Valley. Uncle Abu Rakim went to work on horseback, when flooding made dirt roads too difficult for wheeled traffic. Her father wrote saying he and Kamal were back in their respective apartments, although there was still a great deal of unrest on the other side of town.

"If your father is going home, so am I," her mother declared.

"If you are going, it had better be at once before the main roads become impassable," Uncle Abu Rakim advised. "Our car can still get to Damour. The road from there to the border is clear and the bus service to Haifa is still running. A British military vehicle escorts it from the Palestine border. Travelling by bus may be less comfortable than hiring a taxi but it will be safer. Better not carry too much money or jewellery, just in case, however."

"Your jewellery will be safe left here," Aunt Bahia said. "Besides, there's no telling when owning something valuable outside Palestine could be useful."

Chapter 19

Maftur wasted no time re-enrolling for the next beginners' course in the Premier Secretarial School. Starting again from scratch would be useful as she hadn't taken the typewriter to Chateau al-Zeid.

Returning home along Kingsway, she bumped into a woman from her previous typing class, now working as a part-time paid secretary for AWA. Maftur noticed that although the heads of most Arab women were still swathed in black, this woman wore a very pretty hijab.

"I haven't seen you for ages," the woman said. "What have you been doing? When did you get back from Lebanon?"

Maftur described her stay in Chateau al-Zeid. The woman went on to fill her in with the latest gossip and informed her that most of their old class still met up at Edmunds. They would be glad to see her back.

Before they parted Maftur asked, "Is it official, not having to wear black headscarves?"

"Absolutely! We want to show Jews and the British that we've won, don't we?"

Maftur hurried on, intent on sorting out her hijabs and hats, but as she approached home, Miriam, who had only recently returned from Egypt, hailed her and she stopped to chat. Maftur told her she had just re-enrolled at the Premier.

Miriam looked interested. "Would you recommend it?"

Maftur considered the question. "I have nothing to compare it with, but I only dropped out last year because Ai'isha needed me."

Miriam looked puzzled.

"You did hear that her father-in-law was assassinated?"

Miriam took a step back, her face paling. "No. That's terrible. I knew things were awful back here but we didn't get details in Alexandria. Poor Ai'isha! Was that before or after she had her baby?"

"Before."

"What happened exactly?"

Maftur filled her in with the details. That led them to talking about the whole political situation. It was some time before Miriam reverted to the subject of typing courses.

"My father wants me to run the office at his store when he's finished modernising it, so I started a typing course before we went to Alexandria, but the school closed while we were away. Would you mind if I enrolled in the same class as you? My parents would be much happier if I could walk to and from it with someone else."

Maftur explained about going to Edmunds for an hour or so after class. If Miriam enrolled she might like to join them and walk back under the protection of Mahmoud and Zubaida.

Miriam's face lit up. "I'd love that."

On the day the class started, they both dressed extra carefully in smart dresses and couture hats as became aspiring secretaries. Mahmoud and Zubaida escorted them downtown and Maftur arranged for them to meet her and Miriam outside Edmunds an hour and a quarter after classes finished. In the foyer, the receptionist who kept the register, ticked them off her list and pointed them upstairs. They arrived in class just as it was about to start. Maftur looked around after the introductory lecture. Most women seemed very young, but were far from beginners, judging by the way their fingers flew over the keys. She suspected the political situation had forced them to leave school before taking their exams, so this was a refresher course. Only one woman acted as if she had never seen a typewriter before. Judging by her rather dowdy but well-cut clothes she could be British. Maftur gave her an encouraging smile but the woman only scowled back as she threw a screwed up piece of paper into a bin and inserted a fresh sheet. It must be humiliating being the dunce of the class, especially if you were British. She probably wouldn't turn up again.

Maftur was wrong, however. The woman returned the following week, still very much behind everyone else and still scowling.

The third week, however, the woman's typing had improved dramatically. Maftur saw her smile as her fingers clicked over the keys. Encouraged by the woman's more relaxed stance, she introduced herself.

The woman frowned. "Maftur Noor al-Zeid? But I know you, don't I? You came to a garden party at our house. It must be six years ago. I just didn't recognize you, wearing that hat and elegant dress."

Maftur realised who the British woman was. "You're Patsy Quigley! I remember that garden party. We climbed up a ladder to the roof of the tower. But what are you doing in Haifa at this time of the year? Shouldn't you be back at school?"

"You're right, but I had to give up my last year in the sixth. My father insisted I spend a year at home here before going up to university."

Patsy Quigley called Palestine home? But the British had promised Palestine independence by 1949. They would be leaving then. Maftur's AWA antennae quivered. Was this more British treachery? It was her duty, as an AWA member, to investigate. She gave one of the toothy smiles she usually reserved for her doorstep canvassing, and asked Patsy to join the rest of the class at Edmunds.

"Thank you so much," Patsy said. "I would love to join you but what languages will people be speaking?"

"Just English," Maftur replied. "That's the one we have in common."

At Edmunds the other women found it difficult to draw Patsy into the general conversation. Any questions directed at her were answered in monosyllables, although she appeared to be listening intently. On the other hand, Arab and Armenian women weren't saying much either. Jewish women dominated the conversation, or rather Western Jewish women. Arabic-speaking Jews listened, as fascinated as true Arabs, to a complicated conversation about dating, choosing boyfriends and how to stop one's boyfriend going further than one wanted.

Maftur hadn't realised real women talked that way. She had thought it was just part of the Hollywood fantasy world. She didn't like the idea of being left out of the conversation amongst friends through naivety, however, so, although greatly embarrassed, during a pause, she slipped in a contribution.

"I know I can trust you not to breathe a word about this to anyone outside our group."

She looked fixedly at Miriam, who nodded as eagerly in assent as did everyone else, then went on, with much hesitation, to tell them about a neighbour's son, a friend of her brothers who, she thought, fancied her. She admitted that she really fancied him and knew her face must be anemone red.

"Of course," she added hastily, "it can come to nothing. In my family we always marry relatives. I will marry this Syrian relative my parents have chosen."

All except the Western Jews and Patsy nodded in sympathy.

One western Jew who had been brought up in the USA said impatiently, "It's your life, Maftur. You just tell your parents you are not marrying the Syrian guy."

To Maftur's surprise, Miriam rounded on the woman.

"Golda, you are so American. You do not understand our Palestinian ways."

Maftur felt uncomfortable after her confession. She couldn't understand why she had brought her private life into a discussion bordering on the taboo topic of religion.

However, when she looked at Patsy, she felt better. The British girl was visibly thawing. Anything that would make it easier to find out what Patsy knew about British plans for the future of Palestine was worth it.

A little later Miriam surprised her by asking Patsy if she had a boyfriend.

She watched Patsy's wry smile.

"I had to leave my boyfriend behind in England. Not that we were engaged or anything. I want to be free to follow a career after leaving university."

Maftur found herself exclaiming, "But you British women have so much freedom already." On impulse she fumbled in her crocodile skin clutch and pulled out a photograph. "This is the man I am marrying. I have never even met him."

Not strictly true, she reflected as soon as she closed her mouth, but she hadn't met Great-Uncle Ahmed since she had become a woman. As a child, however, she had seen more than she wanted of the obnoxious adolescent.

Golda put out her hand, took the photograph, and immediately changed her tune about Maftur standing up to her parents.

"Wow! That guy looks like Adonis. I'd grab him if I were you."

A woman looking at the photograph over Golda's shoulder added, "If he were handed to me on a plate I'd be over the moon. I take it he has money?"

Maftur shrugged. "He's well enough heeled, but lives in Damascus. I know no one there. Ismail, on the other hand—" She smiled at her memories "—lives in Haifa, and his family is not exactly poor either."

The photo passed from hand to hand, with everyone very impressed by Ahmed's good looks until it reached Patsy. The photograph shook in her hands as she studied it. Eventually she muttered, "Handsome is as handsome does. You must go for what you want."

Surprised by Patsy's reaction, Maftur replied, "That would be easier if I could only discover something about this man that would displease my parents."

On the way home, she only half listened to an indignant Miriam, waxing voluble over foreign Jews born outside Palestine considering themselves more Jewish than those who had lived here for centuries, and how even Arab Palestinians carried more of the seed of Abraham than these Ashkenazi so-called Jews.

She looked back with embarrassment on her contribution to the evening's conversation. Disgraceful though her behaviour had been, putting previously half-formed thoughts into words had shown her what she really wanted. Was there any way she could take more control of her own future, instead of drifting along, accepting what her parents had planned for her?

She felt a twinge of guilt. All must come out as Allah willed but, she argued against herself, that didn't mean you left fields to sow themselves. Allah expected you to work his will, not just wait for it to happen.

She thought of one thing that might persuade her father to cancel her betrothal. If she could prove that Great-Uncle Ahmed had been the leader of a terrorist squad that included her brothers, her father would be angry enough to consider ending her betrothal. Her mother, however, was more likely to approve of Ahmed playing an active part in the Rebellion, so she would have to play this game without backing from anyone.

Her first step must be to confirm her suspicions that Great-Uncle Ahmed had led a patriot squad, and that her brothers and Fizzy had joined it.

She spent the evening working out how to prise the information she needed from Ai'isha, without actually telling a lie, then went to visit her the next afternoon.

She duly admired Ai'isha's child without too much pretence. Children were much easier to like once they were no longer babies. She then learned that Ai'isha was expecting a second baby, so she had to waste time on that uninspiring topic before she managed to turn the conversation to Fizzy.

"Mother is so glad to have him home," Ai'isha told her.

"He's home—for good?"

"Ah, you are interested in him after all," Ai'isha teased. "Shall I let him know?"

"You have a wonderful brother, Ai'isha, but I couldn't marry him, even if I weren't already betrothed. He's not part of our clan."

"Pity! He really fancies you, and your great-grandfather seems to have taken a fancy to him."

"How's that?"

"He gave Fizzy a glowing reference, and spoke up for him to the managers of the Palestinian Railways. The result is he has his old job back in the workshops and his prospects are looking good."

'So," Maftur said in an off-hand manner, "my fiancé has finally disbanded his squad. I thought he might, now he's concentrating on the political side of things."

Ai'isha gave her a startled look. "So you know about that. Fizzy said I was never to talk about it with you."

Maftur gave a shrug that she hoped looked natural. "Of course I know. My father is very proud of Ahmed. Mind you," she added hastily, "he doesn't know about my brothers being part of the squad, so best keep that between ourselves, eh?"

That should start the ball rolling, she thought on the way home. *If nothing happens in the next few days, I'll have to give things another push.*

Chapter 20

Maftur was enjoying a rare leisurely afternoon at home. Replete after a warming winter meal of mutton shawarma, she sat on a cushion at the low dining table with her mother, lingering over coffee.

"Maftur," her mother said in a casual tone, as she settled further back on her cushion, "Umm Fikri said something very strange today. She had only recently found out I approved of Ahmed being a squad leader in the rebellion. Fizzy had told her your father and I were so much against the rebellion we would break off your betrothal if we discovered Ahmed was the Ghost of the Black Hand."

Maftur, who had picked up her coffee cup ready to finish the last of the treacly liquid, held the cup still in mid-air. Her mother was treating the subject with surprising calm.

She had an earth-shaking revelation. "You knew Ahmed was a squad leader!"

"Well, I had my suspicions, of course. My only comfort was that so long as the Old Man was alive your father wouldn't dare cancel your betrothal, however much he might disapprove. To tell the truth, I was more worried he would find out about Dodi and Dindan." Her mother looked at her sharply. "Surely you knew your brothers were sabotaging the IPC oil line?"

Disorientated, Maftur clutched both sides of her cushion and focused on a beautiful zoomorphic calligraphy of an elephant that hung on the wall behind her mother, disentangling the text *Have you not considered how your Lord dealt with the possessors of the elephant?* before turning her attention to answering her mother's question. "I knew about my brothers, and suspected about Great-Uncle Ahmed from things Ai'isha let slip, but didn't want to make trouble."

Her mother nodded her approval. "However, the difficulty now is that the Tatas believe he already knows, so I can't see him staying in happy ignorance, unless we act straightaway."

The last thing she wanted was her mother enlisting her in a campaign to keep her father in the dark. She sidestepped the issue. "Umm, why are you so keen that I marry Great-Uncle Ahmed?"

Her mother leaned back in surprise. "You need to ask? Who else in the family would you rather marry? Who else owns a house here in Haifa?"

"But, Umm, do I have to marry someone in our family?"

Her mother clutched the table edge with both hands and leaned forward again. "I knew something like this would happen if they delayed your marriage too long. You've set your heart on someone else, haven't you?" She gave a sigh and added. "I suppose it's Fizzy?"

Maftur was not prepared to confess how she felt about Ismail, so seized on an accusation she could deny. "No, Umm, I have not fallen in love with Fizzy. It's just that Great-Uncle Ahmed doesn't seem to care for me at all, except..." She struggled to find words for her feelings. The film *Pygmalion* she had seen with her mother sprang to mind. "Except as an Eliza to his Higgins."

Her mother shook her head. "Of course he doesn't care for you yet, silly girl, but he will once you are married. Now, about our current problem—"

Maftur broke in. "Why didn't you just tell Umm Fikri that Baba doesn't know about Ahmed being a squad leader, and wouldn't approve if he did?"

"And let Imm Fikri know I keep secrets from my husband?"

Maftur, confident that Umm Fikri would already have told everyone she knew that Fizzy had been in Ahmed's squad, felt it safe to suggest, "Perhaps you could tell her now, saying you had only recently found out yourself and were waiting for the right time to tell your husband. Would she wait before telling other people?"

"Too late for that. Umm Fikri will already have informed her friends that your father supports the Grand Mufti in his stand against the British. If I prompt her to go around telling people that he is in fact anti-Husseini, he could suffer the same fate as Ai'isha's father in-law."

Maftur hadn't thought of that. Her plans to end her

betrothal didn't seem so clever now.

When her father came home that evening she watched his face as her mother removed his street shoes and replaced them with slippers.

"I saw Abu Fikri today," he said. "He congratulated me on having a son-in-law who had done so much to save Palestine from partition. I just thanked him—but Maffy, have you been boasting that your fiancé was involved in the negotiations with the British? I am sure Ahmed will be an influential politician one day, but that day is not yet."

Maftur avoided her mother's eye. "No, Baba, I haven't said anything. Abu Fikri must have heard rumours from someone else—Fizzy perhaps."

"I'll have to look into it. Now, on a more serious matter, I've had a letter from your great-grandfather. You must qualify as an efficient secretary by October so you can apply for work at the secretariat. Then a year later you and Ahmed will marry."

Her mother sniffed. "So he remembers Maftur exists then. At least he has set a date for the wedding."

Maftur did some quick calculations and realised she had only a year and a half to get her father to cancel her betrothal, when it had taken her mother all of three years to covert him to the idea of a private kitchen. On the positive side, however, her father now had to let her do a full-time secretarial course that summer.

* * * *

Maftur came home from her first full day at secretarial college, to find her mother in a state of excited joy.

"Guess what? Abu Mussa phoned your father this morning. Dodi and Dindan are coming home."

"Did he say why?"

"The Old Man wants them to tour Palestine's smaller towns and villages, creating new outlets for rugs and scarves."

Maftur suspected her great-grandfather had created these tasks to camouflage her brothers' roles as recruiting agents for the Husseinis. Her mother, however, showed no misgivings.

Next day her father came home with even more startling news. He looked angry as he announced, "The Old Man wants us to arrange Dodi's marriage."

Her mother laughed then raised her eyebrows. "Why has that upset you? It's high time Dodi married."

Her father clasped his hands together until his knuckles showed white. He spoke slowly as if the words hurt him. "The marriage is to a woman Da'oud met in Damascus." He emphasized his next words. "No relation of our family."

A frown replaced her mother's smile. "A woman from outside our family, and he already knows her? Surely the Old Man won't stand for that?"

"So I'd have thought, but he has finally realised that he hasn't long left in this world, so now he's concentrating on leaving our family with useful political connections. He's not going to stop me having words with Da'oud, however."

Her mother clasped her hands together. "Habibi! Please don't start on about this marriage as soon as Dodi returns. I just want to enjoy my boys without any unpleasantness for a while. Promise?"

"For your sake, all right. Anyway, I need a few days to decide how to handle this. As a dutiful son I can't disobey my grandfather."

Not long after her brothers had returned, while all in the family was still sweetness and light, Kamal burst into Maftur's office at the warehouse.

"Abu Mussa has phoned. Great-Grandfather has passed away. We're closing the warehouse for a week. A taxi will take you home. Tell Umm and Janan. We men are catching the next train and will phone through from Damascus, so you women must take a taxi to the warehouse for seven tonight."

Kamal turned on his heel and left as abruptly as he had entered. She heard him running down the wooden stairs. She typed the most urgent invoices with increasing fury, tears dripping onto the keys. She wasn't sure why she was crying. It wasn't grief, more like fear. Her great-grandfather had loomed over every aspect of her life. Nothing important had ever happened without his consent. She no longer knew the rules.

* * * *

It was a strange time, staying at home instead of going to

work—so quiet in the apartment block without men.

Members of AWA, local neighbours and Umm Fikri all dropped in to offer condolences. The atmosphere was so sombre at home, Maftur almost wished she could return to work. Instead, she tried to escape by flinging herself into AWA activities, but found no joy there. The women from all political parties, who worked so co-operatively, found they could do nothing useful to achieve national independence while the all-male delegates in London were behaving stupidly. Maftur could scarcely believe that not only had the Arab delegates refused to meet in the same room as the Jews, but the Arab Husseini Party and the Arab Defence Party had also refused to meet together. The British colonial secretary was racing between three separate rooms to pull off some sort of agreement to forward Palestinian independence.

She retreated to her bedroom and immersed herself in the *Complete Works of Dickens*, a birthday present from Ahmed. It was just as well there was a lot of it because it was a long wait until the al-Zeid men returned from Damascus.

Maftur accompanied her mother to the foyer to welcome home her father and brothers. The boys followed behind their father looking sullen. After they had dutifully embraced their mother, her father, in a harsh tone, ordered them to go straight to their room and unpack.

His face when she greeted him, however, softened and he spoke to her gently. "Maffy, ask Mahmoud to fetch mint tea and cakes into my study, will you? Your mother and I need to talk."

She suspected that, while in Damascus, her father had discovered her brothers' involvement with the Ghost of Sheik izz-ad-Din. Had he, at the same time, found out who the Ghost really was? If so, what was his reaction? She needed to speak to her brothers.

In the kitchen, while relaying her father's request to Mahmoud, she asked him to check if Dodi and Dindan wanted her to set them up some food in the living room.

Mahmoud returned with the message that the boys claimed to be starving, and would come along as soon as they had unpacked.

With the help of Zubaida, she prepared a salad, raiding

the pantry where food for all the visitors they had been receiving was kept, and set out a large plate piled with meat pastries. She then sat patiently embroidering a cushion intended to be part of her dowry.

She was confident her brothers would be eager to blow off steam while they ate. The boys when they arrived, however, could talk of nothing but the reading of Great-Grandfather's will.

"You won't believe this, but there's no one in overall charge of the family business," Dodi told her as he grabbed a meat pastry. "The Old Man's carved it up into national units."

"We had to sit there for an hour while the lawyer read out Great-Grandfather's reasons," Dindan added, his mouth full of pastry.

There was only one aspect of the will that interested her. "Who got the house on Mount Carmel?"

Dodi was too busy stuffing his face to answer but Dindan told her. "That was nothing to do with the business."

Maftur took a deep breath. "But who got it?"

"Ahmed received all the Old Man's personal property," Dindan said, "an estate in the Baalbek Valley, an apartment block in Baghdad as well as the Carmel property. You'll be rich enough sister, if that's what's worrying you."

"It's all very well making Ahmed the family's political champion without him having a vested interest, but the main result of the Old Man's will is that our business has been weakened." Dodi gulped his tea in one swallow and handed his glass over for a refill.

Dindan looked at his brother. "Dodi, I keep telling you the division isn't necessarily a bad thing. The Old Man knew what he was doing. The Holy Quran tells us to respect our elders."

Maftur raised her eyebrows. Dindan disagreeing with Dodi's verdict! Damascus had certainly changed him.

Dodi sneered. "You should tell that to our father. The Old Man made our father head of the independent Palestine business. He trusted him to follow the plan laid out in his will, but our father's intent on going his own way."

Maftur, torn between pride for her father's promotion and her innate sense of justice, stood to wipe a splash of tea from the table. She sat down and tried to look as if she was really concentrating on her embroidery, asking in as offhand a manner as she could manage, "Shouldn't Grandpa have been head of the Palestinian firm?"

"Grandpa's done all right in the will. The Old Man gave him Chateau al-Zeid and the silk mill, so long as he applies for Lebanese citizenship and leaves the Damour Valley property to Uncle Abu Rakim when he dies," Dindan said.

That, Maftur thought, sounds as if Grandpa has been treated fairly but the decision is still illogical. "If Great Grandpa was dividing the firm into national units," she asked. "Why didn't he give Great-Uncle Harun all the Syrian assets?"

"That was another part of Great-Grandpa's long explanation." Dindan got in while Dodo still had his mouth full. "With Lebanon trying to cede from Syria, he thought it safer to divide Beirut from Damascus, but wasn't sure which way the Damour Valley would go."

The family at Chateau Al-Zeid could be in a vulnerable position if Lebanon and Syria quarrelled, Maftur reflected. She looked up to say something and noticed Dindan staring at her embroidery with disapproval. She checked it for irregular stitches but it seemed fine.

"So we've stopped being a real family?" she asked.

Dodi banged his fist on the table, making the crockery tremble. "That's not what Grandfather intended. He made it clear in that lengthy preamble we had to listen to that he was dividing the firm temporarily for political reasons. He asked the new owners to merge again when Pan Arabia comes into being but, of course, our father didn't bother to listen to that bit, did he?" He banged his fist again. "He doesn't care a mil for any of Great-Grandfather's wishes. Only last month Great-Grandfather told him to let me marry Elif, because Elif's father is highly influential in Syria, not just academically but also politically, but now father says, if you please, that Dindan and I must marry Jaffa cousins to keep the Palestine business stable."

"I don't mind marrying a Jaffa cousin, so long as she's devout and respectful of tradition," Dindan said.

Dodi flung him a contemptuous look. "Well I do."

All this was bringing Maftur no nearer to finding out what she really wanted to know. Shilly-shallying any longer would serve no purpose. "Did Baba find out about your part in the Rebellion?"

"You know what?" Dindan said in an awed whisper. "The Grand Mufti himself came to pay respects to our grandfather after the funeral."

She watched her brothers' pride struggle for dominance over their anger.

Dodi took over, puffing out his chest as he spoke. "He introduced a colonel from the German army, a close friend of Herr Hitler himself, to our father. The colonel told our father that Great-Grandfather had been his best adviser and a close friend. Then, you know what? The Grand Mufti laid his hands on our shoulders and told our father how proud he was of our military discipline and expertise as sappers."

"You would have thought our father would have felt honoured," Dindan said.

"Pha!" Dodi exploded. "Was he? Not on your camel."

Maftur dropped her embroidery in alarm. Had their father made an enemy of the Grand Mufti?

"What did Baba say to him?" she shot out.

"Well, it was an occasion to honour Great-Great Grandpa after all, so he had to be polite, but when he got us alone he went majnoon. That's when he told me I couldn't marry my sweetheart."

Maftur gazed at Dodi in disbelief. "You're sweethearts already!"

Dodi smirked. "Yes. This arranged marriage business cuts no ice with Elif. She's really modern. She even goes out with her brothers to cafés in the evening. That's how I met her. She's brave, too, and will fight for Pan Arabia until death."

Maftur could understand why this woman might not be her father's ideal daughter-in-law. Before she could ask about Ahmed, her mother came into the room, interrupting the conversation.

"Boys, your father wants you in his study."

Dindan hung back and asked in a stiff voice, "Umm, why are you letting Maffy embroider in cross stitch?"

Her mother looked puzzled. "Why shouldn't she?"

"The cross is a Christian symbol," Dindan explained. "Our imam in Damascus said women shouldn't do this embroidery."

Maftur put down her sewing, wondering uneasily if her brother was right.

To her surprise her mother laughed. "Men, what nonsense will they come up with next? They'll be abolishing crossroads soon. Dindan, you're going into your father's study, yes? Look at the tapestry hanging over his desk, the one that says 'In the name of Allah'. Don't forget to look at the stitch that's embroidered in." She laughed again as Dindan left the room, and then her face grew grave. "Maffy," she said. "I have some bad news for you. I don't want you to take it personally."

Maftur clasped her hands tightly. She kept her gaze directed at the black and white dining room tiles, trying to hide her excitement.

"I'm so sorry, Maffy, but your father has taken initial steps to break off your betrothal."

"Why?" Maftur asked, hoping her voice sounded sufficiently sad and bewildered.

"It's nothing you've done," her mother hastened to assure her. "He's found out that it was Ahmed who, as he terms it, 'led your brothers astray'. I think, even so, I could have persuaded him to tear up the letter he's written to his lawyer, if he hadn't also found out that Ahmed has allied himself with the Germans. You know how bitter your father has always been against the Germans for supporting the Turks. He's become a lot worse ever since he's made friends with Mr. Shawwa. I'm so worried. Ending your betrothal to Ahmed is very dangerous."

"What grounds is Baba giving?"

"He's going to consult Mr. Shawwa professionally, but I hope it will be the long delay between betrothal and wedding date."

"You mean if Ahmed promises to marry me next week, the wedding would still go ahead?"

"That's our only chance, but don't set your hopes too high. I gather Ahmed is still flying around Syria stirring things up politically, while pretending to be surveying archaeological sites."

Maftur knew that if she stayed in the room any longer she wouldn't be able to disguise her feelings. She threw her embroidery across the room and mumbled, "I'm sorry, Umm, I just want to go to bed now."

Her mother hugged her. "I know how hard this is for you, Maffy. I'll talk to you again in the morning."

Chapter 21

Maftur walked into the kitchen next morning not at all anxious to resume the previous night's dialogue. Instead of sitting down to talk, however, her mother said that her father wanted to see her in his study straight away.

That was more worrying than an informal chat with her mother. She made her way across the liwan and through the door into the men's quarter, gulping down an excess of saliva while nerves pinpricked the walls of her stomach.

Up to this moment she had never been in her father's study. She found him sitting on a throne-like chair behind an olivewood desk, puffing on an antique brass hookah. Above his head hung a tapestry with the words 'In the Name of Allah' embroidered in red on a black background. This had to be the embroidery her mother had spoken of the night before.

Her father followed the direction of her gaze. "You are looking at the tapestry? Your mother embroidered it when we first moved into the apartment block. A very talented woman, your mother."

A memento of her mother's victory in the tussle over private kitchens! The thought gave her courage for the coming interview.

Her father waved her to a chair with an embroidered cushion, presumably another of her mother's creations—this time depicting a view over Haifa Bay with clouds scudding across the sky, and Mount Hermon rising in the background, a more suitable design than sacred words for supporting one's bottom.

Her father waited for her to be seated and then said, "Your mother has told you I intend breaking off your betrothal to your Great-Uncle Ahmed."

It was safer to say nothing. She nodded.

"I am sorry to have to do this to you, Maffy, especially since you have worked so hard to turn yourself into a good politician's wife. If you marry Ahmed, however, I fear there will come a time when you will find yourself on the opposite side of a political chasm from your mother and myself." Her father paused, taking another puff on his hookah.

She wondered if he expected her to make a protest. She kept her gaze on the floor's brown ceramic tiles.

Her father continued, "Your mother may be angry at my decision now, but it is nothing to the grief she would experience if she were unable ever to see you and your children. Please don't make matters worse for her by sulking."

Maftur assured her father she would do her best to remain cheerful even if he did break off her betrothal. As she left the room she felt a rising excitement.

During the week that followed, she worked full days at the warehouse, catching up with orders and invoices that had accumulated during the closure. At home, she spent more evenings than usual alone in the sewing room, while her mother and father talked. She knew her mother would be arguing strenuously against breaking off her betrothal. For once, she hoped her father remained firm.

Days went by. Her mother made no mention of anything she and her father had talked about. Maftur felt increasingly anxious, constantly on the verge of nausea. She couldn't concentrate on reading, and why bother sewing if she didn't need a trousseau?

One evening, however, her mother returned earlier than usual from her father's study. Maftur looked up eagerly, hoping her parents had made up their mind, but she realised her mother had her mind on other things when she announced that one of her Jaffa cousins, Safia, had agreed to be betrothed to Dindan.

Maftur knew she ought to be pleased for Dindan, but couldn't help wishing her mother had brought news of her own situation.

Her mother remained shut away again with her father the following night. Since Dindan was no longer a problem, the subject of their conversation had to be either herself or Dodi. When her mother appeared again, she could contain herself no longer. She waited only until her mother had settled with her embroidery, before bracing herself to ask, "Has Baba heard from Great-Uncle Ahmed yet?"

Her mother pursed her lips and stabbed her needle

through her embroidery. When she opened her mouth, she said, "There have been complications. Let's leave it at that."

Maftur looked at her mother's set face. Why wouldn't she discuss the cancellation of her betrothal? She wondered if her mother had promised her father not to talk about it and, if so, why?

The atmosphere in their apartment felt strange throughout the following week. Dindan was out and about with his friends, celebrating his new status. Dodi moped in his bedroom, except when he was in the kitchen railing against his father to her mother, either for not letting him marry the Syrian woman he loved or for disrespecting his great-grandfather's wishes by attempting to break off his sister's betrothal.

"My great-grandfather only made Father Head of the Palestine firm because Maffy was to be Ahmed's wife," he ranted.

Her mother naturally refused to listen to Dodi's complaints but went about the house with fewer smiles than usual.

Maftur wished her mother realised how much the uncertainty about her own future was affecting her. She feared Dodi had told his cronies about her father's attempts to break off her betrothal, and they had passed on the information to their families. She couldn't face going down to AWA's HQ. Some women there would gloat over her humiliation.

She went to typing class, but worried all the way that Miriam might ask about Ahmed and dreaded someone after class would mention her handsome fiancé.

She just about managed to concentrate on her work at the warehouse, but at home even the news on the wireless couldn't grab her attention.

Often in the evenings she sat in her chair doing nothing, just waiting for her mother to return in hope of some information about her betrothal.

News from London pierced Maftur's apathy and even roused Dodi from his gloom. Despite the uncooperative attitude of the majority of the Arab delegation or, perhaps, even because of it, the British government had agreed to the creation of an independent Palestine governed by both

Palestinian Arabs and Jews in proportion to their numbers in the population as of 1949.

"Nineteen-forty-nine," her mother snorted, putting down her paper. "I don't see how you call that victory. The rate these Jewish refugees are immigrating into Palestine, the Jews will be in a majority long before then. When we finally get independence we'll all be living in a Jewish state."

She stood up and started collecting used coffee cups.

Maftur put down the Palestine Post she had been reading and picked up her mother's paper to check it gave the same details.

"Sit down again, Umm, and read section two in your paper."

She said it so forcefully, her mother obeyed instinctively. Maftur stationed herself behind her and pointed at the relevant paragraph. "See. The British have set a limit of seventy-five thousand Jewish immigrants for the five-year period nineteen-forty to nineteen-forty-four. Now go down to section three. There's to be a regular yearly quota of only ten thousand and, to cover refugee emergencies, a supplementary quota of twenty-five thousand spread out over the same period."

Her mother looked relieved, but Maftur hadn't finished.

"Now, section four, Umm. After nineteen-forty-four, further immigration will depend on our permission. See, there's absolutely no danger of us losing our majority. Finally, just look at section five. The British Government has placed restrictions on the rights of Jews to buy land from Arabs. Now, that's what I call a real victory."

Zubaida interrupted them with a note from Mrs. Shawwa. There was to be a celebration at AWA HQ that evening.

Of the parties all over Palestine that evening, none, Maftur reflected, could be as gay as the celebration at Haifa AWA HQ. Inside the hall every member of AWA danced and sang their triumph. Outside the hall, Maftur knew her brothers were amongst the men dancing in the street. She suspected her father and Mr. Shawwa would be celebrating together rather more quietly in a coffee shop.

Maftur was still feeling cheerful next morning when she joined her mother in the kitchen. They were telling Zubaida about the party, and exchanging snippets of gossip when a blaring loud speaker distracted them. They ran to the french windows in the liwan. Her father had already opened them and stood on the balcony.

"Another curfew," he informed them, "starting at eight-thirty am and going on to six am tomorrow."

"But why?" her mother demanded. "Surely not a terrorist attack, now we've won?"

"There are some people in Palestine who won't be celebrating," her father reminded them.

"But what exactly has happened?" Maftur asked.

"We'll find out when Mahmoud returns from the suq," her mother said. "That is if he makes it back before curfew."

"Let's hope he bought our vegetables before hearing the announcement," Zubaida added, "if we have to stay indoors until tomorrow."

Mahmoud was not back before curfew. By ten o'clock they still had no news of him.

They turned on the wireless. Haifa had made the headlines.

"...Over twenty Arabs died and forty were wounded when a bomb exploded in Haifa suq at six-thirty this morning. The wounded have been taken to the government hospital..."

Maftur felt her whole body go numb, but at the same time her sense of hearing seemed enhanced. She heard Zubaida and her mother draw in their breath and gasp out loudly.

"If it please Allah, don't let Mahmoud be dead," Maftur whispered.

She couldn't imagine the household without him. He'd been with them all her life, even before they had moved to the apartment block.

Her father stood up, looking around uncertainly. "I need to get to the hospital to check if Mahmoud's there. What do the British think they are achieving by this curfew?"

A rhetorical question, but Maftur felt impelled to answer it, if only to distance herself from the possibility of Mahmoud's death. "Preventing a riot. I wouldn't fancy being a Jew out on the streets, would you?"

She thought of Miriam. Would she be grateful for the curfew?

Her mother, wiping her eyes with a corner of her hijab,

stood up unsteadily. "I must go upstairs to Mahmoud's wife."

Her father went to answer a knock on the outside door.

Her mother stood still. They heard voices in the hall but not words.

Maftur felt herself trembling.

He father returned, his face grave. "That was the police. Mahmoud is in hospital. He had his youngest with him. The boy's in hospital, too."

"Anything else?" her mother asked.

"There'll be a break in curfew between two and four this afternoon. I will take Mahmoud's wife and eldest son to the hospital then. You, Maffy, go upstairs with your mother and see what you can do to help."

While her mother broke the news to Mahmoud's wife as gently as possible, Maftur put her arms round Mahmoud's eldest daughter, Azza. Before Azza, at the age of ten, had become Janan's maid of all work, she and Azza had been inseparable. How unimportant her own troubles seemed now.

Together they set about packing things Mahmoud and Azza's little brother would need in hospital.

Just before curfew re-started, her father and Azza's eldest brother returned, bringing both good and bad news. Mahmoud had shrapnel wounds to his back, and his arm had broken when he had fallen onto a metal stall, but it was a clean fracture and he would soon be out of hospital. The cheerful little boy, however, who had been doing so well at school that her father had promised to pay for his secondary education, would never see again, and his face would be scarred for life.

At a family meeting later that night, Janan agreed to release Azza to look after her brothers and sisters while her mother spent time at the hospital. Dindan would accompany Zubaida when she went shopping. Looking further ahead, her father agreed to pay for the little boy to attend a school for the blind.

Chapter 22

It was a whole week later before anyone mentioned her betrothal. Her mother broached the subject as she sank into her sewing chair after the news had finished, and picked up her latest tapestry, a wedding present for Dindan and Safia.

"Your father and I are not at all sure what to do for the best, Maffy. We've not heard from Ahmed. Apparently he is somewhere inaccessible, looking at an archaeological site. Abu Mussa is trying to contact him." She paused to thread her needle. "Meanwhile, we have had another very unexpected proposal for you."

This did nothing to calm her stomach. "One of the Jaffa cousins?"

"No, I hope none of them know yet that your father is contemplating breaking off your betrothal."

"Then who?"

"I'm not at liberty to say, except the man who put the proposal forward on behalf of his son is not a member of the family. He is, at least, however, a Palestinian."

It had to be Fizzy's father! One of her brothers would almost certainly have told Fizzy about her father's reactions to the Germans. She knew he had glimpsed her occasionally, when she had visited Ai'isha, and Ai'isha had more than once teased her about the effect she had on her brother.

"Not Abu Fikri?"

Her mother glanced at her suspiciously.

"I repeat, I am not at liberty to say until your father and I have made up our mind about allowing the suit. Apart from not having heard from Ahmed, and the new suitor not being a member of our family, the proposer has put forward some rather modern ideas, which your father is not too happy about."

Maftur wondered if she had made a big mistake. She wanted to marry Fizzy even less than Ahmed. She had listened to Fizzy talking to her brothers, and found him dull, an accusation she couldn't lay against Ahmed.

During the next few days she became despondent, becoming even less interested in what was going on in the outside world, although she had to make an effort to look cheerful when her father unexpectedly announced at breakfast that he had reconsidered the matter of Dodi's wedding, and was willing to receive a formal proposal from Elif's father.

Dodi sat stock-still looking at her father in disbelief then, standing up, left the remnants of his breakfast and disappeared into the men's quarters. When he emerged half an hour later he had become a different person, lively and courteous. For the first time he seemed a proper grown-up.

That evening her mother came to the sewing room and said her father wanted to talk to them both. Her heart raced as she followed her mother to the study. She was about to learn her fate at last! Her father again sat behind his desk, smoking his hookah. He held an envelope in his free hand. Her mother seated herself in the visitor's chair and indicated a stool next to it.

"Maffy," her father started, "you know I put the legal aspects of breaking off your betrothal into Mr. Shawwa's hands?"

"Yes, Baba. Has Great-Uncle Ahmed agreed?"

"On condition I allow Da'oud to marry this Elif he's been going on about. Apparently her brother is a close friend of Ahmed's. However, Abu Mussa vouched for the respectability of Elif's family, and said the alliance would be of considerable value to my business. That's why I have accepted his advice. Now that I am allowing one of my children to marry out of the family, I must give serious consideration to the proposal I have had for you."

So, she would have to pay the price for Da'oud's happiness by marrying Fizzy. It wasn't logical. Her father must know Fizzy belonged to Ahmed's squad.

"Can you tell me more about how this proposal came about, Baba?"

"Mr. Shawwa and I have talked about your case a great deal, not just as lawyer and client but also as friends. Mr. Shawwa has indicated that he would like to submit a formal proposal for a betrothal between his son and yourself."

Maftur jerked upright. Was she hearing her father

correctly? She couldn't have won her struggle, not this easily.

"However, there are two significant difficulties," her father said.

There would be. She swallowed hard, trying not to show the depth of her disappointment. "What are they?"

"The first has been created by the young man in question."

Ismail didn't fancy her! It was all her imagination. She slumped down, only just managing to keep her tears at bay.

"Mr. Shawwa's son apparently doesn't believe in arranged marriages. He has asked to write a proposal to you directly. Then, if you are agreeable in principle to the proposal, he wants a face-to-face meeting with you, so you can lay down your conditions."

Maftur sat up straight. "He wants to write a proposal to me?" she checked.

"Yes. Your mother and I have talked long and hard about this."

"I've also spoken to Mrs. Shawwa," her mother put in. "She thinks Ismail should be concentrating on his Jerusalem course, rather than concerning himself about his marriage."

So, Mrs. Shawwa didn't think she was good enough for her son.

"Mr. Shawwa, however, is pleased with his boy's attitude," her father said. "He says it is very English."

She mustn't ruin things now she so nearly had her own way. She thought carefully before she spoke, casting her eyes down, the very image of a dutiful daughter. "Umm, Baba, what have you decided?"

Her mother said, "If you consent to read it, we will allow you to do so."

Maftur scanned her mother's face. Did she expect her to refuse?

"If you agree to read the proposal, you must show it to us," her father said.

She didn't look at her mother. "I am willing to read it."

"Not so hasty, Maffy," her mother said. "If you allow Ismail Shawwa to put his proposal to you directly, and then you reject that proposal, it will humiliate him and insult his parents. Our firm needs the services of a lawyer on good terms with the British."

Conscious that it was too late at night for her father to speak to Mr. Shawwa immediately, Maftur considered it diplomatic to delay her answer.

"I'll sleep on it then, Baba, and let you know my decision in the morning."

Her mother gave a smile of approval.

Sleeping on it, however, was not the right term for the way Maftur passed that night. It seemed the longest she had ever spent. When morning came at last she decided to confess to her mother that, ever since she had been twelve, she had wanted to marry Ismail. She found her in the kitchen and asked to speak to her in the sewing room.

Her mother burst into tears after she had said her piece. "Oh, I'm so glad. I was sure you had set your mind on Fizzy, and Ismail would be another unwanted husband we were forcing on you. Now you will still live near me when you marry. I will fetch Ismail's letter at once."

* * * *

"Don't say anything about this to your friends, or even your brothers, until everything is settled," Her mother warned, handing over an envelope with her name inscribed on it in calligraphic Arabic.

When Maftur opened it, she was surprised to find the letter written in English, presumably because Ismail had guessed her parents would demand to read it.

Dear Maftur,

Ever since I first saw you when you were still a child I have treasured you in my heart. I was desolated when I heard of your betrothal.

When your father entrusted the legal case to my father's firm and my father discussed it with me in a professional capacity, you can imagine the emotions awakened in my heart. I urged my father to allow me to propose to you.

Precious Maftur, I want to marry you more than anything I have ever desired, but my parents have forbidden me to marry until I have acquired my attorney qualifications, which won't happen until 1941 at the earliest. If I was so fortunate as to receive a favourable answer from you, and you were prepared to wait that long, we would then have to spend at least the first year of our marriage in England. After that we would return to Palestine as my father requires me to take over his firm.

So now you know my career, but I know very little of your life plans apart from your brothers telling me that you are training to be a secretary. Your plans are of course as important as mine.

If my suit is not repugnant to you in itself, I would like to meet you face to face, under the supervision of your parents, of course, so we can discuss if there is a way we can both feel fulfilled. I realise this proposal is very unconventional, but you won't be reading it if your parents have not already discussed the matter with mine and agreed to the request.

If you are not interested in my proposal then please just write to say so and I will sadly comply with your wishes.

If you think there is a possibility you could agree to marry me, I hope to meet you soon.

Your humble suitor,

Ismail Shawwa.

The letter confirmed that Ismail was the one man she really wanted to marry. She floated round the house in a haze of happiness.

That evening, after Dodi had translated the letter for her father, and he had asked for her response, she had difficulty hiding her eagerness as she told her father she would like to meet Ismail under supervision. She asked if he and her mother would sit where they didn't intrude on the conversation. It was going to be difficult enough talking to a man without being conscious of their presence.

"We must sit where we can hear what you say, and you must both speak in Arabic," her mother decreed.

If that was the only way she could talk to Ismail, then so be it. She just hoped she didn't speak so formally, with her mother listening, that it would put Ismail off.

Chapter 23

Maftur sat in Edmunds, hugging her secret, although she wanted to shout aloud, *Ismail loves me. He's proposed. I'm going to meet him.* However, even if she had decided to say something about it, she would have found it hard to get a word in edgeways.

Miriam, for once, was taking centre-stage, enthusing over her new glass office; a terminus for a system of conveyor belts attached to all sales counters in her father's department store. She described the system in great detail.

"It sounds like something out of a fantasy story," Golda said, "with you the Queen spider at the centre of your web."

"I am enjoying accounting at the moment, but I—" A loud crash outside in the street drowned her voice.

Maftur felt a rush of wind and heard glass crashing to the floor. At the same time her body slammed forward onto the table, bruising her breasts. Coffee spilt into her lap. She looked over her shoulder. The plate glass window on the other side of the cafe had shattered. Jagged splinters covered the nearest tables—luckily no one had been sitting there. The heavy but now tattered curtains had fallen back into place.

One of the younger women was crying, but didn't seem wounded. Her companions, as far as she could see, were shaken but not injured. Golda had even taken her compact from her bag and was powdering her face.

Patsy walked towards the window, stepping high over broken glass, and drawing open the ruined curtains to reveal a Union Jack lying on rubble spread across the pavement.

A loud clanging signalled the arrival of a fire engine. The firemen busied themselves unrolling hoses, although there didn't appear to be a fire. Two ambulances rolled up. The drivers went into Khaiyet House and came out with walking wounded—three policemen holding white gauze to their faces, another, his arm supported by a tea towel knotted round his neck, and one leaning on a walking stick and hopping on one leg. No one came out on a stretcher. The wounded climbed into the ambulances which drove off.

A kitchen boy swept up the glass, and a waiter approached their table to replace the stained tablecloth. He brought clean cups and poured more coffee.

Through the broken window Maftur saw police come out of Khaiyet House and press-gang Arab businessmen from nearby up-market shops into clearing debris. She felt angry, sure Jews were responsible for the bomb, but the police had not forced any Jews to work like fellaheen. She hoped they would not pounce on Kamal when he came to fetch her.

Patsy turned her back on the window, returned to the table and picked up a cup of coffee. Maftur followed her example.

"How are the marriage plans going?" Patsy asked.

She smiled proudly. "Negotiations have begun with Ismail's parents."

Golda overheard and raised her well-plucked eyebrows.

"What happened to that good-looking man whose photo you showed us?"

Maftur couldn't help grinning. "That Ahmed Al-Zeid? He went off the list."

Miriam gave her an admiring glance. "How did you wangle that?"

"My father discovered something about him he considered unsuitable."

"What could have made him unsuitable?" Patsy asked in a sharp tone.

Maftur remembered she was supposed to tell no one about this new betrothal plan until it was finalised. She shrugged and made her answer deliberately vague. "Politics, perhaps."

Just then Kamal entered the restaurant. He must have seen the police press-ganging passers-by, and had the good sense to take a back route. He looked relieved to find everyone behaving normally.

Maftur nudged Miriam. "Whatever you say on the way home," she whispered, "don't mention anything about Ahmed or Ismail. I am not supposed to tell anyone until the betrothal is official."

"You can count on me," Miriam whispered back.

They joined Kamal and walked to the front entrance.

Outside, policemen with loudspeakers were climbing into armoured cars.

"We must hurry," Kamal said, "before getting caught up in another curfew."

* * * *

Her meeting with Ismail took place in the liwan three days later. Her parents sat on the balcony with the french doors open. She sat on one side of the wide table, with Ismail facing her. Conscious of her mother's gaze, she kept her eyes demurely on the table top. They both kept their hands in their laps.

She heard Ismail say, "Maftur, I cannot describe the joy it has given me that you have agreed to this meeting."

She wanted to say how much it meant to her too, but with her parents listening she confined herself to saying in a low voice, as if addressing the table, "It has pleased me too."

"Maftur, you have read my plans for the future. Can you tell me about your own ambitions?"

For a moment she was at a loss. A truthful reply would be that her chief ambition was to marry the man sitting opposite, but she couldn't display such immodesty before her parents. On the other hand, she didn't want to appear empty-headed. She considered answering that she wanted to be his office manager when he qualified, but that might sound as if she only wanted to marry him because of his professional standing. She continued to stare down at the table gathering her thoughts.

Eventually she said, "A few weeks ago I would have said that my main ambition was to achieve independence for my country, but we have achieved that ambition, even if it is deferred until nineteen-forty-nine, so now I want to become a worthy citizen of that country."

Did that sound too priggish and vague? She looked up to read his face and, meeting his eyes, felt a jolt run through her body, interrupting her verbal flow. She swallowed and forced herself to carry on, "I want to gain secretarial qualifications so I can become economically independent if ever circumstances make it necessary."

That sounded as if she was looking forward to becoming a widow. The thought of Ismail dying was so painful she could hardly continue, but felt she had to explain further. Returning her eyes to the table, she said, "Suppose you were taken away to be a soldier. My mother has told me of so many women left destitute and unable to feed their small children when the Turks press-ganged men into their army."

This wasn't going well. The Turks only conscripted fellaheen. She looked up to see Ismail's reaction. He must think she was an idiot, but Ismail just smiled and said, "Tell me the steps you have already taken towards this financial independence."

"I'm working in my father's warehouse, doing his accounts and correspondence, and studying at a secretarial college, but I want experience working for a firm that will help build up the infrastructure of our country. My great-grandfather was going to help me find work in the Government secretariat."

From the balcony, her father broke in, "Take no notice of this nonsense, Ismail. My daughter will not work in Jerusalem while you live there."

"Oh, Baba," Maftur felt herself flushing with embarrassment. "I hadn't thought of that." Tears sprung to her eyes. "I didn't mean—and anyway Great-Great Grandpa is dead so…"

"It's all right, Maftur," her mother said softly, "I know you did not intend to be immodest."

"I know that too, Umm Kamal," Ismail reassured her mother.

Her father muttered, "Maftur continues working at the warehouse until she marries, or else she stays at home, helping her mother."

"Maftur," Ismail said, "your father's word must be of paramount importance to you, but if you would do me the honour of accepting my proposal, I promise to let you qualify as a secretary so you can earn enough to keep yourself and our children if ever I was dragged off to war, or any other calamity occurred. This should be every woman's right."

"It is time to bring this interview to an end," her father

stated, she suspected because Ismail had uttered the fatal words 'our children'.

She looked into Ismail's eyes, hoping she wasn't being too immodest. "Looking after my husband will be my first priority."

He gazed back. "And looking after my wife and children will be mine."

"Maftur!" her father warned. "You and your mother may retire now."

"Just one more minute, please, Abu Kamal," Ismail said. "If Maftur agrees to my proposal, will you allow us to write to each other during the two years before we can marry?"

Maftur pleaded with her father, using her eyes rather than her tongue.

"So long as you both promise not to use your correspondence to make arrangements for clandestine meetings, and Maftur shows us all the letters she writes and all those she receives," her father conceded.

She was tempted to ask if she could talk to Ismail again once they were betrothed, but decided that was a concession she would have to wrest from her father later. She made a formal farewell and left the room.

Chapter 24

The Shawwa's man-servant delivered Ismail's letter while they were all sitting at breakfast next day. When her father handed the envelope over, and she had opened it, she was once again surprised to find it written in English.

She saw her father glance at the script and feared an outburst, but his face remained impassive, his only comment an order to Dodi to stay seated, as his services would soon be needed. She read the letter in silence, slowly, savouring it, knowing she would only too soon have to surrender it.

Dear Maftur,

I cannot express how pleased I am that you accepted my proposal. You have made me the happiest man in all Palestine.

You may be surprised that I am writing in English but it was my father's suggestion. He and your father met up at the coffee shop after our meeting. My father's only just come home to tell me the results of their discussion. I gather they consider English a less romantic and, therefore, safer language than Arabic and decided it will help us maintain our language skills since, if I pass my exams, we have to spend the first year of our marriage in England. What a long way off that is. Anyway, they chose your brother Dodi as your father's official translator.

It is very late now and I have to catch the early bus to Jerusalem in the morning, but I am returning a calmer and happier man than the one who travelled to Haifa yesterday. Please write to me as soon as you can.

All my love,
Ismail

"You must have read it by now," her father said. "Hand it over to Dodi."

To her relief, her father allowed her to keep the letter after Dodi had translated it.

She took it to her room and pressed his firm handwriting to her lips before putting it in her scarf drawer.

When she returned from secretarial college that afternoon clutching a certificate, her mother had set up a small bureau in the sewing room and an office chair.

"It'll come in handy for AWA work," she said, "and you

might prefer writing your letters to Ismail here rather than in the dining room." She then presented her with an olivewood box etched with a drawing of the Al-Aqsa Mosque. "Keep Ismail's letters safe in that. When you are old they may bring you great comfort." Her mother looked wistful as she added. "I wish I had something like that to remember your father by."

Sitting at the new bureau later that evening Maftur wrote the date –

May 5th 1939

The rest of the letter was not going to be so easy.

She wrote *Dear Ismail,* echoing Ismail's greeting to her. Her father had not demurred at Ismail's greeting, but then society allowed men so much more license.

Thank you for your letter. I do hope you have returned safely to Jerusalem and your studies are now going well. Your mother is very proud of your prowess.

Our manservant, Mahmoud, had his plaster cast cut off today and is back on light duties; it makes our household seem more complete. His little boy, however, is still blind. The doctors say he will never recover his sight. My father is going to send him to the school for the blind when he is out of hospital.

You will be pleased to hear I am now the proud possessor of a piece of parchment certifying I can type at 50 words a minute. My father has had it framed and it hangs above my desk in the warehouse along with my matriculation certificate.

After we are married, I hope my new skills may be useful to you.

I am looking forward to our year in England. You are not the only one who will know people there! I have made friends with Patsy Quigley. You may remember the girl who once showed us the view from the tower attached to their house when we were at her parents' garden party—it must have been all of six years ago now—she is back in Palestine for a year before starting a degree course at Oxford University. I met her again on a typing course earlier this year. She will have finished her studies by the time we arrive in England. Patsy says when we are living in London we must keep in touch, and get together during her vacation.

What else could she write that wouldn't upset her father?

Is the khamseen in Jerusalem as bad as it is in Haifa? Zubaida says the temperature on our roof was over 100° today but I don't think it was as bad as that at college, even though we can't have a fan because it would blow the paper about.

She could think of nothing else safe to say and was ashamed of her short letter especially when there was so much she wanted to write. Now for the next really difficult part.

'All my love' certainly wouldn't get past her father! She settled on a formal,
Your obedient betrothed, Maftur

* * * *

All activities in the al-Zeid building now revolved round Dodi and Dindan's weddings. They began by swapping apartments.

Maftur and her parents moved into the largest one on the ground floor, because the huge liwan there was more suitable for the large business meetings her father called on a regular basis. Her mother turned the former women's only living room into a family dining room and installed Zubaida, whose legs were not as good as they used to be when it came to tackling stairs, into a large room which she furnished as a bed-sit. The room on the top floor that had been Zubaida's became a study, where Mahmoud's youngest son could work on a Braille typewriter during his holidays from the newly founded Hebron School for the Blind.

Left alone in their old apartment, Dodi began readying it to receive Elif.

Kamal and Janan moved into the opposite second floor apartment formerly occupied by Uncle Abu Rakim and Aunt Bahia. Dindan took over from Kamal and Janan on the third floor.

Maftur's full-time secretarial course had finished, so while her mother was pre-occupied with rearranging rooms, Maftur wrote out wedding invitations, using her warehouse office facilities. Her mother kept the same wedding lists as all the other married women in the al-Zeid clan, adding to it as people married, deleting from it after funerals. For Dindan's wedding the only extras she had to add were Palestinian business associates.

Dodi's invitations were more complex. Elif's mother had a list of her own. That had to be added to the al-Zeid list while Elif's father had submitted a separate list of academic colleagues from Syria and the newly independent Lebanon.

Maftur also wrote out the invitations for the boys' Sahra Parties (roughly the masculine equivalent of Henna parties, although what went on at them Maftur hadn't the faintest idea.) Dodi's and Dindan's lists differed considerably. When she commented, Dodi explained that Dindan had taken up with a religiously orientated set of young men close to the Grand Mufti while shunning more sophisticated social events. And that, she thought, explained the cross-stitch incident.

No sooner had Maftur sent Mahmoud out to post the invitations than she received a letter from Elif asking her to be a bridesmaid and perform a presentation dance at her Henna party. All right and proper, of course, but it meant she would have to be in Damascus the day before the Henna party. This was taking place a day earlier than Dodi's Sahra Party to allow the women time to travel to Haifa for the wedding reception.

The train service between Haifa and Damascus was excellent, but her father decided she couldn't travel with just Zubaida to a place neither of them had visited. He phoned Parveen's husband and discovered the Lebanon al-Zeid women hadn't booked a coach to Elif's Henna party, because Parveen was the only one to receive an invitation, although, of course, all the men had been invited to Dodi's Sahra party. Parveen's husband readily agreed to drive to Haifa two days before the Sahra party, so Parveen and the children could accompany Maftur and Zubaida.

What time she could spare from other activities Maftur spent embroidering a Henna party thob made from the roll of dark green silk Dodi had given the bridesmaids. She assumed the embroidery pattern Elif had sent was traditional Damascene, although her mother had not seen anything like it, and she had been to enough Henna parties in Damascus in her youth.

Wedding organisation gave Maftur plenty she could safely include in her letters to Ismail, although she wished she could tell him how much she wasn't looking forward to being a bridesmaid in the midst of complete strangers, or that she was sure she was going to dislike her new sister-in-law. However, that wouldn't go down well when her mother read it.

She could hardly contain her excitement when Ismail

wrote that he had finished his first year exams and would be in Haifa for both Dodi's and Dindan's weddings, although she knew that the most she could expect from this holiday were glimpses of Ismail on his balcony and at both wedding receptions. Now that they were betrothed, would she be allowed to wave at him, or would they still have to keep these greetings secret? She didn't like to ask her mother's permission in case she guessed how much waving had gone on before the betrothal. Whichever, there would be no opportunity to speak to Ismail unless a miracle happened.

The miracle happened, but in a way she had least expected. Mrs. Shawwa invited her mother to bring her husband, both daughters and her son-in-law to dinner the night before Maftur set off for Damascus, casually saying it would be nice to see Maftur and Ismail together.

Mr. Shawwa must have warned her father in advance and elicited his approval because he made no fuss, just treated the invitation as an everyday event.

When they arrived at the Shawwa's for the dinner party, Mrs. Shawwa proudly ushered them into a dining room containing a western-style high table surrounded by eight chairs. The men sat at one end, surrounding Mr. Shawwa. The women surrounded his wife. The numbers were small enough to allow a single conversation dominated by Mr. Shawwa and her father. She knew her parents would expect her to keep quiet, so while the older people talked, she gazed soulfully at Ismail as he gazed adoringly back at her. She hardly followed the conversation until Mr. Shawwa asked her opinion on whether protest marches really achieved anything. She hesitated, looking at her mother, who nodded, which she interpreted as permission to speak.

Conscious of Ismail's intense gaze, she replied that it wasn't so much that AWA expected to influence British opinion but they hoped to back up the activities of male Arab Palestinians and make other members of the League of Nations aware of their position.

Ismail replied that he had heard her speeches had been well received and hoped she would continue with her work for AWA. It seemed to him women acted more responsibly than men when it came to politics.

When they left, she was afraid her parents might reprimand her for talking, but her mother's mind was fully occupied with Mrs. Shawwa's new dining suite. She said that it was time they too furnished their dining room western style but, now they had moved into the larger apartment, they would have room for an even longer table and at least sixteen chairs.

Chapter 25

As she sat on the train to Damascus the next day, pointing out to her niece and nephews their Great-Great-Uncle Azza's silk mill in the Jezreel Valley, Maftur reflected that if they had dared to make this journey the previous year, shuttered windows would have prevented them being able to look outside. Once over the border into Syria, they enjoyed views over the lake of Galilee, with the children excited to see a flying boat drop down onto the water.

When they stepped out onto the platform at Damascus, Parveen pointed out a taxi driver wearing a fez and long striped tunic, holding up a board saying Maftur Nour. As she climbed into the taxi, she felt incredibly lonely, a stranger in a strange country.

She had always imagined Damascus to be a giant version of the Old City of Jerusalem, but even darker and more mysterious. However the taxi drove through wide palm-lined boulevards before reaching the suburbs and climbing a narrow road lined with whitewashed walls, punctuated at intervals of about fifty yards by plain doors. It stopped outside one door halfway up the hill. The driver dismounted to ring a camel bell suspended above it. A doorman in a white tunic with a red cummerbund opened the door, revealing a courtyard painted in broad stripes of red, white and blue. Orange, lemon and pepper trees surrounded a splashing fountain. A whitewashed house took up three sides of the courtyard, two storeys high on the left and right, but, straight ahead, a wide flight of marble steps led up to a rooftop terrace on top of a single storey, privacy guaranteed by stone fretwork screens.

The doorman paid the taxi driver, collected her luggage and escorted her inside.

A tall, young woman with bobbed hair appeared at the top of the stairs. "Maftur, my last bridesmaid, bonjour!" she called out in French. "I am Elif. Come and join us. You must be hot after your journey. We have lime juice here with ice. Aziz, take the luggage inside and ask one of the maids to carry it upstairs." Elif ran down the steps, walked forward and kissed her on both cheeks. A strong waft of rosewater assailed her nose.

She followed the girl up the steps and stopped at the top, partly to admire the view of Damascus's minarets and domes rising above the housetops far below, and partly to put off having to meet the gaze of a group of young women in gauzy dresses, seated on cushions beneath a white awning.

She had to turn to look at them though as Elif began introductions. She was surprised to find only Elif's sister was younger than herself. She knew Elif to be the same age as Dodi, but hadn't expected the majority of her bridesmaids to be her contemporaries.

"We made friends at high school and persuaded our parents to send us to the same finishing school in Paris," Elif explained, "so now we are firmly cemented together."

The group resumed the conversation they had been having before her arrival.

As she sipped her iced limejuice she learned they had all taken part in a mass demonstration, only the day before, against a Turkish annexation of part of Syria. The size of the all-women demonstration made her Haifa ones sound puny in comparison.

"We shall miss you so much, Elif," one of the bridesmaids said. "Who is going to organise AWA for us now?"

"You'll manage." Elif waved a hand, dismissing the subject. "Maftur, is this your first visit to Damascus?"

She nodded, shyness temporarily leaving her unable to speak.

"And yet it was nearly your home," Elif's sister butted in. "I am so looking forward to meeting your new fiancé. He must be a real dish to make you break off your betrothal to Ahmed Al-Zeid."

Maftur felt the other bridesmaids' astonished gazes turn on her.

Elif glared at her sister. "Maftur's fiancé is called Ismail," she said, "and he is the one she has always wanted to marry. The betrothal to Ahmed was a family arrangement. So, Maftur, what do you think of our city so far?"

"It is far more beautiful than I expected."

Another bridesmaid chimed in. "Yes, one thing about the French, they cleared away many of our slums. Now all we have to do is clear the French away."

"Maftur, come with me to look at the view properly, now the sun is going down," Elif said.

Maftur followed her to the far end of the terrace where they couldn't be overheard.

Elif pointed over the marble balustrade as if telling her about the various buildings. "I'm sorry about my sister," she said. "She hasn't grown up yet. All those women are ardent fans of your great-great-uncle. I should imagine they are secretly relieved he is now an eligible bachelor."

"I am sure I would have done well with him if it hadn't been that I wanted to marry Ismail," Maftur replied, "but I have really, really wanted to marry Ismail for six years now. It has been hard not being allowed to go about with him, but at least we are allowed to write to each other."

"Well, you'll have a lot to write about after your journey today. If you give your letter to my brother before he gets onto the coach tomorrow, he will deliver it to your Ismail at the Sahra Party."

Maftur was strongly tempted but she had made a promise. "I wish I could do that," she said, "but my parents have to read it first, so I haven't bothered to bring writing paper and envelopes."

"What!" Elif turned away from the view, her eyes wide in shock, her hands clenched. "You have to show your letters to your parents before you can post them?"

Maftur nodded, not sure why she looked so angry.

Elif visibly forced herself to relax. "You will want to rest before supper. Listen, I will send paper and pen. Write your letter and tell your parents you showed it to me. After all, I am very nearly a respectable married woman now."

Maftur followed her through a door at the end of the terrace leading into a corridor overlooking the courtyard. She opened the door to the next huge room filled with two enormous beds covered with mosquito nets, and seven chests each laid out with a green silk thob. Maftur recognised hers by the embroidery, and realised Elif had given a different embroidery pattern to each bridesmaid. "Are these all traditional Damascene patterns?"

"No," Elif replied. "I created them. Yours was inspired by Indian embroidery I saw in Paris. I'll leave you to rest now. The others will wake you in time to change for supper. We're eating on the terrace with my parents so it will be a bit formal."

A few minutes after Elif had left, a maid came in carrying paper, an inkpot and a pen.

Maftur resisted the temptation as long as she could, but it was too great. Because no one but Ismail would see this letter she started it *My dear darling Ismail* and gave a long description of her day.

She gave the letter to the maid who came in later with ewers of hot water to pass on to Leif's brother.

Squashed in the bridesmaid's bedroom after supper, she fell asleep while the others were still reminiscing about their schooldays and giggling about some great secret planned for the next day's party.

She felt very much the odd one out next morning amidst the easy banter of the others while they were dressing the bride. Elif had turned Dodi's gift of pale fawn satin into an exact replica of a Schiaparelli dress that Maftur had admired in a French fashion magazine. Scarcely traditional wear, she thought, but then, by all accounts, Elif was anything but a traditionalist.

The party started off in the time-honoured way, however, with bridesmaids performing typical presentation dances. Parveen and her two older children arrived before it was Maftur's turn. That made her feel a little less isolated. She danced last, relieved she had only a pair of tiny diamond earrings to present. Once, when a bridesmaid in Beirut, she had had to lift a silver jug so heavy she had nearly dropped it.

After her dance, the mood changed abruptly. The drummer stopped playing. The chief bridesmaid jumped onto a stage supporting a grand piano and yelled, "Elif, Your last day of freedom. Bring on the band," and thumped out a jazz tune from 'Hollywood Hotel', while all the Damascene bridesmaids skipped over to a pile of odd-shaped boxes and pulled out trumpets and saxophones.

She found herself standing alone, the only bridesmaid not

in the band. Nothing could have made her feel more of an outsider. She sidled over to Parveen who had her eye on her two children who, along with some of their new little cousins, clapped their hands to the music. She was surprised to find Parveen smiling. She had expected her to be shocked.

"Come on, Maftur," Parveen called above the noise, "don't look so glum. This is a wedding."

Several guests were jitterbugging in couples. The children began imitating them, but not too well.

Parveen took hold of her eldest son's hand. "You do it this way," she said and started shaking her body, strutting steps to the music.

Maftur gazed at her sister, astonished. "Where did you learn?"

"At a night club with my husband, but don't tell our father."

Elif stepped down from her throne and walked over. "Hey, Maftur, you're deserting your post. You're supposed to be looking after me." She held out a hand. "I want to dance. I'll lead, you follow."

Maftur took a deep breath and did as she was told, wondering what her father would say if he heard about this.

"Hey, you're a great dancer," Elif said a few minutes later. "I thought I would have to spend time teaching you. Dodi said you wouldn't have a clue."

"We do have cinemas in Palestine," Maftur replied as she tried a twirl. "But," she admitted, "this is the first time I have actually jitterbugged."

An hour later, as she sank down on a chair, exhausted after dancing with many other guests, Elif's mother, waving a cigarette in a long holder, sat down beside her.

She had to shout to make herself heard above the loud music. "I was hoping to catch you on your own, Maftur. I am so pleased you made it to Damascus. My Elif has been delighted. You are so different to what she imagined. She's really frightened of going to live with a conformist, living-in-the-past mother-in-law."

Maftur thought of Umm enjoying the concert on board the European cruiser, and attending protest meetings. "My mother living in the past?" she exclaimed.

"Yes," Elif's mother said. "When my daughter told me you couldn't send your fiancé a letter while you were here because your mother had to read it first, she was so upset she burst into tears, wondering what she had got herself into."

Maftur bit her lip. Not only had she disobeyed her parents writing that clandestine letter, she had brought them into disrepute.

"It was my mother who insisted on my staying at school until I took matric," she burst out. "She's the one who persuaded my father to let Dodi marry out of family. She's the one who fought my Granny for three years to get our family women to have their own kitchens. I was wrong to write a letter without showing it to my parents, because I promised I wouldn't."

She was nearly in tears. All right, she would like to write to Ismail without having to show her father the letters, she would like to meet Ismail privately and go with him to the cinema, but when she thought of all her mother had done for her, she realised how lucky she was.

Elif's mother shifted her cigarette holder into her left hand, leaned over and patted her arm. "My dear, I didn't mean to upset you, and if it makes you feel any better you can tell your mother you showed the letter to me. You don't know how much happier I feel now about Elif going to live in Palestine. I do hope you and my daughter become good friends."

She kissed her on both cheeks, before extinguishing her cigarette in a tub containing a young cedar tree. "I must go now and hand out sugared almonds. See, I too am not totally immune to tradition."

Chapter 26

Maftur dozed in the coach on its way to Haifa. They were passing through Tiberius when she woke. She tiptoed down the aisle and found Parveen awake, feeding her baby next to a sleeping Zubaida. She would have liked to confess about her letter to Ismail, but didn't want to risk Zubaida hearing. Instead she whispered her other worry. "Parveen, if we tell our mother that we jitterbugged at the Henna party, do you think she'll tell our father?"

Parveen pointed to her two eldest children in the seat in front. "You can't imagine he isn't going to hear about it. Those two can hardly wait to give a demonstration to their father. I wouldn't worry about it. It won't be the last shock our parents will receive now Elif is part of the family."

It was late in the evening before the coach reached the hotel where the wedding reception would take place the following day. Along with the bride, bride's mother and the other bridesmaids, Maftur dismounted, leaving the rest of the women to go on to sleep-over in the Al-Zeid building.

Her mother came down to the hotel after she had greeted and settled her other guests, and they enjoyed supper together. Maftur slipped away from the other bridesmaids at bed-time and went along to her mother's room. She sat on the side of the bed, while her mother brushed her hair in front of a mirror, and confessed she had written to Ismail while she had been away.

"I just hated he wouldn't get a letter from me for so long."

Her mother stood up and gave her a hug. "Thank you for having the courage to tell me. The rules about no communication with one's betrothed are really for much younger people. You and Ismail are both old enough to make more decisions on your own. I'll have a word with your father."

Maftur went to bed, her conscience much relieved, and was up early the next morning, along with the other bridesmaids, to fit Elif into her white western-style long-sleeved wedding dress. The air was redolent of face powder as they renewed the henna on the bride's hands and feet.

While a professional hairdresser set to work, their chat was almost drowned out by the banging of drums and the hooting of car horns. The men from Dodi's Sahra Party had gathered in the street outside.

Elif's father arrived in a large limousine to escort his daughter and her bridesmaids to the mosque. There the chief bridesmaid and Elif's sister removed the bride's shoes. They waited in the limousine until Elif, holding her head high, came out of the mosque beside a grinning Dodi, behind them the two fathers, Fizzy and the local imam. Maftur, now the bride's sister-in-law, put Elif's shoes back on. Then Dodi entered the limousine with his bride amid a convoy of hooting cars and motorbikes.

At the reception there was much speculation at the women's tables about a possible war in Europe, and how it would affect Palestine. People from all the German colonies were already returning to Germany.

"Perhaps," Janan said, "if the British do get rid of Hitler, a lot of Jewish refugees might go home."

"I'm sure of it," Mrs. Shawwa said. "They don't like our climate, they don't like our food and they can't find the jobs they want."

As expected, Maftur didn't get a chance to speak to Ismail but, incredibly, before she left to help escort Elif to Dodi's apartment, her mother had invited Mrs. Shawwa, her husband and Ismail to a dinner party to welcome the happy couple from their honeymoon the following month.

Next morning, after they had all waved goodbye to the bridal pair, Maftur accompanied her father and Kamal down to the warehouse, almost glad to be back to normal routine.

She was surprised when her father climbed the fire stairs with her. He sat on the office's second chair, his legs apart, leaning on his cane.

"Maftur, your mother talked to me last night, praising your honesty. She pointed out that by your age most women are married with several children so we should no longer treat you as an impressionable youngster. From now on we will allow you to keep your correspondence private. Please do not let us down."

Maftur had sense enough not to reveal her feeling of triumph. She bowed her head. "Thank you, Abba. I will not betray your trust."

Her father rose and pointed to the pile of correspondence on her desk, far more than she had expected. "Now, back to work. We've had more orders than usual from the German colonies. You are going to have to work a full day here for the rest of the week."

That evening for the second time she started her letter –
My dear darling wonderful Ismail,

Great News! My parents have at last agreed that I can be trusted to send and receive letters from you without anyone else having to read them. Of course, my mother will expect me to pass on any news from Jerusalem but I will no longer have to read out anything private. Now I can tell you how much I really love you—more than anything in all the world.

Ever since your last letter telling me you expect to hear your final exam results on August 15th 1941, I am counting the days until you are qualified and we can marry. I make it 751 from today. It would have been only 750 but unfortunately for us 1940 is a leap year.

Two pages later, after a long description of Damascus and the Henna party, she wrote,

Now that my parents can't see inside the envelope, I hope you don't think me too immodest if I add a few kisses after my name.

All my love,
Maftur xxxx

* * * *

Her mother had decided that, apart from the meat pastries to be served as appetizers, they would be eating French style at their dinner party.

"It's all very well, Mrs. Shawwa, aping the English," she told Maftur, "but it's the French who are renowned for their cuisine."

On the day of their dinner party, her mother wouldn't allow Maftur to work at the warehouse. "It's important," she told her father, "that I can assure Mrs. Shawwa Maftur supervised the preparation of the meal and made the meat pastries. Dindan's got his matric. Let him do the bills and correspondence for once."

"But Adad can't type," her father protested.

Her mother gave an expressive shrug. "So, what did you do before the Old Man sent that typewriter?"

Normally Maftur would have welcomed the chance of a day spent with her mother, but as she tied on her apron she wished she were sitting in front of her typewriter. The thought of Mrs. Shawwa judging her housewifery skills as she surveyed the table setting, and checking every mouthful of food for flavour and texture, made her stomach queasy.

She was clumsier than usual, dropped flour on the floor, flattened her dough balls between trembling hands so they came out in odd shapes, and cut a finger while chopping suet.

Mahmoud came in to say the mercury in the courtyard thermometer had touched 100°, but it felt even hotter in the kitchen. She was more than ready for the two hour lunch break.

In the afternoon she demonstrated to the kitchen maids how to serve vegetables, standing at the right shoulder of each guest. Using the china dinner service and cutlery she had advised her mother to buy, she set about laying the table. They weren't having soup. It was far too hot, so she used the soup bowls instead of their brass finger bowls.

Dodi and Elif returned. Elif looked at the table, obviously impressed.

"Where did you learn to set up western style?"

"At school," Maftur replied. "It specialised in turning girls into suitable wives for influential men."

Elif laughed. "Brain-washing a new generation of anglophiles!"

"No worse than French education in Syria turning out Francophiles."

Elif grinned. "Touché! We'll see you tonight." She lowered her voice. "Would you like me to come down early to give you support? Dodi told me your future mother-in-law can be a bit overbearing."

"Thank you. That might be helpful."

As Maftur watched Elif leave, however, she couldn't

make up her mind as to whether her new sister-in-law was trying to be kind or merely patronising. If she was genuinely kind it would make her life far more pleasant.

She turned her attention to folding the double fan napkins she had been famous for at school. After she had placed them on the side plates, she remembered Mrs. Shawwa had placed her napkins in the water glasses but double fans didn't fit inside glasses. They would have to stay where they were.

She went to shower and change into her new frock. It was a sapphire-blue, long-sleeved dress made from scalloped-edged chiffon. The silver and turquoise pendant ear-rings she had borrowed from her mother complemented it beautifully. She went into the living room to find her father wearing his fez for the first time for nearly a year.

Elif and Dodi came down soon after and, miracle of miracles, Dodi was also wearing a fez. Elif gave a thumbs up after surveying Maftur from head to foot.

There was a ring at the outside door. Her father opened it. Mr. Shawwa, also wearing a fez, preceded his wife and Ismail through the lobby door and embraced her father.

"Praise be to Allah! My son has received his first year exam results. He has passed with distinction."

Maftur felt her chest swell with pride and smiled her congratulations at Ismail. He gave a wonderful smile in return.

"Then we have two things to celebrate tonight," her father said. "Da'oud's and Elif's return home, and your son's triumph."

Maftur went to the kitchen and brought out the meat pastries to be eaten in the living room before everyone went into the dining room. She found Janan had arrived during her absence, along with Kamal and Dindan, also wearing their fezzes. It looked as if the good days had returned.

The visitors praised the meat pastries, although Mrs. Shawwa did mention that in their household they always used more cinnamon to good effect.

When they went into dinner, Janan exclaimed how beautiful the table looked with displays of yellow carnations and ferns down the centre. Mrs. Shawwa commented that when Ismail and Maftur spent their year in England they must never substitute soup bowls for finger bowls. Ismail assured his mother that the middle classes in England no longer used finger bowls now they had bathrooms with running water. They only used them in the Levant to reassure the natives.

Although she and Ismail exchanged the occasional meaningful glance when they thought their parents weren't looking, with more people at the dinner party than there had been at Mrs. Shawwa's, the women played no part in the serious discussion going on at the men's end of the table.

Elif was a good conversationalist and soon charmed her mother as she described the highlights of her honeymoon. Mrs. Shawwa, however, was still busy analysing the meal. She commented that delightful though French cookery was, Maftur was going to have to learn basic English cookery if she wanted to please her husband, who had acquired a taste for spotted dick and also tomato soup at boarding school. Maftur assured Mrs. Shawwa that she had had lessons in basic English cooking at Haifa High School. Elif backed her up, saying her husband had told her how much he had enjoyed the cookery Maftur brought back from school. Mrs. Shawwa looked at them both haughtily and turned to her mother to talk about the next section meeting.

From what Maftur could hear going on at the men's end, the subject matter was mostly about the possible consequences of a war in Europe. Apart from Mrs. Shawwa, the women seemed to be having a more cheerful time.

"Thanks for speaking up for me," Maftur said to Elif after the visitors had left.

Elif laughed. "That's all right. I guess I'm just grateful for having received the better mother-in-law deal."

Chapter 27

Three days after Dodi and Elif's welcome home party, Maftur, along with other bridesmaids, escorted Dindan's bride, Safia, into the hall in Jaffa where they were holding the Henna party. She hoped this was the last time she would have to be a bridesmaid. She had had enough of other women's weddings.

This Henna party, of course, served its purpose in bringing together the women of the al-Zeid family to provide an opportunity for prospective mothers-in-law to look over potential daughters-in-law, and to learn about available sons-in-law, but it wasn't nearly as much fun as Elif's Henna party.

Once she had finished her presentation dance, she raced over to Sabeen and Yalda standing close to Aunt Bahia, her mother, Parveen and Elif. She was pleased her mother had already introduced Elif. She noticed Parveen's children showing Sabeen's eldest daughter how to jitterbug behind their mothers' backs, although having difficulty with unhelpful drumbeats.

"Tell us all about this new fiancé of yours, Maftur," Yalda demanded. "He's Mrs. Shawwa's son, isn't he?"

"Yes. You met him once at the garden party where Patsy Quigley took us up to the top of the tower. I'll point him out to you at the reception in case you've forgotten."

"Be careful what you say at the reception, though," her mother warned. "Mrs. Shawwa is seated next to me."

"Oddly enough," Maftur told Sabeen and Yalda, "I've been seeing quite a bit of Patsy Quigley recently. She's been in Palestine all this year, but is going back to England next month. We did a secretarial course together, and still meet up with the rest of the group at Edmunds once a week. Did you know we were there when the Police HQ next to the cafe was bombed?" She turned to Elif. "If I get a chance before she goes back, I must introduce you to Patsy. I know you'd like her."

"If she has any sense she'll go back to England early," Elif said. "War in Europe is getting more likely by the day. The

Germans have an effective submarine fleet. British liners would be prime targets."

"I hope the war's over then before Ismail and I sail to England," Maftur replied.

"You're going to England for your honeymoon!" Sabeen sounded impressed.

"Not just a honeymoon," Maftur said. "Ismail will be working there for a year."

Her mother introduced a cautionary note. "So long as he passes his finals. I've heard that the Government Law School sets too high a standard."

Maftur didn't bother to reply. Her Ismail couldn't fail.

By the end of the week, war in Europe was almost a certainty. Anticipation caused chaos at the warehouse. French and English tourists, cutting their holidays short, wanted their orders early. Germans who had returned home, had placed huge orders before leaving. Now their relatives in Palestine were insisting these should be shipped immediately. Kamal, Dodi and Dindan were too busy fulfilling orders to make their routine visits to customs to apply for export licenses, so their father sent Maftur with Zubaida to accompany her. They found a queue snaking all the way round and round the dock area. As they stood in the boiling sun, they watched tugs creating a boom to seal off the harbour mouth, and soldiers placing corrugated iron sheets against fencing to obscure the view of passers-by.

"I can't see the point of that," Zubaida said. "You only have to stand in Allenby Park on Mount Carmel with a pair of binoculars and you can see everything that's going on in the docks."

When they hadn't returned for lunch, her mother came down and left them with flasks of coffee and egg sandwiches. They took it in turns to go to the lavatories on site but their wait was in vain. They hadn't reached the door before the offices closed for the day, but their mother sent Mahmoud down with a sleeping bag so he could keep their place in the queue.

When they returned home, hot and frustrated, Maftur found her father fuming, because there had been a run on the banks and the government had ordered them to close until things calmed down. Hearing she had failed to get the export papers processed only fuelled his anger.

He had simmered down a little by the time Elif and Da'oud came downstairs to join them to listen to the wireless. The presenter reminded them of a mock 'daylight raid' taking place on Kingsway in Haifa at eleven o'clock the next Sunday morning.

"Mr. Shawwa's volunteered to be an ARP warden," her mother said, 'so he will be on the roof of the Palestine Police HQ in the middle of it all, although I can't think why the government here is taking the prospects of European War so seriously. I can't imagine German planes flying all the way to Palestine."

Her father looked thoughtful. "I don't think it's planes we would have to worry about. The British Navy has to stop German warships reaching the Mediterranean, or the harbour and refinery will be vulnerable to long-range gun fire."

Maftur felt thankful that Ismail was safe in Jerusalem.

Next afternoon, she and Zubaida were almost home after finally getting the export papers processed, when Miriam came out of her house. Zubaida went ahead, leaving Maftur to chat.

"I've been looking out for you," Miriam said. "We're all going to be watching Sunday's air-raid practice from the roof of our department store. My father asks would your family like to join us? We'll have a grandstand view and I'd like to meet your new sister-in-law."

"That's wonderful. My mother has been grumbling that we won't see much from our roof. Thank you so much."

Elif was almost as delighted as her mother so that Sunday, the first in September, they were all on the roof of the department store by ten-thirty with a clear view of Kingsway below. Drinking Miriam's homemade iced lemonade and her mother's cinnamon cookies made it seem like a proper party.

Looking down, they could see the police had already closed the road to civilian vehicles. The pavement in front of several large doorways was marked out to show the position of air-raid shelters.

Looking up, they identified Mr. Shawwa on the roof of the seven-storey Khaiyet building in the midst of a group of ARP wardens all wearing tin hats.

At eleven o'clock the sirens sounded for two whole minutes. Cars with placards marked 'Take Cover' in Arabic, Hebrew and English drove slowly down the road. The police inside ordered pedestrians to take refuge in air-raid shelters. Mr. Shawwa left the Khaiyet building roof, emerged onto the street, and busied himself helping the police.

Loud crackers imitated the sounds of bombs, as clouds of smoke rose from the street. Lorries drove in, depositing rubble on road and pavement alike. A group in civilian clothes sprawled amongst the rubble in contorted attitudes. Firemen raced to put out the 'fires'. First-aid squads demonstrated their ability to deal with 'the wounded'. Repair squads cleared rubble in double quick time.

The raid was made even more realistic when an RAF plane from the east flew along the Carmel slope, and an Alla Littoria plane came in from the opposite direction. "That's just a coincidence," Miriam's father said. "They are both on routine schedules."

After the practice, while the men went off to a coffee shop, the women walked home.

Everyone agreed it had been a most entertaining show but, fortunately, something very unlikely to happen for real since the British had such a strong navy.

Maftur sat down to describe the air-raid practice to Ismail, but her mother called her to listen to the wireless before she had finished.

Britain had declared war on Germany.

"Let's just hope things go back to normal at work now it's finally happened," her father said.

"They announced a blackout practice in our area for tonight," Maftur said.

"Our present curtains should do just for one night," her mother said. "We'll start on proper blackout ones tomorrow, if you, Abu Kamal, can send up two bales of heavy black silk."

"There's been a run on it," her father said. "Mrs. Shawwa ordered one last week. I saved two for you in case you needed them, but only use what you really need. I'll take back anything left. We can sell it ten times over. That bale of Palestinian black cotton I sent up last week will do for bathrooms, kitchens and servants' rooms."

That evening, when Dodi, Elif, Janan and Kamal had joined them to listen to the wireless, they heard a banging on the door. The night watchman handed over a note from Mr. Shawwa in his capacity as ARP Warden.

You face prosecution unless you switch off all lights in the building.

"Right," said her mother. "We'll have to sit in our kitchen. I'll light the old coffee brazier. The glow won't be visible from the basement windows but it should give sufficient light for sewing. Kamal, go upstairs to the servants' rooms, and tell them all to turn off their lights and come down to the kitchen to help with the cotton blackout curtains."

"I'll ask Azza to put nightlights in the children's rooms, fetch Dindan and Safia and then I'll be back," Janan said.

Chapter 28

Maftur wouldn't have believed a war far off in Europe could make so much difference to Haifa.

The people worst affected were the German Templers evacuated from their homes.

Liners were requisitioned as troop carriers, so many British tourists found themselves stranded in Palestine. Most took on war work. Maftur's friend, Patsy, found a job at Khaiyet House in the police typing office, where Leila Boutaji was in charge. Maftur was envious. She would have applied for the job if she had known it was going and if her father had allowed her to take it. Patsy told her about a first-aid course the police were sending her on in one of the wedding halls. She and Elif joined it, as did several other AWA members.

The first-aid course brought them all a lot closer as they practiced splints and bandages on each other. Maftur and Elif felt disappointed when Patsy told them her father had been promoted to a post in Jerusalem.

"I'll miss you," Maftur said.

"It's okay. I'm not going with them," Patsy replied. "I've found digs with a police sergeant and his wife on the Stella Maris Road."

"What's happening about the house your parents rented?" Maftur asked.

"The owner's renting it out for the duration, but might sell it after the war."

As she lay in bed that night, Maftur thought about the house on Mount Carmel. If Ismail could buy it after the war her future would be perfect.

She wrote about it to Ismail.

My dearest darling Ismail,

Do you remember the house on Mount Carmel where the Quigleys live and where we met at a garden party in 1933? The Quigleys will be leaving Haifa soon. I loved that house and the view from its tower. Did you like it too? If so, wouldn't it be wonderful if we could buy it after we are married? I know we may not be living in Haifa when we come back from England (if we ever get to England, the way this war is going) but you told me when your father retires, you will have the choice of basing yourself in the Haifa office, Nablus or perhaps a new office in Jerusalem. If the house came on the market while we were living somewhere else, we could always let it out until we needed it.

I thought Patsy would move to Jerusalem with her parents but she wants to keep her job. (I don't blame her, I would.) She will be rooming with a British Police family in the big block of flats on the Stella Maris Road, so I will see her at Edmunds just as often as I do now. Incidentally, since so many of us are now at work, our Edmunds group is now meeting in the evenings instead of the afternoons. Things in Haifa have calmed down since the war started so my father has given me permission to go so long as Mahmoud accompanies me.

All my love, darling,
Maftur xxx

In reply Ismail wrote –

My very dearest Maftur,

What a romantic little darling you are. I would have thought your ideal house would be a brand new one complete with all modern cons, much nearer the centre of Haifa, but if you are sure you want to live in an ancient Ottoman house with all its inconveniences, it would suit me fine. I must admit I was strangely attracted to that house as well. It will be an ideal place to bring up a large family.

Until it comes onto the market, however, and if you still want to go out to work at the beginning of our marriage and while there are only two of us, a small apartment that can be heated properly in winter may be more convenient.

Heating has become very important to me recently. Here in Jerusalem last winter I almost froze to my chair as I sat studying great legal tomes.

All my love, darling,
Ismail, your adoring fiancé

* * * *

Over in Europe the war was going badly for the British. Dodi had a hard time disguising his delight from their father, especially when France surrendered.

Maftur was glad he waited until their father had left to commiserate with Mr. Shawwa in their favourite coffee shop, before saying gleefully to Elif, "Now your country will have its independence, darling."

Dodi was proved wrong. Vichy French government remained in control of Syria.

Of more concern to most people in Haifa was Italy entering the war on the German side. The Italian Alla Littoria Air planes flew a regular service between Rhodes and Haifa. Their pilots knew Haifa as well as their own homes. In fact, several had married local girls.

So now everyone took air-raid precautions seriously. The government rushed to finish nineteen huge public air-raid shelters. Everyone Maftur knew was building air-raid shelters in their homes. The Al-Zeids constructed a large one behind the cistern and beneath the back courtyard, just one big room at first, but after her mother had heard about Mrs. Shawwa's superbly equipped shelter, she persuaded Kamal and her father to divide theirs into kitchen and dormitory areas. Maftur couldn't help laughing when she thought of her mother actually demanding a communal kitchen after she had spent so many years struggling to get a private one. The war seemed to be turning everything inside out.

She thought that again when she found herself, her mother, Elif and Safia working at the police station, alongside Jewish and British women, putting together gas masks for ARP wardens.

"Only a year ago who would have dreamt we'd all be co-operating like this?" she whispered to Elif.

The gas masks weren't finished by the time the first air-raids started. The raids were spectacular, noisy, and destructive of oil tanks at the refinery, but killed or injured very few in comparison to the bombs that had exploded in the city before the war.

Once the masks were finished, she and Elif continued to go down to the police station once a week to join women from all communities in putting together emergency first-aid kits for use by the ARP, Red Crescent, MADA, Red Cross and St John's Ambulance .

One evening in November, after they had done their stint at the police station, they slipped into the nearby milk bar. Maftur introduced Elif to some of her old school friends. They were chatting away, catching up on each other's news, when Elif nudged her and indicated a young man queuing at the counter.

Maftur raised an enquiring eyebrow.

"Don't you know who it is?" Elif whispered.

She looked again, then recognised him from the photo her mother had made her keep in her clutch bag during her first betrothal. She whispered that her former fiancé had just walked in, but that it was all right, as he wouldn't recognise her now she had grown up.

"Didn't he have a photo of you?" the ex-netball captain asked.

"I shouldn't think he looked at it much."

The next time she glanced to the front, she saw Patsy entering.

"Ask her to join us," Elif said.

Just in case Ahmed recognised her though, Maftur pulled her hijab over her face before she went over. While she was talking to Patsy, Ahmed came up. She thought, at first, he had recognised her despite her hidden face, although it seemed strange he should seek her out after all that had happened.

To her surprise, however, he addressed Patsy. "I've found us an empty table."

Patsy, her face reddening, introduced her as Maftur Nour and then introduced Ahmed to her as her former landlord.

Ahmed bowed politely. "Miss Nour, I am delighted to make your acquaintance. Any friend of Miss Quigley's is a friend of mine."

She could hardly control her giggles. She just hoped the hijab veiled her mouth sufficiently.

"How does Patsy know Ahmed?" Elif asked when she returned.

"He was her landlord."

But she couldn't help thinking it ironic that Patsy, who worked in police HQ, should be having coffee with a man who, less than two years ago, had been masterminding the sabotage of the IPC oil line. Also, come to think of it, what was a Syrian doing in Palestine now the borders between the two countries were closed?

The more she thought about it, the more she suspected

that Ahmed was in Palestine illegally. If so, why? Could he be spying on behalf of his German friends? Could Elif and Dodi be aiding Ahmed in whatever he was up to? Should she warn Patsy?

Ismail was probably the only person who could advise her. She hurried home to write her daily letter. She picked up her new fountain pen, a cherished present from him.

My dearest Darling Ismail,

She then put her pen to her mouth and sucked the end. It seemed indelicate to mention her ex-fiancé to Ismail although she wasn't sure why. It wasn't as if Ismail had any cause for jealousy. Today was the first time she had spoken to Ahmed since she was ten years old.

The courteous gentleman she had encountered that afternoon, however, had been very different from the sarcastic adolescent of eight years before. His manners at the cafe had reminded her of Ismail's, although he had never attended a British public School. Of course, Ahmed wasn't half as handsome and attractive as Ismail, whatever the women at Edmunds might say.

She felt angry with herself for dithering. Only a few weeks ago she and Ismail had promised never to keep secrets from each other, so she should be able to write freely about the incident. She knew Ismail would be as intrigued as she was by today's incident, since he knew Patsy well, so, despite her embarrassment, she picked up her pen and gave him a full account, including her suspicions.

His advice by return of post was as sensible as she might have expected.

My own darling Maftur,

Your last letter worried me. You don't have sufficient facts to warrant saying anything to Patsy, and you could do a great deal of harm. Think, if Ahmed is cultivating Patsy's acquaintance under orders from the Grand Mufti and you warn Patsy, news of your warning, if it came out, as it is almost bound to do, would be interpreted as treachery by the Husseinis and could bring fatal repercussions on you and your family. Not only that, but as my fiancée, you would endanger my family, and especially my father. It is not even as if Patsy is a personal secretary to anyone in authority. Any information she has access to from a typing pool would be of little use to the enemy.

> *On the other hand, have you considered that it might be Patsy deliberately cultivating Ahmed under orders from the British CID? In that case Ahmed may be in danger of being arrested. To cover that eventuality, it might be as well to have a word with Dindan or Dodi, telling them you have seen Ahmed in company with a British woman. You needn't say you know the woman's name. They can pass the warning on to Ahmed if they think the situation warrants it.*
>
> *Please, my darling, don't do anything that puts yourself in danger. I don't think I could live without you,*
>
> *Your loving Ismail*

Maftur put the letter down. Although she had initially suspected Patsy of being a British spy when she had started at the secretarial school, she had long since put those misgivings aside. She hadn't considered that Patsy might be deliberately cultivating Ahmed for a sinister purpose. She definitely wouldn't mention Patsy by name to her brothers, although she would mention casually that she had seen Ahmed with a British woman in the milk bar.

When she managed to drop that fact into conversation, her mother shook her head. "You must be mistaken—Ahmed is at his villa in Baghdad studying Iraq's archaeological sites."

Chapter 29

It was the beginning of March 1941 before Maftur heard the next episode of Patsy and Ahmed's story.

The group at Edmunds were listening to Golda describing a party held in Nathanya to introduce Masky, an aperitif distilled from oranges, which was being marketed as a substitute for whisky. The manufacturers had invited influential people from Tel Aviv to sample it, with hilarious results.

While everyone's attention was on Golda, who had the knack of telling a good story, Patsy came in and whispered in Maftur's ear, "I need to talk to you alone."

Maftur, already slightly uneasy about listening to a story centred on alcohol abuse, slipped out of her seat without too much reluctance, and tiptoed to a table for two on the far side of the room.

Patsy sat down, humping her shoulders, looking as if she didn't know how to start.

"What's the matter?" Maftur asked softly.

Patsy crossed her arms in front of her chest, dug her elbows tightly into her ribs and took a deep breath before whispering, "You know when you saw me with Ahmed al-Zeid at the milk bar?"

"Yes."

Patsy bit her bottom lip before continuing, "You're going to find this hard to believe—"

A burst of laughter from the other side of the room interrupted their conversation. Patsy looked around, seemed satisfied no one was paying attention to them, but lowered her voice even further.

"Last summer, Ahmed took me out for a meal and told me he wanted to write to my father, asking for my hand in marriage. I was so angry that he was treating me like a possession of my father's that I walked away from him. When you saw us, we had just met again by accident in the suq. He asked then if he could write to me directly."

Maftur felt slightly disorientated. This was so unlike the

Ahmed she had been engaged to. Had her brothers told Ahmed of Ismail insisting on addressing his proposal to her, rather than her father?

Patsy continued her narrative in jerky sentences. "I told him I couldn't accept. He asked to write, anyway." She looked down, shamefaced. "I was curious so, eventually, I said he could."

"And did he?"

Patsy laid a finger across her bottom teeth, bit down and dipped her head in affirmation before saying, "Yes, but he gave me a long time to consider it as he wanted to hear my answer in person, and he wouldn't be in Palestine again for some time."

This didn't sound like something a spy would say.

"What was in the letter?"

Instead of replying, Patsy reached into her purse and pulled out a crumpled document that looked as if it had been opened and re-folded many times. Silently, she handed it over.

"You're sure you want me to read this?"

Patsy inclined her head. "It's so formal and full of clichés—it hardly counts as a personal document."

Maftur opened the letter and smoothed it out. It was written in English, as was only to be expected, but in a more cursive style than most English handwriting she had seen. She realised she had never seen Ahmed's handwriting, although she had been betrothed to him for four years. It contrasted strongly with Ismail's firm italic hand.

She studied the letter closely.

I, Ahmed al-Zeid, youngest son of Abu Mohamed al-Zeid, present myself as a suitor for your hand.

As the land longs for water at the end of the summer drought,
As the traveller in the desert longs for the oasis,
As the night longs for the moon,
So do I long for your beauty and wit.

If you consent to marry me, I pledge that, as part of my dowry, I will pay for the education you have set your heart on. It is my earnest desire that we may afterwards work together to reveal to the world the treasures that belong to Syria.

We will run a household in the twentieth century western style, as far as it does not conflict with the way of Islam, and you will be free to practice all your Christian rites. Should Allah grant us children, however, we must bring them up in the way of Islam.

In the attached document, I set out my worldly possessions. You will see that I am capable of keeping you in the style to which you are accustomed.

I am a man of honour. As such, I would be unhappy to marry you without the consent of your father while you are a minor under British law. If you cannot gain his consent, I am willing to wait until you can legally answer for yourself. However, should the Germans prove victorious in this present war, if it pleases you, I will marry you at once to afford you protection.

It didn't strike her as the formal document that Patsy had described, and the phrases were traditional rather than clichés. It was not a document written by someone trying to seduce a woman. It was too practical for that. She interpreted it as a letter Ahmed meant Patsy to show her parents at the same time as he was trying to tell Patsy how he felt about her. She could understand, however, that it might not be to a British woman's taste.

If Ahmed had written to her like that, she reflected, would she have had second thoughts about wanting to break off her betrothal?

She answered Patsy in terms she hoped a British woman would understand.

"Patsy, this means Ahmed's stepmothers have consented to the marriage already. They are women to be reckoned with." A fleeting image of the redoubtable Umm Harun passed through her mind. "They trust his judgment, Patsy. You, with your superior education and all this archaeology you have in common, will make him a perfect wife."

Curious about Patsy's true feelings beneath this strange Hollywood style situation, she asked, "Are you in love with him?"

Patsy's forehead flushed not too becomingly. "I'm not sure what being in love feels like. When I left England, I thought I was in love with a boy there, but know now we were both too young to be in love. Ahmed is so mature, so witty, so physically handsome, I think I may really be in love with him, but that's not the sole reason why I am now seriously considering marrying him."

Maftur felt puzzled. "What other reason is there?"

"I can't give you the full details, Maftur, because it would shock you too much. All I can say is that I'm in terrible trouble."

Maftur felt shocked. "You're not...?"

Patsy gave a bitter laugh. "No, not that sort of trouble! But if I stay in Palestine, my mother is going to be badly hurt. Please don't ask for details. You can, though, answer a question that may help me make up my mind as to whether I accept Ahmed's proposal."

Maftur waited for the question in considerable confusion. She was sure she knew nothing relevant to Patsy's problem.

"You told me once that your father considered Ahmed anti-British? Does that mean he works for the Germans?"

Maftur hesitated before answering.

Was Patsy a spy? If so, she mustn't answer that question. If, however, Patsy's question was genuinely personal, she should tell her a little more. She felt her way cautiously. "For an Arab, being anti-British doesn't necessarily mean being pro-German. Back in nineteen-thirty-seven, while you were at boarding school in England, the British threatened Palestinian Arabs with a partition of our country even more immoral than that of Syria in 1920. Ahmed still regards Northern Palestine as Southern Syria. When the British intended to divide his Southern Syria yet again, he joined Palestinians fighting against further partition. Once the partition threat was shelved and the British had promised Jews would not become a majority before our independence, most patriots returned to normal civilian life. From what I can gather, Ahmed is now a full time archaeologist. But, if you are seriously considering marrying Ahmed, you must ask him yourself if he is pro-German. He is an honest man and will tell you the truth. If he satisfies you, you must invite us all to your wedding."

"I can't invite you to my wedding, Maftur. I cannot marry Ahmed in Palestine."

"Not even if my father tells the British government that Ahmed is part of our family?"

"No. It has nothing to do with closed borders. Without my father's consent, I cannot legally marry Ahmed until I am twenty-one. I don't think he will wait that long for me, despite what he writes."

"His stepmothers will certainly want to break off negotiations if difficulties are prolonged, but are you sure your father won't give his permission?"

"My father will never give me permission to marry Ahmed."

"Why not? Ahmed al-Zeid's family is well-respected and rich."

"Ahmed is Muslim, my father is Christian."

Maftur found that a strange answer. "But Muslim men often marry European Christians. If you really love this man you must work to make your father change his mind. If he knows you are trying, I am sure Ahmed al-Zeid will wait until you are twenty-one. After all, so far he has shown no desire to marry for the sake of being married."

"You really think a marriage like that could work? I wouldn't be a slave to his mother, or something? I've heard Arab mothers-in-law treat their sons' wives as dirt."

Maftur thought of her interview with Umm Harun. "If they know Ahmed approves of your studying, so will your mothers-in-law. You are lucky, Patsy, the Al-Zeid women are very different from my future mother-in-law."

Over Patsy's shoulder, she saw Leila Boutaji's sister, Michelle, who had taken classes with them, jump to her feet, and feared she was going to barge over. She put a finger to her lips, then realised Michelle was looking at Leila, who was standing in the doorway, holding her left hand in the air, displaying a large emerald engagement ring.

"Oh, I am so pleased. Everyone said Leila was too old to get betrothed now, but it looks as if we'll have to go over and congratulate her."

Patsy stood up and pulled on her jacket. "I must go, but I am really grateful for your advice, Maftur. You've made my decision far easier."

Chapter 30

Maftur had no more reservations about Elif. She found herself admiring her the more she knew her. Elif's sense of humour and common sense smoothed the surface of the uncompromising idealism that had seemed so abrasive when Dodi first described it. Elif fitted in harmoniously with the Haifa branch of AWA, as equally willing to help with charitable projects as with political demonstrations. Maftur and Elif had become close friends, and the apartment building once more seemed home to a closely-knit family. Once a week her father stayed home after supper and the whole family, apart from the children tucked up in bed, congregated for after dinner coffee in her parents' living room.

Two days after her encounter with Patsy, Maftur was sitting beside Elif, discussing an AWA project for helping children with sight problems. Ever since Mahmoud's son had lost his sight in the suq bombing this had become a big concern in their family. She looked around to see what the rest of the family were doing.

Kamal, Dindan and Dodi were chatting amicably with their father about sales in the eastern villages, debating whether it was time to add an office in Nablus. Her mother and Janan were giving advice to Safia who was working on a piece of embroidery with just the word *Allah* in shades of blue on a black background, as a gift for her husband to celebrate his imminent fatherhood. It would seem that Dindan had forgotten his objections to cross-stitch.

When the camel bell hanging beside the street door clanged urgently, everyone looked up in surprise. Mahmoud entered the sitting room to say a gentleman wanted to speak to Da'oud and Adad.

Maftur looked enquiringly at Elif as Dodi and Dindan left the room, but her sister-in law just spread her hands apart to express her ignorance.

Dodi returned to give his and Dindan's apologies. "A friend has arrived with some news. We are going to my apartment to talk it over."

It wasn't until the following afternoon that Maftur learnt who her brothers' visitor was, or what he had come about.

As she and Elif were walking to the police station, Elif asked, "Do you know anything about a Christian called Habib who was a comrade of my husband's during the Rebellion?"

"No, but then my brothers never told me anything about their squad. Why?"

"He came last night looking for your ex-fiancé."

Maftur laughed. "Our apartment block would be the last place to find Great-Great-Uncle Ahmed. Anyway, he lives in Baghdad now."

"I know, but this Habib says Ahmed came to Haifa two days ago and stayed at his house. He had deliberately volunteered to take a message from the Grand Mufti to a German agent here so he could meet a British woman he has fallen in love with. He went off early yesterday morning saying he had to attend to the Mufti's business, but was meeting this woman later in the day. He told Habib he hoped they would be celebrating his betrothal when he returned for the evening meal, but he never came back."

Maftur hoped her face gave nothing away when she replied, "Did this Habib tell Dodi the name of the British woman?"

"Ahmed never told him."

"Does he know if Ahmed met her?"

"No. Dodi heard nothing from him after he left yesterday morning."

"My guess would be that he has eloped with the woman."

"That's what Dodi suggested but his spare clothes and wash things are still in the spare bedroom, and his wallet with a large sum of Iraqi money and a passport are in Habib's safe."

"Perhaps he took the woman back to Syria. He wouldn't need Iraqi money there and he probably has several passports."

"That's one possibility but Habib is certain Ahmed would never have done that without telling him. He fears the British have captured Ahmed."

Maftur thought it far more likely Ahmed had eloped with Patsy, but all the same she felt a stab of alarm. "Was Dodi involved in the meeting with the German agent?"

"No, thank goodness. Truth to tell, he was a bit hurt to hear Ahmed had been in Haifa and hadn't contacted him."

"If he has been captured, the British will have to put him on trial. He will need a lawyer. Great-Uncle Ahmed is family, so my father can ask Mr. Shawwa to find out if the police have him in custody. If they have, my father will retain Mr. Shawwa to defend him. The British respect Mr. Shawwa. If anyone can get him off, he can."

Next morning her father informed her mother and herself that Ahmed had visited Haifa and was now missing. He was going to consult Mr. Shawwa, although it seemed highly probable that Ahmed had eloped with a British woman. "Which just goes to show how right I was to break off Maftur's betrothal," he added.

A few days later, her father reported, "Mr. Shawwa has made enquiries, but the British police are positive they have no Syrian by the name of Al-Zeid in custody."

That afternoon she and Elif discussed Ahmed as they walked together down to the police station for another session of packing first aid materials.

Maftur confessed that she had campaigned to make her father break off her betrothal to him.

Elif asked why, saying she had found Ahmed charming and courteous. However, after Maftur had cited examples of his patronising ways, she was more sympathetic.

"It seems you both retained unflattering juvenile impressions of each other. Since your parents allowed the pair of you to meet when you were a child and he a callow youth, they should have arranged for you to meet face to face before your betrothal."

"It wasn't just that," Maftur said. "I already wanted to marry Ismail. My betrothal to Ismail is better in every way except one."

Elif raised one eyebrow. "And the exception?"

"If I had still been betrothed to Ahmed, I would be a secretary in Jerusalem by now, not plodding on in my father's warehouse."

"Maftur, you will have to accept your hands are tied until you marry, but if you and Ismail love each other and treat each other as equals after your marriage, there's no reason then that you can't go out to work and prove you can maintain your children single-handed, always assuming you want children."

Maftur felt uncomfortable. She had never heard anyone suggest a woman might not want children. She had felt so wicked having to pretend to like babies, while here was Elif asking if she wanted children as if it was a perfectly normal question. She found it difficult answering the question truthfully.

"Of course, I want children eventually, but I would really like to have Ismail to myself for at least two years, if it is the will of Allah, of course."

Maftur noticed Elif's lips twitch as if suppressing a smile, but all she said was, "I think now you've clarified things in your mind, you had better discuss both issues—work and children—with Ismail before you marry."

Maftur had already discussed going to work with Ismail but, of course, had never said anything about children. It was an improper subject to discuss with a man. She reminded herself that Ismail had said there should be no secrets between them so, greatly daring, she added a paragraph to her next letter.

I love you so much, Ismail. When we marry I don't want to share you with anyone, not even our children for a while. Please don't think it too awful if I tell you that I hope we don't have children straight away. Of course, I want children eventually as I am sure you do but, for a while, it would be so wonderful if it could be just us two, but of course all is the will of Allah.

All my love, darling,
Maftur xxx

After posting the letter, she wished she had not added that last paragraph. She waited in mental agony for Ismail's reply. Would he be disgusted by her immodest remarks?

Her finger trembled so much when his reply arrived she had difficulty in opening the envelope. She breathed a sigh of relief as she read –

Jerusalem April 1941 – only 120 days now

Darling Maftur, you are the light of my life, especially during these drab days of work, work, work, when thoughts of you are the only bright things in them.

I agree about not starting a family straight away after we marry, and am willing to wait for a year or two to earn the proud name of Father. I am glad you have told me your wishes but, until we are married, I don't think I am the right person to discuss with you the ways and means of achieving this. Do not on any account let your parents or any of your friends know you have mentioned it to me. My life would lose all its zest if we were forbidden to write to each other.

I recommend you speak to your mother and ask her if you may read a book called "Wise Parenthood" by a lady called Maria Stokes. I am sure your mother, as a member of AWA, will know of it. However, your mother may ask how you heard about it, so perhaps, before you mention it, you had better talk to some of your Ashkenazi Jewish friends from the Secretarial course, (NOT your friend Miriam, by the way.) Then you can say the Jewish girls were discussing it with you. Let me know how you get on.

Think of me returning to my drudgery,
All my love, darling,
Ismail

Maftur sat pondering over this letter. She wondered if Elif had heard of 'Wise Parenthood.'

She made her way upstairs to Dodi's apartment and found Elif immersed in a book.

"You should read this sometime," Elif said as she put her book down. "Maryana Marrash is such a talented woman. Have you come about something particular or just for a chat?"

"You know you advised me to write to Ismail? He suggested I read a book by a Mrs. Stopes."

"'Married Love'?"

"No. 'Wise Parenthood'."

"Ah, yes. I have that one too."

"May I borrow it?"

Elif frowned. "Maftur, your family's ways are different from mine. You should ask your mother first before you read this book."

"That's what Ismail said, but he doesn't want me to tell my mother it was his suggestion."

"Sensible fellow."

"May I say I heard about it from you?"

Elif put the back the back of her hand to her mouth, and bit the skin. "I'd rather you didn't. It may make your mother angry with me."

"I wouldn't want that!"

Elif considered again. "I want to help you, though. May I tell your mother you are hoping it would be Allah's will that you don't have children straight away?"

"I don't think she'll like that."

"What if I said you meant only for a year while you and Ismail settle down together?"

"Yes, I'd be pleased if you did that."

"All right, then. Leave it to me!"

A few days later, as Maftur sat darning stockings in the sewing room, her mother looked up. "Maftur, you've been engaged far longer than most women so there is no need to keep you ignorant of the details of wedding night rites—" Her mother looked down at her lap "—and yet, perhaps just because you are older I find it more difficult to discuss these things with you."

Maftur could think of no suitable response, so remained silent but attentive.

"Luckily," her mother continued, "there are now books that give you the information you need. I happen to know that Elif owns at least two that you would find useful."

Maftur put on her most innocent expression. "What are they called?"

"I forget their names, but they are by a Mrs. Stokes. If you ask Elif, I am sure she would lend them to you."

"Thank you, Umm."

"Anything you still want to know after you've read them, don't be afraid to ask." Her mother was not being too successful in hiding her embarrassment. Her cheeks had gone pink. "Oh, and by the way, because you did gymnastics at Haifa High, other mothers tell me you may need some chicken blood on your wedding night. I will tell you how to use it after your Henna party. There will be no need to feel shame. I know you are unsullied."

It wasn't until Maftur had read the books Elif had lent her that she understood why chicken blood and gymnastics had entered the conversation.

Chapter 31

Two months after Ahmed disappeared, Habib once more knocked on the apartment door. Again Dodi and Dindan took him upstairs. Dindan returned with a drawn face and told the family that Dodi was going out and didn't know what time he would be back.

"He's not getting into more political foolishness?" Baba asked. "I thought you two had put all that behind you."

"I promise you, Father, he's doing nothing illegal," Dindan said.

Dodi had still not returned home when Maftur, with her father, Dindan and Kamal, set off to work the next morning.

She was tapping away on her typewriter when she heard footsteps on the fire escape. She always locked the door once she was in the office so she wasn't unduly alarmed.

There was a knock on the door. "Maftur, it's me, Elif, with Mahmoud, please let us in. We've news for your father."

Maftur recognized her sister-in-law's voice and unlocked the door. The room felt crowded with three in it.

"What news?"

"Not good. Sit down first, Maftur."

Had something happened to her mother? But although Elif's face reflected real sadness, Mahmoud seemed calm. She sat obediently. Elif took the other chair.

"It's Ahmed, Maftur. Dodi and some others from the squad found his body. He's been dead so long they could only identify him from his clothes and watch."

Maftur felt a wave of sadness wash over her. Not grief—she hadn't known Ahmed that well, just sadness at the waste of a young man's life.

"Your mother says we must keep everything from Safia because we don't want to alarm her in her condition."

Maftur nodded. "Mahmoud," she said, "go downstairs and break the news to my father, then tell him we would be grateful if he would come up."

After Mahmoud had left, she asked, "Did Dodi tell you

anything else?"

"Yes. Habib knows who killed Ahmed but we're not going to let Beau-père know that, or he may order Dodi to avenge him. Habib is claiming that honour. He and Ahmed were blood brothers."

"Dodi is happy with that?"

"Yes, praise Allah. He and Dindan will help Habib lure the murderer into a place where the revenge can take place without danger to spectators, but they will leave the action to Habib."

Maftur heard the tread of heavy feet climbing the stairs. Her father entered the office while Mahmoud waited outside.

Elif told him what Dodi had discovered.

"The grave was shallow," she said, "no more than an inch of soil over his body. The murderers erected a large cairn of stones over it."

Her father listened in silence until she finished, then asked, "Why have you come instead of my son to tell me this? It is not women's business."

"Dodi worked with his friends all night removing stones so they could identify the body. I asked him to allow me to bring you the news while he bathed and changed his clothes."

Her father gave Elif a curt nod. "Mahmoud, you will escort my daughter-in-law home. I will follow with Kamal when I have finished a discussion with a client. Dindan will remain here so we don't alarm Safia. Maftur, you will come home with Dindan and tell him what has happened on the way."

Dindan was grief-stricken when she gave him the news, but she warned him to act normally in front of Safia. Once inside her parents' apartment she and her mother discussed Ahmed's death. Elif had told her mother-in-law the bare minimum before hurrying down to the warehouse, so Maftur provided more details.

She was glad she had left Patsy's name out when later in the evening her mother told her that her father had reluctantly agreed that Habib should have the honour of killing Ahmed's murderer. That left Dodi, Dindan and other members of their band with the task of identifying the woman who had lured Ahmed to his death, and exacting their revenge.

Maftur tried to sound indifferent as she asked, "What will they do to the woman when they find her?"

"By rights they ought to stone her but, with British laws being what they are, it may be more practical to shoot her, even if it does mean a quicker death."

Maftur wanted to shout that this was barbaric, but realised she only felt this way because she still doubted that Patsy had deliberately betrayed Ahmed. She needed to discover the facts before jumping to conclusions.

"How did Habib find out where Ahmed was buried and who had murdered him?" she asked.

"From his step-sister. One of the British children she looks after repeated a conversation she'd overheard between her parents and the murderer as they passed by Ahmed's grave."

Maftur wanted to ask Ismail's advice, but didn't dare include details in a letter. Although censors were supposed to leave internal mail alone, if the British knew Ahmed had worked for the Germans they might make their family an exception, and she didn't want the British arresting her brothers for treason. She could only hope her brothers didn't discover the British girl's identity until they had proved her guilty.

A week later, for the first time in over two months, Patsy walked into Edmunds while the secretarial group was meeting. The British girl had lost weight and there were deep shadows beneath her eyes. Maftur ran over to cut her off before she joined the rest of the group.

"Patsy," she whispered in her ear, "I am so glad to see you. We must talk at once." She drew her over to the far end of the room. "First, I must tell you that I do not believe what people are saying about you."

Patsy opened her eyes wide and burst out, "Not you too, Maftur!"

Maftur looked around to make sure none of the other women were looking their way and whispered, "Quiet, please, Patsy."

"But how did you hear of it?" Patsy demanded.

"Through my brothers."

Patsy raised her eyebrows. "Your brothers? How do your

brothers know my father?"

Now it was Maftur's turn to feel puzzled. "Your father? I thought you didn't want your father to have anything to do with it."

"To do with what, Maftur?"

"Ahmed al-Zeid's proposal."

Patsy wrinkled her face in bewilderment as if this were the last thing she had expected. "Maftur, please forget what I told you about Ahmed. I decided not to turn up for that meeting."

Maftur leaned back and stared. Could her brothers be right? Had Patsy deliberately lured Ahmed to his death, or was it possible no one had told her Ahmed's body had been found?

"Patsy, about Ahmed al-Zeid? You do not know?"

"Know what?"

This was terrible. She didn't want to be the one to break the news. Even if Patsy had not turned up to the meeting with Ahmed she was sure she had been really fond of him.

She closed her eyes. "I thought you would know."

She heard Patsy say in a frosty tone, "If you are going to tell me he is marrying someone else that is no concern of mine."

She looked up to see Patsy rising. "No. That's not what I'm telling you." The next words jerked out of her mouth of their own accord. "Ahmed is dead, Patsy."

Patsy slumped heavily back onto the chair. "Dead?" She covered her face with her hands.

Maftur sat quietly in front of her.

After a few minutes Patsy took a handkerchief out of her bag, wiped the tears from her face and blew her nose. "When did he die?"

The question threw her. She had expected Patsy to ask how he had died.

"My brothers think it happened the day he told a friend he was meeting a British woman."

Patsy pressed the sodden handkerchief back on her eyes. "So all the time I spent in the milk bar, Ahmed was already dead!"

Maftur remained silent.

Patsy looked up. "I thought he had stood me up." She

blew her nose again and asked the expected question.

Maftur gave the blunt answer. "A British policeman killed him."

"Why?"

"According to my brothers, he volunteered to deliver a message from the Grand Mufti to a German agent in Palestine because he wanted an excuse to meet a British woman. The police ambushed him."

"He died because he wanted to see me?" Patsy's hands covered her face again.

The women on the other side of the room were staring now. Maftur knew she would have to concoct some sort of story later to satisfy their curiosity.

Patsy wiped her eyes again. "You said that you don't believe what people are saying about me. I don't understand."

Maftur twisted the end of her scarf round her little finger working out how to answer that question. "It's not about you as such, because they don't know you're the woman Ahmed al-Zeid was meeting, and I haven't told anyone." She unwound the scarf and twirled it round a finger on the opposite hand. "They are saying that Ahmed al-Zeid wanted to marry a British spy."

Opposite her, Patsy clutched her hands together. Staring into her lap, she whispered, "Maftur, that's not true. I lied to you just now about not going to meet Ahmed." She suppressed a sob before continuing. "I did go, but he didn't turn up." Her fingernails dug into her kneecaps. "I had decided to say yes to his proposal."

Maftur leaned across the table. "I believe you, Patsy, but I'm not the one you have to convince. Ahmed's friends have vowed vengeance. They'll kill the policeman who committed the murder and then they will go after you. They think you lured Ahmed to his death, but have not yet found out who you are, but that won't last long. Please, Patsy, understand. Your life is in danger. You must leave Palestine before they find you."

Patsy stood up and kissed Maftur on the cheek. "You know something? I don't really care if they do."

Maftur watched her walk slowly out of the café. She had done all she could to warn Patsy. She just hoped she would heed her advice once she had had time to think it over.

On the way home, she promised herself that from then on everything would take second place to her wedding.

Chapter 32

Maftur and Ismail had finally accepted there would be no question of travelling to England, not with the way the war was going. An exam pass that year would qualify Ismail to practice law in Palestinian courts, so they would spend their honeymoon at the Shawwa estate in Nablus, not London.

A fortnight in Nablus would be paradise enough for Maftur, so long as she had Ismail to herself.

Mrs. Shawwa had already embarked on a campaign to persuade her mother to stop her working outside the home.

"Maftur needs to concentrate now on honing her housekeeping skills."

Thankfully, her father had insisted he needed her at the warehouse to train Safia's younger sister, Naveen, who had come up from Jaffa to take over Maftur's job.

Cheerful and organised, Naveen picked up the office routine so quickly that Maftur was spending the morning handwriting Henna party invitations. As she wrote to her friends from school and secretarial college, thoughts of Sabeen, Yalda, Aunt Bahia and her sister Parveen occupied most of her mind. Their invitations had already been written and dispatched but she doubted if they would be able to attend.

Mighty battles between Allied and Vichy forces currently raged round both Damour and Damascus. A two-day long procession of military vehicles, heading for the Lebanese border, had given her some inkling of the number of troops involved.

She glanced over at Naveen frowning over a handwritten order from Egypt and felt a pang of conscience. She had been too obsessed with her Henna party to give her the support she deserved. "Anything I can help with?"

"I think I'm all right. You've set up a well-organised system. By the time you leave I should have the hang of it all. Anyway, I can concentrate better here in Haifa. It's so relaxing living with your peaceful family—not like the domestic chaos back in Jaffa."

She wondered if the girl would feel like that if she knew about the current family drama. Everyone had agreed to keep Naveen in the dark about plans to avenge Ahmed's murderer, as part of the campaign to protect Safia during her pregnancy.

She returned to her invitations and, after some hesitation, added Dalia Leitner's name to her list, although unsure of her current address.

Michelle Boutaji, Leila's sister, who now also worked at Police HQ, had told everyone at Edmunds that Dalia's family had disowned her because she was marrying a British police officer.

She had also sent Patsy an invitation, but had warned her that some guests were married to men out to kill her. Their husbands would be present at the wedding reception.

She felt tears pricking her eyes as she thought of how many people she really wanted at her Henna party who just wouldn't be there. Then her thoughts turned to Ismail. His situation was far worse. He would have neither English schoolmates nor fellow students from Beirut at his Sahra party, and he hardly knew his Saudi cousins.

Chapter 33

On the morning of her Henna Party, Maftur felt sad as she surveyed her bedroom. Her big sister, Parveen, should have been applying henna to her hands and feet, not an aunt from Jaffa. Sabeen and Yalda's younger sisters should have been her bridesmaids, not these strangers from Egypt and Saudi Arabia. At least Elif popped in now and then to give her moral support.

"Smile," Elif ordered. "None of this really matters. The important thing is that tomorrow you and Ismail will be married."

She ran her hands over her gold jewellery, an engagement present from Ismail, so different from Levantine over-elaborate filigree work. Darling Ismail had consulted her mother and had taken the relevant page of a pre-war Cartier catalogue to a Yemenite goldsmith. He had not only had him replicate the necklace and earrings she and her mother had admired, but had instructed him to make matching pairs of bracelets.

Her mother came in to say that the coach was waiting.

The young bridesmaids, who had not had enough time in Haifa to be instructed properly, picked up her train awkwardly.

Inside the coach, she bent down and kissed Ai'isha as she passed her going up the aisle, grateful to her for keeping her schoolgirl promise, by designing both her wedding dress and the crimson Henna day thob she was wearing.

"Ai'isha, I felt like a million piastres when I looked in the mirror this morning."

Ai'isha inspected her. "I said that thob would be just right for your jewellery." She fingered the red gossamer silk head scarf, interwoven with gold thread. "And that is exactly right too. You are so lucky to come from a centuries-old urban family rather than a rural one. Remember that awful money-hat I had to wear?"

"Indeed," Maftur replied. "I have so much to be thankful for." She hung on to that thought.

As they dismounted from the coach she could hear the drummer. Her bridesmaids ushered her to a dais and seated her on a comfortable chair. They then proceeded to dance their solos and present the bridegroom's wedding gifts. The only part of his gifts she had seen so far were the loose pearls sewn onto the bodice of her western-style wedding dress. She had told her mother she wished she had a pearl necklace to go with it. Ismail had obviously consulted her mother again, because a bridesmaid presented a braided triple-stringed necklace, even more beautiful than the one she had envisaged. She was still reeling with pleased astonishment when the next bridesmaid presented a pearl-studded tiara to hold down the following day's white veil. Besides the pearls, they presented cut glass bowls and a Sheffield steel cutlery set. The one whose task it was to present a gramophone, removed the wrappings slowly to music in imitation of a strip tease.

Once the gifts had been displayed, Maftur looked around the hall. Her school friends were all there, apart from ones who had just had a baby or were expecting one imminently. Most were accompanied by two or even three young children. The secretaries were there, the Ashkenazi Jews a little hesitant about joining in the dances, but Miriam taught them the steps. She couldn't see Dalia, and wondered if she had stayed away because Patsy had not come.

When Michelle danced within speaking distance, Maftur called her over to ask after Dalia.

"Nobody knows where she is," Michelle replied. "She left work without handing in her notice, saying she had to prepare for her wedding, and then just disappeared. She's not at her lodgings. Her landlady assumed she had gone home, until her mother came looking for her."

"Her mother didn't know where she was?"

"I told you Dalia quarrelled with her when she converted, but her mother said she wants to make it up."

Michelle drifted off. Other people came to congratulate her on her appearance and Maftur settled down, determined to enjoy the day despite the missing guests.

She woke early next morning. THE DAY. She wanted to be as beautiful as possible. Before going to bed she had bleached away the henna pattern on her hands. Beautiful as it looked, it didn't go with a Parisian wedding dress. She had left the henna on her feet, since they would be hidden by her long dress and silk stockings.

After her morning prayers, she waited patiently for her bridesmaids. They came in, yawning, and helped her into the wedding dress. The pearl beads sewn onto the smocked bodice glowed in the morning sun shining through the window. She sat in front of her mirror and let Elif work on her, using her huge collection of Parisian cosmetics.

Elif applied pale pink varnish to her nails and then plucked her eyebrows into clean, well-defined arches and accented them with a dark brown pencil. She worked on the skin of her face and neck, patting in a moisturizer, and smoothing on a warm foundation matching her skin. She touched up her cheeks with rouge that had soft fuchsia undertones, before applying a lighter sweet-smelling powder, and then concentrated on the area around her eyes, using dark brown mascara and muted brown eye shadow with a narrow eyeliner.

The hairdresser dressed hair Maftur had allowed to grow for the past six months. The bridesmaids placed the white lace veil over her face and positioned the pearl tiara.

When she drew on her arm-length fingerless gloves, her mother kissed her and placed a bouquet of white gardenias in her hands.

By the time the wedding limousine arrived Maftur was trembling, whether with excitement or nerves she wasn't sure.

"Relax, Maftur," Elif urged in a whisper. "You love Ismail. Ismail loves you, so this is the happiest day of your life. Just think what a bride must feel who knows nothing of her groom, except what she has seen in a photo."

Waved off by all the women and children from the apartment and most of the neighbours in the street, the limousine bore Maftur and her bridesmaids off to the mosque, followed by a taxi bearing her father and, as witnesses to the wedding ceremony, her mother, heavily veiled, and Mr. Shawwa.

She leaned back as the bridesmaids rearranged her veil. Her heart thumped heavily as, through the lace she saw Ismail, in a top hat and tails, waiting by the mosque entrance. The bridesmaids took off her shoes. Her father led her over to her bridegroom. Side by side, without touching, they entered the mosque, followed by the three witnesses, to meet the elderly sheik from the Shawwa clan who had travelled up from Saudi Arabia to perform the simple marriage ceremony.

Maftur listened to the recitations from the Koran in a daze, conscious only of the proximity of her beloved. This continued, while the sheiks advised them on their duty to treat each other courteously at all times, as they followed him into a small room to sign a register.

Feeling almost mystically solemn, Maftur walked silently out of the mosque beside Ismail, into ear-splitting chaos. His friends tooted motorbike horns and shouted congratulations. He took her hand. A tingling sensation swept all the way up her arm and down into her stomach. Her legs felt weak. She thought she was going to faint, but managed to keep up with Ismail, clutching her bouquet in her free hand as he rushed her to the limousine. He let go of her hand and took his place beside the driver. A bridesmaid rescued the shoes from the mosque entrance while the others wiped her stockings free of dust. Three motorbikes revved up and took their position in front of the limousine. Vehicles of all descriptions crowded behind the taxi, the drivers still tooting their horns while their passengers blew trumpets and whistled or just shouted. The whole noisy procession made their way to the reception.

The bridesmaids led Maftur into a cloakroom, checked her makeup and drew back her veil so her face was exposed, before leading her to the salon, down an aisle separating men from women and children, to a dais where Ismail sat on a red velvet sofa behind a low table. She stepped up to join him, and the bridesmaids retreated.

A waitress brought a dish of saffron-flavoured rice and lamb cooked with mint and cumin, and set it on their table. Feeling shy, Maftur raised her eyes and looked at Ismail.

He grinned broadly. "Come on," he said, "I'm starving."

Together they dipped their right hands into the dish and scooped rice and meat into a ball. Maftur carefully transferred the food to her mouth, terrified of soiling the front of her magnificent dress.

"No one can separate us now, habipti," Ismail said in a

low voice.

"No," she whispered back. "I am so, so happy."

When they had cleared the plate, she looked around at the other women, all eating a European style meal with knives and forks. She was surprised to see so many British ladies. She found her mother and mother-in-law sitting together. Her mother looked up and smiled reassurance. Mrs. Quigley sat on the other side of her mother-in law but Patsy wasn't with her.

When everyone else had finished their meal, a waitress cleared the empty dish from their table and replaced it with a three-tier white and silver wedding cake. She and Ismail stood up together and with his right hand on top of hers, they cut the first slice.

The waitresses then took over and distributed slices to the guests. Her father, Mr. Shawwa, her brothers, her new brother-in-law from Nablus, and the religious Sheik from Riyadh made speeches before her new brother-in-law clapped—and in came a line of highly-esteemed professional belly dancers.

After their performance, waitresses moved the tables to the sides of the hall, and a curtain was drawn revealing a stage on which was seated a European string band. They struck up a note and played a waltz. Luckily her parents had warned her about this European practice that had become popular at weddings. She and Elif had practiced in her mother's sewing room for several weeks, so she confidently allowed Ismail to lead her onto the dance floor. What she hadn't expected was her reaction when his arm went around her waist. It was so different from the feel of Elif's. Her legs turned weak again, but Ismail's arm held her up. Conscious of all eyes on her, she concentrated on following his lead and breathed a sigh of relief when her parents, the Shawwas and other married couples joined them on the dance floor.

The waltz finished, her bridesmaids led her from the room, up carpeted stairs to the bridal suite. Supervised by her mother, they dressed her in a white satin nightdress and propped her up on large lace-bordered cushions on a four-poster bed.

When the bridesmaids had departed, her mother said, "Mrs. Shawwa will inspect your sheets tomorrow morning, as is her duty." She fumbled in her clutch bag and brought out a small vial containing a red liquid—the chicken blood. "If there is no blood on the sheets by the time your Ismail falls asleep you must place a few drops from this vial on the sheet beneath your legs. Make sure you do not wake him."

Maftur watched her place the vial in the upper drawer of the nearer of the bedside cabinets that contained the chamber pots.

"Bless you, my child, and may your marriage be happy and fruitful." She bent down, kissed her and left.

Lying there on her own, Maftur felt much as she had done first thing that morning, only in an exaggerated form. She was trembling with a mixture of nerves and happy anticipation. The feeling increased as the minutes dragged on. Before long, she heard raucous laughter on the stairs, and men singing coarse songs. Heavy footsteps clomped down the corridor towards her bedroom. She cowered back against the pillows.

The door opened and Ismail entered. He slammed the door in the faces of his companions, locked it and turned to face her. The raucous singing continued outside.

"Maftur, my darling, I am so sorry about the noise. I hope my uncouth friends aren't frightening you."

She sat up. "I'm not frightened now you're here, Ismail."

"Would you like a glass of mint tea?"

She realised how dry her mouth was and nodded.

Ismail picked up the handset of a phone sitting on the bedside cabinet and ordered mint tea and cakes. He also asked the receptionist to send up the manager to get rid of hooligans outside the bedroom door.

"Is it all right if I sit on the bed and hold your hand while we're waiting?" he asked.

"Oh, Ismail, please! I would like that more than anything."

He lowered himself onto the edge of the bed and took her hands.

She sat up and pressed her head against his chest. "Ismail, you don't know how much I have been longing to be with you."

An authoritarian voice barked orders outside. The singing and bawdy comments ceased. A few minutes later there was a knock on the door.

Maftur lay back on her pillows as a waitress appeared with a tray, and placed it on a small table next to a basket of fruit.

"It's like having a midnight feast in a boarding school book," she giggled.

"We didn't have midnight feasts at our boarding school," Ismail said. "The prefects were too strict. So it will be fun starting now." He brought over the tray and placed it beside her.

She remembered the vial in the drawer beneath the tray. She didn't want to start her marriage keeping secrets. She sipped at the tea. "Ismail, I have something to tell you which you may find funny, although it's rather rude, but we agreed not to keep secrets from each other."

She told him about her mother's worry over gymnastics and the vial of chicken blood.

He laughed. "Oh, my darling, you must be the first bride to tell her husband about the chicken blood. Oh, I do so love you, habipti." He stopped laughing. "About us waiting before having children—I think it may be best to leave it in the hands of Allah for this one night. Afterwards we will see to it ourselves, I promise. Are you willing to take the risk, my darling?"

She flung herself into his arms, spilling his mint tea. "Oh, Ismail, just now I don't care about anything except that I am with you at last."

An hour and a half later, as she lay, almost exhausted but peacefully content in Ismail's arms, they started giggling when they realised the chicken blood was redundant, and gymnastics weren't as great a danger to virtue as the mothers of Haifa High School girls feared.

Chapter 34

The Shawwa farm estate, where they were spending their honeymoon, lay on the lower slopes of fertile Mount Gezerim, overlooking Nablus town. Their taxi drove up a dirt drive, passing clusters of beehives and men on ladders picking apples, lemons and late season peaches from trees with green leaves, above parched ground. In their shade, women packed fruit into baskets. A building came into view, a two-storeyed red-roofed stone house. Cloths spread round the house were covered with figs, peaches and tomatoes drying in the hot August sun.

They drew to a halt in front of a veranda, protected by a wooden canopy covered in climbing asparagus ferns and hoyas displaying clusters of pale velvet flowers. Maftur stepped out onto the drive. Heat struck her, almost as a solid force, although it was already late afternoon. She followed Ismail onto the veranda, cooler there, and smelling of damp earth from well-watered plant tubs.

A middle-aged woman in a blue thob and white scarf ran towards them from an open doorway and hugged Ismail, kissing him on both cheeks. "Oh, my precious, you have brought a beautiful wife with you. Welcome, welcome, both."

Ismail turned his head with a rueful grin. "Maftur, this is Umm Saleh, the nurse who looked after me from the moment I was born until I went to school in England."

"And I will look after you both now. Come and eat. I have prepared a wedding feast."

The next three weeks were magical, despite Maftur's initial fears during the first week of the honeymoon that the wedding night ritual might have left her pregnant. She never thought she would ever have been pleased to see a period but she cried with joy when it put in its appearance a few days early. After that she had no worries. Ismail kept his promise and used protection on every occasion when they made love.

Although it was the hottest time of the year, they made the most of early morning and late evening when a fresh breeze blew through the estate.

Each day, as soon as it was light, Umm Saleh laid out their breakfast of warm stone-baked pitta bread, homemade jams, coffee and hard-boiled eggs in Ismail's favourite boyhood retreat, a hut with three stone walls and a wooden roof, once used by shepherds to shelter flocks from winter rain. Afterwards she and Ismail wandered around the estate, talking, exchanging small secrets while watching workers pick fruit in the orchards—tomatoes, melons, lettuces and cucumbers in well-irrigated fields, and figs from trees surrounding a small vineyard. They visited two cool, stone outbuildings, one where men boxed fruit and vegetables intended for the local market, and the other where women cut apples into rings, halved peaches and tomatoes before taking them outside to dry under the blazing August sun next to whole figs and bunches of grapes.

Later in the day, as the sun rose higher and the heat became unbearable, they retreated to the house, where thick walls and tiny windows lowered the temperature by ten degrees. After a light lunch they headed for their bedroom to make love, exchange deeper secrets and sleep until the day grew cooler.

During one of these intimate siestas, Maftur told Ismail how her brothers were supporting their friend Habib in his mission to avenge Ahmed's death, and spoke of her concerns about Patsy's safety when her brothers found out that Ahmed had intended to see Patsy on the day of his death.

Ismail couldn't believe that her urban-raised brothers were still going in for blood feuds in the twentieth century, and disputed the fact that Ahmed had been murdered.

"Let's face it, Ahmed was a German agent killed in action. There was no great conspiracy."

"Then why didn't the police bring his body back for an investigation and decent burial?"

"Diplomatic reasons, I should imagine. Remember, the British were on the brink of invading Vichy-controlled Syria. They wouldn't want to upset the native population."

"That's not the way my brothers see it."

She wasn't sure that was the way she saw it, either. She wasn't against the idea of her brothers avenging Ahmed's death, her only concern being that Patsy was probably innocent of bringing it about.

"I suspect your brothers and this Habib are more bluster than action," Ismail replied. "It's four months since they discovered Ahmed's body, and since they have done nothing about it so far, except talk, I don't think you need worry about Patsy Quigley."

For the first time she realised how differently she and Ismail viewed the world. She must attempt to see things from his point of view, but did that mean she had to agree with him about everything? The uncomfortable thought worried her. So she banished it to the back of her mind. What mattered was working to make her marriage a success.

The day after that conversation, when they came back to the house for lunch, they received a forwarded letter addressed in English to both of them. The original postmark was Haifa, but neither of them recognised the handwriting.

"If it's addressed to both of us, it can't be work," Ismail said, "so you open it, Maftur."

Full of curiosity, Maftur tore open the envelope and pulled out a wedding invitation.

Mr. & Mrs. Shepard request the pleasure of the company of
Mr. and Mrs. Ismail Shawwa
at the marriage of
Miss Dalia Leitner to Inspector Peter Monteith
at Bethesda Hall, Allenby Road, Haifa
on Saturday 4th October at 11.30 o'clock
and afterwards at 137, Pine Street, Mount Carmel.

Ismail smiled. "That will please my parents."

"I would have thought they would be upset at our going to a British function to which they weren't invited."

"If it were an invitation to a funeral or tea-party, they would have been," Ismail said, "but we're going to this wedding because you're a friend of the bride. They'll be pleased, because we'll be increasing our circle of British acquaintances."

They received another invitation that day—to dinner with Ismail's sister, Khawlah, and his brother-in-law, at their modern house in Nablus town.

Despite Maftur's initial reservations, it proved an enjoyable occasion. The meal was well-cooked, and Ismail and his brother-in-law obviously got on well. While the two men talked law, Maftur became better acquainted with her sister-in-law. They arranged to go shopping on the day Ismail had set aside to audit the estate accounts.

After two hours of wandering around shops, where she bought gifts for her family, and toured a huge soap factory, Maftur was glad when Khawlah suggested they stop for a light lunch in the cool interior of a cafe in the square.

While they were eating tabbouleh and pitta bread, Maftur asked Khawlah, who was five years older than Ismail, if she could remember moving to Palestine from Saudi Arabia and why they had moved.

"I remember it well. It was just after the First World War. Ismail was only a toddler. My father wrote to my mother saying the British had given him a fine piece of land with a house outside Nablus, and we were to join him straight away."

"Why did the British give your father land?"

"He had been with Lawrence fighting the Turks."

"I didn't know that."

"Oh, quite a hero, my father. The emir of Transjordan thinks very highly of him."

"When did he train as a lawyer?"

"That was before the war. Even after the British had given him the land, he wanted to go on being a lawyer but, instead of selling the land to Jews and going back to Saudi, he opened up a solicitor's office here and employed an estate manager. When Palestine officially came under British government he took out Palestinian citizenship."

"Did your husband come from Saudi?"

"Yes, but he has Palestinian citizenship now. He was studying law at Cairo University when we were first betrothed. My father gave him a job in his office when we married. Once he was a Palestinian citizen, he studied law under the government. When he qualified, my father made him manager here and opened up an office in Haifa for himself, because my mother fancied living there. I hear Ismail will run an office in Jerusalem once my father has finished negotiations for suitable premises, or more likely—" Khawlah laughed as she picked up an olive "—when my mother thinks she has trained you sufficiently to run your own household."

Maftur sighed. The main drawback of not going to England was that after the honeymoon she would return, not to a home of her own, but to the Shawwa's house in Haifa. Mrs. Shawwa had stipulated the couple live there until Maftur was capable of running a household in the style to which her son was accustomed.

"Have you any idea when that is likely to be?"

"If it were left to my mother—never. However, my father's hoping to get negotiations over the office in Jerusalem finished by the end of December."

Chapter 35

The day after they returned to Haifa, Maftur's father-in-law whisked Ismail off to the office, and her mother-in-law presented her with a rigorous six month training plan, from domestic cleaning, through cookery to household accounts.

"You can't expect servants to work their best, unless you can do everything better than they can."

Maftur, terrified of causing a rift between her husband and his mother, did her utmost to prove herself a competent housewife and keep any unpleasantness away from Ismail.

Her mother-in-law kept her hard at work all day, except for the one day a week when her father-in-law closed the office, or when she made her twice monthly visits to her mother. Otherwise, Mrs. Shawwa released her from housekeeping chores only for the half-hour after Ismail returned from the office, so she could go up to their bedroom where, as a good wife, she was expected to act as her husband's valet.

All day she looked forward to that half hour alone with Ismail, a break from the stifling atmosphere of the women's quarter, when Ismail could fill her in on news from the outside world.

She so missed having her own copy of the Palestine Post, and hated having to rely on Mr. Shawwa's brief comments as he skimmed through the paper before taking it to work. While the others listened to the wireless after supper, her task was to supervise the maids' washing-up, to make sure they put things away correctly, and left an immaculate kitchen for her mother-in-law to enter the following morning. By the time she returned to the living room, Ismail had usually accompanied his father to the coffee shop where they would discuss the daily news with her own father and other men opposed to the Grand Mufti's party.

When Ismail returned, she was usually already in bed. He wouldn't want to waste love-making time on trivial matters, such as the battles in Russia and the Western Desert that had already been discussed in full at the coffee shop. Nor would she want him to. Loving Ismail was the most important thing in her life. Domestic slavery to her mother-in-law would not last forever. Soon she would set up her own home with Ismail, and would go out to work. She was already getting him to study job vacancies in Jerusalem. Meanwhile, to relieve the strain, she had fortnightly meetings with her mother, Elif and Safia, and then there was Dalia's wedding to look forward to—an event she and he would be attending without her mother-in-law.

The silver-printed invitation now occupied a prominent place on the Shawwa's mantelpiece. Ismail had been right in thinking it would please his parents. Her mother-in-law had even asked to take it to a local AWA meeting being hosted in her mother's apartment, but she had persuaded her it was too precious to risk losing.

It seemed strange at that AWA meeting to be sitting in her parents' living room as a guest, while Elif and Safia served the mint tea and cakes.

Once the meeting proper had started, Elif came and sat beside her. While the rest concentrated on Mrs. Shawwa's opening speech, Elif slipped a piece of paper into her hand. Under cover of looking through Janan's agenda, she read –

Ahmed will be avenged tonight.

Her immediate thought was that once Habib had killed Ahmed's murderer, her brothers would start looking in earnest for the woman they believed had lured him to his death.

She showed the note to Ismail as soon as he came upstairs to change that evening.

He withdrew his arms from around her, without taking the house-robe she was holding, sank on the bed and buried his face in his hands.

She hadn't expected the news to affect him like that. She sat beside him, not sure what to say.

He looked up at last. "Habipti, I'll have to go and talk sense into your brothers. Tell Umm I have to see a friend in trouble and don't know when I'll be back." He sprang up, gave her a perfunctory kiss, and was off.

She dropped the house-robe on the bed, and went out onto the balcony, watching him run over the road and down the steps to her family's backyard, before going down to pass his message on to her mother-in-law. That lady was not best pleased, especially when Maftur claimed she didn't know what the trouble was.

Ismail returned only a few minutes later. He can't have achieved much in that time, she thought. He brushed aside his mother's questions.

"I'll discuss it with my father later. Right now I need to change."

Maftur followed him upstairs. "How did it go?" she asked as he removed his jacket.

"Your brothers aren't at home. They've gone camping up north. I should have taken you seriously when you first told me about all this. I could at least have found out the name of the policeman being targeted and warned him."

She flung his house-robe at him, making him duck. "You'd have risked my brothers' lives to save a murdering British Policeman?"

He lifted his head and eyed her warily. "Of course I wouldn't, habipti. I'd have spoken to the man off-record."

She clenched her fists. "You can't do that with the British. They'd have arrested you."

"No, habibti, they wouldn't arrest me."

"What makes you so special?"

He gave a wry smile. "I went to a British public school, remember?"

Maftur picked his house-robe from the bed and handed it to him.

"I just hope your brothers fail," he said as he pulled it on.

She picked up one of his shoes.

He added hastily, "And get away safely, of course."

Two days later, her father-in-law read aloud a piece from The Palestine Post, reporting the death of an Inspector Peter Monteith who had been mortally wounded in an exchange of gunfire with smugglers near Al-Bassa in Northern Palestine. While Maftur gazed at Ismail in horror, her mother-in-law looked across the table at the mantelpiece, her face revealing her disappointment. She walked over and took down the wedding invitation.

That's when the enormity of what her brothers and their

friends had done hit her. Her friend Dalia had broken with her parents because of Inspector Monteith, so she must have loved him dearly. How would she be feeling now? Would she go back to her parents? If not, what would happen to her?

She sat down at the desk in their bedroom late that evening to write a letter of condolence to Dalia, but could find no words to put on paper. Guilt overwhelmed her. She put her head down on the desk and sobbed.

That was how Ismail found her when he came back from the coffee shop. He put his arms around her. She buried her forehead in his shoulder.

"It's all my fault, Ismail. I knew what was happening. I even thought it right."

Ismail stroked her hair. "I'm to blame as much as you, habibti. I didn't take your warning seriously. I shall have to warn the police now before we have a second tragedy."

Maftur lifted her head in alarm. "No, my darling, please don't go to the police. They'll put my brothers in prison."

"It's your friend Patsy I'm thinking of. We can't allow your brothers to harm her. Is there any way we can stop them, apart from telling the police?"

Maftur put her arms round him. "Our only hope is to prove Patsy innocent."

"I'll start enquiries tomorrow morning."

When Ismail returned from work the following evening, however, he had had no success. None of his British friends in the CID would talk about a mission in which two German agents had been killed.

Maftur wrote to Patsy again, urging her to leave Palestine. She received a brief note back, thanking her for her advice, saying she had found a job in Cairo and would be leaving for Egypt the next day.

For obvious reasons, I won't be returning to Palestine in the immediate future. I'll send my address when I have found digs.

She was glad Patsy had taken her advice, but felt sad her friend would be cut off from her parents. She was sure Ismail was right and Patsy was innocent. She must continue in her attempts to prove it.

She asked Elif if there had been any developments in her brothers' attempts to discover the identity of the mystery woman. Elif said they were still working on it. They thought it might be a policewoman.

Ismail laughed when she took that back to him. "There are no women in the British section of the Palestine police, except for the very respectable middle-aged wife of one of the police inspectors, responsible for the women's prison. Even your brothers couldn't suspect her of being a Mata Hari. However, it sounds as if they are getting closer to finding out who Ahmed had hoped to meet in Haifa."

There was just one other person Maftur felt might be able to help, and that was Habib's sister Suzannah, who worked for Mr. Shepard's family. Patsy's mother had helped Suzannah when she was a child, but was it safe to let Suzannah know the name of the woman? Her loyalty to her brother might overcome her gratitude to Mrs. Quigley.

She wrote to her in Arabic. It was a forlorn hope at the best but she had to try.

Dear Suzannah,

I am the sister of two friends of your brother. Your brother and mine believe a woman was responsible for the death of one of their mutual friends. I do not believe that was so. Is there any way you can find out the true circumstances in which their friend died?

Maftur Nour bint al-Zeid

Towards the end of December, Ismail brought a letter addressed in English to her at the Shawwa Law office, care of Mr. Ismail Shawwa. It had a Jenin postmark.

Ismail gave a grin as he handed it over. "What is this you are trying to hide from my mother?" he asked.

Maftur was genuinely mystified, and said so. She looked at the address carefully but didn't recognise the handwriting. Turning to the back of the envelope, she saw it was from a Miss Suzanna Hadad.

She tore the envelope open and read.

Dear Maftur Nour,

Since receiving your letter I have made enquiries amongst relatives of Christian Arab policemen to find out the truth. I found one policeman who was a member of Inspector Monteith's team when Ahmed al-Zeid died. He is the fiancé of a woman you went to school with, Michelle Boutaji.

Michelle's fiancé told her family about the operation in which

Ahmed al-Zeid was captured although he didn't know Ahmed's name. He told them how his squad, led by Inspector Monteith, spent weeks trailing a hashish smuggler hired by Germans and, as a result, they ambushed him when he was meeting a spy employed directly by the Grand Mufti. Unfortunately, the smuggler pulled out a knife while Inspector Monteith was cautioning him. The other police shot the smuggler. The spy was caught in crossfire and killed by accident.

I gave this account to my brother, who has talked with Michelle's fiancé. He now realises whatever woman Ahmed had been intending to meet before he died was irrelevant to his murder.

Please could you pass this letter on to your brothers and ask them to get in touch with Habib to confirm the truth of this.

Yours sincerely,
Suzanna Hadad

There was a separate page containing a short paragraph –

P.S. I found out who the woman is but haven't told my brother. Her mother was very good to me when I was a child so that is why I started making enquiries. Do not give this page to your brothers.

Maftur showed the whole letter to Ismail.

"Right," he said. "Put on your coat and hijab. Tell my mother I have an important legal matter to discuss with Abu Kamal and I'm taking you on a surprise visit to your mother." He placed the postscript in a drawer and handed her back the letter.

After Maftur had delivered her message to a tight-lipped mother-in-law, she and Ismail walked around the corner to the al-Zeid family block. She was silent on the way, feeling guilty that she hadn't been the one to resolve the situation.

While Ismail spoke to her father, Maftur showed the letter to her mother, who agreed that she should give it to Dodi.

"It would be terrible to have an innocent woman killed. One death is sufficient to avenge Ahmed al-Zeid."

Dodi was out when she went up to the apartment, so she showed it to Elif.

"I am so pleased," Elif said after reading the letter. "I could not believe my husband still clung to these barbarous notions of family honour. Perhaps, realising he could have murdered an innocent woman will give him occasion to reflect. I will certainly see to it that he contacts Habib—and tonight if possible."

The next day Maftur received a brief note from Elif saying that Ahmed's friends were no longer searching for the mystery British woman and wrote a letter of gratitude to Suzannah straight away.

She started a letter to Patsy, telling her it was now safe to return to Palestine, but realised she couldn't tell her why.

"Leave it," Ismail urged. "You can't write to Egypt about it, anyway. The censors will read your letter, and then where will your brothers be?"

"But I should do something. I should have been the one to prove Patsy innocent. What sort of friend am I, leaving it all to someone else?"

"Maftur," Ismail said, "this is real life, not a romance. In real life one person doesn't solve everything. People take turns in being heroic. Proving Patsy's innocence means even more to Suzanna than it does to you. Peter Monteith was a frequent visitor at the house where she worked. How do you think she felt when her brother murdered him? How much worse do you think she would have felt if she knew her brother had aided and abetted the assassination of the only child of a woman who had befriended her?"

Maftur bit her lip. Ismail was right. She had been intent on her own feelings when she should have been concentrating on other people. She determined to learn from the incident.

She wrote, instead, asking Patsy if she could name her as a referee when she applied for jobs, and added that she had good news which she would tell her when Patsy was next in Palestine.

She felt a lot happier when, a week or so later, she received a cheerful letter from Patsy.

"I'm so relieved Patsy seems happy in Egypt," she told Ismail. "She is visiting museums in her spare time and still hopes to go to university in England after the war. She's climbed a pyramid and been on picnics in the desert. She's in the most awful digs, though, cockroaches all over the bathroom floor and traffic noise all night, but the woman she shares the apartment with is really nice." She couldn't help adding, "But she doesn't say anything about coming back to Palestine to see her parents. I'm sure she would have spent

Christmas at home if she had known it was safe."

A few days after Christmas she read in the paper that Patsy's father had died suddenly of a heart attack. At least Patsy could come up to her father's funeral without danger of being assassinated.

She wrote to her straight away, sending condolences, and adding it was safe for her to make the journey to Jerusalem. She found out afterwards that Patsy did not receive that letter until she had returned to Egypt after the funeral.

Chapter 36

A full end-of-year moon shone through open french doors on furniture stripped of all cloths and ornaments. Large cubes filled the middle of the room. Woken by a screeching siren, Maftur surveyed the room in befuddled bewilderment, until she remembered it was the day for which she had been waiting, and the cubes were merely packed tea chests. Having successfully orientated herself in time and space, she sat up and shook Ismail.

"Wake up, habibi."

"Ya lel!" he muttered. "Couldn't the Nazis leave us alone for our last night?"

He turned and kissed her before sitting up. She swung her feet over the side of the bed and winced as they hit stone-cold tiles. By the time Ismail had peeled off his pyjama top, Maftur had already donned a headscarf and was kneeling on the floor, shivering, as she wrestled with the stiff hasp of her overnight case. She looked up. "What's the time?"

Ismail consulted his luminous watch. "Ten past two."

Ack-ack guns thundered. The hasp sprung on the case. Maftur found her dressing-gown, tugged it over her head, and took out her slippers. The first bombs whistled down.

"What will be, will be," she told herself firmly, in an attempt to quell her churning stomach. She put on her slippers and moved across the room, intending to close the blackout curtains before opening the door to the corridor where her mother-in-law kept a light switched on all night. Before she reached the curtains, a crash—louder even than the ack-ack guns—rocked the room. The sky turned red.

She pulled open the french doors and ran out onto the covered balcony, hearing the tattoo of shrapnel on its roof, smelling winter sharpness in the air. Leaping flames from the harbour far below pushed up a plume of black smoke that blocked the stars. Fire danced across the water. Ack-ack guns crashed out in defiance. Searchlights criss-crossed the sky, highlighting barrage balloons. High above the balloons, something flared red, before plunging brightly into the sea.

Ismail, dressed in his house-robe, took her hands and pulled her inside. She kept one hand in his for comfort but freed the other to draw the curtains, creating instant darkness.

Groping their way across the room, they bumped into packing cases and chairs. Another string of whistling bombs curdled the contents of her stomach. Her fingers found the door handle. They could see again. In the corridor they hastily closed the door.

"Hurry," Ismail urged, "before Umm sends out a search party."

They raced down marble stairs, still holding hands. Ismail opened the heavy oak door guarding their air-raid shelter, dug deep into the mountainside. The air inside hung heavy with paraffin fumes from a portable stove.

Her mother-in-law poked her head through the curtains surrounding the women's sleeping quarters. "What kept you?"

"I had to unpack my dressing-gown, Belle Mere."

She wondered why every explanation she made to her mother-in-law came out as an apology. She comforted herself with the reminder that by the end of the day she would be a hundred miles away and mistress of her own household.

Ismail reached for a tin hat hanging from a peg on the rock wall. "It's bad this time, Umm. The whole harbour's on fire."

"Well, we're safe enough here, Allah be praised," his mother replied. "Ismail, put back that hat. I told your father that he has to get used to patrolling alone. Now settle down and get some sleep, both of you."

Maftur parted the curtains and entered feminine territory. She dropped onto a comfortably-mattressed camp bed next to her mother-in-law, happy that Ismail would not be walking the street in a hail of shrapnel. Thick rock shut out the sound of both gunfire and bombs.

She woke to a fragrance of roasting coffee beans, and peeked through the curtains. Four elderly neighbours, an Arab, two Jews and a Guatemelan sat on chairs, clutching tin mugs. Her mother-in-law, still in her dressing-gown, was supervising two servants as they boiled eggs and cut bread at the kitchen end of the shelter. Her father-in-law, fully clothed but without his tin helmet, sat at a small table beneath a telephone extension. No sign of Ismail. Presumably he was still sleeping, or else engaged in prayer. She looked at the clock near the phone—six am.

"Umm Ismail," she called out. "You should have woken me. The removal van is due."

It was her father-in-law instead of her mother-in-law who replied.

"Maftur, oil is burning across the harbour. Tugs are towing an ammunition ship out into the bay. If it blows up, every vehicle and building in town will be destroyed. The police have blocked all roads into Haifa. Until the ammunition ship reaches clear water, everyone must remain in the shelters."

She visualised her parents, her brothers, her sisters-in-law, her nephews and nieces in their basement shelter with no escape tunnel. If their apartment block collapsed it would bury her family alive. She remembered the ferocity of the flames in the harbour. The ammunition ship stood no chance. Her bowels loosened and she rushed to the commode in the corner of the partition.

Afterwards, she washed carefully in the prescribed manner with water from a ewer that stood on a marble washstand. It seemed important to focus on ritual.

She had almost finished when Fatima, one of the servants, brought in the day clothes she had left out on a tea-chest in her bedroom the previous night.

"Fatima, you shouldn't have risked your life getting those for me."

"I didn't, Miss Maftur. Your husband went upstairs for them, despite what the mistress said to him."

She slipped on the dress she had reserved for this long-anticipated day, but the shimmering blue silk felt wrong, unsuited to struggling through rubble.

She laid aside her frivolous matching straw hat with its Hollywood-style half veil, and tied her hijab back over her dampened hair with trembling hands. She performed her prayers, concentrating on the meaning of the over-familiar words. Afterwards she peered again through the curtains. Ismail was there, in his office suit with his briefcase at his feet, going through legal papers with his father as if he were at the office. How could they be so calm?

She dropped back on the bed, her fists clenched as she anticipated the big bang signalling the destruction of everything she knew and held dear.

The telephone rang. Her father-in-law answered it. He looked around the shelter, his face beaming.

"The all-clear is sounding outside."

Maftur's dress felt right again. She tore off her scarf, pinned on her hat, and left the women's partition, smiling broadly. Ismail packed away his papers. She couldn't kiss him goodbye in public, so let her eyes beam her love.

His eyes signalled a response, as he spoke staidly. "Ya Maftur, remind the taxi to pick me up at the office."

He went off with his father.

Her mother-in-law placed a boiled egg and a slice of buttered bread on the table. "It will save the servants extra work if you eat here. Afterwards you can go upstairs and brush your hair properly."

Maftur hardly tasted the food as she gulped it down.

Upstairs she combed her hair and then stepped out onto the carved stone balcony to stare down at the harbour. Apart from blackened decks and the smashed bridge of one cruiser, there were no obvious signs of damage. Even the black smoke had dispersed. It was a fresh blue-skied day.

From here she could see right across Acre Bay, to white-capped Mount Hermon guarding the Northern horizon. Over the road, slightly below the balcony, her young cousins raced round the rainwater tanks on the roof of her own family's apartment block, just as she had done at their age, except that now, instead of playing tag, they were collecting shrapnel.

She had been on that roof opposite in the summer holidays nine years before, the first time she had met Ismail, when he had acknowledged her as a real person by offering her one of his sweets.

She stored the memory back for future use and looked farther down the slope, picking out Haifa High School where she had first mixed with Christian girls as well as Muslim. From there her gaze wandered over the secretarial school with memories of more friends. She followed the road down to Kingsway near the harbour and smiled as she remembered the carefree hours she had spent gossiping in cafes and milk bars.

She loved that town. Before her marriage, she would never have believed she would be happy leaving it. If only Ahmed had been Ismail, then they could have had their own home there on Mount Carmel.

A large removal lorry rumbled up the street, followed by a taxi. She picked up the overnight bags. The one hundred mile journey might go without a hitch but, with cars and lorries frequently breaking down, and spare parts like gold dust, who knows where she and Ismail might have to spend the next night?

Downstairs, her mother-in-law took time off from supervising the removal men to say goodbye.

"I don't like the idea of you running a house on your own. You still have so much to learn," she said for the umpteenth time that week.

Maftur combed all indignation from her tone as she stooped to kiss her. "Ya Umm Ismail, I won't be running it on my own, not with Umm Saleh there to help me at the beginning. You know she'll put me to rights. And that maid, Ishfaq, you found me, she seems reliable. Anyway, it's only a small flat, not a big house like this."

"But you still need more training, dear. Don't mistake me. Your parents were quite right to give you an education but…" She paused as she looked to see how the removal men were doing.

Maftur tried not to smile. How difficult her mother-in-law found combining traditional matriarchy with the modern outlook demanded by her husband.

Her mother-in law returned her attention to the conversation. "It's not too late to change your mind and stay on for a few weeks. The servants can look after Ismail in Jerusalem. It will make him all the more pleased to see you when you join him."

Maftur hid her laughter well. "Now you don't really expect me to do that, Umm Ismail. If your son becomes unhappy with the way I run our household I'll give him permission to grumble to you."

Her mother-in-law caught sight of one of the removal men knocking a desk against the side of the van. Taking advantage of the subsequent altercation, Maftur handed the overnight bags to the taxi driver and climbed into the car's back seat.

Her mother-in-law poked her head through the window. "You will tell me just as soon as there is any *news*, won't you?"

"Yes, Belle Mere of course," Maftur replied, careful still not to show her feelings.

Her mother-in-law signalled the driver to start.

Maftur sank back against the leather seat. Independence at last! She doubted if she could have kept her temper with Ismail's mother for even another month, but she dutifully waved out of the window until the taxi swung round the bend.

She stopped it outside her own family's apartment block. Her mother, sister-in-law, nephews and nieces, school friends, and the next-door Jewish neighbours were waiting on the pavement to bid her farewell, the younger women armed with hand-embroidered tapestry bolsters for her new living room. To her relief, the taxi driver succeeded in stowing all the bolsters in the boot.

As she climbed back into the taxi, her mother said, "You will let me know when you change your mind and let me have any *news*, won't you?"

Maftur didn't need to be so circumspect with her own mother, "For Allah's sake, Umm, I'm not a baby factory, you know."

Looking at her mother's crest-fallen face, she relented, came out of the taxi, and hugged her. "Umm, you have always told me a woman should have qualifications, so she can earn her own living if left to look after children by herself. With Ismail's full approval, I have sent off several applications for jobs in Jerusalem. Patsy Quigley is one of my referees."

She saw the conflicting emotions on her mother's face.

"You already have seven wonderful grandchildren, Umm. There's no real urgency for any more. But I promise, if I do get pregnant, you'll be the first to know."

She stopped the taxi again outside her father-in-law's office on Kingsway. Ismail stood on the sidewalk, wearing the pin-striped grey suit, with toning trilby, in which he had left home. His briefcase bulged and several paper bags, overflowing with files, lay at his feet. She felt her chest swell with pride. She had the most handsome husband in town.

The driver couldn't fit the files into the bolster-crammed boot, so he proceeded to stack the files beside her on the back seat until Ismail interfered.

"I will be sitting beside my wife."

The driver, his back signalling disapproval, transferred the files to the front passenger seat.

Twirling his military-style moustache, her father-in-law strode out of the office to make his farewells. "I will be up next week to see how the new office is doing, ya Maftur. I'll be bringing Umm Ismail with me, so make sure your guestroom is in order. Don't say a word about it to her though, as I haven't told her yet. It's to be a surprise."

And just who had put the idea of that 'surprise' into her father-in-law's head, Maftur wondered in irritation, as she smiled politely.

The taxi moved off. Ismail glanced through the dividing glass to check the driver was concentrating on the road, before he nibbled her ear. "You're looking really beautiful this morning, habipti," he whispered. "Is that a new outfit?"

Maftur slid a complacent hand over the blue silk. "I bought it for our honeymoon but saved it for this day."

She squeezed his arm and lay back against the cushions. "Now that we're moving into our own home, I feel truly married at last."

Chapter 37

Maftur was enjoying a leisurely breakfast alone with Ismail, recovering from her in-law's last visit. A brief respite—her mother-in-law had threatened another visit in a week's time. She wondered in what area she would be found wanting, then.

Ishfaq, their maid, brought her a letter, postmarked 'Jerusalem'.

Mystified because she was sure no one in Jerusalem knew her address, she turned the envelope over. "Ismail, it's from Patsy Quigley."

"Open it, then," he said, putting down his newspaper.

"She's on compassionate leave after her father's funeral, and wants to meet up with me tomorrow afternoon at that milk bar on Ben Yehuda Street."

"That's good. It's about time you had a bit of social life."

"Ooh, and listen to this, she says the Post Office asked her for a reference and she's sent it."

"Well done, habipti." Ismail rose from his chair and kissed her. "Now I will have a working wife who can entertain me with fresh gossip every evening." His voice held a slightly wistful note as he added, "I shall miss you not being here to greet me when I come up from the office, though."

A smile surrounded her answer. "I haven't got the job yet and, even if I do, you needn't walk upstairs until I've come home."

The following afternoon, Maftur walked the short distance to Ben Yehuda Street, its cafés and shops still busy despite the war, but there were more service uniforms than tourists' cotton frocks and linen jackets. Patsy stood outside the milk bar where they had arranged to meet.

At first she didn't recognized the stunning woman in an ecru linen suit and matching straw hat, all broad curving brim in front and collapsing chimney pot on top. As well as looking elegant, Patsy appeared confident, very different from the tense woman she had known six months previously. The change surprised her. With her father dying so recently, she had expected Patsy to look even unhappier.

"I was so sorry when I heard about your father," she said.

"Yes, it was quite a shock. It was worse for my mother, of course. There he was, sharing Sunday dinner with her one minute, and dead the next."

"How is she coping?"

"Far better than I expected. She's even applied to go back into nursing."

"That's really brave of her."

They entered the milk bar, narrow and ill-lit, so unlike the one with large plate glass windows that she and her friends had patronised in Haifa.

After they had ordered milk shakes and found a table, she told Patsy that she'd got an interview at the Post Office, and thanked her for giving her a reference.

Patsy held up her hands in protest. "That was the least I could do after all you've done for me." Then she leaned across the table and lowered her voice. "I can't begin to say how grateful I am to you putting me in the clear with Ahmed's pals. It would have been so difficult staying on with my mother while they were gunning for me. I only found out what you had done when Suzanna told me last week."

Maftur's conscience twinged. "Suzanna put in all the detective work. All I did was notify Ahmed's friends."

Patsy looked surprised. "That's not how Suzanna tells it. She just said she was passing on a message from you."

Suzanna, Maftur realised, would be even more anxious than she was not to reveal her brother had any part in the affair. She wished she hadn't been so quick to give credit where credit was due, and hastily changed the subject. "How did Suzanna seem when you saw her?"

"Enthusiastic about her new job."

"Too enthusiastic, I'd say. Did she tell you the teacher at a local village school asked to marry her?"

Patsy raised her eyebrows. "No! When's the wedding?"

"Not for some time. Suzanna told her uncle she didn't mind being betrothed so long as she didn't have to marry until she qualified. Her mother backed her up. Would you believe it?"

Patsy laughed. "You were a bit like that yourself at one time."

"I wasn't betrothed to my Ismail then."

"Your Ismail is one in a million, Maftur. Even in England, most husbands don't like their wives going out to work. At least, they didn't before the war. Many don't get much say in it at the moment."

"I just hope I get this job."

"Nowadays, British admin don't send for references until security has cleared the candidates and they only interview people they intend to appoint." Patsy lowered her voice again. "I was surprised you applied for a Post Office job, though. Aren't you worried about working for the British with the Germans so close to invading?"

Maftur detected a false note. It wasn't like the British to voice the possibility that Rommel could occupy Palestine. She gave a cautious answer. "The Germans wouldn't sack native workers just because our previous government was British, and Ismail, praise Allah, has always refrained from expressing political views."

Patsy nodded. "True, but the Germans might target you and Ismail because of your father-in-law's indiscretion."

Maftur shivered. Patsy had touched on her worst fear. "I've not really thought about that aspect. I don't think I need worry, however. Ismail himself is the soul of discretion." She was not comfortable with the direction the conversation was going. She had to change the subject. "Have you seen Dalia recently?"

"Yes. Oddly enough at the same time I saw Suzanna. Dalia was on a field trip to Megiddo from her university. I hardly recognised her in shorts and blouse. She looked really fit. So different from when I last saw her at Peter's funeral."

"What's she doing at university?"

"A degree in agriculture."

"That's a bit different from secretarial work!"

"Well, she owns her own orange grove in el Tireh. She's probably thinking of settling there."

They chatted on, gradually relaxing into the carefree comradeship of their younger days.

Patsy suggested they meet up again the next time she was

in Jerusalem.

Reflecting on their conversation as she walked home, though, Maftur wondered whether Patsy had really wanted to see her, or had merely been checking out her political loyalties, on behalf of the Post Office, perhaps.

Chapter 38

The letter inviting Maftur to an interview arrived the day following her in-laws' latest visit. Praise Allah, she thought, the letter didn't come while my mother-in-law was still here.

If Ismail still had reservations about a working wife, he hid them well. He seemed almost as ecstatic as she was.

After she had waved him goodbye from the top of the stairs, Maftur moved on to their bedroom and took two gift-wrapped boxes of sugar-coated almonds from a cupboard, before walking towards the kitchen.

As usual, after one of her mother-in-law's visitations, she had to remind herself that this was her kitchen, and threw back her shoulders. She found Umm Saleh sitting at the scrubbed table, shortening the velvet curtains Ismail's mother had brought up 'to make the guestroom presentable'.

Umm Saleh returned her greeting with a smile, putting down the curtain and pulling a notebook and pencil from the pocket of her starched apron. Behind her, at the deep sink, Ishfaq looked up from washing the extra crockery Ismail's mother had considered essential to every well run household, and gave a respectful bob.

Maftur placed the almonds on the kitchen table. "I want to thank you both for the hard work you have put into making the apartment so comfortable. Umm Ismail was very pleased with your efforts. Once those curtains are ready for the guestroom, and we have the right crockery for every occasion, I am confident she will find no fault with our housekeeping next time she comes." She looked at the new crockery. "I suppose we need to keep a tally of that lot. Ishfaq, when you've finished washing them, will you add them to our crockery inventory."

She reached into a drawer and pulled out the relevant notebook from several her mother-in-law had made her write up as they had packed chests back in Haifa. In this one she had already had to cross out three plates, broken since her arrival.

She held the notebook out to Ishfaq, who looked at her

in dismay and put her hands behind her back.

"What's the matter, Ishfaq? Have we had more breakages? If so, don't worry. These things happen."

"It's not that," Umm Saleh put in. "Ishfaq has never been to school. She can't write. Most country girls who start in service so young can't write."

"I am so sorry, Ishfaq, I didn't know."

She was about to say she would teach her, when she remembered that if the Post Office took her on she wouldn't have the time. She sat at the table beside Umm Saleh and waited until Ishfaq had returned to work, before asking in a lower voice, "Umm Saleh, has my mother-in-law told you how long you will be working here?"

Umm Saleh replied in an equally low tone, "Not exactly, Maftur Nour. She said that unless you were expecting, I was to go back to Nablus in a month's time."

Maftur nodded. She knew that Umm Saleh's main role in the family was taking over the household reins for women with new babies, and training young nursery nurses to the standard her mother-in-law demanded. Umm Saleh was only there because her mother-in-law thought she hadn't acquired the skills needed to train her own servants.

"Well, I'm not pregnant, but I hope I can rely on your assistance when I am. While you're with me, however, I would very much appreciate it if you would train a housekeeper for me in the ways of the Shawwa family. Do you know anyone you can recommend?"

Umm Saleh gave the matter some thought. "The Shawwa family nearly always choose their staff from families on the Nablus estate. I have a cousin there, recently widowed, whose children are now grown. Before she married, she assisted the cook in your mother-in-law's kitchen. I am sure she would prefer to be working again rather than having to live under her son's roof."

"There's one thing you need to know. I may be going out to work before you leave."

She watched the older woman carefully. Observing the consternation on her face, she told her prepared lie. Glancing at Ishfaq, she lowered her voice still further, "My doctor recommended it. He said that it might help me to get pregnant if I stopped worrying about it."

Umm Saleh seemed satisfied. "A sensible man, that doctor. I can see with my own eyes that things are right between you and Ismail, so perhaps it is that you are both trying too hard."

The new cook/housekeeper arrived three days later, a friendly woman who, Umm Saleh said, needed very little training, so all Maftur had to worry about was her interview.

Ismail found out from a friend that the appointment of shorthand typists at the Post Office was left to the supervisor of the typing pool. "She'll give you tests to check on your shorthand and typing skills. And ask you a few basic questions."

"Oh, Habibi, I've no office experience of shorthand."

"That's all right. I'll send my clerk out on errands and dictate my office letters to you."

On the appointed day, despite Ismail's assurance that her clothes were right for the occasion and her shorthand was excellent, Maftur set out feeling nervous.

The imposing Post and Telegraph building was only two hundred yards or so farther up the Jaffa Road but each step eroded her confidence.

As directed in her letter, she crossed the main Post Office hall with its Italian marble counters and went through a side door, framed in black basalt that opened onto a lobby with stairs leading up from it. An elderly man, in post office uniform, sat on a bentwood chair behind a small wooden desk. He checked her appointment and told her in English that the typing pool was on the first floor.

At the top of the stairs, double doors fitted with glass panels allowed a view of rows of young women, most with uncovered heads, sitting behind typewriters at individual desks. Large windows set high gave the room plenty of light. She pushed open the doors. At the front of the room, behind a large desk, a hard-faced middle-aged woman faced the typists. The woman looked up, beckoned her in and consulted a piece of paper.

"Mrs. Maftur Shawwa?"

Maftur nodded, scarcely able to speak.

The supervisor rose. "Follow me," she said in English

with a strong Polish accent, and led the way to a small cubicle behind her desk.

The typing and dictation tests took quarter of an hour.

The supervisor perused the results. "These are fine but, before I can offer you the job, for some reason best known to himself, the chief engineer wishes to see you."

Maftur received the impression that the supervisor resented this intrusion into her sphere of responsibility, and felt bewildered. Why would the chief engineer, the man in charge of the whole Post and Telegraph service in Palestine, want to interview her? This was not going the way Ismail had told it. Her nervous tension returned fourfold as she followed the supervisor to the top floor.

The chief engineer's secretary had a room to herself, a reception area with a frosted glass door shutting off an inner sanctum. Maftur gazed around in awe and envy. The secretary gave Maftur a professional smile and picked up a phone. "Mrs. Shawwa has arrived, Mr. Grant."

The glass door opened. A large man said, "Mrs. Shawwa, please come in."

He left the door open and motioned her to a comfortable leather armchair, some distance from the large polished desk where he seated himself. She had expected to be perched on a hard chair or high typing stool.

He complimented her on the results of her typing and shorthand tests and seemed impressed by the duties she had undertaken in her family offices. She had to concentrate hard to understand what he said—his accent was similar to a Scottish teacher at Haifa High, although more pronounced.

She was beginning to relax, until he said, "We dinna have any Muslim ladies on our staff. Most ladies are Christians from Beit Jala, although we have some Jews." He picked up a pipe from a metal plate on his desk and rammed tobacco into it. "How do you think you will fit in, lassie?"

Maftur wasn't sure how to answer. In Haifa, or at least that part of it in which she lived, it had not seemed important if a family was Muslim, Christian, or even come to that, middle east Jewish. Ismail had warned her things were different in Jerusalem, but she had assumed that would not apply to the government's Post and Telegraph service.

"I have many Christian friends," she tried. "I go to their weddings, they come to mine."

She had to stop talking to control an urge to giggle, as she visualised herself marrying and remarrying Ismail several times just so she could keep inviting Christian friends to her weddings.

The chief engineer held up his still unlit pipe after waiting a few seconds. "It may be best if we take you on for a trial period of three months and then review the situation. What do you say?"

Maftur hesitated only briefly. If she hadn't managed to fit in by that time, she wouldn't want to stay, anyway.

Chapter 39

It took some time for Maftur to fit into the typing pool at the Post Office. Her colleagues were not glamorous, independent role models like Dalia, Golda and Patsy. Such women did exist in Jerusalem, Ismail assured her, but mostly in private firms. The only government institution that employed women with superior skills was the secretariat housed in the West Wing of the King David Hotel.

The Arab women were all Christian and came from the same village. Most were younger than herself, very much under the protection of a few older married women who chaperoned them into work each day, and hustled them out to catch the Beit Jala bus as soon as the workday finished.

The Jewish women were more sophisticated but tended to keep to themselves.

Gradually, however, she managed to join in conversations during the short lunch break, and became accepted by both groups.

Her skills impressed the supervisor and she found herself being sent to take dictation from those male Post and Telegraph employees, high enough in the hierarchy to have private offices, but not high enough to have their own secretaries. The office doors on these occasions were always left reassuringly open.

She felt pleased to be gaining useful experience, and the money she earned came in useful.

Once Ismail was sure she had settled in, he bought a car, a red, third—or perhaps even fourth—hand Alvis Speed 20 SB.

For the first Saturday afternoon after the purchase, Maftur requested two hours unpaid leave, and they made a visit back to Haifa.

They drove down along the Seven Sisters to the coast road, crowded with military vehicles heading for Egypt. Although traffic in the opposite direction was comparatively light, long conveys of army lorries, travelling south, made overtaking trains of donkeys and camels a tricky business, so it was already dark before they drew up in front of the Shawwa's house. All Maftur's family had been invited over for a celebratory meal that evening but, scarcely had they walked in, when the air-raid alarm sounded.

So, instead of eating western style in her mother-in-law's expensive dining room, everyone clustered around old-style low tables in the Shawwas' huge air-raid shelter, men at one end, women and children at the other. The mountain rock kept out the crashes of ack-ack guns.

Maftur sat between her mother and Elif, who filled her in on all the local gossip. She was grateful to be back with family. Later in the evening, she, along with the other women, listened in some trepidation as, at the male end of the table, her father-in-law railed against Haj Amin al-Husseini whom he claimed had fled from Iraq to join Hitler. He followed the rant by an equally long paean of praise for Lawrence of Arabia and the British defeat of Germans and Turks in the First World War.

Maftur watched her brothers' faces. Although she knew they would disapprove, she hoped they were too loyal to betray her father-in-law to their Husseini party friends. However, if her father-in-law often spoke like this in coffee houses, he was putting himself and his family in danger. She looked at her mother's face and realised she was not the only one experiencing alarm.

Eventually, the night watchman came in to say the All-Clear had sounded. The women left to enjoy coffee in the living room while the men adjourned to the liwan.

She and Ismail rose late the next morning. Because of the heavy military traffic still rumbling south along the coast road, Ismail decided to take the old road to Jerusalem.

As they drove across the Plain of Esdraelon and up the dangerously steep road beyond, Maftur remained deep in thought over her father-in-law's rant. He was entitled to make himself a martyr but someone had to stop him endangering his son. She determined to say something to Ismail in as tactful a way as she could.

Back home, after a cold supper in their sitting room, Ishfaq placed the coffee pot on the brass table by the hand-embroidered bolsters.

Maftur poured the coffee and stirred in sugar, then snuggled down against the bolsters to rest her head on Ismail's shoulder. He placed his arm round her waist and they sat in companionable silence enjoying the privacy of their own home. She felt overwhelmingly fortunate to have him, and wondered if so great a love for one's great husband was sinful. She couldn't bear the thought of losing him.

As Ismail reached out for his coffee, she retrieved her own. "Habibi," she asked, "what makes your father so pro-British? Surely, it's not just because the British gave him land?"

Ismail smiled down at her. "Back into politics, are you? Even though you haven't attended an AWA meeting since we came to Jerusalem."

Maftur put down her coffee and gave him a playful punch. "I wasn't asking a political question."

Ismail laughed as his cup rattled on his saucer. "You're lucky my cup was empty or you'd be crying over a stained carpet. What do you mean you weren't asking a political question?"

Maftur thought hard as she tried to put her meaning into words. "People don't feel things for political reasons. It's more to do with their upbringing or personal experiences. They just use political slogans to justify their feelings."

Ismail kissed the top of her head. "You're right as usual, habipti. My father became pro-British because he wanted to get rid of the Turks."

"I know that much, but there has to be a personal reason for him still being pro-British. Many of his old war comrades support the Grand Mufti now."

She could tell by his frown of concentration that Ismail was thinking. Eventually he said, "I guess it was because of what happened to my father's elder brother. My uncle was already a conscript into the Ottoman army when my father joined the British."

"So they had to fight each other?"

"Fortunately, it never came to that. My father fought in the Sinai and round the Red Sea. My uncle never left Syria."

"Why does your father never speak of this uncle?"

"When my sister and I were little, Umm told us we weren't to ask about him because our father found his memory too painful." Ismail looked into his cup. "I'm getting myself more coffee. Do you want a refill?"

Maftur smiled. Her father-in-law might spout pro-British sentiments but it was his son who had imbibed British manners.

She felt a frisson of guilty pleasure as she handed over her cup. What would her mother-in-law say if she could see her now, allowing her husband to pour her coffee? While he poured, she thought how sad it was to have two brothers on opposite sides in a war.

Ismail returned with full cups and settled down.

Maftur snuggled back close. "Was your uncle killed in the war?"

He sat up straighter. "You could say so. He went down with dysentery. His men took him to a hospital in Damascus but the German and Turkish medical staff fled before the British took it." He stared at the pattern on the precious Persian carpet, a wedding gift from her in-laws. With his gaze still lowered, he said, "Lawrence found my uncle's body piled with many others on the foul floor of the abandoned hospital. He ordered Turkish and German prisoners to clean up. Later, he wrote a full account of what he found in the hospital."

He stood up, went to the bookshelf that completely filled one wall of their living room, and took down an imposing leather-bound volume. "It's all in this book, 'The subscriber's edition of Lawrence's Seven Pillars of Wisdom'. Only two hundred copies printed. This was my father's. He gave it to me as a wedding present, only, I suspect, because he knows it off by heart. If you read the last chapters you will understand why my father has never forgiven the Turks or the Germans, and why he felt grateful to Lawrence for cleaning up that hospital. It was too late to save my uncle, but at least he had a decent burial."

Maftur wasn't sure how she could use this knowledge in her campaign to keep Ismail safe. She took the book and started reading, but looked up, conscious that he was still standing in front of her. He gave that sudden grin, which never failed to make her remember why she loved him so much.

"Whatever you do, habipti, don't let my father know I've shown you that book. He would not consider it suitable reading for a woman. I suspect my mother doesn't even know of its existence." He resumed his place against the bolsters. "My father still keeps in touch with his wartime comrades. Did my mother ever tell you what he did when this war broke out? She was absolutely furious."

"Your mother never criticizes your father in front of me."

"He only went to see Emir Abdullah.'

"I thought Lawrence and the emir didn't get on!"

"That was during World War One, but my father made a hit with the emir later at the Cairo Tea Party."

"What Cairo Tea-Party?"

"The nineteen-twenty-one meeting, otherwise known by Churchill as Ali Baba and the Forty Thieves, when the French and the British carved out Syria and Palestine."

"Your father was there?"

"In a minor capacity as a legal adviser. The emir gave him some of the credit for getting him Transjordan—quite mistakenly I'm sure—but it was my father's skill at camel racing that cemented their relationship."

"What did your father go to see him about?"

"He asked to re-join the Arab legion."

Maftur laughed. "Not at his age!"

"That's what the emir said, but—" Ismail paused and took a sip of coffee "—he did add that if I possessed half of my father's camel riding skills, I would be most welcome in his army."

Maftur experienced a pang of alarm. "You can't ride a camel, can you?"

"No. I've never ridden one in my life."

Chapter 40

She and Ismail had a little ritual when she came home from work. As soon as she opened the street door and the bell hanging over it rang, Ismail would call out, "Won't be long, habipti. I'll just tidy my desk before coming up."

One Friday evening soon after the desert war had turned against the British, and Jerusalem was full of refugees from Egypt and wounded allied soldiers, Maftur came home and opened the street door as usual. The bell rang, but there was no response.

She tried the handle of the office door. It was locked. She plodded upstairs without her usual 'glad to be home' feeling, went straight to the bedroom, brushed her hair and put on fresh makeup ready to welcome her husband home.

She started towards the kitchen to speak to the new housekeeper and Ishfaq, but, as she passed the open sitting room door, she saw Ismail already there, his head between his hands.

"Habibi!" she exclaimed. "Whatever is the matter?"

He lifted his head, heaved himself up, and came over to hold her tightly.

She caught her breath. "It's your father, isn't it?"

He nodded.

She felt numb.

Ismail picked up a letter by the cushion where he had been sitting. She recognised her father-in-law's handwriting and felt calmer. He couldn't have been assassinated.

"What does he say?"

"You remember my telling you that Emir Abdullah would have welcomed me into his Arab Legion if I had been a good camel rider?"

Maftur felt an anticipatory shudder run down her spine. "Yes, but you told me you'd never ridden a camel."

"He's setting up a Desert Mechanized Brigade."

"Oh!" Maftur leant against her husband, feeling too weak to stand alone. "Your father hasn't…?"

All happiness squeezed out of his voice as he replied, "He has. If I had children to provide for, he would not have done so but…"

Maftur lifted her head from his shoulder and attempted a smile. "We can remedy that."

"Too late, my darling. The emir has already booked me into an officers' training course the week after next. My father is sending his chief clerk to run the Jerusalem office as from next week, and says I have to take you back to Haifa."

"He can't make us do this, Ismail. Write at once and tell him no."

Ismail hugged her so tightly she could hardly breathe. "You know as well as I do, habipti, that sons must obey their fathers."

"Oh, Ismail, I don't want you to go!"

Then it came to her. Could this be her father-in-law's way of ensuring his son's safety from assassination? If so, she mustn't hold him back.

She pictured the bleakness of her own future life, and then lifted her head from his shoulder. "If you have to leave, I'm not going back to Haifa. I want to keep my job."

Ismail kissed the top of her head. "I wish you could stay, but my father has promised this flat to the chief clerk. With all the refugees here, it's impossible to get accommodation in Jerusalem. Besides, I need you in Haifa for my first six weeks in the army. The officer's training course is at Acre. I can drive into Haifa whenever I'm off duty. It will be almost the same as living at home."

She stood on tiptoe and laid her cheek against his. "I'll give my notice straight away."

At the back of her mind, a thought popped up. Now might be the right time to start a family. She found the idea unexpectedly appealing. She would discuss it with Ismail on the way to Haifa.

Since she had chosen Sunday as her weekly day off and the Jewish supervisor had Saturdays off, she had to wait until Monday to hand in her notice.

The supervisor tore the letter open and read it straight away. "So! You're one of these 'here today, gone tomorrow' types."

Maftur clenched her fists. "I don't want to leave, but my husband's joined up. I have to go back to Haifa."

The Chief Engineer sent for her halfway through the following morning. Maftur felt nervous as she made her way up the stairs to the next floor, assuming that he too would be scathing. She was surprised to find a military officer sitting beside him. A tray containing coffee, biscuits and three cups sat on the desk.

The officer rose to his feet, leaning heavily on a stick. The Chief Engineer introduced him as Major White, asked her to sit down, and poured coffee. He gave no explanation for the major's presence, before saying, "I understand, Mrs. Shawwa, that the only reason you are resigning is because your husband is joining up, and you have to return to Haifa."

Made uneasy by the presence of an army officer, Maftur replied, as composedly as she could, "Yes, that is correct. I have enjoyed working here, especially now I have progressed to taking dictation, but I have to leave."

"The Post and Telegraph service have a vacancy for a secretary in Haifa," the chief engineer continued, "a new post. It requires someone capable of the utmost discretion. Would you be interested?"

Maftur felt tempted, but her first duty was to Ismail. "While my husband is training in Acre, I need to be free whenever he has leave."

"I understand. I hope my wife would feel the same."

The major entered the conversation. "As my colleague said, this is a new post. It covers special wartime needs, which is where I come in. The terms of employment can be flexible. Suppose you were to be paid only for hours worked and we agreed you could take time off whenever your husband had leave. Would such an arrangement be satisfactory?"

Maftur stared at the major, too stunned at first to reply. Eventually, she looked at the chief engineer. "Why is a soldier talking to me about a civilian job in the post office? It is a civilian job, isn't it?"

The chief engineer smiled but let the major answer.

"It is a civilian job, but very much part of the war effort. We are offering you the job, partly because you have demonstrated your ability to get on with people outside your own culture, and partly because the post office gave you a rigorous security check before appointing you to your present job. We don't want to waste time and effort checking other applicants, only to end up with security refusing them."

"I must speak to my husband. If he agrees, I will be very happy to work in Haifa under the conditions you have suggested."

She hoped Ismail would let her take up the job offer. It would mean she would not be under her mother-in-law's thumb twenty-four hours a day. Only on her way home did she remember she had been contemplating starting a family. She was glad she hadn't yet mentioned it to Ismail.

Ismail hugged her when she told him. "I am so proud of you, habipti, and so grateful. It will make it so much more fun for me when I'm stationed in Acre. I can come and pick you up straight from work and we can go off where we like, without suffering the third degree."

Chapter 41

It came as no surprise, of course, that her mother-in-law did not take kindly to the prospect of a working daughter-in-law, especially one living under her own roof. Maftur had unexpected support, however, from her father-in-law. He was proud that the British had entrusted his daughter-in-law with special war work. Since both her husband and father-in-law agreed to her working, her mother-in-law had to acquiesce, in front of the men folk at least. She gave way to her true feelings, however, in the women's quarter.

Maftur started her new job the day Ismail left for Acre. She accepted his offer of a lift to Kingsway, even though she would have to hang about for nearly an hour before the Post Office opened, but leaving with him would shield her against cutting remarks from her mother-in-law.

"Drop me off at the suq and I'll walk back."

She longed to throw her arms around him and kiss him goodbye but, of course, couldn't do that in public. She stepped out of the car and shut the door, put her hand on the frame of the open window and whispered, "May the blessings of Allah be with you."

"And with you." His hands tightened on the steering wheel. "I shall miss you so much tonight, habipti." His face contorted as he revved the engine. "I must be off. Keep cheerful."

The red Alvi shot away, throwing dust onto her office dress. She brushed it off and walked slowly back down Kingsway, regaining her composure. Edmunds was not yet open, so she gazed into shop windows until the Post Office's watchman opened the staff entrance.

A policeman, not a civilian, guarded the small door leading to the back stairs. Haifa was considered a strategic zone, she remembered. He told her to sit on a chair. Someone would come for her soon.

A portly lady, probably in her forties, wearing a blue silk dress, with a crucifix suspended conspicuously across her bosom came down the stairs.

"Mrs. Shawwa, my name is Mrs. Essa. I have prepared a desk for you in the typing pool, although your duties will be under the supervision of Mr. Shepard."

Maftur followed her up one flight of stairs. As Mrs. Essa pushed open a door, several women stopped typing to stare. No one smiled. Mrs. Essa led her to a station at the back of the room, badly lit and isolated from the rest of the work force. The typewriter on it looked as if it belonged in a scrap yard.

Mrs. Essa turned to face her. "You must understand this set-up is unusual. The man you will be working for is a telecommunications inspector. Telecommunication inspectors do not have private secretaries. Only the assistant engineer has a private secretary and that secretary has her own office."

Maftur smiled apologetically. "I was told that the person I would be working for is often away on war work, which is why the assistant engineer made this arrangement."

Mrs. Essa sniffed as if doubting the necessity and handed her a folder. "I understand your hours are fluid, so I have prepared a special time sheet. Please bring it to me for signing every time you enter and leave the building, so I can ensure you receive the correct wages."

She consulted a watch pinned to her dress front. "It is time for you to meet Mr. Shepard. I will escort you to his office."

Mr. Shepard? That was the name of Suzanna Hadad's former employer, and the husband of the woman who had sent out invitations to Dalia Leitner's wedding.

Mrs. Essa paused on the bottom rung of the next flight of stairs. "It is a department rule that while a typist is in the private office of any employee, the door must be kept open at all times."

Maftur dropped her eyes, insulted by the insinuation. "Of course, Mrs. Essa, that is understood."

They walked along a narrow corridor. Mrs. Essa knocked on a door, labelled in English, Arabic and Hebrew, INSPECTOR SHEPARD – TELECOMMUNICATIONS.

A small man in a brown striped suit with sagging pockets, his hair plastered flat across his head and his eyes distorted by pebble-thick glasses, opened the door. She remembered seeing him at the garden party in aid of the blind, nine years previously. He had seemed taller then.

He held out his hand. "Mrs. Shawwa, I have been looking forward to meeting you."

Confused, Maftur handed him the directions she had been carrying.

"Come in, come in, Mrs. Shawwa. Mrs. Essa has probably told you that, in the past, members of her excellent team have dealt with any shorthand work or typing I needed. However, currently not all my work pertains to the Post and Telegraphs. I have had some government work thrust on me. Please make yourself comfortable in that seat there." He pointed to an armchair in front of his desk. There was only just room for it in the six by eight office. "Thank you, Mrs. Essa, I think we will be all right now. I have confidential matters to discuss with Mrs. Shawwa. Please close the door after you."

Maftur glanced around wildly, but luckily Mrs. Essa was made of stern stuff.

"Mr. Shepard, war or no war, may I remind you of the department rules. While you have a female member of staff in your room, the door must be kept open. If you need to change the rules, you must consult the assistant engineer and he will advise me."

Mr. Shepard smile ingratiatingly. "Yes, of course, Mrs. Essa. I was forgetting. You may leave the door open."

Maftur settled more comfortably as Mr. Shepard lowered his voice. "This job comes under the Official Secrets Act. I will have to ask you to sign it before we go further." He picked up a thick document, held up his hand and recited something very fast, put down the documents, handed her his fountain pen, showed her where to sign, put the document away in a drawer and locked it. "It would be more convenient to have you working here rather than in the typing pool, but my office is too small to hold another desk, so Mrs. Essa is placing you in a corner of the typing pool where no one can accidentally read any documents on your desk. It is your responsibility to ensure no documents are left unattended when you leave the room. If I am in the building, you may return all finished work to me. However, since I am often away, I have taken over one of the Post Office boxes downstairs."

He unlocked the top drawer of his desk, taking out a key on a steel necklace. "You must lock all documents in the box if you have not already handed them to me in person. I will leave the work and instructions for you in the box before my periods of absence." He passed over the key. "You and I are the only key holders. Keep the key around your neck." He unlocked a large drawer at the bottom of his desk, and hauled out a sheaf of hand-written papers. "Here is today's work. I have pencilled instructions at the top of each document. If you need to ask questions, I am in all day, but remember not to leave paper on your desk before coming up."

Maftur returned to the typing pool. The other women watched her. Still no one smiled as she made her way to her isolated desk. This was going to be a lonely job, but at least it kept her away from her mother-in-law.

* * * *

Acre was only seven miles from Haifa. Once the first fortnight of Ismail's training course was over, Maftur and Ismail went out together even more frequently than when they were living together in Jerusalem.

Mr. Shepard grumbled about her frequent absences, but she pointed out that she had only taken on the job because her conditions of service allowed her unpaid leave whenever her husband was home.

She and Ismail went for long walks along the Carmel range, and also took the car to Khaiyet Beach with its rows of wooden changing rooms. Daringly, Maftur donned the one-piece bathing costume with short sleeves and skirt that Ismail bought her. He led her across the wide sandy beach into the water and through two sets of breakers. In the deeper water beyond the waves, they made love and he taught her to swim. At the end of each visit she was careful after changing back into her clothes, to dry out her costume in the strong summer sun and leave it hidden in the car boot.

Soon after the first rains, the idyll ceased. Ismail was posted to an army camp at Sarafand, south-east of Jaffa, with the rank of first Lieutenant, not due for home leave for at least six months.

Maftur had never felt as lonely as during that winter. The women at work only spoke to her if she spoke to them first, and then they answered in monosyllables. After work, her mother-in-law would present her with a basket of darning or patching, and comment on the quality of her needlework. At least the comments became less harsh as the days grew longer.

She wondered frequently whether she was doing the right thing by staying on at work, especially after the Germans were defeated at al Alamein, and the threat of invasion was over. Perhaps now was the right time to start a family. She would talk about it to Ismail when he came home on leave.

In spring she received a letter from Patsy, saying she would be visiting Palestine, possibly for the last time in a while. Was there any chance of Maftur organising a reunion of the women who used to meet at Edmunds?

Maftur broached the subject with her mother-in-law with some trepidation, but found her enthusiastic.

"Of course you must do this. You haven't had any social life since Ismail was posted. The Quigleys' daughter works in Egypt? Invite her to stay overnight. We have plenty of room."

Maftur suspected her mother-in-law wouldn't have been so enthusiastic if Patsy's mother hadn't been part of the British community.

She passed on the invitation to Patsy who wrote back saying she was delighted to accept, and had told Dalia Leitner about the reunion, so she would probably be getting in touch as well.

In due course, a letter arrived from Dalia.

"That's the Jewish woman whose wedding Mrs. Shepard was organising until her British fiancé was killed. She converted to Christianity, I suppose?" remarked Mrs. Shawwa.

"I'm not sure. She and Patsy seemed very close after Patsy's father died, then after al-Alamein they seemed to drift apart, but they're obviously friends again now."

"Why not invite her as well?"

"You mean that?"

"Yes. Abu Ismail will be pleased that you have friends among the British community, and so will your husband."

"Thank you, Umm Ismail. I'll really be looking forward to having them here."

After her long period of social isolation, Maftur enjoyed sending out invitations to the reunion, and receiving replies, even if there was an unexpected flurry of extra work at the Post Office. Judging by the papers Mr. Shepard was giving her to type up, he was transferring from one secret project to another, although what either projects were about she couldn't work out.

She was thrilled when she counted the replies. Almost everyone, however far they lived from Haifa, was making a special effort to attend.

Chapter 42

A week before the reunion, she returned from a hectic day at work to find both her in-laws waiting to greet her. Her father-in-law, still in suit and fez, had delayed his evening trip to the coffee shop to announce Ismail had phoned to say he had three days unexpected leave, and would be home next evening.

"You'll have to stay tomorrow to help me get everything ready," her mother-in-law declared.

Maftur visualised her brass box at the Post Office stuffed with unfinished work.

"I have to go into the office tomorrow, but I'll leave early."

Her father-in-law gave an approving smile. "That's the spirit that will win this war! We've enough servants to cope."

Her mother-in-law glared at her and flounced out of the room.

Maftur left work two hours early the next day, looking forward to changing into something more glamorous than her office clothes before Ismail arrived. Then, when he arrived, they could have at least half an hour together. That would be the right moment to tell him that she was ready to start a family. She was sure he would be pleased. In fact, she felt a bit guilty at withholding the dignity of fatherhood from him so long.

When she entered the house, however, she found Ismail already there, tucking into piles of meat pastries his mother had placed in front of him while she bombarded him with questions. Maftur was unable to get in a word edgeways.

Her father-in-law came home and immediately commandeered Ismail's attention, only staying for the lavish meal her mother-in-law had prepared before taking Ismail down to the coffee house.

Maftur retired to bed early, totally miserable.

When at last he entered the bedroom, he rushed over and held her tightly, and everything was all right again. He started kissing her, stroking her body and it didn't seem the right time for talking.

"Habipti, what have you decided?" he whispered.

She felt glad Ismail had introduced the subject, not her. "I'd have to hand in my resignation, but that doesn't matter anymore. I've proved myself. I'm ready to move on now."

"No, you won't have to resign. It's the same job," he replied, "only full time."

She raised herself on her elbow. There was something out of kilter with that response. If he knew having a baby was a full time job why did he think she could keep her job on.

"Habibi, I am sorry. What are we talking about?"

"The new project, of course."

"What new project?"

"Hasn't Mr. Shepard said anything to you about your job extension?"

"Extending it? No, thank you. It was bad enough missing your arrival today. If I'd known you were going to arrive early I'd have taken the whole afternoon off, even if it meant Britain losing the war."

Ismail laughed. "You don't mean that! Anyway, it's not quite like that. I wanted to talk to you as soon as I came home, but couldn't do so in front of my parents, with it being so hush-hush. If you go for it, we'll have to make up a cover story."

Maftur lifted her head from his shoulder and looked at him blankly. "Why all the mystery?"

He smiled teasingly and pressed his lips to hers. She was torn between returning his kiss and questioning him further. She chose the first option.

Eventually Ismail let go of her mouth. "You'll never guess in a million years."

"We haven't got a million years, so just tell me."

"All right. We've a chance to be together for a fortnight each month, miles away from my parents."

She screeched in excitement and flung both arms round him. "They've given you married quarters at last?" She pushed herself back. "But why only half the time?"

He sat up and pulled her onto his lap, stroking her hair. "I can't believe Mr. Shepard hasn't discussed it with you, already."

"Stop teasing. Tell me."

"The army have seconded me part-time to the hush-hush project your boss is part of."

"Why you?"

"Because I've studied copyright law. A week ago Mr. Shepard told the Commanding Officer that it would be very convenient to have you working on the project as well. The CO was in favour but said because of the nature of the project you would have to be checked again in even greater depth. He thought it would be a mere formality because I'm already part of the project."

"They'll find out about my brothers during the Troubles."

"I am sure they knew about your brothers before they interviewed you last time. The only danger is that they may connect you with Ahmed, but I don't think that's likely."

"What's the project about?"

"We can't talk about that. All I can say is that if you take the job, you'll find the location a long way from either Haifa or Jerusalem, and you won't see much daylight. However, now the threat of invasion has receded, there's no danger involved. I would never let you take it if there was. There are no other young women there, although there's an older British lady, a widow, who will see you properly chaperoned while I'm in Sarafand. You'll like her. She has a sense of humour and would really welcome another woman about the place. The big drawback of the project is, apart from our days off, you'll be living underground away from family, shops, and cafes."

She drew him back down into the bed. "So long as I'm with you, habibi, I don't care about anything else. You do want me to get the job, don't you?"

"Of course I do, habipti, I've missed you so much. Amman's the only place with married quarters for lowly officers like me, and I don't know when, if ever, they'll transfer me there."

"Habibi," Maftur replied, "I would rather be in prison and have you with me half the time than be free full time without you. I hope I get accepted."

"And I hope the project won't last long and that the war

ends soon. My father has told me that he intends going into politics when peace comes, leaving me to run the Haifa office—and there's something else. You remember saying once that you wanted to live in the house Abu Mussa owns on Mount Carmel?"

"Of course, but with your army pay we can't afford to buy it, even if it comes onto the market."

"My father handles the letting. I asked him if he would be prepared to buy it for us if your great-great-uncle decided to sell it. Do you think, habipti, you'll be ready to start a family when I'm back on civvy street?"

She, Ismail and their children living in that house—it would be almost as good as paradise.

"I can't wait for you to be demobbed," she said, and buried her face in his shoulder. He held her tight, kissing her hair.

Ismail left the following evening. Her only consolation was knowing that she would soon find out if she had passed the security checks.

Mr. Shepard was away, however, when she arrived at work, and had left a stack of typing instructions but no other messages in her locker.

Chapter 43

Maftur searched through the sheets Mr. Shepard had left her to type up, hoping to find more about the project but, as usual, they contained only unintelligible comments to be typed onto hand-drawn diagrams.

By the morning of the reunion she had still heard nothing, so was sure security had turned her down. She placed her time sheet on Mrs. Essa's table with a heavy heart and told her she would be leaving early.

"Good of you to come in at all, I'm sure," Mrs. Essa remarked in a sarcastic tone. "Mr. Shepard has also honoured us with his presence today and wishes to see you."

She almost ran upstairs.

Mr. Shepard looked up from his desk with a smile and asked her to take the armchair. "Your husband told me, when I saw him yesterday, that you were happy to join our project team. I hope to get the clearance sometime tomorrow. Now, I mustn't keep you because I need you to type up these reports."

She left carrying a huge pile of documents. She succeeded in typing all Mr. Shepard's reports in time, and took them upstairs, feeling pleased she would be at home to greet Patsy and Dalia herself instead of leaving them to the mercy of her mother-in-law.

Mr. Shepard looked through her typing as she stood in front of his desk. With head still down he said, "These seem fine. I won't keep you tonight. I gather you're leaving early because you have a ladies' reunion at Edmunds."

How did he know about that? She hoped he hadn't told Mrs. Essa the reason for her early departure.

He looked up. "You'll be seeing Miss Quigley at the reunion?"

Just how much did her boss know about her private life?

"She's staying with me overnight, sir." But she guessed he knew that already.

"Good. Would you be so kind at to pass on a message. I would like to see her here in my office first thing tomorrow morning." Her face must have revealed her puzzlement, because he added, "Miss Quigley was part of our project in its former existence but, now the Allies have routed Rommel, she is going on to other things. However, we have a few odd threads to tie up before she leaves."

She hurried off and was home a few minutes before Dalia and Patsy arrived.

Dalia looked confident and well, far more cheerful than she had expected, but it was eighteen months since Peter Monteith had died. Patsy, however, exuded an aura of sadness.

They didn't have time for a real conversation, however, before leaving the house.

The reunion proved a great success.

When the initial communal session had finished and women were mixing in smaller groups, Maftur suggested to Patsy that they go outside for a breath of fresh air. She passed on Mr. Shepard's message, adding, "I know you and Dalia are intending to leave early tomorrow morning but if you come down with me to see Mr. Shepard, you can be back by nine."

Patsy smiled. "Dalia would just love the opportunity to mooch round your house, talking to your mother-in-law about cookery."

"How well do you know my boss, Patsy?"

"Fairly well. When they lived in Haifa, the Shepards and my parents attended the same church. Why?"

"This morning he told me that, subject to security clearance, he wants me to accept a job that would allow me to live part-time with my Ismail. Do you know anything about it?"

"A little. If you take the job, you'll be roughing it, but the people are okay. The most important part for you, I guess, is that you'll be seeing more of Ismail."

"Patsy, if Mr. Shepard says anything to you about me, please stick up for me."

Patsy looked hurt. "After all you've done for me, what do you think?"

Next day when Maftur popped into Dalia's bedroom to say goodbye, she found her propped up on huge feather pillows, enjoying breakfast in bed. A tray in front of her was loaded with orange juice, boiled eggs and dainty rounds of toast.

"I haven't experienced such luxury since leaving Munich," Dalia told her. "I'll take my time eating this, then dress in a leisurely fashion and have a chat with your mother-in-law. It's been great seeing you again. When this war's run its course, you and Patsy must come and spend a holiday on my place at el Tireh."

"That's the second time you've invited me," Maftur reminded her.

"Then you're duty bound to accept the invitation."

In the Post Office building, Maftur led Patsy to Mr. Shepard's office, before signing her time sheet. She found a message in her PO Box from Mr. Shepard that he needed that day's work by lunchtime.

Mr. Shepard beamed at her when she brought it to him on time.

"Ah, Maftur, good news. Your clearance has come through. You'll start work with our new project on Monday, and you'll need this."

She took the folded work pass he handed over.

"Someone will collect you and, remember, you must say nothing about this to anyone, not even your parents."

Maftur wondered what sort of world Mr. Shepard lived in. How could she keep so momentous a secret from her mother-in-law, if she had to get everything washed and packed by Monday?

She needn't have worried though. Her mother-in-law greeted her as she returned.

"Ismail phoned. He's found married quarters. He wouldn't tell me where—says its restricted information and I must write to both of you care of the British army, giving just his name and army number. He'll pick you up in a military vehicle early Monday morning, but you're only to pack one suitcase, as the married quarters are tiny. He's staying for breakfast so we'll invite all your family round and have an early morning feast."

Up in her bedroom, Maftur opened up her work pass and found Mr. Shepard had made a mistake. It gave her occupation as 'nurse'.

Chapter 44

The Shawwas and the al-Zeids stood on the pavement outside the lawyer's house, replete from a magnificent breakfast. Ismail placed Maftur's not so small suitcase into the back of a camouflaged open-topped Austin 8, on top of his kitbag. Two brown paper carriers occupied the rest of the space.

Maftur made her final farewells and climbed into the passenger seat. With both families waving, they set off down the road into town and took the coast road north.

"Where are we going?" Maftur asked.

"Somewhere beyond Safad not marked on the map. We have to double back to it through Lebanon because this car's not sturdy enough for the direct route."

Sitting beside Ismail, Maftur felt in holiday mood as she looked out on scenery she had last seen on the way back from Chateau al-Zeid.

Around eleven o'clock, before they reached the boundary, Ismail pulled up by a small restaurant. He took one of the carrier bags from the car and pointed to a beach on the far side of sand dunes held together by marram grass. "Fancy a stroll? We might as well make the most of fresh air and sunshine while we can. They're going to be in short supply where we're going."

They walked along firm, damp sand, stopping like children to pick up seashells. Although it was only the beginning of April, the noontide heat felt like summer.

They had not gone far when Ismail steered her back into the sand dunes where they found a hollow the size of a bomb crater. He reached into the carrier bag. Instead of the picnic she had anticipated, he produced two beach towels, laid them on the ground and took her into his arms. An hour later, she felt all she needed to make the day perfect was a shower before dressing. As if he knew what she was thinking, Ismail reached into the bag again and brought out their swimming costumes.

She wriggled into hers and ran across the beach. Dipping

her feet into the water, she gave a little scream. The air might be summer-warm but the sea was winter-cold. A few strokes out beyond the waves and they sprinted back to land, clean but chilled.

"I don't know about you," Ismail said as they shook the sand out of the towels to rub themselves dry. "But I've worked off my breakfast and could do with some lunch. Let's try that restaurant."

They spread out their costumes and towels on the car seats before entering the simple wooden building.

Inside its dark interior, the Jewish owners served them fried herrings, salad and freshly baked bread. They assumed Ismail was a soldier on home leave from the front, and gave them each a free glass of wine. Maftur was horrified to see him drink his and even more horrified when he drank hers too after checking their hosts weren't looking. What would his mother have said?

"The war has changed you," she remarked in a carefully non-judgmental way, as they walked back to the car.

"It has changed everyone," Ismail replied.

Before they drove off again, Maftur leaned over and kissed her husband. "I didn't expect the journey to be so delightful. Thank you so much. Now tell me about the project."

"How much has Mr. Shepard told you?"

"Not a lot."

"We're quite literally an underground unit, devoted to scientific research, hidden in the basement of a military hospital. Our code name is Magog."

Maftur remembered the name cropping up in documents she had typed up for Mr. Shepard. Being horrified the first time she had seen it, pulling her out of her usual policy of allowing information from papers marked 'Top Secret' to pass through her fingers rather than her brain. For a while she had recalled the terrible legends and prophecies associated with that name.

"I assume the British who named it are not aware of the connotations," Ismail commented.

They reached the border with Lebanon where Ismail showed their joint passport to British soldiers before being waved on. After a steep uphill climb through wooded country, they arrived at another section of the border. Ismail showed their passport again and they drove along a recently widened road. He stopped the car when they were out of sight of the check point and took the second carrier bag out of the boot.

"Time for you to change into uniform."

"But I'm a civilian."

He smiled. "Of course you are," and produced a Red Crescent uniform.

"I'm not a nurse," she exclaimed, remembering her pass, and wondering what sort of bureaucratic mix-up had occurred.

"I know, habipti, but you're going to have to get used to this disguise."

When she had changed, Ismail drove on. Soon she saw a timber-built military hospital, with a prominent red cross on its roof. It sat on a mountainside, above a wadi with almost vertical sides.

Ismail drove up to double gates, let into ferocious rolls of barbed wire, and they both showed their work passes to two armed soldiers. One, a corporal, took out his duty book and made a note of the van's registration, while the other checked the interior of the van and swept a bomb detector under the chassis. The corporal gave the thumbs up to a third soldier on the other side of the fence. The gates swung open.

"Best leave the car by the reception area," the soldier advised with a cheerful smile. "Someone's waiting for it."

After parking, Ismail lifted their cases out. "I'll take these," he told Maftur. "You bring the carriers."

A pretty, civilian woman, Arabic in appearance and standing behind a plain reception desk, examined their work passes and consulted a list. An armed soldier unlocked a door into the main section of the hospital.

Maftur followed Ismail down a concrete stairway that angled out of sight after only three steps, and continued down a further thirty. At the bottom, Ismail took a right turn along a narrow and dimly-lit corridor, sloping slightly upwards with doors on both sides. Most were shut, but one that stood ajar revealed wheelchairs and crutches.

The corridor continued for almost one hundred metres, the last forty passing between blank walls. The corridor ended at a door labelled 'Isolation Ward 2'. Flanking it, two doors respectively labelled 'Isolation Wards 1 & 3' faced each other. All three doors had notices saying, 'NO UNAUTHORIZED VISITORS' in three languages.

Ismail used a buzzer on the end door to spell out his name in Morse code. An eyelevel shutter opened. A pair of eyes stared out.

"I've brought your new nurse," Ismail told the eye. He held up his work pass. The shutter closed. A key turned. The door opened.

A middle-aged woman wearing the uniform of a nursing sister let them in.

"Mrs. Porter," Ismail said. "This is my wife, Maftur Nour."

Mrs. Porter smiled. "Welcome to Magog, Mrs. Shawwa."

Maftur stared around at an artificially-lit room containing two rows of hospital beds, half-filled with patients in pyjamas, not desperately ill judging by the way they were sitting up reading, writing or just talking.

"I didn't realise I'd be working in a real hospital!" she exclaimed.

Ismail laughed.

Mrs. Porter explained, "The hospital upstairs is real enough, but the men here aren't patients. Most are scientists. Dressing up is part of our security system. While Ismail shows you your bedroom, Mrs. Shawwa, I'll brew up."

Ismail headed for a door hidden behind a screen. It led into a narrow lobby, carved from rock. When Ismail closed the door, they were left in total darkness. She felt him squeeze past. He opened another door to reveal a well-lit cavern furnished as a comfortable common room and dining area. Men clustered round a table, poring over a large diagram.

"Bonjour, Lieutenant. And who is this beautiful nurse you have brought with you?"

Ismail introduced her. They looked genuinely pleased that she was joining them, all except one, a Dr Katz, who, after an initial grunt, pulled the diagram towards him and continued studying it, while everyone else listened to Ismail's news from the outside world.

As they left the group Ismail pointed to the doors on

both sides of the cavern. "Offices, kitchen, labs. The dormitory's straight ahead."

The dormitory proved to be another cavern, this one dimly lit and filled with far more beds than the ward. One corner had been partitioned into two cubicles with curtains and cardboard walls.

Ismail pushed aside the curtain of the larger cubicle to reveal two narrow camp beds, made up with coarse army blankets, khaki sheets and khaki-encased pillows. A gap between the beds, eighteen inches wide, allowed access to a narrow washstand that held an enamelled ewer and basin on top, and a metal bucket with lid below. Beneath each bed peeped the handle of an enamel chamber pot.

Maftur made a brave attempt at a smile. If sleeping there was the price for being with Ismail, she would cheerfully pay it.

Chapter 45

Maftur had been in Magog for four weeks and was now on first name terms with Dorothy Porter. Apart from Dr Katz, all the scientists, French, Jewish and British, treated her well, although they teased her terribly, but in a kindly way.

She wasn't sure why Dr Katz had taken such a patent dislike to her. He had not been exactly friendly to either herself or Ismail during their first fortnight there together, but as soon as Ismail returned to Sarafand, he had turned downright hostile, never satisfied with her typing, constantly complaining that she hadn't listened to his layout instructions, and making her re-type whole documents. He complained about her spelling as well. She was certain she had spelled words like 'centre' and 'realise' correctly, but he insisted she retype the pages changing those words to 'center' and 'realize'. The previous day he had threatened that, if she didn't improve, he would go to the Commanding Officer and demand her dismissal.

That day, however, she was trying to forget his threat. Ismail was due back late that afternoon. She had organised her workload to ensure she went off-duty early. As she sat in front of her typewriter, screened off at the back of the ward, she congratulated herself on keeping to schedule.

Then Dr Katz entered the ward and, without saying a word of greeting, slapped down a pile of work carrying the label 'TOP PRIORITY'. She bit her lip to prevent herself from crying as she realised her plans were in ruins.

A few minutes later the bell attached to the door leading to the hospital corridor rang without sounding a code. Behind her own desk, Dorothy frowned as she consulted the daily schedule. Before walking towards the door, she signalled for all men in pyjamas to get into bed and lie down, looking ill. Maftur jumped up to push a thermometer into the mouth of a patient half way down the ward, and took his pulse.

A masculine voice with an Arab accent sounded loudly through the voice tube. "I have a message."

Dorothy lifted the flap over the spy-hole and gave her standard response. "I am sorry, this is an isolation ward. I cannot open the door."

The voice from outside answered, "The message is from reception. There's a very large parcel for Nurse Shawwa. Could you send up two men to carry it down, please?"

Maftur felt a spasm of alarm. Could this be an assassination attempt aimed at Ismail? She left her desk and went over to Dorothy.

"I'm not expecting a parcel."

The armed soldier cocked his rifle.

Dorothy raised her eyebrows. "I'll consult the Commanding Officer."

"Maftur," Dorothy said on her return, "the captain says the soldiers on guard duty will have checked the parcel before allowing it into the building. You can go upstairs and tell reception that, although we're expecting a very contagious patient this afternoon, you, yourself, are not in quarantine until he arrives. If the parcel's genuine, ask them to get two porters to carry it down and leave it outside the door."

The soldier unlocked the door and let her out. Her heart pounding, she ran along the corridor and up the stairs.

"Whatever is it?" she asked the young lady at reception. "I haven't ordered anything."

"No mystery," the receptionist told her. "It's a double mattress from the bedding shop in Safad. You must have received an extra large patient. One of your staff asked a doctor on leave to bring it back. I'd have sent it down, but I know how fussy they are about quarantine on that ward."

Embarrassment replaced Maftur's fear. She and Ismail had had to make love standing up in the narrow space between their two beds, because the camp beds had bounced up and down noisily at the slightest movement. Ismail had promised he would buy a mattress. She had assumed he would bring it with him. She didn't want everyone to see it being brought into their room.

After two porters had put down the parcel, she gave them five piastres each and watched them depart before ringing in her code.

"What was it?" Dorothy asked through the speaker.

Maftur tried to whisper but the system broadcast her reply. She heard raucous laughter as the door opened. Two British marines, armed with rifles and a metal detector, took in the parcel.

Trying to keep a straight face, Dorothy told them, "When you've checked it, you can carry it into the dormitory." She turned to Maftur. "Why don't you take your lunch break early so you can set it up?"

"I daren't," Maftur whispered. "I haven't finished Dr Katz's work yet. He'll make another complaint."

"What have you done to upset that man?" Dorothy asked. "You get on so well with everyone else."

"I don't know."

"Hi, Maftur, how are you going to use the contents of that enormous bag?" one of the scientists called out from the nearest bed.

She retorted with a phrase she had heard Patsy use. "That's for me to know and you to find out."

The scientists all gave good-natured laughs.

They were a decent bunch of men, she thought. If only Dr Katz were as friendly, she could be happy here even when Ismail was away.

When she had shown the marines where to leave the mattress, she returned to her desk to discover Dr Katz had placed yet more work on it. Her fingers flew desperately over the keys of her typewriter.

By her official lunch break, she had finished the first section of Dr Katz's work and took it through to his lab. He greeted her with a grunt and carried on studying a meter gauge.

She placed the papers on a bench top. "I'll finish the rest after lunch."

He looked up. "You have already had your break. I wasted enough time earlier waiting by your desk while, for no official reason, you left the premises. If you need another break, you will take it after you have finished my work."

She turned on her heels without replying and hurried to the dormitory. Inside the cramped cubicle, brushing aside her tears, she manoeuvred her camp bed next to Ismail's and slid the washstand to the side. With difficulty, she unpacked the bulky feather mattress and hauled it on top of the hard army biscuits. She bounced up and down on it a few times, relieved to discover the camp beds now produced no embarrassing squeaks, and looked forward to Ismail's return.

She picked up a cheese sandwich from the canteen and took it back to the ward.

Dorothy smiled and put a mug of tea on her desk. "Comfortable?"

"Very! I shan't know I'm not back home. I'm in trouble again with Dr Katz, though." She retreated behind her screen and picked up the work still to be completed. "Oh, no."

She hadn't realised how loudly she must have exclaimed because she heard Dorothy say, "What's up?"

"Dr Katz has told me to retype the work he gave me this morning. He says he left a note saying he specifically told me to use three-and-a-half inch margins, but I know he didn't."

She had only just taken the cover off her typewriter when Jim Shepard bustled through with a bunch of rather dog-eared papers.

"I need these typed up urgently."

Her heart sank. "I'll do it as soon as I've finished this for Dr Katz."

Mr. Shepard peered at the papers she was working on. "I've a meeting in Jerusalem this evening. My stuff's more urgent."

She could see the work was complicated and would need intense concentration as the notes, as usual, made no sense.

Mr. Shepard picked up Dr Katz's work and strode off.

Maftur had no choice but to start on her boss's work, typing the codename 'Manhattan' at the top right hand of the sheet and rolling the diagram through the machine to start on the notes.

Dr Katz strode in.

She assumed he was going to insist she stop working on Mr. Shepard's documents and type his, except he was carrying no papers.

Instead he said loudly so the whole ward could hear, "I have had to report you to the Commanding Officer, Mrs. Shawwa, and demand your dismissal, and not just for your customary inefficiency. You deliberately disobeyed my command to type up my work without delay. If you had done as you were ordered you would have finished the most urgent of my work before Mr. Shepard gave you his."

He looked down at the paper in her typewriter and stopped, almost as if in shock. Then he pressed his lips firmly together, swivelled round and left the ward.

Maftur carried on typing, biting back tears. Dr. Katz had said nothing about the extra wide margin, but she couldn't prove it. She could lose this job and, with it, her monthly fortnight with Ismail, and also her claim to be qualified to earn her own living.

Dorothy came around the screen. "Take no notice of that bully, dear. The rest of the staff have the highest regard for you."

A few minutes later an orderly came onto the ward and told Dorothy that the Commanding Officer wished to speak to her.

"I'll leave you to answer the door if it rings again," Dorothy told Maftur.

Maftur watched her leave, convinced that the Commanding Officer was about to tell Dorothy he would have to dismiss her assistant. Her fingers lost their speed, her stomach churned.

By the time a soldier summoned her to the Commander's office, she could hardly walk she felt so anxious.

"Sit down, Mrs. Shawwa," the Commanding Officer said as she entered. He pointed to a comfortable armchair, and picked up a teapot. "Do you take sugar, milk, lemon?"

He poured her tea into a porcelain cup, decorated with roses, and offered a chocolate digestive, a treat from the NAAFI. He waited until she had taken her first mouthful before he came to the point.

"Now, Mrs. Shawwa, about this misunderstanding with Dr Katz, Mrs. Porter has explained that she ordered you to take your lunch break and, as she is your immediate superior, you had no choice but to obey her orders. Regarding Dr Katz's other complaints, I have requested him in future to put down in writing any special requests he may make, and to place that paper prominently on top of his documents. He mentioned that he has been concerned about your spelling as well, but when he showed me instances, I found you had been using the correct British spelling. Dr Katz apparently learnt his English in America. I have informed him that in Palestine we use British spelling, and have lent him a dictionary. Has anyone else been complaining about any aspects of your work?"

"No, sir, they have all been very kind."

"Good. We don't want you getting upset. We rely on you too much for that."

Chapter 46

Maftur had been at Magog nearly ten months, and was tired of living under artificial light, breathing stale air, getting only four days a month respite, most of that taken up with the journey to and from Haifa and the rest of it, spent with her in-laws, fending off embarrassing questions about her social life.

The last ten days over the Christian festival of Christmas had been the loneliest since she had arrived at Magog. Ismail had been at Sarafand. Dorothy had taken annual leave. Maftur wished she were a man. Then she could have enjoyed the festivities associated with Hanukah and Christmas, but with so many alcohol-fuelled men on the premises, she felt it safer to isolate herself in her cubicle every evening. She had never written so many letters in her life, sitting on the end of the mattress with the washstand turned into a desk. In her daily letter to Ismail she tried her hardest to sound cheerful. She wrote longer letters to Patsy who was now working in Italy, because Patsy knew Magog, Dorothy, Dr Katz and Mr. Shepard so she could tell her a lot without having to mention anything secret. She wrote to Dalia too, because she had also worked for the project.

She wrote to her mother, Elif, Miriam and Ai'isha but those were more difficult letters, since she couldn't let them know what she was doing, or where she was. When she received replies, however, she could write back commenting on their news. So she lived life vicariously as Elif told her of the trials of living with a baby who had just learnt to crawl, Miriam wrote reams about her destructive toddler, Ai'isha grumbled about the local kindergarten, Patsy described the poverty of war-torn Italy and the comradeship amongst the ATS, while Dalia grumbled about her experiences on her last farm practice.

A couple of days after New Year she woke by herself in her partitioned bedroom, wanting to roll back over and continue dreaming of trees, fresh breezes, sparkling sea and Ismail. As she reluctantly climbed out of bed, a female voice from the other side of the partition called cheerily, "So you're awake then, Maftur. I'll see you at breakfast."

Dorothy must have returned late last night. That cheered her up.

"How was your time off?" she asked as they queued up at the canteen counter for porridge, coffee, and scrambled egg on toast. One thing about being fed by the NAAFI in Palestine, the food was good.

"Brilliant. I am so glad I rented that apartment in Safad, even if it is costing an arm and a leg. The views over Galilee are spectacular, and I spent Christmas at the Tegart with police friends we made when Danny was alive. I wish I'd been able to afford it earlier."

"It sounds like heaven," Maftur said wistfully.

"Any news from this end?" Dorothy asked.

"The rumours about moving location are growing stronger."

"Has anyone mentioned which location? Luckily Zamzum's been handed over to an agricultural group. David would suit me best but I expect it will be Ark and that would be too far for me to keep up my place at Safad. I shall be loathe to give it up now I've found it."

"David? Ark? Zamzum? The names seem familiar."

Dorothy raised her eyebrows. "You worked for Jim on our last project, didn't you? You must have heard of Ark, David, Zamzum and Armageddon?"

A vague memory stirred. "Subsidiary bases linked to Magog, but I know nothing about them."

Dorothy lowered her voice. "Guerrilla bases created when we expected a German invasion. Probably still hush-hush. After El Alamain, the powers-that-be handed Magog over to the present project and supposedly dismantled the rest, but I suspect they spent so much on setting up Ark they were loathe to ditch it."

"Where is Ark?" asked Maftur.

"Jerusalem. How do you feel about working there?"

Maftur thought about that. "Only if they keep Ismail on."

After breakfast she sat at her typewriter while Dorothy took back the jobs she had undertaken during her absence, taking in the Commanding Officer's mail and receiving the daily instructions. She sped up her typing. She didn't want a backlog when Ismail arrived.

"I've had an idea," Dorothy said when she returned from the office. "Your monthly breaks and mine never coincide. How would you and Ismail like to sublet the flat for three days a month? I have an Arab girl come in to clean, air and change sheets every time I leave. She would do the same for you. It would help me financially."

Maftur took her hands from the keyboard. "That sounds too good to be true, especially now they've made up that track across the wadi, so you don't have to be certified mentally insane before using it. I'll have to speak to Ismail, of course, but I'm sure he'll be all for it."

"If he agrees, why not try it out at the end of his next stint? Even though it's winter, the kerosene heater keeps the flat warm and the views are stunning."

Maftur carried on typing, her mind now on the prospect of three days completely alone with Ismail in an idyllic environment.

Dorothy interrupted a few minutes later. "A post card for you from Italy. It's strange seeing cards from abroad instead of flimsy OHMS airmails."

Maftur gazed at a picture of the Basilica of St Nicolas on Bari and turned it over to read the message. "It's from Patsy Quigley. Guess what? She's engaged to someone she knew before she left Britain."

"Fancy that! I remember Patsy swearing she would never get married."

Maftur smiled. "I'm glad she's seen sense at last, but I must get on. I have a pile to finish before Ismail arrives tomorrow."

The following evening, after Ismail had settled in, Maftur told him about Dorothy's proposition.

Instead of displaying instant delight, he looked thoughtful. "I am as keen as you are on the idea, habipti, but we can't make a long term commitment. My secondment to Magog is drawing to a close. Even if the army decided I should continue, my mother would be quite rightly angry if we put off too many visits to Haifa."

She felt her eyes fill with tears. "Please, habibi, you don't know how miserable I've felt the last fortnight. I'm so desperate for a real break and just to be together, only the two of us. Do you realise, ever since we've been married, I've never once cooked a whole meal for you?"

He took her in his arms. "Oh, habipti, I'm being so selfish after you've been so brave working here. I'll explain the situation to Dorothy and ask if we can pay for just the times we use the flat. If she says yes, we'll go at the end of this fortnight."

He went straight off to speak to Dorothy.

While he was out of the room, she brooded. All her friends except Dalia and Patsy had children. It was time she and Ismail started a family. Since their future together at Magog was drawing to a close, if they could take a break at Safad, just the two of them alone, she would tell him there that she was ready to start a family.

Ismail returned. "It's all arranged, habipti."

Chapter 47

Maftur's hopes of a quiet three days alone with Ismail were dashed when, towards the end of his fortnight, heavy snow painted the hills white. Although the track to Safad had improved enormously over the past months, there was no way Ismail could drive across the snowbound wadi in the military car he had brought with him. She was relinquishing all thought of Safad when Ismail managed to hitch them a lift with a jeep going for urgent medical supplies, and arranged for a lift back with another jeep collecting post.

Maftur kept her eyes closed and her hand in Ismail's until they were safely on the dirt road across the wadi.

In her thin coat, she was thoroughly chilled by the time the driver dropped them outside Dorothy's flat. All the same, she insisted on crossing the road to the grocery opposite.

While Ismail went to find a newspaper, she bought crusty bread, goat cheese, a large pat of butter, flour from a tub on the floor, a tin of evaporated milk, a tin of corned beef, purple olives from a display at the front of the shop, red onions and a tight cauliflower. She then asked the grocer to grind her one hundred grams of real coffee beans and breathed in their aroma. Ismail returned while the shopkeeper's wife was packing her purchases into an orange box.

She was still shivering when they entered the freezing flat. Ismail pointed to a double bed, covered in a plump maroon comforter that occupied a corner of the large room and gave a lecherous grin.

"Get under the covers. I'll light the kerosene heater, then join you. We'll soon have you warmed up."

Maftur, with the eiderdown drawn up round her ears, braced herself for what she had to say. The words came out in a sort of squeak between her shivering. "Ismail, I think I am ready to have a baby now."

He turned with his shirt half off, and stared. "Did I hear correctly?"

She nodded.

"Oh, my darling." He tugged his clothes off as fast as he could and climbed into bed beside her. Their lovemaking was longer and gentler than usual.

Two hours later she disentangled herself from his arms and sat up in bed, the air, redolent of kerosene fumes, warm against her bare skin. She had never before felt so calm and contented. Once she had cooked the evening meal she would feel really and properly married at last.

She was all geared up to hand in her resignation a fortnight later when her next period arrived as usual. She couldn't believe it.

Ismail just smiled when she told him of her disappointment. "These things don't happen to order, habipti, we have to be patient."

It was warmer the next time they stayed in Safad. The grass was tender green and the scarlet anemones had just begun to flower. They drove down to Tiberias and sat on the quay in the sunshine, looking over water sparkling back at the sun while they ate fish from that morning's catch.

After what seemed a magical break, she was sure she must have conceived, but again was disappointed.

Ironically, it was after a rather staid visit to Haifa that she missed a period. She decided to say nothing about it to Ismail until she missed a second, as she didn't want to raise false hopes and anyway, if she was pregnant, she wanted to tell him at Safad. They had to waste their next break attending a wedding in Jaffa.

Ismail's secondment was ending. Their next break in Safad would be their last but by that time she was sure she was pregnant.

The day before they set off for Safad, she received a letter from Patsy in an envelope with an Egyptian stamp.

Dear Maftur,

Big news! I am expecting a baby and have had to leave my job in Italy. I have a small job to do here in Egypt but should be back in Palestine within the week to stay with my mother in Jerusalem. I do hope the war ends before our baby is born, so Tim can be with me.

I would love to see you. If you are still working at you-know-where, I have to make a delivery there before I leave my unit for good. After that, I will no longer be authorised to visit.

Maftur put the letter down and smiled. What a coincidence. She would tell Patsy about her baby soon, but Ismail must be the first to know.

That time, when they made their trip to Safad, the weather was so warm they had to leave the car windows open. The hills were yellow with dying grass and the flowers had disappeared from wild areas, although the houses in Safad were bright with geraniums and bougainvillea.

When they arrived at the flat, she flung open the french doors onto the balcony and flopped onto one of a pair of cane chairs. Beyond was a panoramic view of irrigated fields and vineyards, set against a backdrop of the tawny flanks of the Golan Heights, with just a glimpse of blue lake showing in between and far below.

Ismail came out to join her, bearing two glasses of water, each with ice and slices of lemon, and placed them on the rattan tabletop.

"You did use the boiled water in the clay jar?" she checked.

"Of course," Ismail said. "I may be only a man but I'm not stupid enough to drink water straight from a tap, and I rubbed the lemon over with permanganate. Since Mrs. Porter is British, I am sure she used boiled water to make her ice cubes." He gave her a quizzical look. She hadn't been so scrupulous about the water the last time they had been here.

She put her hand on his sleeve as he sat down.

He looked sideways at her. "Habipti?

She had practiced a long introduction but the words had gone. "Habibi," she blurted out, "I'm almost certain you are going to be a father."

Ismail sprang from his chair, knelt in front of her, and laid his head on her knees. "Oh, habipti," he whispered. "If it is true, you will have made me the happiest man in the world."

He rested his head for a few minutes, motionless and silent before resuming his seat, his face tinged now with all the dignified authority appropriate to a father.

"You must see a doctor here in Safad tomorrow, habipti, and you must leave Magog straight away. I know how much that Dr Katz has been sniping at you whenever he thinks he can get away with it. You mustn't be upset in any way from now on. It won't be good for our child."

Maftur laughed gently. "I have to give at least a month's notice before I can leave, Ismail. I don't need to see a doctor to do that. I would rather consult our family doctor in Haifa next month. Please let us just enjoy our last break here together."

And then she realised something strange. She did not feel unhappy about returning to a traditional woman's world, spending her time knitting, buying prams and mixing with friends who already had children. Her chief sorrow was being parted from Ismail once again.

Chapter 48

Maftur had always known that the key to acceptance in her mother-in-law's household would be a healthy pregnancy, but hadn't realised pregnancy would cause her so much contentment that she could even find satisfaction in routine domestic duties.

That afternoon she was in the living room sitting opposite her mother-in-law and knitting a baby matinee jacket. Fatima entered carrying a tray with warm towels and brass hand-washing bowls. Behind her, Ishfaq wheeled in a trolley with glasses of iced tea, delicate china plates, silver forks, towels and a platter of sticky honey and date cakes—a delicacy her mother-in-law had taught her to bake that morning.

Mrs. Shawwa raised puzzled eyes when she saw a tidy hand-written label beside each item on the tray and trolley.

"I'm teaching Ishfaq to read," Maftur explained, and added with a smile of approval at Ishfaq. "She's a quick learner."

She hoped her mother-in-law wouldn't be too scathing and was relieved by her reply. "A good idea. I have always found it useful that Umm Salah can read and write." She turned to the maid. "Ishfaq, if you make good progress, my daughter-in-law will promote you to nursemaid when Umm Saleh leaves."

At one time Maftur would have deeply resented her mother-in-law organising her domestic arrangements. Now she just felt pleased Umm Ismail had announced what Maftur had intended to do anyway.

Fatima felt in her capacious sleeves and pulled out the afternoon's post.

Both Maftur and her mother-in-law opened their letters from Ismail first, the older woman with an ornate brass-handled letter opener, and Maftur with her fingers. Both carefully preserved the envelopes for re-use. They gave a simultaneous gasp when they started reading and, in unison, exclaimed, "He's being posted to Mafraq in Transjordan!"

"But whereabouts in Transjordan is Mafraq?" Maftur asked.

Her mother-in-law shrugged as if it made no difference.

Maftur put down her knitting. "I'll fetch an atlas."

The door of the library was ajar. She stepped inside and found her father and father-in-law so deep in conversation they failed to notice her presence.

Her father was saying, "But, Abu Ismail, I beg you, please take more care. We have already lost too many of our best minds to the Husseini assassins. Now if only—"

Her father-in-law's louder voice broke in, "No, dear friend, I will not keep silence. My country means too much to me."

Maftur stamped her feet to warn them of her presence and explained why she was there.

"About time the emir put my son into action," her father-in-law commented as he handed over a tome that had her staggering under its weight.

It was not only her arms that felt burdened. The overheard snippet of conversation weighed on her mind as she walked back to the sitting room.

She put her worry aside, however, as she and her mother-in-law discovered Mafraq was a town on the Hejaz railway close to the Syrian border.

"I didn't realise Transjordan was so large," her mother-in-law said when Maftur worked out how many miles Ismail would be from Haifa. "But at least he'll be safe. If only the emir had accepted his father, I wouldn't be worrying every day if Abu Ismail will come home alive."

Maftur stared at her mother-in-law with increased sympathy. "It's not fair," she burst out, realising her mother-in-law was aware of the danger her husband was in. "Abu Ismail has not sold one dunam of his lands to Jews. How many hypocrites in the Husseini party can make that claim? The Grand Mufti over in Germany, recruiting Muslims for Hitler's army—he's the one who should be assassinated."

Her mother-in-law looked up, her face distorted with fear. "Maftur, stop that at once! I have enough to worry me without you joining my husband in rash talk."

Maftur hung her head. Umm Ismail was right. "I can't

think what got into me," she apologised.

Her mother-in-law put her hand on her arm and spoke more gently. "It's what happens when you are expecting a baby. One moment you feel more peaceful than you've ever been. The next you're acting like a tigress. Well, aren't you going to open the rest of your post?"

Maftur looked at the back of the first envelope.

Her mother-in-law looked expectant. "Who's it from?"

She wished Umm Ismail understood the concept of private correspondence. "Dalia Leitner, the friend who came here with Patsy last year."

"I remember her well. A nice girl. She liked my cooking. You wouldn't believe she was Jewish. What does she say?"

"It's written in English so you wouldn't understand."

"Then translate."

Maftur skimmed the letter. "She's inviting Patsy Craine—that's Patsy Quigley as was—and me to spend a week with her next month at her orange grove in el Tireh."

She wasn't too sure she wanted to go. It was comfortable here in Haifa having nothing to do but prepare for her baby. A memory of Ai'isha flashed through her mind. Ya lel! Was she really turning into a self-centred bore like Ai'isha had been when pregnant? She must accept this invitation.

Her mother-in-law frowned. "I didn't know Jews owned orange groves at el Tireh."

What would her mother-in-law say if she knew those groves had once belonged to her great-grandfather, especially as only a few minutes before she had been denouncing the Husseinis for selling their land to the Jews?

She must justify the sale in case her great-great-grandfather's part ever came out. "Dalia's father kept on the Arab manager."

"Ha! Typical Jewish subterfuge. However, I still like Dalia, and a holiday in the country can only do you good—so long as it doesn't clash with Ismail's leave."

She wouldn't even have to fight her mother-in-law to accept this invitation. "I'll accept the invitation then. El-Tireh is so close, you can always send a taxi to bring me back if Ismail wangles unexpected leave."

"You can read out the rest of your letter now," her

mother-in-law said.

Maftur concealed a sigh behind her hand and started into a long round of explanations about people her mother-in-law didn't know.

Umm Ismail waved a hand. "Enough. Now for the next letter. Who's that from?"

Maftur opened it. "Patsy Craine."

She skimmed through that one before divulging its contents.

"Patsy must have written this before receiving Dalia's invitation. She hasn't heard from her husband since leaving Italy, but everything else is fine. Her mother is well, too. She would like to see me and wonders if I would spend a few days with her in Jerusalem."

"Jerusalem is too far for you to travel in your present condition," her mother-in-law stated, "but a holiday in el Tireh should be fine."

The thought of her approaching holiday burst the bubble that had isolated her from the outside world ever since she had found herself pregnant.

Once again she followed the Allied progress in Europe and dreamt of the war being over, with her and Ismail living in their own house on Mount Carmel.

She started visiting Elif on a regular basis. Together they began drawing up plans for an informal school for young girls entering domestic service with AWA members.

Chapter 49

July 1944

Maftur remembered the cob-built house in El Tireh from her childhood visit. She paid the taxi and dismounted carefully, conscious that she now had another human being to care for besides herself. The strong perfume of citrus blossom assailed her nostrils.

The manager's wife, thinner and more wrinkled than before, stood next to Dalia on the veranda.

"Maftur, I'm so glad you could come," Dalia said, "and Umm Ibrahim here is delighted."

Umm Ibrahim greeted her in Arabic. "Maftur Nour al-Zeid, it is an honour to welcome a member of your family. Your great-grandfather, even after he sold these orange groves, ensured my husband would continue to work for a good employer. Allah has been good to us."

Maftur was touched, and kissed Umm Ibrahim on both cheeks before following Dalia across the grove to three seaside-type chalets facing a fly and mosquito proof shelter, four metres square, built from narrow wire mesh. Inside the shelter stood a table covered with a white damask cloth weighted down with blue beads, cutlery and shining glasses.

"See, Maftur, our picnic area, built to my father's design. Wrong time of the year for orange blossom though, so you'll have to make do with lemon."

Rather more luxurious than the picnic she'd envisaged at the age of twelve, Maftur thought.

Patsy arrived an hour or so later, even more heavily pregnant than herself. Umm Ibrahim served a feast of grilled chicken, accompanied by a variety of salads, and they reminisced over chilled glasses of home-made lemonade well into the night.

They agreed to spend most of their holiday lazing about on secluded beaches, making full use of the car Dalia had borrowed from her father.

Maftur hadn't brought her swimming costume. As far as

she knew, it was still in the back of Ismail's car, but she borrowed one of Patsy's spares plus a 'mother and baby' book, which extolled the benefits of swimming as an exercise for pregnant women.

It was just as well her mother-in-law couldn't see her, Maftur reflected the first time she put on the swimming costume, and she and Patsy ran inelegantly across virgin sand to join Dalia, already swimming out beyond the breakers.

Once in the sea, however, bulging bumps beneath swimming costumes didn't show, so she and Patsy could swim and lark around without embarrassment, even when passing fishermen intruded on their privacy.

In the shade of a portable umbrella, they picnicked from the hamper Umm Ibrahim made up each day, and caught up on each other's ambitions.

In autumn, Dalia was joining an experimental agricultural project in the Negev. She waxed enthusiastic about irrigation and turning desert into fertile farmland. Patsy, who would have to return to England when her visa gave out, intended to study palaeontology, with special reference to Neanderthals at London University, once her children reached school age.

When the other two enquired about her plans, she replied that she and her sister-in-law, Elif, were determined to organise literacy classes for maid-servants.

"My mother would be interested in that," Patsy commented. "What gave you the idea?"

"Finding my first kitchen maid unable to read or write."

As she discussed her proposals with the other two, vague ideas took more definite shape. She would have a lot to take back to Elif.

Dalia asked them if they would mind having a brunch instead of breakfast and a packed lunch on their last day as Umm Ibrahim was seeing off her two grandchildren, who had been staying with her over their school holiday. Maftur immediately volunteered to help prepare it so Umm Ibrahim would have time to sit and eat with them, if she could be persuaded to do so.

Umm Ibrahim welcomed her help and seized the opportunity to talk. After lauding her great-grandfather again, she praised Dalia's father. "In nineteen-thirty-seven," she said, "when there was talk of transferring Arabs from this part of Palestine, Albert Leitner came down to el-Tireh and told them to sign a contract, entitling them both to live for the rest of their lives on a patch of land in the Jezreel Valley that he had bought for his own retirement. He asked them to hide the document and only bring it out if needed, as it would make him unpopular with his own people if they knew about it."

"Praise Allah, you never had to use it," Maftur said, remembering the pre-war uncertainties.

Dalia and Patsy had already laid the table and were drinking from glasses of chilled white wine when they wheeled the laden trolley to the picnic area.

Dalia pulled two bottles of coca cola from the icebox beside her chair, poured the contents into frosted glasses, and made her and Umm Ibrahim sit down to enjoy their drinks, while she and Patsy proceeded to lay out the food.

When the trolley was cleared, Patsy produced a Brownie camera from her bag and took a photo of the others.

Umm Ibrahim then put her arm across the table. "Please, if you give to me the camera, I will take the picture of all you girls."

They grouped themselves with their arms around each other, and Umm Ibrahim pressed the camera button. They heard a car rumbling down the drive. Dalia raised her eyebrows. Umm Ibrahim shrugged her ignorance.

The car proved to be a taxi. When Dalia ran across to wave it down before it drove on to the empty house, Maftur saw Fatima and Ishfaq on the back seat.

"Ismail must be home on leave," she exclaimed, and ran over but, as she drew nearer, she realised both servants were weeping into handkerchiefs.

Her stomach rolled over. She called out in Arabic, "Not Ismail? Please Allah, not Ismail."

Fatima called back, "No, no! Not Ismail! Abu Ismail."

Ishfaq climbed out of the taxi. "He was in his office, at his desk," she explained between sobs. "They shot him. You must come. Your mother-in-law needs you."

"Is he...?"

"He died at once."

Chapter 50

Maftur sat in the taxi, oblivious of servants and landscape, waves of guilt almost overpowering her grief.

If only she had asked her brothers to protect her charismatic but infuriating father-in-law before coming away, he might still be alive. A horrible suspicion flashed across her mind. Could her brothers even have been involved in his assassination?

When the taxi drew to a halt, she ran into the living room, crowded with female friends and relations. Her mother-in-law clung to her hands. "Ismail is washing his father. Praise Allah that I did not have to give this task to a stranger."

Had grief affected her mother-in-law's mind? How could Ismail be washing his father? He was stationed in the depths of rural Transjordan.

Then, looking over Umm Ismail's shoulder, she saw her husband, in military uniform, walking past the open door, carrying a shroud, his face so white and drawn she wanted to break away from the crowd of women and run after him to offer comfort. She couldn't insult her mother-in-law, however, by scandalising the mourners.

Later she caught a glimpse of Ismail, along with other male relatives, carrying out the bier on which lay her father-in-law's shrouded body.

The women, led by Umm Ismail, followed the men at a distance. Since her sister-in-law, Khawlah, had not yet arrived from Nablus, Maftur walked beside her mother-in-law.

The procession was halfway to the burial ground when a taxi drew up. Khawlah and her husband jumped out. Maftur relinquished her place and walked back to her own mother.

"I am glad that Umm Ismail is coping so well," her mother said, without breaking step or turning her head. "It will be a comfort that your Ismail arrived so quickly."

Keeping her own eyes staring at the bier so far ahead, so as not to seem dishonouring the dead, Maftur asked, "How did he manage to get here?"

"From what I've heard, his commanding officer phoned the emir, who ordered the pilot of his personal plane to fly him straight to Haifa."

An assortment of conflicting emotions swirled through her mind—relief to have Ismail home, fear he was in more danger here in Haifa than in Transjordan, grief at the loss of her vibrant father-in-law, guilt over her failure to contact her brothers and worry over their possible involvement.

Her mother spoke again, still staring straight ahead. "Your brothers asked me to tell you how devastated they are by Abu Ismail's death. They do not know who hired the assassins, but if your Ismail wants help tracking down his father's murderers, he can count on them. Perhaps this will relieve you."

In matters like this, Maftur thought, my mother is wiser than my father.

Still without turning her face, she squeezed her mother's arm. "Umm, thank you so much. I'll tell my husband."

Ismail, red-eyed with grief, came up to their bedroom late that evening. She sat up in bed and held her arms out wide. He fell into them, rested his head against her bosom and sobbed. She passed on her brothers' message.

He jerked his head in rejection of the offer. "There will be no more blood-letting. That was my father's wish. He knew he was putting himself in danger. He made me promise that if ever someone murdered him, I would leave the matter to the police. If we want to keep our country, we Arabs must stop killing each other. Jews have as many political differences as we do, but Jew does not kill Jew. That way, they make themselves strong, while we, with our long feuds, make ourselves weak."

* * * *

Maftur had never felt so exhausted in her life.

Ismail had returned to Transjordan. Her mother-in-law had given up the will to live, sitting all day in an armchair staring into space, saying she wanted to leave Haifa, despite refusing to live in the house on the Nablus estate where she and Abu Ismail had brought up their children.

"You can't expect me to go there. It's too full of

memories."

So Khawlah had returned to Nablus with Umm Saleh to prepare a suite of rooms in her townhouse. "I'll send Umm Saleh back to you nearer the time your baby's due."

Maftur hadn't realised what running a large household entailed, with everyone needing her permission before getting on with anything. In addition to that, Ismail had asked her to visit the law office two or three times a week and help the junior clerk answer letters. No new cases could be taken on in Haifa or Jerusalem, of course. Existing cases, if the clients agreed, had to be dealt with by her brother-in-law in Nablus, or farmed out to other solicitors. Ismail's army salary didn't even cover the cost of keeping the office open, let alone employing another clerk. They were living on the capital left to Ismail in his father's will. It wouldn't last forever.

In addition to her unexpected workload, the summer heat was affecting her as it had never done before. For the past fortnight during the siesta, instead of writing letters or darning, she had fallen asleep. She didn't know how she would have coped without the support of her mother and Elif.

Things couldn't go on like that.

The emir, however, was notorious for impulsive acts of generosity. She began a letter begging him to release Ismail so he could save the law firm, but fell asleep before she had finished. When she woke, she realised the letter would be dealt with by the emir's secretaries who would redirect it to Glubb Pasha. He was sure to refuse.

Her only hope of getting Ismail back was to go to Amman herself and ask for an audience. She couldn't do that until after Khawlah had taken her mother-in-law to Nablus, but she could start planning. Elif had visited Amman several times. While it wouldn't be fair to ask Elif to accompany her when she had a toddler to look after, plus another baby on the way, she could still give invaluable advice.

She went over to her mother's apartment. Both her mother and Elif were horrified at the idea of her travelling so far in her advanced state of pregnancy, but since the firm needed saving, and they could come up with no better suggestion, they agreed to help.

"Find out if the emir will be in Amman before you

leave," Elif advised. "He spends much of his time away from the capital. Write asking for an urgent audience. His secretaries will have to pass that on."

"You'll have to have a taxi," her mother said. "The train takes too long."

"You need to go to Thomas Cook's to book taxis and hotel rooms. There's only one decent hotel—the Philadelphia," Elif added.

As soon as Khawlah had carried off her mother-in-law, Maftur wrote to Emir Abdullah, requesting an urgent audition on a personal matter. Elif had warned her that if the emir were out of town it might be weeks before she received a reply. She was in luck, however. The reply came almost by return of post, giving her an appointment for the following week.

She rushed down to Thomas Cook's who, with amazing efficiency, organised her whole trip while she waited.

On the appointed day she and Zubaida stepped out of a local taxi, which had taken them from their hotel in the centre of Amman to the Royal Palace, built on a hill outside the town. They paused to admire stonework and windows of coloured glass reminiscent of Jerusalem's al-Aqsa Mosque.

An aide greeted them and escorted them into a hall with magnificent woodwork. Maftur had read about the splendour of the royal throne room, so was disappointed when the aide conducted them through wood-panelled corridors to the rear compound, where tiled paths criss-crossed gardens, planted with palm trees and lush grass. The aide led them to a smaller building at the back of the compound and ushered them into a comfortable office.

The emir, dressed in a black robe with a white keffiyah wound round a blue fez, turban style, sat behind a western-style desk. He motioned Maftur to an upholstered armchair facing him and waved Zubaida to a stool at the rear of the room.

"Your father-in-law was a very good friend of mine," he told Maftur. "An excellent lawyer, a competent camel rider and a good chess player. I was desolated to hear of his death."

He clapped his hand and a servant brought in glasses of mint tea. While they sipped it, the emir reminisced on the 'Tea Party' in Cairo where he had become emir of Transjordan.

It was several minutes before he asked, "Now tell me, please, dear lady, what I can do for you?"

Maftur explained the difficulties she was experiencing with the law firm while her husband was away in the army.

"But, dear lady, there was no need for you to put yourself out by coming all this way. You could have explained all in your letter. We are no longer in danger of invasion. I would have sent your husband home straight away."

He picked up a phone and asked to be put through to the commanding officer at Mafraq. A few sentences later he put down the phone.

"There, that's done. Now your husband is on indefinite leave and will only be recalled if an emergency arises. The way the war is going, there is very little danger of that happening."

The lightning speed with which the emir had solved her problem disorientated her. It would be rude to question if it had really happened.

Back outside the palace, she couldn't remember the rest of her interview with the emir, but Zubaida reassured her that she had behaved impeccably. The reality of her success only struck as she paid the hotel bill.

Uneasiness set in again on the long journey home. The men who had organised her father-in-law's assassination were still at large. Everyone knew who they were, but the police could prove nothing. By bringing her husband back to Haifa, was she luring him to his death? She must persuade him to move them both out of Haifa as soon as possible.

Incredibly, when she reached home, Ismail was already there. The Emir had ordered a plane to fly him home. Despite her delight at seeing him, she sobbed on his shoulder.

Ismail held her tightly and stroked her hair as she confessed her fears. "I shan't have a moment's peace, habibi, while we are still in Haifa."

"My poor darling, we will move out quickly. I'll transfer the chief clerk back here and take over the Jerusalem branch once more. The men behind my father's murder have little influence in Jerusalem. Now stop worrying and let's enjoy being together again, just the two of us."

Later over supper, he said, "My taking back the Jerusalem office and turning it into our head office will be better for the firm as well as us. The chief clerk has far more experience of our business in Haifa and I still have many useful connections in Jerusalem."

Maftur felt herself relax for the first time since returning from el-Tireh. "Habibi, I can think of nothing I would like more than having you working beneath me all day."

He gave her a long tender kiss. "Now we're starting a family, the flat above the office is too small for us, habipti. We need somewhere with a large garden where children can play. We'll spend a couple of days together at a hotel in Jerusalem next week and, in between my discussions with the chief clerk, we'll go house hunting."

Chapter 51

They found a traditional-style stone house with a large garden that reminded Maftur of the house she hankered after on Mount Carmel. The house was in the centre of Deir Yassin, a village on the outskirts of Jerusalem, close to a frequent bus service into the town centre. During the course of Deir Yassin's evolution from fellaheen village to dormitory suburb, the residents had formed reasonable relations with those of a neighbouring Jewish settlement. If they had to live in Jerusalem they couldn't do better than that. Once they had found a nearby doctor and Maftur had visited a local midwife, they closed the deal.

Not long after moving into her new home, Maftur received a note from Mrs. Quigley, saying Patsy's baby had arrived. She took a bus into town and visited the maternity hospital in the Russian compound.

She wondered afterwards whether it was holding gorgeous little Johnny so close to her womb that had persuaded her own baby to make an early start.

Whatever the reason, she went into labour a good fortnight earlier than the forecast date. The midwife had not yet sent over the birthing chair. Umm Saleh dispatched porters to collect it while Ismail took the car to fetch the midwife.

Meanwhile, her mother, who had come up to admire the new house, sat her on an ordinary kitchen chair and timed the intervals between contractions.

Maftur was unprepared for both the severity and character of the pains. She had expected them to be sharp and stabbing but they were more like crashing waves pounding her stomach from the inside. She found things easier to bear when she stood up and clutched the kitchen door.

She was glad her mother was there to give her moral support, better than the original plan which had involved her mother-in-law supervising the birth of her son's first child. Patsy had told her she had been made to lie down the whole time she had been in labour and she had thought that a comfortable way to manage the event, but now she couldn't imagine how Patsy had put up with it.

The birthing chair arrived before the midwife. It resembled a wooden garden bench with slotted back and sturdy arms she had seen at the Quigleys' garden party, except it had a circular hole cut into the seat.

Once she was in the chair, able to push her shoulders against its solid back during each contraction while stretching out her arms to grip its sides, she felt calmer.

Ismail arrived, but the midwife he brought with him banished him to the downstairs office.

She had been in labour two hours (for the last hour of which, in more agony than she had thought possible, she had been bearing down under the midwife's instructions) when she had the worst pain she had yet experienced, like a knife being slashed between her legs.

The midwife exclaimed, "See, the crown already," and then her mother was chanting the names of Allah.

Maftur gave another push and the rest of the baby slithered out almost painlessly.

"It's a boy," she heard the midwife declare.

That will please my mother-in-law, she thought. For some reason, she could feel none of the anticipated excitement. She just wanted to crawl into bed and go to sleep. She wondered vaguely why she didn't feel disappointed because her baby wasn't a girl as she and her mother had wanted, but, of course, her baby had every right to be the sex Allah decreed.

Her son let out a great wail, reassuring everyone that there was nothing wrong with his lungs. The cry roused her from her drowsiness.

He's real, she thought, not just something we keep talking about.

She wanted to hold this real baby but the midwife was washing him.

"His given name is Rafiq," Maftur announced, having kept that part of the child's name secret until now. "A good friend as well as a son."

"I'll give Abu Rafiq the news as soon as Umm Saleh has you looking pretty," her mother said, filling a washbasin with warm water and fetching a new nightdress.

Abu Rafiq, she thought. No longer Ismail, but I'll love him even more and, imshallah, he'll love Umm Rafiq as much as he loves me.

At last they allowed her to hold her son, and as she breathed in the smell from the top of his head, she felt a surge of almost sexual emotion race through her body.

"Come now," said her mother, "I need to brush your hair."

A few minutes later, when Abu Rafiq put in an appearance with a broad smile on his face, Umm Rafiq was sitting, brushed and sweet smelling, propped on new lace-trimmed pillows, a sleeping child in her arms. She held little Rafiq out to his father like an offering.

"Rafiq al Jamal ibn Ismail ibn Abdul Rashid al Shawwa, meet your father."

Abu Rafiq accepted his son, and carried out his first paternal duty. He bent his head and whispered in his right ear, "Allahu Akbar, Allahu Akbar, Allahu Akbar, Allahu Akbar, Ash-hadu al-la Ilaha ill-Alla, Ash-hadu al-la Ilaha ill-Alla, Ash-hadu anna Muhammad-ar-Rasulullah, Ash-hadu anna Muhammad-ar-Rasulullah, Hayya' ala-a-salah. Hayya' ala-a-salah, Hayya'ala-a-falah, Hayya'ala-a-falah, Allahu Akbar, Allahu Akbar, La Ilaha ill-Allah."

Rafiq opened his eyes. Umm Rafiq was afraid he was going to bawl, but he gave a little burp-induced smile as his father went on to whisper Allāhu Akbar in his left ear.

A tear ran down Abu Rafiq's shaven cheek as he handed the baby back.

Umm Rafiq knew he was mourning a father who would never know his grandchild.

"Abu Ismail would have been so proud today, Abu Rafiq," she said softly.

Her mother and Umm Saleh silently left the room.

"Thank you so much for this greatest of gifts, habipti," Abu Rafiq said as he kissed her forehead.

"He is your gift to me as well, remember," Umm Rafiq replied, "and I am equally thankful to you."

They sat together in silence, holding hands just staring at their son, then her beloved husband kissed her again, rose and said, "I must send a message to my mother and ask her to get our shepherd to pick out the two fattest sheep for our son's aqeeqah."

Umm Rafiq smiled. This birth, she reflected, was not the end of something, but the beginning. Abu Rafiq was right to be planning ahead. She looked at her baby and imagined him in his pram under the shade of an apricot tree in their new home, while she managed her own household.

The conclusion to Maftur's story will appear in 'Dalia', the third book in this Trilogy…

About The Author

Margaret spent her childhood in Palestine during the 30s and 40s of the last century.

During the pre-WW2 Palestinian Arab Rebellion, she watched her father strap on a revolver before leading night squads off to repair sabotaged telephone lines. When WW2 started, she watched police and army struggle to rescue passengers from the capsized SS Patria. Later, she and her mother spent an anxious few weeks when her father, covertly recruited by Eastern Mediterranean Intelligence Centre, disappeared in Bulgaria. He turned up in Athens weeks later, after escaping from a rural Bulgarian prison, and joined the last allied convoy from Greece. Fifteen months later, with the Axis poised to invade Palestine, her father, due to a domestic crisis, left her in sole charge of a fake army camp set up to deter Germans from landing on a beach near Haifa. After the war, when the Irgun blew up the West wing of the King David where her father worked, she sat in front of the radio biting the back of her hands while awaiting further news. At the end of the mandate, her father gave her the last Union Jack to fly over Jerusalem. These experiences left her with a lifelong interest in the British Mandate of Palestine and the turmoil the land has experienced since.

Nowadays, when people ask which side she is on in the conflict, she replies – it depends on which character I am currently writing.